KANGAROO HOUSE

by

L. G. CRAWFORD

This is a work of fiction set in a background of history. Names, characters, businesses, places, events, and incidents are either the products of the author's imagination or are used in a fictitious manner. Any resemblance to actual living persons is purely coincidental.

Editor: Maggie Taylor

'For those of us…' from a poem written by the author's grandfather, Cleo Crawford, in memory of Mabel, in 1964.

Book and cover design: Vladimir Verano, VertVolta Design
vertvoltapress.com

Cover: San Juan Islands ⓒⓒ Jonathan Miske via Flickr.com
u-boat via wikimedia commons

First edition, 2019, Kangaroo House

Published in the United States by L. G. Crawford

Author contact:
budcrawford@comcast.net

Print ISBN: 978-1-7328635-0-7

e-book: 978-1-7328635-1-4

For those of us who must live on,
When the one we love has come and gone.
There's nothing left, or so it seems;
But – just our dreams.

So, I love and dream, day after day
Tis time drags on; in its own slow way.
Yes, loving on; and dreaming too,
Of all the things I'd have liked to do.
With the one I knew at the very start
Would remain forever, within my heart.

Will time drag on down through the years?
Each thought, each heartbeat drenched in tears?
Will each day's effort seem in vain,
As I carry on, all wracked with pain?
If this be true, Dear God above:
Why was I sent this consuming Love?
Why cannot I be set free?
Why, oh why, do this to me?
Must I hold forth just empty arms,
That long to enfold her dear sweet charms?
Must all my thoughts, and all my schemes
End – just in dreams?

My dear, I want you just to know,
That though we're mortal here below.
There's one above who knows all things,
And who to some, much happiness brings.
So, knowing that He is always there,
To Him my Dear, I pray my prayer.

God, please watch over this Lady fair
Each day and hour, no matter where.
And see that you – her so bless,
That each day will bring her happiness.
No matter where or when she go.
Dear God, I love this Lady so.

≈ CLEO CRAWFORD ≈

CHAPTER 1

1914

Hazy shafts of morning sun seeped through crooked orange-barked madrona trees onto the beach. The air smelled of a low tide. Faded and patched clothing draping off his slender frame, a barefoot boy crouched to pick up a flat rock as a retreating wave parted around his ankles. Shaking off a fleeting shiver, he fingered the stone's smoothness as he sought the warming sun along the water's edge. Taking a stance, he skipped the rock across the placid water leaving a trail of dimples amongst lazily floating kelp ribbons. The stone's 12 ricochets nearly equaled his age. The next rock sliced into the water on the second hop. Spying his mother making her way up a rickety dock in the distance, he set off down the beach. Barely five feet tall, not weighing much more than her trailing mail pouch, she wrestled it through the General Store's rear screen door. Letting it slam, it interrupted the bay's tranquility scattering a nearby group of skinny legged shorebirds darting to and fro at the surf's edge.

"Damn it," Bud said, knowing he should have retrieved the island's morning mail. The streaked hull mail boat, sometimes gillnetter, was now abeam of the youth as he waded knee deep to retrieve a wayward wood net float. Prize in hand, he exchanged a wave with the boat's operator before continuing towards the whitewashed store perched above the beach.

Bud Fowler and his mother Mabel resided above and operated the unassuming island store originally built by his grandfather in the late

1890s. Bud did not remember his father. There was nothing around indicating he had ever been there. The only thing he had been told was that he had not returned from crewing on a tramp steamer.

For the most part, the Shaw Store served a sparse local community other than the odd customer who might venture from a nearby island or a passing boat. At the rear of the store facing the bay, a small walled corner proclaimed itself the United States Post Office. The area was off-limits to everyone except Mabel, the Shaw Island postmistress. A nearby warehouse extending partially over the water on piles stored hay bales and gunnysack feeds.

Scampering precariously up the bedrock at the beach's end, Bud walked the narrow, worn path snaking amongst soil starved plants. Off to the west was his favorite haunt, Blind Island. The sparsely vegetated rock outcropping was so uninviting that hardly anyone other than himself ever ventured near. Canada lay beyond in the distance.

Stepping onto the porch, he flung the screen door open and disappeared within.

Scuffed and chipped paint attested to the fact that the rowboat's current color scheme hadn't been her first. Water seeping between the boat's planked bottom cooled Bud's feet—a welcome respite from the hot August day. Scarcely a whisper of a breeze, the oar blades dipped through the water leaving a trail of rivulets. The stern settled slightly, triggering a rusty bailing can to wander aimlessly in the bottom of the skiff. Distancing himself from the store, his destination was Blind Island. A leisurely thirty-minute row transported him into the hideaway's skewed entrance. Undetected by most who might ply the nearby area, he had drifted upon the non-descript inlet fishing for rock cod one lazy afternoon the previous summer.

Stripping off his shirt, giving one last pull on the oars, Bud rolled over the side into the shallows while the rowboat continued of its own accord until it caught the bottom. Emerging from the frigid waters, he dragged the skiff partway onto the beach. Tipping the boat on its side, the accumulated seepage from the row over disappeared into the pebbled surface. Seizing a coiled line attached to the bow ring, he tossed it towards the beached logs in a haphazard effort to secure the boat from the incoming tide. A wood contraption in hand, he set off for one end of the beach where a rocky finger jutted into the cove. Having already baited the trap with the skeletal remnants of the previous night's cod dinner, he looked forward to taking a bounty of crabs home. Flinging the trap with all his might, it settled slowly into swaying waves of eelgrass. A red streaked wood float bobbed above.

Bud next wandered the upper tide line in search of any stranded bounty that might have come ashore since his last visit. Grasping a piece of weathered board with traces of blue paint, he turned it over in his hands before discarding it. Spying something out of the ordinary peeking out amongst a collection of seaweed floating nearby, he veered into the water and waded up to his waist to capture the elusive treasure.

"Damn, that's cold," Bud yelled out.

It was a bamboo fishing rod missing its tip. Despite questioning if it was too far gone to ever catch another fish, Bud brought it ashore and headed for a makeshift fort under a lone craggy fir tree. Virtually undetectable, his hideout was an assortment of driftwood spanning a pair of upland logs. Vaulting from log to log towards his encampment, he stopped and back tracked to retrieve a yellowish board similar in size to the one he had rejected previously. For some reason, unlike the earlier find, the board passed muster.

Dropping to a sandy area amongst the last rows of beached logs, he arrived at his destination. Taking little deliberation, the board was wedged on end against the fort's framework narrowing its entry. Balancing the bamboo rod precariously across the top of the entrance, it fell away as he maneuvered inside. An accumulation of beach finds cramped the cozy interior. Propped above the sand, a derelict deck hatch created a makeshift table. Sitting on the board were some shells, a dried purple starfish and a greenish glass fishing float that had made its way unscathed across the Pacific from Japan.

Doodling with a stick in the sand, he smiled thinking about the night he spent on Blind Island a few weeks prior—an adventure never to be repeated. As the orange and red sunset skies had faded away, an onslaught of sand fleas had rallied. The resulting mayhem drove him to spend a good part of the night entombed in an old castaway blanket trying to defend his barracks before finally retreating to the comfortless accommodations of the old rowboat.

Bud headed back to the beach. Poised atop a recent arrival that still had traces of bark, he jumped off the log's end with outstretched arms as if taking flight. Tumbling onto the warm beach, he buried his feet in the loose sandy gravel to methodically watch the waves rhythmically pushing and pulling against the shoreline.

Wondering how to while away some time until the bay's pinched crustaceans were drawn to the trap, he grabbed a handful of pebbles and thrust them out over the placid water. The noisy eruption caused a nearby heron to take flight with a boisterous squawk. Cupping another mixture of gravel, Bud let some of the sand sift through his fingers. Tightening his fist around the remainder, arm arched, preparing to launch, he hesitated. Opening his fingers, a slate-black arrowhead stood out amidst the gray and white stones. Wondering how it had come to be on his beach, he turned the triangular object over and over inspecting his find. Maybe a young Indian brave had also been drawn to the solace of his island haven. Squinting, aligning the arrowhead up against the brilliant sun, the blocked rays silhouetted a near-perfect form. Gazing out across the water, he imagined a make-believe canoe entering the inlet.

A squadron of geese winged above as Bud lay back on the beach. In unison, as if given a command, the gaggle dropped toward the cove. With a slight dip of a wing, their leader made minor course corrections guiding the final approach. Noisily, hordes of webbed feet skimmed atop the water as tucked wings settled them into their customary boat-like position.

Bud's eyelids drooped. The rumbling noise of a powerful engine broke the stillness. Instantaneously wide-eyed, Bud realized the sound was coming from the opposite side of his island. Then there was silence again.

Springing to his feet, Bud raced across the logs past his fort and up the rocky embankment. Hunched on all fours, he scrambled over the rocks to see who was invading his sanctuary. Perched undetected some ten feet above the water, he saw a man without a shirt and a younger girl in a bathing costume sitting in a runabout drifting in the current. The boat was a glistening varnished mahogany inboard—not the likes of any Shaw Island craft. A small red flag fluttered on her bow.

Bud couldn't make out what was being said, but the passengers seemed to be in the midst of an argument. The boat's driver advanced, pulling his passenger near in an attempt to kiss her mouth. Resisting, the girl turned her head away and pushed back. The man was undaunted.

Holding her tight with one arm, his free hand began to forcibly explore the girl's breasts before descending in an effort to pry her legs apart.

"Stop!" the struggling girl screamed in terror.

The boat was a mere 25-feet from Bud's roost and drifting closer.

Hugging the earth, Bud's pulse pounded.

Suddenly the man stood up in the cockpit and began violently tearing at the girl's attire stripping her to the waist.

Wildly fighting back, the girl's teeth found his arm and bit down.

"You bitch!" her assailant yelled in pain.

Viciously wrenching her loose, he grasped her auburn colored hair and torn bathing costume and flung her over the side. Dunking her underwater, obscenities raged from his mouth.

Bud knew he had to help the defenseless girl. Audibly emitting quick labored breaths, his unsteady hands raked the surface around him until his fingers grasped a rock the size of his palm. The sharp rocky surface biting into his flesh through the holes of his pants, Bud rose to his knees and hurled the projectile. Ricocheting off the bow's deck into the windshield, a volley of glass shards exploded across the cockpit.

Wrenching back in disbelief, the assailant released his prey. Quickly regaining his wits, he calmly craned up at Bud. If looks could kill, his expressionless dark eyes would have ended the island boy's life that very instant. Bud held his ground.

Gasping, the girl flailed at the side of the boat trying to stay afloat.

Sizing up his predicament, looming above his prey, he seized her arms and dragged her back aboard. He then nonchalantly swept the glass from the seat with his shirt and started the engine with a deafening roar. Whimpering, the girl cowered in the stern attempting to cover herself with the tattered pieces of her swimwear. Hauntingly, she locked her eyes with Bud's.

The craft began to maneuver away. Struggling, the girl stood as the boat accelerated rising out of the water. Her horror-stricken face searching Bud's, she launched herself off the stern into the kelp entangled waters. Gaining speed, disappearing around the island, the driver seemed unaware his passenger was gone.

Teetering at the cliff's edge as the girl surfaced, Bud yelled out, "Can you swim?"

"Yes," the frightened girl responded struggling through the kelp. "Help me!"

Bolting back to the beach, he cried out with all his might, "Hang on!"

Racing down the bank, stumbling along the way and cutting his ankle, Bud crossed over the logs onto the beach. Frantically grabbing the bow of the rowboat, he wrenched it around into the water with unaccustomed strength. Vaulting aboard, fumbling to slot the oars in their locks, he strained with all his might as the blades dug in. Clearing the cove entrance at a record pace, he rounded the shoreline and had the girl in sight.

Gasping for life, clinging to the barnacle encrusted rock face below where Bud had made his stand, the wide-eyed girl watched her rescuer's advance.

"I am almost there!" Bud yelled.

Barely audible, she whimpered, "I can't hold on much longer."

Bud furiously closed the distance between them—40 feet, 20, ten, the rowboat slammed against the rocks near the girl.

Exhausted, scraped and bleeding from the sharp barnacles, the girl went limp as Bud grabbed her arms pulling her to the boat.

"I don't think I can climb in," she moaned.

Likewise, Bud was unsure he could lift the girl into the boat without her assistance. He also wondered if the boat might tip with both of their weight concentrated along one edge.

Taking her delicate hands in his, Bud guided her around to the back of the boat and placed her fingers on the stern rail.

"Now hang on. I am going to tow you."

The girl nodded.

Aware the water temperature of the Sound was bone-chilling 50 degrees, Bud pulled steadily and swiftly back to the cove.

Leaping from the boat before reaching the shore, Bud found he had misjudged the water's depth. Stumbling for footing, he plunged beneath the surface for a split second before resurfacing.

"Take hold of me," Bud said reaching out to the girl.

Her bathing costume partially torn away, she threw her arms around Bud's neck as he dragged her through the shallows. Their bare skin against one another, Bud felt the girl shivering wildly.

"Over there the gravel is warm," Bud said softly in her ear as he hauled her up the beach. Crouching, he placed her on the sun warmed pebbles trying not to look directly at her nakedness.

Attempting to rake her torn bathing suit up across her snow-white skin, the girl rolled into a tight fetal position.

Bud sprinted back to the water to capture the drifting rowboat. Pulling it ashore, he snatched the shirt he had discarded earlier and raced back to the girl.

"Put this on," Bud directed as he placed it over her bare shoulders.

Paying no attention to her naked torso, the girl moved her arms, so Bud could help align her hands through the sleeves before pulling the shirt around her.

"Thank you," the girl whispered in a trembling voice.

Not knowing what to do or say, Bud blurted, "My name is Bud Fowler and live over at Shaw."

"I'm Mary," she said with glistening green eyes.

Finally, the girl spoke again, "My parents and I are visiting the Rosario Estate on Orcas Island."

Bud sat down near her and said, "Move over a bit. The gravel won't be wet and will be warmer."

The girl chose to push up against her rescuer instead of moving further away as he had anticipated. Bud clumsily placed his arm around her shoulder and pulled her even nearer for added warmth.

After a few more minutes had passed, Mary's shivering subsided, and she said, "My cousin was the one who attacked me. I owe you my life."

Unsure how to acknowledge her declaration, Bud said, "I'll take you over to Shaw. My mother will find a way to contact your folks."

Standing, streaks of red marking her scraped hands and legs, Mary silently followed.

His passenger seated in the stern, Bud positioned the bow to his liking then pushed away. Jumping aboard, the drifting skiff headed towards the wood float with nary a course correction. The caged crabs clambering about exhibited their displeasure as Bud hauled them from the watery depths.

Rowing steadily towards Shaw, the couple sat in close proximity with their legs overlapping in the confined space. Little was said. Eyes welling, Mary looked directly into Bud's face as if wanting to say something but unable to form the words. Noticing Bud's bleeding ankle, she bent over and dabbed the torn flesh with the tail of Bud's shirt.

Bud rowed with a sense of urgency. From time to time, both looked around—silently fearful the cousin would reappear. Sweat beading off his face, his arms tiring, he maintained an unwavering steady course. Stealing glimpses, he thought Mary might be a bit older even though they were of similar height. Her auburn hair, greenish eyes and lightly freckled face radiated a beauty that was unfamiliar. He wondered if maybe they might become friends.

Pointing, Mary called out, "Is that the store?"

No need to make visual contact, Bud said, "Yes."

Finally within a few hundred yards of their destination, Mary, seeming calmer, the first indication of such, said, "Bud, I think you can slow up. We should be safe."

Reaching the store float Bud hastily tied up the rowboat. Mary remained seated until Bud beckoned her. Walking briskly up the planked incline to the sanctuary of the store, they bolted through the door. There was no one there. A note scrawled on the small blackboard next to the store counter said, "Gone to make a delivery. Back soon."

Bud handed Mary a candy bar. She accepted it without reservation, "Thank you."

He then found a piece of gauze to wrap his ankle, slowing the blood to a trickle. Mary declined any first aid since most of her cuts and scrapes had stopped bleeding.

Considering the awkwardness of the circumstances, time passed slowly. Intending to leave Mary in the store, Bud started for the door, "I'm going to run upstairs and find you some other clothes to wear."

"I don't want to stay here alone," she replied catching up to him.

Outside on the stairway landing at the top of the stairs, Bud said apologetically, "It's not much, but it works for my mom and me."

Bud was able to find a well-worn pair of his pants and one of his better shirts. Handing them to Mary, he said, "You can go in my room to change."

They had made their way back down to the store when Bud's mother appeared through the feed warehouse door. Realizing that something unsettling was gripping the room when neither her son nor the nameless girl said anything, she was about to ask when Mary rushed to her in tears. Instinctively Mabel held the girl noting she wore the shirt she had given her son on his last birthday. "Your son saved my life. Can you help me contact my parents at Rosario?"

While Bud quietly stood nearby, Mary detailed the horror of the day's events. It was then that Bud learned that she was nearly two years older than him. She was almost fifteen.

At his mother's direction, Bud headed down the bay trail to fetch her brother Frank. His uncle worked as a deckhand aboard the steam driven tugboat *Lorne*. A bit crotchety, living alone, the solace of the water seemed to shape his very existence. Like his sister, Frank had thick dark hair with barely a trace of gray. Only Frank's weathered face and telltale salt and peppered beard gave light to the fact that he was the oldest sibling.

Frank moored his 22-foot working class boat at the store float. The boat didn't get used all that much, but provided him with an option to putter about, go fishing or whatever struck his fancy when not onboard on the tug. A heavy wood planked boat, what it lacked in speed, it made up in reliability—the two-cylinder steam engine never missed a beat.

It had been Mabel's initial intent to have her brother run Mary over to Rosario. But while they waited for Frank's boat to build up a head of steam, Mary clung to Mabel making it evident she needed the reassurance of a woman until returning to the security of her parents. Once all were assembled on the float, Mabel said, "Bud, it's almost closing time. Lock up at 5:00. I'm going to ride along with Frank and Mary to Rosario. Find yourself some supper."

Mary looked gratefully towards Mabel.

Before boarding Frank's boat, Mary stepped to Bud. Hugging him, she said, "I owe you everything. I have no way to repay you for your kindness. Hopefully, I will see you again. Good-bye for now."

Slightly embarrassed, Bud bid a reserved "Good-bye."

Noting the caged crabs in the rowboat, Mabel added, "You'll also need to tend to your catch."

Bud remained dock bound until he could no longer make out the steam-boat's trail of wispy smoke.

Rosario, the huge estate built by Robert Moran, was named after the strait that separated the islands from Canada. A distinguished ship-builder in Seattle, he purchased the former lumber company on Orcas in 1905 and began its transformation into his personal residence. He spared little expense during its reconstruction. The dominant feature of the palatial setting was a five-floor mansion. The interior was a lavish mix of marble, dark paneling and ornate rugs cast upon highly varnished wood floors. Leaded-glass windows invited gentle breezes laden with the scents of the season into opulent fireplace-adorned rooms. Influenced by the owner's ship building days, highly detailed millwork and brass castings lent just a hint of a nautical flavor. A nearby lake with a dam powerhouse furnished the estate's sizable electrical needs.

The estate had become a destination point for Moran's wealthy and powerful guests—the socially privileged. The kind of place or wealth the Fowlers or other island inhabitants knew little about.

Billowing smoke announced the coming of the Shaw Island craft long before it reached its destination. Drawing the attention of estate employees, they watched near the boat basin wondering who was intending to land. The Fowlers and Mary were still a hundred feet or so away when a man and woman approached the sloped gangway to the dock. Seeing her parents, tears surfaced in the corners of Mary's eyes and crept down her cheeks.

"Mary, are you alright?!" hailed the woman as she saw her daughter arriving with strangers and wearing unfamiliar clothes.

Mary choked, unable to form words in response.

As the craft slid alongside the pristine wood planked float, Mary sprang from the boat and into the arms of her mother.

Mabel followed while Frank remained in the boat.

"Where's Jonathan?" Mary's father asked in a concerned voice.

Mary looked at Mabel for help.

"Let's find a place to talk," Mabel suggested.

Mabel, Mary and her parents walked up the freshly whitewashed gangway to a benched seating area located just above the beach. Mary recounted the happenings at Blind Island and the help she received from the Fowler family. Mary's mother cried while her father became enraged.

Jonathan Pickard, the cousin, had not returned to the estate since he and Mary had left hours earlier. The twenty-year-old had come to visit his relatives from his family home in Olympia, where his father, Mary's uncle, was a judge.

After a time, Mabel stood to bid her farewell indicating that her son's clothes could be returned at another time.

"Mom, can we find something for the Fowlers to eat before they head home?" Mary asked.

"That's okay. Another time," Mabel replied.

"No, please stay," Mary pleaded.

"Yes, do stay. We haven't eaten either," Mary's mother said shooting a disapproving glance at her husband.

Arms entwined, Mary and her mother walked ahead of her father who lagged trying to shoulder the burden of the ordeal. Distancing themselves, out of their element, Mabel and Frank trailed the others up to the huge covered veranda that encircled the mammoth residence. Once assembled, Mable again suggested that it might be best if her and Frank just headed back to Shaw. After spotting Mary's pleading eyes, Mary's mother declined the Fowler's offer.

At the fringe of other guests gathered about, the solemn group found a table while Frank sank into a nearby cushioned chair to peruse the mansion's details.

Dinner was a nice sampling of salmon, freshly baked rolls and salads in addition to the availability of both red and white wine. The spread was likely typical for the mansion's daily fare, but extraordinary for the Fowlers. To Mabel's embarrassment, her brother was not bashful about consuming his share, and then some, of the bottled spirits.

Towards the end of dinner, word came that the estate's sleek runabout was moored at the public dock on the other side of the island. After further inquiry, Mary's father learned the young man who arrived in the boat had promptly boarded a passenger ferry bound for Seattle – his fury towards his nephew would have to wait.

Mary excused herself to change out of Bud's clothes. Returning, she handed the borrowed attire to Mable and exchanged a warm hug. Before departure, Mabel received a less enthusiastic imitation from Mary's mother.

Mary and her mother remained on the porch while her father prepared to accompany the Shaw Island outsiders back to the boat basin. Frank had already started down the steps not wishing to spend any time with formalities.

"Give Bud a hug for me and thank him again," declared Mary.

"Of course, I will," responded Mabel.

Sensing Mrs. Pickard's reserve, Mabel stepped down the stairs near Frank and said, "Mr. Pickard, please stay, we can find our way."

The Pickard family watched from the veranda as Frank opened the steam valve to the engine and navigated his launch away from the float.

Bud had the crabs cooked, cleaned and had already eaten his fill upon hearing the sharp shrill of the steam whistle. Running down to the dock to greet his mother and uncle, he helped secure the boat. Frank extinguished the boiler fire and released the remaining pent-up pressure in a steamy hiss.

Over the next months as the summer warmth faded away, Bud often thought fondly of Mary.

During those reflections, he envisioned the nakedness of their bodies touching as he helped bring her to shore.

CHAPTER 2

1915

THE WINTER OF THE FOLLOWING YEAR ARRIVED EARLY AS MEASURED BY the return of the winged coots that frequented the bay. Over a year had passed since the encounter on Blind Island.

Rising each morning as the night shadows retreated, Bud braved the cold to revive the embers of the store's potbellied stove. Always prepared for the morning ritual, split and stacked kindling stood at the ready near the stove from the previous evening. Sheltered overnight from the woodshed's dampness, the dry wood brought the previous night's embers back to life. The crackling fire rekindled the spirit of most all who ventured near – hypnotic flames casting a spell beyond the warmth.

Regardless of the season, there were always regulars who gathered in the store's curved-back spindle chairs scattered near the stove. If for no other reason, it was a place to go. They were drawn to Mabel's coffee as well as to catch up on the island grapevine. An empty soup can, its label peeled away, sat on a nearby table with an assemblage of mismatched coffee mugs. Throughout the day, a few coins would appear in the can to help offset the cost of the dark brown liquid flowing from the speckled porcelain pot reigning atop the stove. Those who made the trek would often leave with a few goods, contributing to the store's well-being.

Once the stove was stuffed with wood, Bud made his way to the chicken coop to feed the feathered flock and gather their eggs before making his way back up to a filling breakfast. On this particular morning, he was greeted with fried eggs and leftover dinner cod. Once the morning dishes were washed and left to dry, Bud and his mother descended to the store to prepare for another day of activity, not unlike the day, week or month before.

It was nearly time to be leaving for school. After stacking more wood, Bud lingered by the stove's radiating warmth.

"Bud, you better think about heading off to school or you'll be late," his mother cautioned.

"I know. Let me take a minute to warm my coat," he answered, caressing it over the stove.

"See you later, mother," echoed back as Bud closed the door behind himself and stepped into falling snowflakes.

Sounds of fresh snow crunching under his boots broke the stillness as he set out for the half-mile trek to the one-room schoolhouse. While snow in the islands was not routine, it was also not uncommon to have a few days of wintery transformation during late December or early January.

At fourteen, Bud was the oldest student still attending the island school. Another boy, one-year Bud's senior, had recently dropped out to work at the lime kiln located on one of the nearby islands. The boy had stepped up to help when his father had taken a fall off a rail car on the mainland, hurting his back. Bud knew his mother didn't always charge the family the entire amount owed for the few staples they got at the store. He had learned early in life she was a giving person who never had second thoughts about helping those in need.

There were only a few other students, let alone any boys, near Bud's age on the island. But, for the time being, it didn't matter. A girl named Helen had recaptured his interest.

Bud had known Helen for as long as he could remember. Their mothers were friends and he and Helen were introduced at an early age crawling around the store's fir-planked floor. Later, they chased each other on the beach or waded in the warm tide pools in search of bullheads. As they grew older, they played tag with the waves, swam in the cold water and fished for rock cod off the nearby point on Harney Channel. In those early years, Bud knew she was a girl, but paid it no mind. She seemed to be able to do everything he did and was often the first to suggest they test themselves with some new adventure. She had not been squeamish about poking a dead seagull with a stick, nor drying the eyes of a dogfish on a flat rock to later use as wobbly marbles. They kissed each other on the mouth when they were about eight or nine just to see what might happen and immediately dismissed it as a waste of time. But by 11, their adventures together became infrequent.

Sitting at his classroom desk, Bud watched the last arrivals shake off the snow from their outerwear before closing out the cold January winter. Helen shed her heavy woolen coat and hung it on the last wooden peg next to the door. As luck would have it, his coat hung on the next hook. Smiling, he thought that at least something of his was touching hers—feelings he found himself thinking more about lately.

She crossed the room and sat next to a girl her age. Since summer's end, he had noticed a difference in Helen. She and a girlfriend had rowed over to the store from her house around the point and arrived just about the time the weekly mail pouches were being exchanged. Helen, clad in a blue woolen bathing costume, had drawn Bud's attention. A pair of roundish bumps on her front had appeared since the close of the school year. Her long hair, the color of dried field hay, had been tied back in a long ponytail. Both girls had bid him hello, but he had only noticed Helen. Her hair blowing about in the warm summer breeze, he found it difficult to take his eyes off her as she walked up the dock. Startling him, the arriving mail pouch had landed at his feet beckoning a response. Still clutching the outgoing bag in his hands, Bud's inattentiveness forced the mail boat to make a circle for another pass.

Helen glanced at Bud and smiled as she sat down and gave her attention to the teacher. Bud's mind drifted back to the summer day on the dock.

"Bud," the teacher called out for the second time. "Do you understand what I just said or are you having difficulty joining us today?"

Feeling a wave of intense warmth creep up his face, Bud stammered, "Yes."

Luckily, the teacher did not ask him to repeat what she had just said.

Later that morning, Bud was paired up with Helen and another student to discuss the events that led up to the Civil War. Other groups were formed to discuss related topics. Clustering their island-built chairs, the trio reviewed the war's pertinent points. Helen led the discussion. Bud watched intently during her dissertation as she formed words from lips that he thought about touching with his own. He also found himself dropping his eyes to the ruffled front of her blouse. Looking up and into her smiling blue eyes, he knew she had discovered his wandering thoughts as she tried to hide a flirtatious smile.

The teacher assigned a spokesman from each group to provide a brief recap. As chance would have it, probably due to his earlier lack of concentration, Bud was chosen. He didn't do a great job of highlighting the issues but got through enough of the relevant points so as not to embarrass himself. Helen would have provided a clear and concise recap of the day's studies that would have rivaled the lesson's author.

Scheming, Bud seemed preoccupied the rest of the day.

Donning their coats at day's end, Bud asked, "Helen, would you like to stop by the store for a soda? My mother just got a shipment of a new drink called Moxie."

"All right, but, Nellie needs to come too," she replied coyly.

Bud was both elated and disappointed with her acceptance. Exhilarated that she said yes but wishing Nellie wouldn't be tagging along. His intentions were further foiled when Nellie chose to walk between the two of them on their journey down the snow-covered road to the store.

Loudly stomping, hoping to leave the accumulation of snow on their boots outside, they announced their arrival on the store's planked porch.

Inside, the girls moved quickly to the warmth of the stove while Bud sheepishly stepped to the small oak framed postal office and asked, "Mother, can we have three bottles of soda?"

Looking up from sorting the mail, Mabel smiled and nodded.

Unsure of himself, Bud uneasily handed Helen and Nellie their drinks and said, "I hope you like it. It tastes a bit odd. Sweet, with a bitter tang."

Both girls said, "Thank you," in unison.

"How do you like it Helen?" Bud asked, hardly aware of Nellie.

She withdrew the bottle from her lips, swallowed and replied, "It's pretty good. What do you think Nellie?" she asked without breaking eye contact with Bud.

Nellie said something, but neither of the other two paid much attention to what it was.

Bud nervously smiled and looked to see if his mother was watching. She was not.

Between short awkward attempts at talking around the stove, the party finally consumed the last of the odd tasting liquid. Returning their empty bottles to the wood crate, Bud said, "Do you want to take the shoreline trail to get home? I can walk along for some way."

The two girls looked at each other. Helen said, "Okay."

Passing his mother sitting on the counter stool, Bud shyly announced, "I'll be back soon to finish up my chores."

"Hurry back," Mabel called out as the silence of a snow fall overtook the store.

The narrow snow-laden trail only permitted the bundled threesome to walk single file. Bud positioned himself in the middle while Nellie led. Other than a few failed communication efforts by Nellie, the others seemed buried in their own thoughts—the silence broken with little more than snow crunching under boots.

Heart pounding, Bud removed one of his gloves and reached his hand behind into the cold unknown. After what seemed an eternity, about to withdraw his offering, the gentle touch of a naked hand encircled his. For a time, Bud's total being was embodied in the touch of her fingers. Approaching a junction in the trail, her hand retreated. Both wayward hands were gloved by the time they halted.

Exchanging goodbyes, Nellie headed off on an inland route toward home. Helen's house was only a short distance further.

Gentle trace amounts of snow began to fall.

"It is either now or never," Bud thought as he fidgeted to face her and took a small step forward. In unison, they closed the narrow space between them. Their closed lips met awkwardly before quickly parting. They held each other loosely not quite knowing what to do next. Bud maneuvered his face to hers and kissed her again. Their mouths caressed as her petal-like lips surrendered ever so slightly. Withdrawing, they stammered uncomfortably, backing away from each other.

"Thanks for walking me home Bud. It was nice."

Bud nodded his agreement.

Helen turned, and half walked, half ran, down the trail toward home.

Bud watched her fleeting silhouette disappear into the whiteness before racing back down the trail. Jumping up as he went, he slapped at laden fir boughs triggering a sparkling avalanche.

Bud and Helen continued to capture brief periods of time as their own. Whether walking home from school or just sitting on the beach watching winter storms pound the shoreline, their fondness grew. They were at an awkward point in their lives. Bud was approaching fifteen, a month older than Helen. Still basically kids at heart, but with yearning feelings. Their relationship blossomed into a comfortable exchange through the winter and into the summer. One minute they might be skipping rocks from the shore, while the next exploring their feelings with a kiss. Bud once intentionally brushed his hand across Helen's clothed breasts hoping for a sign of acceptance. Instead, he was told in no uncertain terms that such liberties were inappropriate.

Embarrassed that his mission had been exposed, he apologized with a simple, "I'm sorry," without trying to contrive an explanation. Helen kissed the offending hand, rose from the beach and set off to explore a tide pool.

CHAPTER 3

1916

THE MID-SUMMER AFTERNOON SUN CASTING A SHADOW OVER HIS WORK area, Bud clung near the top of a ladder painting the store's exterior clapboard siding. From his vantage point, he noticed an approaching boat, but paid it little mind. Continuing his toils, he hoped to finish the eastern wall before evening supper. He would tackle the west face first thing in the morning before the sun's rays reached their height.

The boat's engine fell silent as it reached the float.

Dipping his brush into the paint, Bud glanced down at the dock. The gleaming runabout looked strikingly similar to the Rosario craft he had encountered a couple of summers back. A girl with flowing reddish hair sat at the wheel. It was Mary.

Seemingly unsure of her mission, Mary remained in the boat as it began to drift away from the float. Looking around, she spied Bud on the ladder and waved.

Bud let the brush plop into the paint bucket as he quickly descended the pole ladder. Reaching the ground, he briskly made his way to the gangway.

Part way down, Bud greeted Mary with a grin, calling out, "Hello Mary, nice to see you." Mary returned the greeting.

Reaching the float, Bud said, "Throw me the line and I'll pull you in."

The uncoiled line landed haphazardly in his arms. While it took no time to close the gap between the runabout and the float, it was enough time to see Mary was even more beautiful than he recalled. A bit taller with longer hair, what drew Bud's eyes was her tailored clothing defining a more mature figure.

Once the boat was resting at the dock, Mary jumped out and gave Bud a hug. His arms instinctively captured Mary with the line still in his hand.

"It's so good to see you again," Mary said. "I've thought of you often."

Transfixed on her twinkling green eyes, Bud released her saying, "You look wonderful."

"How have you been," they asked in unison.

Laughing, Mary said, "I am doing well, but I wanted to see you again."

Feeling his face start to flush without provocation, Bud struggled to control his emotions as they walked back toward the store.

The squeaking screen door caused Mabel to look up from her stool at the counter. Smiling, she left what she was doing to greet Mary with a mutual warm embrace.

They talked about nothing particular, just enjoying each other's company. Mary was nearing seventeen and would finish high school next year in Seattle.

"Yes, my parents are also at Rosario and doing well," Mary said when Mabel inquired. "We arrived the day before yesterday for just a week. I hope we can return before the summer ends."

Bud considered inquiring about the fate of her cousin but thought better of it.

Finally, Mary indicated, "I need to be heading back to Rosario. I told my parents I was coming here but promised I would be gone for only a short time."

Unbeknownst to Bud, Mary's mother was not in favor of her coming to see the Shaw Island boy. Not that she didn't feel indebted but having made it clear to her daughter that he was not of their kind. Besides, her family was Irish Catholic and his lineage, based on the Fowler name, was likely Protestant. Not an ideal match, to be sure.

Mary dismissed her mother's comments, "I am just going by to say 'hello' mother. For crying out loud, he did save my life."

Mary, Mabel and Bud strolled towards the dock. At the top of the gangway, Mabel hesitated and said, "I am going to say good-bye here and get back to the store."

Mary and Bud continued leisurely toward the boat.

Untying the boat, Bud knelt to hold it against the float while Mary, using his shoulder to steady herself, stepped into the Rosario runabout. Once aboard, Mary turned to Bud and kissed him briefly on the lips.

"It has been great to see you again Bud. Let's try to keep in touch. If I get back up this way before the summer ends, I will let you know."

"That would be nice," Bud proclaimed wishfully.

Watching from the dock until Mary disappeared around the point, he turned to see his mother's back going through the screen door.

Bud was conflicted for the remainder of the summer. Still carrying on much more than a friendship with Helen, but often thinking of Mary. As late summer whittled towards an end, Helen ran up to him on the beach. Tears welling in her eyes, she sought the comfort of his arms.

"Mom's on the porch Helen," Bud whispered, somewhat standoffishly.

Helen said softly, "Father has taken a job to run a cannery in Alaska." Her father would be abandoning the dangerous and unpredictable work of fishing to others.

Saddened by the news because she had been a memorable part of his life, Bud also harbored feelings that there was more to life beyond the confines of Shaw Island.

The day before Helen's departure, Bud decided to show her his secret retreat on Blind Island. He had thought about taking her there before but hadn't. Besides, after she left, his secret would remain his own.

Pulling on the oars, Helen sat in the stern watching him. Sweat glistening off him in the mid-day sun, Helen's eyes began to tear.

It reminded Bud of the time Mary sat in that very seat.

"I don't want to leave Shaw or you. I know we're still young. But, I wondered if someday we might be together forever," she confessed.

Bud let the oars go limp in the water and attempted to brush away her tears with his hand. His gesture seemed only to add fuel to the fire as her eyes brimmed over.

Except for creaking oar locks, the pair remained silent for the rest of the crossing.

The beach came into view as the couple cleared the inlet. Nearing the shore, Helen bounded out of the boat's stern and disappeared into the clear water amongst the eel grass. Rising from the depths, she shouted she saw a crab and submerged in a futile chase of the crustacean. Resurfacing near the protective reef, she admitted defeat and swam to shore.

Bud dragged the skiff onto the sand as Helen emerged from the frigid water to entwine him into her cold wet arms. Surrendering, Bud embraced her with a kiss before setting out to explore the tide line. Finding nothing significant on their exploration, Bud took her hand guiding their way across the logs to his fort.

Words between the two seemed strained somehow. Trying to lighten the mood, Bud recreated the frightful night he spent on the island with the unmerciful invading regiments of sand fleas. Helen laughed at Bud's description of his exploits.

Cuddling in the fort, they kissed more passionately than ever before. Taking his hand, Helen placed it against her lips and then lowered it upon her covered breast proclaiming, "I love you."

Bud wasn't sure what to say, but felt the need to respond, "You know I feel the same."

"Someday I hope we will be together again," she confessed, breaking away teary-eyed.

The next day, Bud watched from the dock as a passenger boat's bow parted the waters ahead and carried Helen out of his life. Gripping the arrowhead from Blind Island tightly in his palm, Bud followed the vessel's progress until Helen disappeared from sight.

CHAPTER 4

1917

A WINTER AND SPRING HAD PASSED SINCE HELEN HAD LEFT THE ISLAND. Sensing her son's restlessness, Mabel sought her brother's counsel. Rarely around, Frank chose life aboard the tug *Lorne* as his preferred lifestyle. *Lorne* was one of the most powerful tugs plying the waters of the Pacific Coast. She was 157 feet long powered by a 1300 horse steam-driven engine. It was a place where clean clothes and a shave were considered an inconvenience—a life insulated from the challenges most endured to keep a roof over their head and food on the table. While Frank still maintained his small cabin on Shaw, it was a rarity to find him there for more than a few days a month. With a steady income, he helped his sister financially manage their departed parent's store.

From time to time, at Mabel's urging, Frank arranged for Bud to make runs with him if the towing consignment did not take them too far out of the area. The trips generally never exceeded a couple days, ensuring that Mabel didn't have to fend for herself for too long. Bud missing a few days of school was not an issue.

Lorne's steam whistle sounded across the bay. Responding to the tug's broadcast, Bud left a customer dallying about and briskly made his way to the rear screen door. Seeing the *Lorne*, Bud called out to all within earshot and ran down to the end of the dock.

The massiveness of the tug was impressive. Perched on the bow was Uncle Frank.

When *Lorne* was within hollering distance, Frank yelled, "Are you up for a run to Victoria to pick up a tow bound for the south sound? After that, we have another tow to take back to Vancouver. We should only be gone a few days."

Bud flashed a wide-eyed grin, turned and raced back up the ramp.

Bounding into the store, he excitedly exclaimed to his mother, "They want me to make a run to Canada, then south and then back to Canada. I'd only be a few days. Can I go?"

"Go get your bag," she answered knowingly. Having quickly gathered the necessary belongings from upstairs, Bud returned to give his mother a fleeting kiss before heading toward the back porch.

Mabel called out, "Wait a minute. I have something for you. You don't think I forgot about your sixteenth birthday tomorrow?"

Bud ripped open the brown paper string tied gift to find a dark blue woolen seaman's cap. Adjusting the cap on her son's head, she gave him a hug and said, "Now be careful."

Taking a few steps to make his leave, he stopped and ran back. Bending down to meet her short frame, he planted a kiss on her cheek and said, "Thanks Mom. I love you."

Glancing back as he raced down the gangway, he saw his mother wiping her eyes with the edge of the flowered apron that encircled her waist.

Captain Lyle Block maneuvered the huge tug around ever so gently bring her low freeboard stern up to the float. *Lorne's* captain was a skinny guy with short graying hair and a matching ill-trimmed beard. Gangly arms and legs gave him a distinctive puppet-like gait. His identifiable grin flashed several gold teeth. An ever-present captain's hat looked as though it hadn't been washed since the day he placed it atop his head.

Bud threw his bag to Frank and leapt up to the bulwarks as *Lorne* sounded a long echoing blast signaling their departure. Water frothing from astern, the sound of her departure fading up the bay, *Lorne* began moving toward the channel beyond.

Bud turned and waved a final goodbye to his mother. Frank mimicked the gesture. Bud knew she would make do during his absence, but nevertheless felt a bit guilty leaving.

Pleased that the captain had taken the time to stop as he would any crewmember, Bud considered Captain Block's parting words on the last trip, "The next time you're aboard you need to start earning your keep instead of just taking up space."

Block stepped outside the wheelhouse and yelled down, "Bud, go below. Store your bag in the crew's quarters. Then report to the wheelhouse."

A familiar bunker diesel scent permeated Bud's senses as he stepped into the passageway. Wedging his bag between his legs, he grasped the smooth pipe ladder-like stair handrail with his grubby cotton gloves and launched himself forward. He reached the bottom with a perfect landing. Finding an empty upper bunk in the cramped crew quarters, Bud tossed his bag atop the shoddy thin gray striped mattress. Taking a minute before heading back topside, he perused the bulkhead pictures of scantily clad women. Some were the same as the last time he was aboard, but now there were a couple where the ladies had no clothes at all. Hung with care, it was doubtful Rembrandt originals would receive higher esteem in the same setting.

Bud knocked on the wheelhouse door, hesitating briefly on the small landing before entering. The customary knock was not intended to generate a reply, but to provide Captain Block an opportunity to secure any loose charts that otherwise could blow about when the door was opened.

At the helm, the varnished spoke wheel was nearly as high as Frank was tall. If it weren't for the lower portion of the wheel slotted below deck, it might exceed his height. Multiple wraps of rope encircled the wheel's spool before leading below into the unknown where it controlled the tug's rudder. Bud had been cautioned on previous trips to watch his feet near the narrow deck opening. There had been an instance when a helmsman had gotten his foot caught by one of the spokes when a riptide manhandled *Lorne*. Without warning, the underwater force had caused the rudder, and in turn the wheel, to move violently catching the seaman's foot dragging it into the slot. His foot broken and mangled, the man ultimately had to take a desk job in the Seattle company office.

Block was hunkered down over a chart plotting *Lorne's* course. He glanced at Bud before dropping his head back to the task at hand. Block's demeanor seemed a bit more formal than previous trips signaling to Bud that his sightseeing days were over.

Like most sailors, as a boy, Block had been a recruit not unlike the young man standing in the wheelhouse when he first ventured to sea. Through hard work and persistence, he had climbed his way up to command his own vessel.

Bud's eyes swept the wheelhouse. The sparse, yet meticulous surroundings, delineated the area's one and only purpose—operation of the vessel. It was one of the areas onboard that symbolized formal tradition. The gray painted deck contrasted with the varnished fir wainscoted bulkheads. The gleaming brass floor mounted telegraph, pedestal compass and engine room speaking tube were lined up like soldiers at attention. Only Block's chart table, positioned on high legs so he could comfortably lean over it, showed signs of organized disarray with multiple navigation charts piled atop each other. A stop watch, log book, and parallel chart ruler were positioned along the upper portion. A lit pipe balanced precariously in the middle of it all.

Stepping over to a window next to Frank, Bud scanned the horizon. He had learned that any crewmen in the wheelhouse was expected to add another pair of eyes to the operation unless specifically there for another purpose.

Captain Block moved his attention from a chart to the ship's log where he made a notation. Placing his pencil into a bulkhead mounted holder, he crossed the planked deck to an elevated chair giving him a commanding view of the channel ahead.

Once assured of their heading, Block said, "Bud, are you ready to go to work?"

"Aye, sir," Bud responded.

"Report to Jeb in the engine room."

Not Bud's first choice of assignments for such a nice day, he nevertheless enthusiastically responded, "Right away sir," and headed for the door.

Observing the routine, Bud knocked and paused before leaving.

Deafening noise, heat and the ever-present pungent odor of bunker oil contrasted sharply with the sea air as Bud descended into the heart of the ship. Looking around, it took him a moment to spy Jeb hunched over one of the many reservoirs that lubricated the whirling gears and wheels of the engine. Each reservoir had a needle valve that was tweaked to ensure a precise amount of lubricant was being measured out.

As if expecting the recruit, Jeb nodded to Bud motioning forward to a partition that separated a workbench area from the engine's mechanics. While the noise might have diminished slightly, the heat from the nearby steam boiler works seemed almost unbearable in the confined space. Jeb extended his oily hand as he wiped his brow with a soiled cloth from his rear pocket. Bud took old Jeb's hand eagerly, believing that an oily hand was as good a welcome as any.

Jeb, a nasty-mouth codger, smelling of the engine room regardless of where you might find him, seemed to be in constant conversation with no one other than himself. Substantially over-weight, his wardrobe usually consisted of a low-slung pair of pants and an undershirt stained with the filth of his trade. His unkempt appearance was enhanced by a protruding belly hanging below his shirt and a cavernous butt crack when he squatted or bent over. His dark slicked back hair no doubt received much of its grooming from his oily hand running through it.

Bud spent the next few hours cleaning up the engine room and polishing the brass scattered throughout. There were few jobs more satisfying aboard a workboat than reclaiming the gleam of tarnished brass. Startled, a series of bells broke the rhythmic chug of the steam engine. Still in the midst of polishing the engine room telegraph, the arrow pointer moved to the "STAND BY" position, warning Jeb that the tug's engine revolutions were about to change.

The round clock-like face of the telegraph mimicked that of the wheelhouse. The only difference being that the engine room telegraph hung from the bulkhead instead of sitting atop a floor mounted pedestal. The face of the telegraph was sectioned into "AHEAD" and "ASTERN" separated by "STOP" in the traditional twelve o'clock position. The directional headings were further segregated by "SLOW", "HALF", and "FULL" to denote the wheelhouse engine demands. There were also auxiliary notations for "STAND BY" and "FINISHED WITH EN-GINE."

The cantankerous engineer had served under Block for nearly eight years and instinctively knew the amount of power needed for the various telegraph call outs. He had learned his Captain was a capable ship handler who understood *Lorne's* quirks and anticipated her every move. Jeb had previously told Bud that not all captains he had served understood their vessels. When such was the case, every series of random telegraph call outs seemed a crisis.

The indicator moved from "FULL AHEAD" to "SLOW."

Quickly throttling the steam valve, slowing the engine's revolutions, Jeb moved the engine room telegraph handle to "SLOW AHEAD" signaling Captain Block that he had received and understood the order. The telegraph rang out "HALF ASTERN" requiring Jeb to stop the propeller shaft, change the engine revolution direction and throttle up the RPMs. Not bothering to look at a large brass RPM gauge mounted on the bulkhead, he knew by the engine's sound when the proper setting had been achieved for the task at hand.

About the time the engine's speed reached Jeb's satisfaction, the telegraph signaled "SLOW," then "STOP."

Bud could tell that *Lorne's* forward movement had come to a halt as her tie-up lines went taut and the tug pulled to one side. He could also see the bilge water move forward and then level out as she settled against her moorage.

Block signaled "FINISHED WITH ENGINE."

As *Lorne's* massive steam engine was disengaged, silence spread throughout her.

In the habit of using hand signals in the normally deafening confines, Jeb motioned Bud to go topside.

The shrill of the unleashed boiler steam greeted Bud as he stepped onto the upper deck into the bright sunlight. Blinded, Bud squinted and stumbled over a tie up line, pulling it out of Frank's hand. Saying nothing, Frank's frown communicated volumes. Bud held his tongue even though he wanted to offer an excuse.

Block appeared and bellowed, "We're all going up-town for dinner. Wash up, put on a clean shirt and be back on deck in twenty minutes."

Bud had been to Victoria, Canada only one other time. During that trip, also aboard the *Lorne*, the crew never left the tug—only there long enough to pick up a tow. Having hardly ventured beyond his island surroundings, the fact of the matter was that Bud had never eaten in a restaurant.

As the crew of six gathered dockside and headed up the wharf, Bud wore his new seaman's cap squarely atop his head with a sense of pride. He straightened up with an air of importance when he noticed two boys about his age talking and looking towards him.

Wandering along the wharf area observing the activities, they entered a pile supported tavern that hung over the water. Block ordered a round of beers while his crew arranged wayward chairs around a table. Bud was a dumbfounded when the barmaid set a beer in front of him.

Cautiously, he moved his hand toward the odd-shaped handled mug. But, before he could take possession, Frank scooped it up and gulped nearly half of the golden liquid before sliding it back to his nephew.

The rest of the crew drank another while Bud nursed his first. Inwardly, he questioned why the nasty tasting stuff had a following at all.

Trailing Captain Block back onto the wharf, he steered them into a nearby shipwreck of a structure. The sign nailed to the weathered exterior said it all, "Good Food—Good Prices." The worn fir flooring and small-windowed structure reminded Bud of their store back on Shaw. Noticing his chair rocking a bit, Bud looked down to find a worn pattern to the floor. The random sizes and styles of tables and chairs strewn about suggested the establishment had been cobbled together after having served some other use in the past.

A plain but robust woman made her way through the obstacle course towards the assembled crew. Flashing a white, straight-toothed grin, she unburdened herself of an overflowing pitcher and fistful of mugs onto the planked table. Her full-length dress, probably fitting her at one time, pulled at the seams. Bud couldn't help but catch an eyeful of her abundant tits as she bent and planted a kiss on their leader's mouth.

His declaration that she was his long-lost sister raised a good laugh among everyone in hearing range. It took Bud a second to gather that the lady was in fact not the captain's relative.

Frank made sure his nephew's glass only received a partial filling. Bud didn't like his earlier introduction to the distasteful brew but wasn't about to say so. An array of fish, clams, vegetables and other assorted offerings were brought to their table. Everyone attacked the spread as if they hadn't eaten in days. As the evening progressed, having had their fill, plates were ceremonially pushed to the center of the table. Jeb loosened his belt and continued spooning more onto his plate long after everyone else had all but given up. Still, groans of appreciation spread across the gathering as a piping hot blackberry cobbler landed loudly in the middle of it all.

Finally, after the last berry disappeared, Block, with a twinkle in his eyes, announced, "It's time to call it a night boys."

All responded to the directive by pushing themselves away from the table. Rising, they headed for the door. Block held back.

Bud asked his uncle, "Shouldn't we wait for the Captain?"

Frank did not answer, but turned his head slightly back prompting his nephew to do the same. It was then Bud saw Captain Block, whiskey bottle in one hand and his lady friend in the other, disappearing through an adjoining doorway. Footsteps could be heard making their way to the building's second floor. Bud thought the silhouettes of the twosome reminded him of the Mutt and Jeff characters in the Sunday comics.

Darkness had fallen transforming the mood and appearance of the waterfront district. Crowds of boisterous patrons jostled on the boardwalks flowing in and out of the various drinking establishments. Along the way, Jeb urged them into a pub for a nightcap. Frank hesitated, but followed, placing a protective hand on his nephew's shoulder as they entered.

Bud began nursing a beer when a curtain bordering their table jerkily opened to reveal an empty stage. Wondering why the unassuming action caused an already noisy gathering to erupt into a barrage of whistles and catcalls, Bud looked to Frank for an explanation. Frank said to his nephew, "If you ever leak a word of this to my sister, this'll be the last run you'll ever make."

Piano keys began dancing near the edge of the stage. The crowd's tempo continued to build as the howling was joined by clapping hands and stomping feet. Then, as if the boisterous behavior conjured her up, a young enchantress sauntered from an off-stage wing. Her red hair—a good match for her bright attire—flowed down past her waist. Immediately, Bud thought of Mary's auburn locks as the dancer's gyrating hips caused such unrest that the piano player struggled to be heard over the commotion.

Bud took a sip of beer stopping in mid-swallow as the dancer started to shed a piece of her attire. Unable to take his eyes off her, she began to inch her top down, slowly, very slowly, demanding a response from the crowd.

The stripper looked directly at Bud and winked, but it went unnoticed by the young spectator. Her top floated to the stage as she whirled across the floor inducing sounds of coins chiming on the hardwood around her. Some approached for a better view with the pretense of placing a coin or two into a container strategically placed at the edge of the stage.

She moved suggestively across the platform.

Bud strained to catch sight of unfamiliar nipples while her hair swirled over, past and around them, always hinting at the possibility of a clear view, but never fully delivering. Then, having been tipped off by one of his fellow crewmembers, without Bud even noticing, the pianist began to hammer out the familiar melody of Happy Birthday. Slithering to a point only a few feet from Bud, the seductress focused her attention only on him. Bewitchingly, she began to inch her ruby colored panties down until they dropped to and past her dainty feet. All the while, her flowing hair shielding what Bud knew was there.

Performing for the benefit of the young birthday patron, a patch of reddish hair flashed by, disappeared and reappeared under cascading locks drifting across her naked body. The unveiling, seemingly in slow motion, held Bud transfixed. Fleetingly, Bud glimpsed the contours where her legs branched, as his own crotch began to stir. For just a moment, he was within touching distance. Then the music stopped.

Lingering, the stripper picked up her ruby panties, presented them as a souvenir to her young admirer, blew a kiss, and said "Happy Birthday."

Red faced, Bud shoved the gift into his front pocket as the gathering roared their approval. Crossing the stage, the songstress scooped up the rest of her castoff ensemble, grabbed the coin container and exited as the curtain closed behind her.

Frank looked at his nephew, knowingly raising his brows, and said, "We have to be up early. It's time to be heading back to *Lorne*."

Bud was relieved that a couple of the crew took a few minutes to drain the last of their beer—time spent to rearrange the front of his pants.

Beginning to feel a bit queasy, the walk back became toilsome for Bud. Nearing *Lorne's* moorage, Frank steadied his nephew after he unsuccessfully tried to place his foot onto the tug's rub rail to board. One of the crew and Frank each grabbed an arm and hoisted him aboard helping him down to the crew quarters. In no condition to make the climb to his designated upper berth, he fell atop one of the lower bunks.

Bud closed his eyes, quickly reopening them as his surroundings spun. With little warning, he knew he was about to be sick and hurriedly staggered topside. Nearing the rail just in time, he spewed one of the best meals he had ever eaten. Unfortunately, only a small portion of the projectile cleared *Lorne's* bulwarks.

"You know, if you're just going to feed the fish, I'm gonna tell Block to save his money next time," Frank said standing in the shadows smoking his pipe.

Frank stayed until Bud could no longer gag anything else up. While he waited, Frank grabbed a bucket with a line and dropped it overboard. Repeatedly hoisting the water-filled bucket, he washed down the side of the tug before guiding his nephew back to the crew quarters.

CHAPTER 5

Captain Block roused his crew at daybreak for a quick onboard breakfast before moving *Lorne* down the harbor to pick up their tow. Jeb had been up an hour earlier to fire up the boiler and build-up a head of steam. Bud declined to eat anything.

Sensing the recruit might not be up to returning to the heat and smell of the engine room, Block directed, "Bud, spend the morning cleaning and straightening up the galley area and anything else that could use it. This afternoon we'll do some scraping and painting."

Leaning on the deck rail just outside of the galley, Bud watched as *Lorne* maneuvered to a huge barge of lime destined for a south sound pulp mill. With little fanfare, tow cables were made fast followed by ringing telegraph bells. *Lorne* churned the surrounding stern waters as her tow began to pull away from her moorage. Their roost underway, seagulls took flight noisily squawking their complaints.

Frank winched out the spooled tow cable maintaining a constant tension between the tug and tethered barge as they headed towards the straits. Bud studied the cable connecting *Lorne* to her tow astonished that once the proper length had been reeled, it disappeared in an arc below the surface. He learned that tugs had experienced boats passing between them and their tow without incident if the offending boat was fast and had a shallow enough draft. There were also a few stories of boats unknowingly passing between the two in fog or darkness never to be seen again. Once a tow is underway, there is little that can be done to stop it until it slows on its own accord or a tug comes about to rein it in.

Returning to the galley, Bud discovered that the early morning air and activity had finally broken his bout of queasiness. Finding a dried biscuit and cup of milk, he was able to take the edge off his hunger.

Lorne entered Haro Strait bound for Bellingham.

"It's going to be a hot one," Block surmised. "Look at the Strait. Not a hint of a breeze. And the temperature already feels warm for this time of day."

"Yep," Frank agreed, "We'll likely run into fog ahead in the usual locations."

An hour later, as if Frank had foreseen the future, a seemingly impenetrable veil of fog blocked their path ahead.

"Alright Frank, you know the drill," Block said as *Lorne's* piercing horn sounded.

"Bud, stand watch on the bow. Report anything you hear or see," Frank commanded.

Taking his position, Bud peered intently into the approaching barrier as *Lorne's* horn sounded again. Bud mumbled, "Shit, that's loud," knowing it was one of many encores to follow.

Entering the fringe of the moist blanket, traces of sunlight reflected like a sparkling chandelier. Another loud blast of the fog horn warned others of their position. The return echo additionally provided valuable navigation detail—an understanding of any nearby shoreline. A keen ear could detect near area shorelines by matching the echo patterns with area navigation charts. A quick return echo would mean land was near. A longer or fading echo identified a bay or channel.

Tiny droplets of moisture began to cling to Bud's clothes and drip off his eye lashes. Shivering, he turned up the collar of his woolen shirt wishing he had taken the time to dress more warmly.

Frank dropped one of the wheelhouse windows. Craning his head out, he yelled down to his nephew, "Do you hear the return echo off the port?"

Bud wasn't sure at first. Was he being tested?

"Yes. I hear it now," Bud reported.

"Good. That's Mandarte Island," Frank responded, already having detected the echo and duly reporting same to Captain Block.

"I hear seagulls," Bud yelled up to Frank.

"Good report," Frank shouted back, aware of the constant deluge of squawking seagulls that inhabited the bare rock.

Even with the fog, the trip fell into a constant rhythm. It was clear to Bud that while the fog was always a concern, the crew felt comfortable in their skills to operate without mishap. By late morning, clear blue skies began to unveil themselves.

Nestled in the warmth of the sun once again, Bud and another deckhand broke out scrapers and began preparing the wheelhouse for a new coat of white paint. As paint flaked away under their relentless attack, Bud paused to watch a pod of black and white orcas appear and begin to overtake them. As if choreographed, the graceful mammals broke the surface of the water with their large dorsal fins only to disappear and resurface again. One orca breached totally out of the water putting on a show.

Wondering if the tales were true, Bud thought to himself, "would they really just as soon eat man instead of their routine diet of salmon and seals?"

In time, the pod headed off on a course of their own.

Perched on a wheelhouse stool that evening, Bud scrutinized the shadowy outline of the islands they passed as the moon lit their way. Captain Block had retreated to his cabin a couple hours before to get some much-needed sleep. Frank was left in command. By this action, it was clear the captain had a high degree of trust in Frank. Block would return at midnight for the remainder of the night watch.

Leaning against the wheelhouse window ledge, Bud's eyelids began to weigh heavily. Jarringly, Frank kicked his nephew's stool, shaking him back to consciousness. "If the Captain found anyone sleeping on watch, it might be the last time they ever crewed for him. Move your stool back! That way, if you ever start to drift off, you'll fall forward and jar yourself."

As promised, Block returned around midnight with one of the deckhands. "Frank, go get some shut-eye. I'll send someone to wake you and Bud at five."

Before leaving, Bud pointed out a set of distant lights off their starboard bow that appeared to be another tug and tow. Block nodded his approval.

Under the soothing drone of the engine and waves brushing against the bow just beyond his pillow, Bud drifted toward sleep. He thought about the previous night in Victoria, triggering wanton thoughts of Mary. Maybe it was the dancer's red hair and green eyes. He visualized

Mary's features—her breasts, her skin, her unseen wisps of hair. As he lay there, he could feel his body responding until relief swept over him.

❈

Their destination in sight, *Lorne* slowed and skillfully came about to tie off her tow. Proceeding cautiously in the narrow confines of the busy harbor, they moved towards an unloading wharf. The ritual performed many times, the transition was carried out flawlessly by the crew with nary a word other than the sounding of telegraph bells signaling Jeb. No longer a casual observer, Bud helped with the lines.

After securing the barge alongside a pier and transferring the appropriate paperwork, the mammoth tug moved to a neighboring fuel dock to top off her tanks. During the fueling, Block sent a couple of the crew to a nearby grocery for provisions. Bud stood by with his uncle and was surprised at the enormous amount of fuel required to fire the tug's boiler.

Supplies and fuel onboard, *Lorne* and her crew moved deeper into the wharf area toward a majestic old three-mast clipper ship.

"There's our next tow," Block announced. "We're bound for Vancouver, Canada."

Narrowing the distance to her, Bud studied the detailed figurehead depicting a woman that still graced the ship's bow. Aft of the life size figure, the ship's name, "*AMERICA,*" was intricately carved into the upper planks of her hull. What a fine sailing ship she must have been during her prime to be given such a name. With the advent of more powerful engines, she had become a symbol of bygone years—reduced to a soiled coal hauler.

The once proud *America* slid away from her moorage tethered helplessly alongside *Lorne.* Clearing the constraints of the harbor, *America* was set adrift only to be recaptured as Frank winched the tow cable that shackled her. Forcibly, the figurehead guided ship came about unwillingly like a leashed dog.

Bud kept busy for the next few hours storing provisions, making the galley shipshape and scrubbing down the stern deck. Later, helping to put together the evening meal for those assembled in the galley, he took dinner to the wheelhouse for Captain Block and down below to Jeb.

The helmsman would have to wait until he was relieved. After a time, Bud retrieved their empty plates and returned to the galley to wash dishes and re tidy the area.

Captain Block told Bud that the 232-foot *America* had been built in 1874 in Quincy, Massachusetts. During her prime, her beauty and speed were unsurpassed by no other clipper ship. The larger than life figurehead that still adorned her bow had been recognized around the world as being one of the most artistic carvings ever to grace a ship.

As the day's end cast a glow to the western sky, Bud sat on the stern watching *America's* silhouette against the fading halo beyond. He could only imagine the exotic places and oceans she had sailed. Instead of coal, she would have been loaded with precious cargo. Envisioning white sails billowing from the pinnacles of her masts, her rigging creaking under the burden of captured wind, she sliced through blue-green ocean swells. The constant protector, clothes flowing against the head winds, sword in hand, she scanned the horizon ready to fend off any danger that might be encountered.

The remaining embers of light descending from view, Bud said quietly to *America's* lady, "One day I hope to retrace the seas and ports where you led your crew."

A yellowish band of moonlight glimmering atop the water seemed to beckon *Lorne* and *America* onward as Bud bid the lady figurehead goodnight.

Bud awoke at 5:40 a.m. to the shrill of *Lorne's* steam whistle. Quickly pulling on his soiled work clothes, he headed topside. A blanketing fog accosted him as he stepped onto the deck. He could not see *America*, but knew she was there because of her cable leading astern.

Frank appeared and barked, "Dress warmly and report to the bow for fog duty!"

Bud raced below and donned a sweater that his mother had knitted a year or two previously. The arms were a bit short, but the warmth reassuring. Positioning his new hat down tightly, he scurried back topside.

Finding Frank perched on the bow staring relentlessly into the gray mist, he stepped up next to him as if hunting an unknown danger. Frank explained that the few feet of elevation difference between the deck and the wheelhouse could significantly improve the visibility over the water.

Frank said, "These are some of the most treacherous conditions for a tug and tow. The tidal currents around the reefs and islands we're navigating through require we maintain a constant speed or we might lose control of our tow. We don't have the luxury of slowing to feel our way along."

As the steam whistle continually sounded, Frank and Captain Block identified their location by the return echo. They were just west of Kanaka Bay on San Juan Island.

Frank spoke, "Did you hear the echo of the small inlet? Hear that?" stopping in mid-sentence as his brow furrowed.

"Cap, I don't like the sounding pattern," Frank bellowed towards the wheelhouse. "They're coming back too quickly!"

Block did not second guess Frank as the telegraph bells rang out in terror signaling Jeb to slow.

Knowingly, Frank bolted to the stern engaging the tow winch reeling *America* in as her cable slacked.

Just north of Deadman Bay, the fog horn at the Lime Kiln Point lighthouse sounded.

Bud remained at the bow willing his eyes to penetrate the mist.

America on a short lead, Block began to slowly turn *Lorne* to port away from the echo return.

Suddenly, Bud's heart jumped as he saw kelp patches appear in the surrounding water. Instinctively, Bud knew they were in trouble.

"KELP!" Bud yelled with all his might, "KELP!"

Feverishly, Jeb engaged *Lorne's* massive engine and gears as the brass telegraph commanded.

The waters around *Lorne* boiled as she responded, "FULL ASTERN." Jeb had no firsthand knowledge of what was going on topside, but the telegraph call outs bore witness they were in trouble.

Lorne halted her advancement and began to creep astern. Block signaled the engine room "STOP."

America's tether no longer led astern but was swinging starboard as the invisible sailing ship continued to stand her course.

Lorne sat motionless with her engine idling as Captain Block contemplated his next move. The brief lull fleeting, *Lorne's* stern began to swing in the direction of the cable. *America* was dragging her captor—master of her leash.

Block knew if he was going to halt *America's* march into the unknown he needed to act quickly, but the precarious surroundings dictated caution.

After a brief hesitation, Block ordered, "Release the winch brake now!"

Defeated, his voice trailing off, "Let her go Frank."

Daring hardly to breathe, the crew stood by helplessly, wondering, hoping. A dull scraping sound broke the deafening silence. Unseen, the clipper ship *America* was aground.

"Frank. Get up here!" Blocked called out.

Frank raced up the stairway to the wheelhouse and shot through the door. Captain Block was hunkered over a chart laid out on the table.

"Where the fuck did I go wrong?" Block muttered, not really expecting a response. "Was it the sideward influence of the tide? I know we were on the right compass heading. If we weren't properly positioned, we should have detected a longer echo pattern on the starboard as we entered the islands lining the channel entrance."

A man beaten, Block uttered, "Lift you goddamn fog."

"Frank, go back on deck and drop the sounder weight over the side to check our depth. And for Chrissake don't dally!"

The weighted line hardly had a chance to spool out before it slacked on the water's surface.

Frank yelled back with a sense of urgency, "We only have about four feet of water under our keel."

To make matters worse the tide was ebbing, going out. They would be aground if they didn't find deeper water. The telegraph bell broke the uneasy silence as Block commanded Jeb's attention.

Lorne began to maneuver ever so slowly. They would try backtracking the compass heading they were following before they found themselves in such dire circumstances.

Frank began to spool out the tow cable. Gingerly, they began their retreat.

Moving less than fifty yards, *Lorne* nosed up against a submerged reef and stopped. The unknown draped a suffocating mood over the crew as mysterious rays of sunlight began to slowly dissipate the fog. Kelp bulbs with trailing ribbons were everywhere. The etched outline of *America* began to emerge from the grayness. She was listing on reef some hundred feet away.

Lorne and *America* were trapped, if not condemned.

Block told Frank, "Go below and tell Jeb that the near shore looks to have a soft bottom. We're going to beach away from the rocks before it is too late."

Block turned the *Lorne* toward the eelgrass shallows signaling Jeb "SLOW AHEAD." No sooner had the tug began to move when the telegraph sounded "STOP."

The great tug lifted slightly, halting her march as she settled into the muddy bottom.

A bald eagle glided overhead in a patch of blue sky surveying the unfamiliar stage.

All eyes squinted into the misty remains towards the distant islands that marked the channel's entrance. The outline of one island looked somehow different. As if willing their concentrated focus to part the fog, two large anchored lumber barges began to take shape in the channel. Block had mistaken the return echo off the barges as one of the islands. *Lorne* was some hundred yards off course.

"The sorry fuck'n captain who left his tow in such a narrow channel should be keel-hauled!" Frank protested for all to hear.

The menacing tide's withdrawal continued throughout the morning. *Lorne* settled into the bay mud at an ever-increasing heel until she lay on her keel and side. At low tide, sloshing around in only a foot of water, the crew was able to inspect the tug's underside, rudder and propeller. The bow portion of her keel was gouged, but with a little dry dock carpentry, she should be no worse for the ordeal. With a little luck, they should be able to re-float her at high tide and make their escape.

Plotting *Lorne's* retreat, Bud watched Block sketch the rocky barriers that caged them from the main channel. Once the tide rose, his reef survey would guide their way.

Captain Block remained a pillar of professionalism during the ordeal, yet all knew it had to be a low point in his career. He would survive the professional humiliation and maintain his Coast Guard Merchant Marine Officer License after a formal inquiry pardoned him for extenuating circumstances.

No longer caressed by comforting waters, *America* lay perched precariously on her side atop a rock outcropping. Her keel and ribs creaking and straining under the weight of her cargo, she was doomed. Her final screams of pain noisily spreading across the inlet, she surrendered to the burden she held within. Broken and humiliated, her dirty cargo spilled around her watery gravesite.

Pardoned from her degrading bondage, she was free once more to feel the joy of cutting through caressing blue seas under billowing sun-bleached sails.

CHAPTER 6

1918

A LONE SEAGULL GLIDED EFFORTLESSLY OVER THE WAVE TIPS AS SPORADIC fits of rain began to fall. Dimpling the surrounding channel, the drizzle splattered and sizzled on the steam engine boiler. Bud tucked a corner of the tarp over the supplies that filled his boat before placing a tattered canvas hat atop his head. On a heading into East Sound, his destination was the Rosario Estate located on Cascade Bay, Orcas Island. While most of Rosario's day to day operational supplies came directly from Seattle, the Shaw Store's supplemental deliveries played a significant role in the financial wellbeing of the Fowlers.

The nation was at war. While WWI began in 1914, the United States had managed to remain formally out of the fray until April of 1917 after seven U. S. merchant ships were sunk by German U-boats. Even the death of 128 Americans when the *Lusitania* was destroyed by a U-boat in May of 1915 had not drawn the reluctant United States to declare war. While a constant cloud engulfed the nation, the formal declaration seemed to have minimal impact on the remote island way of life.

Bud had been using Frank's steamboat to make the weekly Rosario deliveries. Well fitted for the task, heavily built, she never labored when loaded. As the short-lived summer shower began giving way to traces of sunlight, Bud witnessed a fleeting rainbow pinpointing the estate.

Now seventeen, feeling restless, his Shaw Island daily activities had become boring. Besides, there were no girls on the island that seemed to peak his interest. The random encounters with Mary over the last two summers were memorable, yet nothing gave him hope they would be anything more than indiscriminate friends. And, the trips to the estate only seemed to ingrain in his mind that he was not up to their standards—seeing was not experiencing. He wondered if he should join the war effort, but dismissed the thoughts knowing such action would result in a significant hardship for his mother.

Making the occasional trip up and down the coast with Frank and Captain Block on *Lorne* helped, but the store responsibilities always came first. He did know there was more to the life than afforded by his narrow upbringing and he wanted, no, intended, to seek it out.

Nearing his destination, the familiar outline of *America's* figurehead prominently overlooked the bay. Bud recalled his first visit to the estate the previous fall when Robert Moran, the estate's owner, had hired Frank to retrieve the figurehead from her reef bound grave. Like others before him, Moran had been captivated with the statue's beauty and workmanship. While glad to see her preserved, helping with her salvage and relocation, Bud was jealous that Moran possessed her. Mounted to a timber resembling the shape of a ship's bow, the only consolation he felt was that she commanded a fitting post where she was able to gaze over the surrounding vista.

Tying up at Rosario, Bud began to off-load the supplies onto the dock. From the float, he would carry the boxed items up the ramp to the upper landing. The final transport to the mansion would be aided by a wheeled cart.

Toiling, Bud watched the progress on a large sailing yacht under construction cradled near the buildings that once housed the Cascade Lumber Company. Down on the adjoining beach, children were at play darting in and out of the water as their watchful mothers sipped drinks delivered from the house. In the distance, Bud could hear the back and forth volley of a tennis ball. Summer brought many visitors to the estate as well as an increase of staff to cater to their needs. Taking note of two girls about his own age heading to the beach, he knew they were socially beyond his reach.

Delivering the supplies to a storage room adjoining the estate's enormous kitchen, Bud learned, as was often the case, that Rosario would be catering to a large group of guests that evening. The kitchen area and adjoining dining room were a buzz of activity. Folks adorned in crisp white aprons went about their assigned tasks preparing a multitude of hors d'oeuvres, main course, and dessert selections. Fresh clams, oysters, shrimp, crab and fish were strewn across one expansive sink counter. Fresh breads and cakes were being mixed and thrust into ovens at the opposite end of the room. Multi-colored fruits and vegetables were sliced meticulously in another area. A large center counter area was piled with stacks of plates and serving trays where the variety of culinary delights would ultimately come together before making their exit through the large swinging doors to the privileged. He acknowledged a plain looking girl a year older than himself who had left Shaw to become a domestic at the estate. Likely having sealed her destiny, he wondered what the future held for himself.

Bud sought out Rosario's overseer, Earl Yansen. Yansen had managed the lumber company prior to its acquisition by Robert Moran. Staying on at Moran's request, he provided continuity for the transformation of the mill to the grand estate it was today. Everyone under Moran's employment reported up through Yansen. Known to be a cranky sort who tolerated little, he was responsible for every operational detail. Nothing escaped his scrutiny from stocking Moran's favorite scotch to ensuring weed free flower gardens. One look around the compound left little doubt Yansen was well fitted for the job.

One could usually find Mr. Yansen in his office off the second-floor staircase landing. From his vantage point, he had a commanding view of the estate and boat basin. Office furnishings included a strategically placed brass telescope that could monitor a worker or an approaching watercraft. However, the scope's alignment often focused on the beach area where female guests gathered.

Quickly stepping aside as Mr. Yansen's office door swung open, Bud faced a plump, pretty-faced woman clothed in traditional domestic attire. Appearing a bit ruffled and red-faced, she hurried past. Yansen, a six-foot bearded Norwegian, with only a halo of graying blond hair, seemed startled to find Bud standing there.

Yansen paid Bud for the delivered supplies with little formality. Thanking the man, Bud headed back down the stairs.

"Hey boy! Come back here a minute," Yansen bellowed.

Re-climbing the staircase, Bud entered the room.

Yansen stood gazing out one of the sunlit windows as a column of cigar smoke choked the alcove above. Barely inside the room, Bud stood awkwardly, unsure if he should announce his arrival. An uncomfortable amount of time passed before Yansen turned and faced Bud. Framed by the sunrays streaming into the room, the veil of smoke gave the overseer a saint-like appearance—a far cry from the truth by anyone's account.

"How would you like to work at Rosario for the remainder of the summer?" Yansen barked. It was more of a command than a question.

Before Bud could answer, the lumber manager said, "I recognize you may have a need to help your mother at the store, but I am willing to schedule you accordingly."

While Yansen's demeanor generally fit his reputation, he seemed a bit friendlier than Bud's previous dealings with the man.

"Your initial duties will be to clean up, fetch tools and run errands for the shipwrights building Mr. Moran's new yacht. From time to time, I'll also need you to help for special events at the mansion. On those late nights, you can sleep over in the staff quarters."

Bud responded, "I appreciate the offer and would like to say yes, but I need to check with my mom first. Can I let you know tomorrow?"

"Sure. Be here ready for work at 12:30 tomorrow," Yansen responded with an air of finality. In his mind the decision had been made.

Walking along the concrete path back to the boat basin, Bud paused to watch a bald eagle soar from its vantage point atop a fir tree. Its stealthy mission no longer in question, it laid back its wings and dove to what appeared to be a watery ending. Spreading its wings at the last moment to slow its descent, the eagle's extended claws barely rippled the water before snatching its prey. Outstretched wings flapping, a squirming rock cod in tow, the magnificent bird struggled to lift its quarry from the water. Slowly gaining height, the eagle triumphantly returned to its perch.

Then Bud saw her. She was emerging from the water down at the far end of the beach. She had not seen him. Unable to take his eyes off her, the distance between them slowly closed. Her loose-fitting swim attire did little to define her features as he had remembered—as he often thought of. She glistened from the droplets on her pale skin. Her auburn hair was tied up with a green ribbon that matched her eyes as well as her bathing costume.

Bud stood motionless as Mary veered off ascending the stairs to the upper lawn area. She probably wouldn't see him unless he made it known he was there. Should he call out to her or let her be? If she had an interest, why hadn't she boated over to Shaw? Maybe he was too young for her? But more than likely, he just wasn't up to snuff.

Stepping onto the manicured lawn, she continued to distance herself.

Bud remained silent. Downtrodden, he walked briskly toward the boat basin. Maybe someday, he thought wishfully, he might be good enough.

Mabel was less than enthralled with the news her son delivered. Not debating the issue outright, she said, "We can discuss it over dinner. Now go clean the salmon you caught."

The fact was that Bud's mother wanted to consider the job offer her son had received before discussing it further. While recognizing there were benefits of her son taking on more responsibility and earning extra money, she was apprehensive. She wondered what life experiences her son might be introduced to—especially if he spent nights at the estate. And yet, she knew she needed to give him room to grow. While she had hoped, it wasn't fair to expect her son to remain tied to the store. Not now anyway. Maybe later, as he got older, he would take more of an interest.

The pair had just dished up the fish when Mabel, pausing to remind herself that her son was already an adult in many eyes, said, "All right, I'm willing to let you try working there for the rest of the summer as long as you do your chores here. I still need your help and if your absence becomes too much for me, we will have to revisit the decision."

"I can do it mom," Bud responded enthusiastically. Fork in hand, a piece of salmon impaled on the prongs, he rose to give his mother a peck on the cheek.

After dinner, they convened at the sink to begin their nightly ritual of washing and drying the accumulation of mismatched dinnerware and an iron skillet. Mabel washed while Bud dried, stacking the dishes in the door-less upper cupboard. As far back as he could remember, washing dishes with his mother was where most of his life lessons were taught. In his youth, Bud stood on a stool to reach the sink. Now, at nearly six feet, he towered over his mother. Topics might cover everything from the next day's chores, schoolwork or a fishing boat that had stopped by during the day. There was even the time she broached the topic of sexuality when she noticed he was spending time with Helen. The dishes had been finished quickly that night.

As the last cup was put away, the two agreed that Bud would work around the store in the mornings before heading off for the thirty-minute run to Rosario.

Having slept fitfully, Bud was up and feverishly sweeping the store's stoop as he heard the 6:10 whistle from the mainland bound passenger boat. It had left the Orcas landing directly across the channel. The boat's destination was Friday Harbor but would stop at a select few islands along the way if there were passengers. Down at the end of the store's dock, Bud could see the Guard family raising the white wood panel flag signaling the boat's captain to stop at Shaw. Bud scarcely noticed the boat's arrival and departure.

By 11:15, Bud left for Rosario. Once underway, he took a bite from the sandwich his mother thrust into his hand as he shoved-off. Glancing back as he rounded the point, the ever-present flowered apron around her waist, he saw his mother poised at the end of the dock. Her hand shaded her eyes a she watched him motor away.

Climbing out of his working man's boat, Bud eyed a large pristine runabout at the end of the dock. At some 25 feet in length, it was longer than Frank's craft by a few feet. She was no doubt fast with her narrow beam and large gas engine. Able to hold a passel of guests, she was used for day excursions to other islands, fishing or just motoring about. Bud considered that the boat might look better if it had a small cuddy cabin to break up her lines.

Daydreaming about how he could own such a boat, Bud headed toward the kitchen with a crate of eggs. He then, unsuccessfully, tried to find Yansen before reporting to the boatyard.

Bud's first workday at Rosario was spent cleaning up wood chips and scrap in and around the new yacht. He went about his task while the shipwrights skillfully carried out their craft. While the workmanship was exceptional, Bud didn't think much of the overall appearance of the 132-foot boat. He doubted the lady of the *America* thought much of the craft's appearance either. Fashioned after a Chinese sailing junk Moran had sailed on during one of his world travels, she would be named the *San Wan* after the San Juan Channel.

Earl Yansen finally stopped by during the afternoon to acknowledge his new employee, but as might be expected, had little to say.

Bud found himself perched on the bow of *San Wan* as his first day in the yard came to an end. Surveying a world he knew little about, he wondered why some seemed to be chosen to lead a more privileged life? Maybe some worked for what they had, but it seemed many around the estate looked as if this life been handed to them or at least, they had been given an unfair running start.

Returning to Shaw in the evening and then back to Rosario each afternoon, Bud fell into a routine that seemed to work for everyone, including his mother. It had only taken a day or two of his hard work for the workers to accept the recruit. When he arrived each day, the shipwrights always made it known they were pleased to see him. And, after a time, Bud's general housekeeping tasks slipped to second rung status between other calls for help. The crew sought him out to trim boards, hold lumber in place as it was attached, retrieve lumber from the shop and the like.

Bud had not seen Mary since the day Yansen had asked him to work at the shipyard. She had either left or, like most guests, just didn't get down to the working end of the property.

Yansen stopped by the *San Wan* on Bud's fifth week and told him that he was pleased with his progress and work ethic. He also asked Bud if he would be able to work the next evening at a large gathering celebrating Mrs. Moran's birthday. His duties would include serving refreshments and dinner to the guests as well as tending to their general needs. The affair was to include a dance which was expected to last into the wee hours. Bud would need to spend the night. Accepting Yansen's request immediately, Bud was confident that he could clear it with his mother.

Leaving his *San Wan* duties after only a couple of hours the next day, Bud reported to staff housing. He was assigned a bed for the night and given a formal looking black and white livery to wear for the evening. By 4:30, he was washed, dressed and crossing the freshly cut yard to the kitchen.

Bud spent the next hours serving drinks to guests as they milled about the grounds and large veranda that encircled the mansion. Under the shade of the veranda, newly white-washed wicker tables decorated with an array of appetizers set the stage. Clusters of matching wicker chairs scattered here and there beckoned the blue-bloods onto manicured yards and the beach beyond.

She saw him before he saw her. "Well, Mr. Fowler, don't you look handsome this evening?" Mary teased. Bud wasn't sure if she was mocking him or flirting with him as she took one of the glasses of champagne from his tray.

"How have you been?" Bud responded somewhat tongue tied.

Clothed nearly head to toe in a floor length pale green dress, her red locks pinned high on her head with a showy jeweled barrette, she looked breathtaking to Bud.

Twinges of embarrassment came over Bud as their chance meeting defined the social order between them. He was in his place and she in hers. A nearby guest summoned him for a drink. Politely dismissing himself from Mary's clutches, he escaped.

Dinner was served promptly at 7:00 in the expansive dark walnut paneled dining room. Cut crystal glassware, fine china, and brightly polished silverware adorned white starched tablecloths. From the nearby ballroom, an orchestra's music drifted lazily across the gathering like a slow-moving morning mist.

By 8:30, guests retreated to the ballroom for an evening of dance and socializing. Not unlike the dining area in appearance, the ballroom had a series of double doors open to the veranda. Except for a massive wood and mirrored bar, the room was sparsely furnished. A large unlit rock fireplace centered one wall.

Bud continued his serving duties throughout the evening. His coverage included the areas around the veranda as before, but also beyond to the beachfront where guests retreated to stroll in the warm August night. Near the beach, a symphony of gently washing waves harmonized with the orchestra music at the house.

The women decked out in their best attire did not go unnoticed by Bud. At times he found it difficult to focus on the task at hand as he filled crystal-cut goblets. A couple of flirtatious women even teased him that he should change out of his starched uniform and join the party. On the other hand, a few prima donnas and stuffed shirts treated him as if he didn't deserve the time of day.

Bud had not seen Mary since eyeing her earlier at a table with her parents. She had not seen him, or least hadn't acknowledged that she had.

It was nearing 11:30 as Bud made his way up the walkway from his latest round of champagne to the lower garden and beach overlook. The last group of guests that had been down at the beach walked ahead.

Midway to the house, a woman's gentle voice, barely audible over the ballroom music, said, "Have you saved any for me?"

Turning his head in the direction of the inquiry, he saw Mary sitting alone on an ornate white metal bench under an orange-barked madrona tree.

"Come sit for a moment," she beckoned.

Bud, lacking self-confidence, obliged her without response.

Her mood mimicking the bubbly spirits Bud had been dispersing, she took the near empty bottle from him and poured the last dregs into her glass.

"I know it must be uncomfortable being around me in this setting. But please Bud, don't shut me out. My feelings for you have only grown over time. Or maybe you just don't want to get to know me better."

"No. That's not it at all," Bud protested.

"Walk me down to the beach and show me the yacht being constructed," Mary blurted.

"Well, umm, I'm not sure that I should take the time," Bud responded glancing up toward the house. "And besides, you really can't see much of the yacht this time of night anyway."

"I'll be able to see all that I need to," Mary said taking his hand guiding him down the moonlit pathway.

Looking back apprehensively, Bud checked to see if anyone was watching.

Once they reached the sand, Mary removed her shoes and set them on a nearby log. Hiking up her dress to her knees, she crossed the beach and waded into the dark cold water. "Brrr," she called out before retreating to the water's edge.

Leading their progression down the beach, Mary darted in and out of the surf, playing tag with the waves while Bud followed maintaining a course just above the tide line. Studying her dance-like antics, moonlit depressions of her dainty naked feet remained behind in the sand momentarily before being erased by the next wash of a wave.

Turning to face him, resuming her progress backwards along the water's edge, she challenged, "Hurry up slow poke."

Bud picked up his pace. Mary did the same, intent on staying ahead. Stumbling, as the water swirled around her feet, she landed butt first in the sloshing waves.

Quickly closing the distance between them, Bud swooped Mary into his arms. Green eyes seductively drawing him, he moved his mouth toward hers. They kissed passionately. Inhibitions unchecked by the champagne, her tongue explored his mouth—retreating, her lips yielded beckoning her partner to reciprocate.

Her mouth caressed Bud's tongue, drawing him deeper and deeper. Bud was in ecstasy. Then without warning, Mary playfully broke the mood by sucking on Bud's tongue with such force that he had difficulty withdrawing himself.

Breaking away, Mary said enticingly, "I still want to see the yacht."

Bud was dumbfounded not knowing quite how to interpret their kiss. Was she just toying with him?

"I left my shoes at the other end of the beach, so you're going to have to carry me across the gravel," Mary proposed.

Bud's mind strayed with anticipation as he lifted Mary, his hand between her dripping dress and upper leg area. The underside of her leg felt silky to the touch.

Moving across the boatyard, the crunch of gravel under Bud's soggy shoes drowned out the diminishing symphony of distant waves. Placing Mary on the second step of a ladder leading up to *San Wan's* deck, Bud wondered if she had detected his hardening arousal. Hiking her wet dress almost to her hips, she scampered up.

Bud's craned neck followed her progress. An owl hooted nearby. Stepping to the ladder, Bud smiled at the thought of what he might see if only he could see in the dark.

The scent of freshly cut lumber filling their senses, Mary led the way to *San Wan's* fore deck to view the moon reflecting off the bay. With only the twinkle of stars gazing down, a screen of stacked boards shielded them from the goings on up at the mansion.

Bud took Mary into his arms.

"You know, I did see you a month or so ago, but you didn't seem like you were interested," Mary cooed.

"Mary, that's not it at all. Our lives are so different. I didn't want to put you on the spot. And besides, I haven't heard from you in over a year."

"That's not true. I wrote you twice last fall," Mary professed.

"I didn't get any letters," Bud replied.

"Well, I sent them. At least, I thought they were mailed," she questioned.

"Take off your coat and lay it down on the deck," she said quietly.

Bud obeyed and then moved toward her.

Boldly, Mary stopped him, "I want to get out of these wet clothes."

Supporting herself against Bud, she slowly slid her dress down and stepped out of it. Handing it to Bud, she asked him to hang it nearby with hopes that it might dry somewhat in the warm night breeze.

Pulling the hair clip from her hair, her flowing locks cascaded over her bare shoulders. She handed the clip to Bud. He placed it in his pocket.

Dropping to the white coat, she lay back clothed only in her undergarments and the moonlight, as her eyes reached out to him.

Bud pulled at his attire. Failing to unlace one of his shoes, he fumbled to remove it with his other foot while struggling to yank his partially unbuttoned shirt over his head.

His undershorts failing to conceal his readiness, Bud knelt.

"Lie next to me," Mary said, sensing Bud's hesitation.

Facing each other, Bud placed his arm around Mary's waist and pulled her tight against his stiffness. Kissing lustfully, his hand explored the roundness of her breasts, her slender hips, her shapely legs, her thighs—every fiber of his being screaming for relief.

Mary rolled to her back as Bud removed her waist high undergarment before shedding his own.

Searching almost frantically, he found the moist warmth he sought. Racing, he pulled himself from her clutches within moments, spilling himself across her snow-white skin. Except for Bud's pounding heart, they lay in silence, the warm sticky fluid binding them together.

Silence followed for a time, each seemingly drawn to their own thoughts.

Never in Bud's wildest dreams had he expected such intimacy. He had thought about Mary in this way, but to experience it left him reeling.

"This deck is hard and I'm getting squashed," Mary protested prompting Bud to roll to her side. Gazing into the star speckled sky, a shooting star crossed overhead.

"Hurry and make a wish," Bud blurted. "My Uncle Frank used to teach me how to identify star formations on clear nights while at anchor aboard the *Lorne*."

Taking Mary's hand, reaching toward the sky, he began tracing the Big Bear constellation. Rambling, Bud said, "Some folks call the formation the Big Dipper. It does look like a dipper, but stars should not be reduced to such simple terms. In ancient times, the stars held great significance to those that looked to the sky. Most star clusters were named after real and mythical creatures."

"See the Little Dipper nearby? Both formations were known to the Native Americans as Little Bear and Big Bear."

Moving Mary's hand across the sky, they traced Little Bear to the bright star at its end.

"The bright star at the end of Little Dipper's handle is also called the North Star. It's the most important star in the heavens if you're a sailor. It also aligns with the extension of the last two stars of the Big Bear that looks like a dipper. If you look toward this star and extend your arms in line with your shoulders, east and west will be at the end of your fingertips with south at your back."

Mary rose and faced the North Star with her back to Bud. If taking flight, she raised her arms turning her head east and then west.

Studying her nude outline against the moon's backdrop, Bud began to harden again.

Turning towards Bud, Mary said, "Come on, you've seen enough. Get dressed. I have to get back before my parents come looking for me."

As they clothed themselves, Mary smiled at Bud's attempt to conceal his renewed interest.

Making their way back up the beach to retrieve Mary's shoes, the two remained quiet savoring their time together. Along the way, Mary asked for her barrette. Bud had thought about the piece earlier but was hoping she had forgotten about it for now. If allowed to keep the barrette, they would have to meet again for its return.

Continuing up the walkway towards the house, reentering their separate worlds, Mary released Bud's hand. Reaching the top of the pathway, they exchanged a light kiss before she disappeared into the night.

Now past midnight, most of the guests had retired except for a small knot of gentlemen at the bar. Bud picked up the empty champagne bottles he had left near the bench along with a few glasses and proceeded to the kitchen. There, he found the staff dealing with the voluminous aftermath of the event. Back to reality, Bud took a wash station at one of the sinks. It was after two in the morning before he headed to his assigned space for the night in the mansion basement. Lying on his cot, savoring Mary's touch, her smell, her nakedness against the night sky, he had difficulty finding sleep.

Bud only caught a glimpse of Mary the next day—her parents hovering. She cast her eyes up towards him on the deck of the *San Wan* but did not acknowledge his presence. Unbeknownst to him, Mary had to face her waiting mother the previous night. Besides the lateness, she had not been happy to find that her somewhat tipsy daughter's dress was damp and her hair in disarray. During the inquisition her mother asked if she had been with the Shaw Island boy. Mary lied.

At 5:15 the next evening, Bud climbed into his boat to return to his ordinary life.

CHAPTER 7

1923

THE EARLY YEARS OF PROHIBITION FOUND BUD LIVING AND WORKING AT Rosario. Five years had passed since he began his part-time stint at the estate. One of the old lumber company's worker's cabins had become his living quarters. It wasn't all that fancy, but it had a good view of the bay and was in easy walking distance of the mansion's compound. Now twenty-two years old, Bud had assumed substantial responsibility at the estate.

By this time, Bud's mother had found a partner to share in the store's operation, relieving Bud from the guilt of spending less time on Shaw. Cleo, a tall lanky fellow, his graying and thinning hair typically hiding under a brown brimmed fedora, had tied off on the store's float one day in his black hull cabin cruiser. His mission was to buy some provisions and fishing gear. He hailed from the mainland where he worked in a shipyard building yachts for the expanding pleasure-boat market. A bit older than Mabel, not as ambitious, they developed a working relationship over a few months. Initially residing in his boat by night and volunteering to do carpentry and other odd jobs by day he slowly became a fixture around the place. Ultimately, becoming more reliant on each other, they found love and married. Mabel still managed the store's day to day activities with Cleo helping, but he mostly stayed out of her way. During the summer, local youths were hired to help with the peak period demand. With time on his hands, Cleo began to build a boat under a lean-to attached to the feed warehouse.

Earl Yansen, the man most feared at the estate, had become a friend as well as a father figure to Bud. Taking Bud under his wing, he provided Bud advancement opportunities that would otherwise have been out of his reach. The young man from Shaw was now responsible for the day to day operation of the shipyard including the maintenance and repair of the estate's extensive fleet of watercraft. Shipwrights became his teachers. And with the skills he was learning, there was little doubt that Bud should have been pleased, maybe even content, but something was still missing.

Mary never returned to Rosario, nor did he hear from her after their memorable encounter on the *San Wan*. While her parents visited the estate from time to time to mingle with their kind, she was nowhere to be found. Bud once passed Mary's mother near the boat basin, but only received a nod of acknowledgment when he said hello. Bud figured Mary was likely married and had a family of her own. Any hope of a renewed relationship with his real first love was apparently not to be.

One project Bud had recently undertaken was the rebuilding of the narrow-beamed excursion boat he had admired when he first came to Rosario. Among other upgrades, he added a small cabin to the boat. As he had first envisioned when he had laid eyes on her, it improved her appearance. In addition to the cabin, he convinced Earl the boat could use a new, more powerful, engine. The engine changeover required Bud to rebuild the engine cradle and up-size the shaft log to accommodate a larger drive shaft and prop to match the increased horsepower.

Earl monitored Bud's progress on the boat's transformation with guarded zeal. Even though he grumbled about the cost of the rebuild, Bud felt he was pleased with the undertaking. Once he even overheard Earl bragging to old man Moran he was overseeing the runabout's improvements.

One afternoon, discovering the excursion boat was no longer in the shipyard shed, Earl headed straightaway to the boat basin. As he neared, he could see her blocked on rails above the tide. Bud, standing in the water up to his knees was tightening the nut and inserting the cotter pin connecting the new propeller to the engine drive shaft.

Seeing Earl, Bud stood back and said with a big grin, "Earl, she may lack wings, but she's going to fly across the water."

Giving Bud a scowl, implying the whole engine change out was a waste of effort, Earl mumbled, "The boat went plenty fast before. Though I'll admit she does look better with new paint and that cabin."

Having liked the looks of Cleo's boat, Bud had painted the boat's hull black.

"Come back in a couple of hours at high tide and we'll slide her back where she belongs," Bud said.

The boat was off her cradle, running and moored against the dock by the time Earl returned. The deep resonating thrum of the exhaust system signaled the boat's metamorphosis. Earl stepped aboard joining Bud. Pushing away from the dock, Bud slowly increased the throttle monitoring the oil pressure and temperature gauges. There was a slight chop and head wind, but the runabout gave it no mind. Rising to a plane atop the blue-green waters of the channel, it was instantly apparent that Bud had chosen the proper engine and propeller combination.

A huge grin spread across the Norwegian's face. "My god," Earl exclaimed, his band of hair thrashing about, "This boat is probably untouchable compared to any other around."

They steered toward the Shaw Store taking a wide circle around Blind Island. It had been years since Bud had been ashore on his old haunt. He glanced longingly at the cove inlet as they sped by, vowing to make a visit in the not too distant future. Eventually, they pursued a course back to the estate. Entering Cascade Bay, Bud's eyes fell on lady of the *America* and hoped she would be pleased with what she saw.

The wake rolling her side to side, Bud maneuvered up against the dock as Earl stepped across. Not waiting, as if on a mission, he headed up the gangplank. Turning at the top, he yelled back, "Come up to my office once you have her bedded down for the night."

Earl was pouring two whiskeys when Bud entered the office. Plopping into overstuffed chairs, they sipped their drinks and reflected on how powerful the transformed boat had become.

Earl said, "This goddamn prohibition has sure made it difficult to keep a supply of alcohol for Moran and his guests. Not to mention that I loathe paying such outrageous prices. There's also the inconsistency. It's making Moran an unhappy fellow."

Bud shirked his shoulders and took another swig—the declaration having had no effect on him.

Earl, brow furled, and jaw squared as if contemplating the fate of the world, turned in his chair and said, "What do you think about making a few runs up to Canada and bringing back some of Moran's favorite whiskey and other spirits?"

Before entertaining a response, Yansen outlined his thoughts regarding the pros and cons of such an undertaking. Of particular interest to Bud was the fact that he would be given a substantial financial incentive for each trip he undertook. On the downside, he could face significant jail time if caught. "I suspect Moran would try to help defend us if the revenuers figured out what we were up to," Earl said with a hearty laugh, "But, I can't guarantee it."

Bud gazed out the window considering the proposition. Finally, turning his eyes back to Earl, he said, "I have a counter offer."

Earl, seeming a bit taken back, said, "I'm listening."

"Don't pay me anything extra. But if, and when, I complete," hesitating as if mulling over the impact of finishing his statement, "say twenty successful trips, the boat is mine. It will be up to you to square the deal with old man Moran. I'll continue to make runs after I own her. We can agree to the ongoing finances at that point, unless we're in jail," Bud said with a laugh.

Earl stroked his chin contemplating a response. Wanting to be fair, aware of the risks Bud would be taking, he blurted, "Twenty-five, but I'll need to clear it with Moran."

Bud extended his hand.

Over a final drink, Earl suggested they needed to find a name that reflected the traits of the excursion boat's transformation. A few names were tossed about until they finally reached agreement.

The runabout would be christened *Channel Runner*.

The next day, Earl did in fact broach the idea to Moran how they might restore a supply of liquor to Rosario's nearly bare alcohol basement storage area. Moran was somewhat familiar with Bud and knew he was the one responsible for the excursion boat's upgrades.

"The young man does seem to have a head on his shoulders. I like what he did to the old boat. How would you intend to reimburse him for the risks he will be taking?" Moran asked.

"He wants to own your excursion boat," Earl said apprehensively.

"Good for him!" Moran responded. "I like that he knows what he wants and is willing to reach for it. I'll leave it up to you to work out a fair deal for us both."

CHAPTER 8

A FEW DAYS LATER, BUD LOADED A DOZEN SACKS OF FEED INTO *CHANNEL Runner*. His excuse to one of the estate's general-labors who helped him was that Earl wanted to test out the boat as if loaded with a bunch of folks on a cruise. Bud was not disappointed. While the boat didn't leap out of the water as she had done the previous day, her speed was still impressive once she was planing atop the surface.

Having obtained Moran's blessing, it was decided a surveillance trip to Victoria, British Columbia would be in order. Bud would take one of the less conspicuous work boats under the ruse of needing to buy some line and an anchor. While shopping for these items, he would make inquiries regarding the purchase of alcohol. Earl had suggested taking the slower boat because the borders were being watched by Federal revenuers and there was no reason to flaunt the high-powered *Channel Runner*.

The surface of the sound was mirror-like. Never tired of being on the water, Bud lay back in the seat and reveled in the peacefulness of the lazy trip north. Motoring near the area where the *America* met her fate, he took time to view the few surviving ribs and planking protruding above the surface like headstones marking her grave. The somber visit seemed to spur a change in the weather as the relatively cloudless sky was swallowed by advancing legions of darkness. Heavy rain followed as he crossed the Canadian border with no sign of revenuers.

Arriving in Victoria Harbor, the rain having subsided, Bud moved along the waterfront amongst the moored boats and shipyards in search of a retailer where he could find an anchor. Finally, he spied a gray clapboard structure perched over the water. A sign on the building's upper roof area read "Marine Hardware."

A bell clanged as Bud opened the grimy glass paneled door. Sitting on a stool amongst piles of coiled rope, an old geezer of questionable character, his beat-up captain's cap askew, glanced up. Nodding to acknowledge Bud's presence, he went back to reading a newspaper. Bud strolled around the store threading his way between the scattered display of new and used marine supplies. The merchandise didn't appear to have any particular order except for a few shelved bolts and screws. It looked as though whenever anything came into the store it was just placed in the closest vacant spot. He smiled, thinking of his mother's store where nary a mouse's whisker would be out of place.

"I need an anchor for a 25-foot boat," Bud said.

"New or used?" the proprietor responded trying to corral a dribble of tobacco juice oozing from his mouth.

"New with 15 feet of chain and 150 feet of line," Bud answered.

"You'll need at least 200 feet of line around these parts," the man responded as if Bud didn't have a say in the matter.

The old salt got off his stool, grabbed a nearby cane and, with a slight hobble, weaved his way amongst the piles. It appeared he knew roughly where he was going but found it necessary to hesitate a time or two to get his bearings.

"There," the cane pointed some distance away to the back of the shop. "There should be a price on the anchor and chain. The line is back by my stool."

Finding a winged-shaped anchor and chain to his liking, Bud sought out the counter with the dangling chain trailing him across the floor.

"There looks to be a few more feet of chain than I need," Bud questioned.

The man looked briefly down at the ringed links and said, "I ain't cuttin' it."

"Oh, it'll be okay," Bud said knowing he had little choice.

Bud measured, cut and coiled 200 feet of line.

"Don't you need a thimble and shackle to connect the line to the chain?" the store proprietor asked with an air that questioned Bud's knowledge of such things.

"Sure," Bud responded even though he knew the items were available back at Rosario.

Once tallied, Bud finalized the transaction with U.S. dollars.

As the old man limped back to his perch on the stool, Bud asked, "Is there a place to buy a bottle of whiskey around here?"

"There's a place uptown a bit or you might get one of the bars to sell you a bottle."

"What if I want a few cases?"

"You'll need to go uptown, but it'll be a bitch to haul back."

"Well, I'm sure you know since I paid you in American dollars that we have a bit of a tough time getting anything worthwhile to drink back home."

While Earl had cautioned Bud to be careful about who he might do business with, the fact remained that as long as *Channel Runner* could dodge any pursuers on the American side of the border, there was little risk having a boat load of liquor on the Canadian side.

"I work for a place that has a rather thirsty need for a reliable supply. My boat could carry a dozen or more cases at a time. Several trips would be necessary over a few weeks to build some inventory. After that, who knows?"

The man rubbed his unshaven stubble, sizing Bud up. The fact was that the proprietor had dabbled in providing liquor to customers south the border from time to time as had many of the other waterfront maritime businesses. But there was no reason this gent needed to know that. "It isn't my normal line of trade, but," hesitating, "I could help you out."

"I would start with 12 assorted cases of whiskey and other spirits. Your choice, but I want the best. No rot-gut. I also know roughly what my costs should be, so I expect a fair price. Can you be ready for me to pick it up the day after tomorrow? Say in the evening after dusk?"

Without getting a response, Bud extended his hand, "By the way, my name's Bud."

"They call me Jake," bringing his hand up to meet Bud's in a callused grip.

Jake said, "There's a float below the store with a door above. It's used for loading and unloading supplies. It's not all that visible to prying eyes. I live in the back room and am usually around."

"I'll be here by 9:30 the night after tomorrow," Bud advised.

The workboat pushed back towards home under clearing skies. While the return trip would take over two hours bucking the ebbing tide, Bud figured the newly powered runabout could make the run at a leisurely pace in under an hour.

Anticipating he might need to take refuge from the revenuers at times, Bud explored a few out of the way bays and inlets along the way. About half way home, a boat some distance away began to approach from the stern at a high rate of speed. It had the makings of the revenuer boat that moseyed into Rosario from time to time. Pushing the workboat's throttle full ahead, creating a billowing plume of exhaust, Bud smiled. While there was no way to outrun the trailing craft, he might as well get an idea about the other boat's capability.

As if on cue, the distant boat picked up speed to overtake Bud. The nearing boat was fast, but no match for the boat moored back at Rosario even when loaded.

The familiar boat pulled alongside and signaled Bud to stop. Acting surprised, Bud throttled back and took the boat out of gear. The heavy workboat settled into the sparkling water almost immediately stopping her forward progress.

There were two men onboard the visiting craft. One man with a turned down rimmed black hat flashed a badge and jumped aboard Bud's craft without the benefit of an invitation.

"Where are you coming from and where are you going?" demanded the officer.

Bud responded, "I'm on my way back from Victoria. Why?"

"What were you doing there?" the same man asked with authority.

"I bought an anchor and line," Bud answered dutifully pointing them out lying in the stern.

The Federal agent looked under the decked over bow area. Finding nothing but a couple of soggy cork life jackets, he said with a look of disappointment, "Okay, we're just making routine checks. Be on your way."

Bud didn't bother to hide a grin of contentment as he motored away.

❈

Rain dimpled the surrounding waters as the last defiant remnants of daylight fought off darkness. Clad in an oilcloth rain slicker aboard his newly christened partner in crime, Bud left Rosario for his first Canadian whiskey run. Guided by a partial moon, along with his upbringing, *Channel Runner* skipped across white topped waves eager to prove herself. In under an hour, the lights of Victoria shone in the distance marking their destination. The maiden trip had gone without incident. Nor were there any sightings that the revenuers were poking about on either side of the border. Still, he was a bit nervous considering what he was about to do. He had a fast boat, knew the islands better than most and had made a commitment—there wasn't any turning back at this point.

Announcing their arrival, *Channel Runner's* rumbling exhaust echoed loudly in the cavern-like space beneath the pile supported marine store.

Bud wondered if the gimpy proprietor had heard the disturbance when the hatched door above opened, emitting a band of light. Along one side of the opening, a rusty steel ladder descended into the watery darkness. By chance, the high tide covered the lower barnacle encrusted rungs below his grip. Grabbing the small nearby float, he wedged a couple of rope fenders against the ragged nailed board face hoping to curtail any chafing of *Channel Runner's* newly painted hull.

"Climb the ladder. You'll have to load the stuff yourself," Jake said curtly.

"And a good evening to you," Bud mumbled under his breath as he finished securing *Channel Runner*. Stepping onto the second visible rung, Bud began his assent. Nearing the top, he inspected the makeshift pulley system used to raise and lower goods. He could see no reason it wouldn't help lighten the task at hand.

Bud found Rosario's wood-cased cargo stacked in an adjoining shed amongst old fishing nets and random marine items. Most of the stuff looked as though it should have been chucked out long ago. Satisfied the estate was getting what had been ordered, Bud hesitated before paying the salty Canadian his asking price.

"Seems a bit steep Jake. I hope you're not trying to gouge me," Bud said, somber faced.

A slight smile crossed Jake's lips. "Alright, take twenty bucks off."

Bud peeled the bills off a roll provided by Earl, "If you're going to be my long-term supplier, you need to be fair or I'll look elsewhere. Also, I forgot to bring gloves."

"There's gloves for sale over with the other clothing. I'll throw a pair in," Jake said with a grin that showcased his stained teeth.

It took Bud nearly three-quarters of an hour to load the bottled payload.

Tying off and lowering one case at a time, he made a mental note to build a platform that could be lashed to the pulley system to speed up the loading. Once the thirst quenching cargo was secure, it was covered with a tarpaulin.

Channel Runner cautiously motored out into the dim lights of the basin amongst the array of moored boats. Clearing the maritime wharf area, Bud throttled the runabout's speed up. Rising to a plane quickly, barely laboring under her load, they rumbled for home.

Nearing the undefined border between Canada and the United States, broken clouds gave way to traces of moonlight. Bud upped the throttle a few notches matching the increased visibility. The familiar outline of the island reefs guarding Wasp Pass at the northern end of Shaw Island came into view. Knowingly, Bud slowed to watch for drift that tended to accumulate in the area. About to nose her up some, he detected the outline of a boat off his port and slightly aft. The craft began to move in his direction.

"Jesus, I guess we're going to be tested our first night out," Bud exclaimed as he turned hard to starboard and slammed the throttle forward.

Channel Runner responded to the challenge. Exiting the confines of Wasp Pass, Bud and his cohort in crime would circumnavigate Shaw Island. It was a much longer route, but it would give them time to shake their pursuer. Besides, there was no one who knew the area around Shaw Island as well as Bud Fowler.

The chase boat accelerated in pursuit, but to no avail. Lagging ever further behind, the other craft finally gave up.

Channel Runner arrived at Rosario's boat basin nearly forty minutes later. Moving the wood crates onto the float, Bud transported them by cart up to the house. Grabbing a bottle of Canadian whiskey, Bud went to find Earl.

After midnight, pacing his office, Yansen was duly concerned about the lateness. Hearing footsteps approach up the stairs, he headed for the landing outside his office. His nervous tension pent up, he growled, "What took you so goddamn long?!"

"The Feds showed, and I had to alter the route home. No worries though, *Channel Runner* left them in her wake," Bud boasted.

"Well then, let's sample the wares!" Yansen beamed as he stepped to a nearby bookcase and extracted two glasses from the clutter.

"To many more successful trips," the bearded Norwegian toasted, holding his glass to the light to better inspect the liquid's color.

A clink of the glasses and the contents were downed in a single swig. Bud coughed as the liquid burn slithered down his throat. Earl snickered and poured them another shot.

Bud and *Channel Runner* continued to make trips to Victoria and back without incident. To minimize the likelihood of anyone detecting a pattern to their comings and goings, he varied the schedule and route. To the satisfaction of all, the liquor storage room in the mansion's basement reached pre-prohibition inventories for both quantity and variety. Yansen was pleased, but, more importantly, Moran was happy. During a recent entertainment function, the guests had taken it upon themselves to try and concoct a drink that the bartenders could not supply. The guests were unsuccessful. One individual who owned and operated a hotel resort on a neighboring island asked Moran if he would give up the name of his supplier.

Moran led his guest up to Yansen's office where Earl typically hung out during such events in case a need arose for his services. The duo found Earl sprawled out in one of his overstuffed chairs asleep. A half empty bottle of Scotch sat on the floor within reaching distance. Resting precariously in his lap was a partially filled glass. Gently awaking the somewhat inebriated overseer, Moran asked him to assist with his neighbor's quandary.

The following morning, Yansen asked Bud, "What do you think about making a few runs for the Roche Harbor resort? The owner claims the feds generally give the place a wide berth because of all the influential politicians and aristocrats that frequent the place."

Bud considered his partner's proposal for a few moments and then responded, "I guess there would be no harm as long as the trips count toward *Channel Runner's* ownership. You know I only need to make seven more runs before she's mine," Bud reported.

Pleased that Bud was nearing his goal, Earl nodded in agreement.

Bud planned to make the next two trips in one evening. Roche Harbor lay directly across Haro Straits from Victoria. He should be able to make the round trip from Victoria to Roche Harbor and back in about two hours. Then he could then pick up his second load for Rosario and be on his way.

Yansen saw Bud off that evening with enough cash to pay for both deliveries. With a twinkle in his eye, Earl told Bud he had arranged for the Roche Harbor payment to come through him. Bud surmised his boss included a hefty carrying charge for his troubles.

Leaving Rosario's boat basin and heading towards the channel, Bud spied a boat some distance away. While unsure, he thought it looked distinctly similar to the revenuer's boat that had stopped him in the workboat a few months back. Bud altered his destination for the Shaw Island Store.

Mabel and Cleo were glad to see Bud even though it seemed odd he was coming for a visit so late in the evening. After exchanging a few pleasantries, they retired to the back porch to enjoy the colorful display of the sun setting to the west.

"You seem to have fairly free reign over the use of that boat you tied at the dock," Mabel said questioningly.

"Do you like her? I'm buying her from Moran."

Not wishing to add further explanation to his mother's line of questioning, Bud changed the subject. Then, the pesky revenuers rounded the point. Motoring slowly alongside *Channel Runner,* the officers gave her a once over. Mabel and Cleo knew the visitors because they had been in from time to time to purchase odds and ends as well as fuel.

The feds cast their attention from *Channel Runner* up to the store. There was still just enough light for them to see the group sitting on the porch. Half-heartedly, the two men in the boat waved. They received a similar gesture in return.

Mabel frowned at her son—what's he been up to?

The revenuers backed their launch away and proceeded slowly into the channel. As they retreated, both men turned in their seats and gazed back toward the store as if conveying a message.

Mabel eyed her son and asked, "They seem interested in that boat. Do you know why?"

Bud shrugged and said, "She's a good-looking craft. Why not take a look?"

Mable scowled, as only a mother could communicate, and said, "You better not be going out of your way to find trouble young man. The feds are not ones to be messing with."

"Mom, there's no need to worry," Bud assured her.

Cleo sat quietly puffing his pipe, studying the rising smoke drifting aimlessly above his head. He wasn't about to get in the middle of the discussion. He knew he had the love of a good woman and had learned life was much easier if he just went along with Bud's mother temperamental mindset when it came to her son—and for most everything else as far as that was concerned. Besides, Bud routinely stashed a bottle or two of Canadian whisky in the warehouse for him to sample as the urge arose. Unbeknownst to either Cleo or Bud, the store's matriarch was well aware of their arrangement.

Bud gave the revenuers a few minutes to continue down the channel before bidding his hosts a good evening. Mabel walked her son down to his boat, gave him a hug and pleaded, "Please be careful."

Motoring away, Bud plotted how he was going to make up the time from the unscheduled stop. Additionally, Victoria was in the opposite direction from Rosario. Once around the point, out of the view of the store, Bud navigated *Channel Runner* to the other side of the channel. In an effort to avoid the suspicious nature of the Federal spoilers, he set an out of the way course for the west side of San Juan Island.

A partial moon cast a glow helping to illuminate the waters ahead as *Channel Runner* darted past the shadowy landmarks of Bud's youth. Hoping to defy detection, warm and inviting breezes urged him to notch the throttle forward as he sped along in the dead calm without aid of navigation lights. Then without warning, a dark shape emerged from nowhere! Cranking hard to port, digging in, *Channel Runner* wrenched wildly to her starboard side spraying out a cascade of water over another boat. It was sheer luck that Bud had been able to avert a nasty collision.

Bud circled and motored up close for a better look. The craft's two occupants looked like drowned rats. They had been running without lights as well.

Taking a calming breath, Bud said to himself, "Well at least it isn't those goddamn feds."

Shouting to the two waterlogged individuals, Bud said, "If we're both going to be poking about without lights, we're going to have to synchronize our schedules. Sorry about the drenching."

Noting what appeared to be a load of crates under a tarp, Bud continued, "It would've been an awful waste to send you and your cargo to the bottom. I imagine a lot of folks would have gone thirsty."

The two men didn't quite know how to respond. Finally, one managed to utter, "That's for sure."

"In case it's of interest, I saw the feds about a half-hour ago in the vicinity of the Shaw Island Store," Bud relayed before disappearing into the night.

Thirty-five minutes later Bud maneuvered alongside the narrow float under the marine hardware store. Stepping onto the float, the hatch opened above revealing Jake's familiar face. Curtly he said, "You're late."

Bud craned his head upward and reported, "I'm running a bit behind. Got side-tracked. I'm only running over to Roche Harbor, so it shouldn't take long. I was hoping to make a second run tonight but will have to see how it goes."

"I ain't going nowhere," Jake answered forcing Bud to dodge a bit of chewing tobacco dribble.

Channel Runner crept into Roche Harbor while Bud scanned the basin for anything unusual. Heading to a distant point near the fuel dock described by Earl, Bud could make out two men mulling about in the subdued lighting.

Bud stopped *Channel Runner's* forward motion. "Do you have fuel?" Bud called.

"I'm the hotel manager. You Bud Fowler?"

Sliding alongside the dock, Bud tossed the men lines and silenced *Channel Runner*. Music could be heard spreading out across the bay from the resort's bar. Bud positioned the rope knotted fenders between the dock and the runabouts glistening hull as his greeters tied the boat.

Vic, the hotel manager, shook Bud's hand and said, "Join me for a drink to celebrate our new business deal while our cargo is unloaded."

Not knowing what business arrangement Earl had made, Bud figured he better find out, "Sure, lead the way."

Vic popped the top on one of the crates and grabbed a bottle of Canadian whisky in each hand before proceeding up the gangway. The manager's office was located just beyond the expansive veranda of the two-story restaurant.

Shouldering through the gathered crowd, Bud felt underdressed. Without a doubt, no one would mistake him for one of the hotel patrons.

Vic pulled the cork from one of the bottles and poured them each a double shot. Downing the golden liquid in one gulp, Vic poured himself another before launching into a monologue. The gist of the rambling was that the resort had retained Yansen to provide a steady flow of liquor from Victoria across Haro Strait.

"Earl and I have already resolved the financial end of things, but I want to be sure you're up to the task," Vic questioned.

Seeming a bit noncommittal, Bud responded, "Sure. But I'll need to finalize some small details with Earl now that I have a better understanding of the lay of the land."

After more discussion, and learning Bud grew up in the islands just like himself, Vic suggested, "It's getting late, why don't you stay the night. I know we have a couple of empty rooms in the hotel. I could get word to Rosario for you."

Bud responded, "Good idea."

Noting Bud's working man's attire, Vic further offered, "I think I can find a change of clothing that should fit if you want to clean up and take advantage of the hotel's late-night activities."

"Yep, I could use some shaving gear as well."

"Let's go find you a room," Vic concluded.

Bud finished washing up and shaving when he heard a knock at his door. Opening the door, he was greeted by a timid young thing who handed him a hanger full of clothing and a pair of black winged-tipped shoes.

Bud thanked her and placed fifty cents in her hand. She bowed slightly and left.

The shoes were a bit tight, but Bud figured since he wasn't intending to dance the night away they would do.

The hotel bar was a lavish setting filled to the brim with elegantly dressed patrons. The controlled group of wealthy guests had arrived either by the passenger boat that traveled between Seattle and Victoria or aboard one of the many luxury yachts moored in the harbor. Few local islanders could financially make the cut.

Bud had no trouble fitting in looks-wise but kept to himself. These people weren't his type. He ordered a scotch with one ice cube and moved out onto the deck overlooking the basin. A seven-piece band played in the background. Although their tempo seemed more upbeat, he was certain they might be the same group Moran used.

Feeling the presence of someone standing closely behind him, Bud winced slightly as the arms of a woman reached around his waist clasping her fingers along his front. She pulled her body tight against his without speaking.

Bud swallowed the sip of scotch he had in his mouth and said, "Whoever you are, I have to admire the way you introduce yourself."

A soft suggestive voice from the past replied, "Spent any time on the bow of any boats lately?"

Bud turned breaking her grip to find familiar green eyes staring up at him.

Immediate infatuation overwhelming him, Bud's voice cracked slightly, "How have you been Mary?"

"Fine. You appear to be doing very well," she said suggestively looking Bud over from head to toe.

"So, I guess we'll skip catching up the last five years," he stated quizzically with an ever so slight bit of sarcasm. "I never got over the night you jilted me."

She laughed and responded, "For crying out loud, you were only a kid at the time. What are you twenty-one…twenty-two now?"

"Twenty- two," Bud replied as he steered her to a nearby table.

"Well, I'm a ripe old lady of nearly twenty-four. Our age difference seemed significant back then," signaling to Bud that might no longer be the case.

Mary went on to explain that her father's yacht had brought several members of the family up to the islands for a summer outing while he stayed in Seattle to work. This was their second night at Roche Harbor.

Bud asked, "Why isn't a nice rich girl like you married yet? Or, are you?"

Mary light-heartedly responded, "No, you ruined me for anyone else."

"So, what have you being doing since we last saw one another?" she asked.

Bud told her that he was now living and working full time at Rosario. Briefly, he touched on the ongoing operations at the estate.

"Yes, the *San Wan* was completed and launched about a year after we christened her. Moran routinely takes guests out for extended trips exploring the islands on both sides of the border. I think of you every time I'm aboard her. In fact, I make it a point to visit the very spot and look up at the stars if they're out."

Mary blushed slightly and smiled.

When asked, Bud relied, "No, I really haven't found anyone special."

Mary warmly inquired about his mother and Bud told her about his mother's good fortune of finding Cleo to share her life. He also mentioned that Uncle Frank was still working on the *Lorne* plying the waters of Puget Sound and as far north as Alaska. Captain Block having retired, the tug's operation was now under his uncle's command.

Bud also shared that he was making a few runs to Victoria for the betterment of mankind. He recounted a few stories and made sure to spice up the particulars to pique Mary's interest. She seemed delighted as well as intrigued with his part-time venture.

After nearly two hours of reminiscing, Bud was surprised how comfortable their conversation flowed. Maybe it was because he was finally feeling more secure in his own skin. Maybe it was because her silver-spoon upbringing no longer influenced her behavior quite so much. Or, maybe it was just that Bud's fancy duds made him look like everyone else.

In time, Bud announced, "You know, it's getting late and I have to make an early morning trip to Victoria. I suppose I should consider calling it a night."

Mary asked, "Can I go along in the morning?"

"I am not sure if you should. There's always the chance the trip could be more than you bargain for."

Bud was about to detail some of the potential pitfalls when she raised her hand to his lips and said, "I could return to our boat to get a change of clothing for an early departure."

Bud took no further convincing.

Walking down to the moorage area under a starry sky, Bud wrapped his arm around Mary's waist and brought her close to shield her from the night chill. Stopping to check *Channel Runner*, Mary continued down the dock to the family yacht.

Waiting, Bud's mind raced with what might be as he thought back to the night on the *San Wan*. Approaching, she had changed into clothes that were a bit of a dress-down from her previous attire—a nautical flair. Still her appearance flaunted wealth. She also carried a small bag. Encircling his arms around her, he bent down and kissed her—his lust renewed as if time had stood still.

As they walked up the dock to the hotel, Mary informed her escort, "Don't get ahead of yourself Mister Fowler. We need to take this a bit slower than the time you plied me with champagne and took advantage of me," tugging at Bud's arm for good measure.

Not knowing quite what to say, Bud didn't respond.

Once in Bud's room, Mary disappeared into the bathroom with her bag. Bud stripped to his shorts and got into bed wondering if he should be waiting in anticipation or expecting to be sleeping on the floor for the night.

His hopes dashed, Mary entered the room covered head to toe in a frumpy looking Mother Hubbard getup.

"Probably not quite what you had in mind huh?" she said with a Mona Lisa smile. "You are required to stay on your side of the bed or one of us is going to have to return to their boat for the night. And, you better have something on under those covers."

"Okay, I'll be good," Bud replied reluctantly. "You're right. I just hoped...," his voice trailing off as he moved to his half of the bed.

Mary climbed into bed. Before settling in, she leaned over and placed her mouth on Bud's giving him a long amorous kiss, then declaring, "That's going to have to see you through the night."

Once settled, Mary moved over and snuggled her back up against Bud's front, no doubt able to detect the protrusion bound in his shorts. "Now try to get some sleep."

Encircling his arm around her and receiving no pushback, he unbuttoned a front portion of her nightgown and slid his hand inside. She cuddled closer signaling that she was surrendering to his disobedient tactic as they fell asleep.

The morning sunlight crept into the room and woke Bud around 6:00 a.m. He raised himself up on one arm and watched his bedmate sleep. With a little help, the cover slid away revealing one of her breasts.

During the night he'd taken the liberty to unbutton almost the entire front of her gown.

"God sure knew what he was doing when he created her," he thought to himself. Leaning over, he covered her flesh with his mouth, gently exploring her nipple with his tongue.

Cat-like, she stirred and stretched, slowly opening her eyes.

"What do you think you are doing?" Mary purred.

Bud pulled her atop him. They kissed longingly as Bud's hands explored her.

Breaking away, her face flushed, Mary said, "Come on. You promised me a trip to Victoria."

CHAPTER 9

CHANNEL RUNNER'S THROATY RUMBLE BROKE THE STILLNESS OF THE dawn as she unsuccessfully tried to sneak out of the harbor. Nestled up against Bud to fend off the damp chill, Mary shared a coffee and roll she had begged from the hotel kitchen crew preparing for breakfast. Glancing over towards her family yacht, Mary could see her mother sitting on the fantail watching them. Clearing the bounds of the harbor, they steadily gained speed leaving the dozing haven behind.

Victoria's harbor was already bustling with activity upon their arrival. A large tug maneuvered ahead near a barge. It was the familiar outline of the *Lorne*. Bud could see Captain Fowler standing watch just outside the wheelhouse on the small railed deck. Frank disappeared inside from time to time, no doubt signaling old Jeb. It was a source of pride to Bud to see his uncle commanding his own vessel.

"Hey, you guys know where I can find a compass key?" Bud yelled to the deck crew as he recklessly motored into the middle of the activity.

Not initially recognizing the intruder forced Frank to take evasive action and abandon his approach. Storming out of the wheelhouse, Frank bellowed, "goddamn it! You stupid son of a bitch, don't you know…," then he smiled, "For cryin' out loud, I should've guessed," he said as he recognized his nephew.

Bud backed *Channel Runner* out of the way, so Frank and his crew could complete the task at hand. Pulling alongside *Lorne's* outboard side to wait for Frank, he told Mary about the time the crew had sent him all over the tug, into every nook and cranny, looking for the compass key.

"Did you find it?" Mary asked.

"There's no such thing," Bud confessed. "It's sort of a rite of passage they run every landlubber through when they first come aboard."

"How in the hell have you been?" Frank said, descending the ladder to the main deck of the tug.

"Not bad," Bud responded. "I'd like you to meet an old friend, Mary Pickard."

Remembering her red locks, Frank said, "It's been a long time. Good to see you again."

"And of course, I'm so happy to see you. Your family was so caring when we last met. I also understand you're the one who taught Bud about the stars. He relayed some of those teachings on the bow of a boat one time."

Frank looked as though he was about to ask a question but thought better of it. "Visited your mom the other day Bud. She and Cleo seem to be doing just fine. She told me she worries about you. I told her you could take care of yourself. But, she worries anyway."

Bud nodded in response.

The three talked for a few minutes before leaving Frank and his crew to their work.

The shadows below the store swallowed *Channel Runner* as she left the sun-drenched harbor. The eerie scene created by the pilings was only enhanced by the muffled sound of her engine. Mary shrieked as pigeons dropped from their roosts to make their escape.

Once tied up, Bud suggested, "We might as well take time for a real breakfast and enjoy the morning before heading back to Rosario."

Tapping the bottom of the trapdoor with a pole used specifically for that purpose, their heads craned upward waiting. Finally, after a second series of taps, the floor yielded.

Once they were sure-footed in the store, Bud asked Jake, "We haven't had any breakfast. Can you recommend someplace to eat?"

"Whatever," he said hobbling back to his stool roost. "There's a place down the main wharf. You can't miss it."

No doubt the result of Mary's presence, Jake's manners seemed a bit more pleasant than the norm.

Strolling down the planked boardwalk, Mary took Bud's hand in hers. Neither spoke—content with the moment.

They almost didn't see the rickety clapboard structure at the end of the wharf. By the looks of the tattered old commercial fishing nets and other discards heaped about, it didn't look like an eatery. So much for, "You can't miss it," Mary said as they passed through the entry while an old bearded salt with a toothless smile held the door. They took seats at a round wobbly table. The place had a décor that no doubt matched their normal clientele—one's appearance was of little importance. A couple of guys sitting at the counter looked as if they might have been painting the underside of a boat. The red paint smattering on their clothes, faces and hands seemed a good match.

"Morning," the waitress said trying to appear upbeat. Assuming coffee was a given, she filled their stained coffee mugs with a dark liquid without asking. Pulling a pencil from her unkempt dish-watery blond hair, she stood transfixed gazing intently at the basin beyond. In all probability, her pencil had done more to groom her looks throughout her shift than her morning brush. If her blouse had been clean before she started her shift, the day had not gone well.

"We have the normal stuff," she offered.

"How about a couple of eggs easy over, bacon and toast," Bud said.

"I'll have the same, but make mine scrambled," Mary indicated.

"We can do that," the waitress said, even though she appeared to be the only one manning the place.

Overall, the food and the service were fine. The toast was a bit overdone, but the homemade raspberry jam helped disguise the subtle burnt taste.

Mary had never been to Victoria and wanted to take time to walk around the area. While Bud had been there repeatedly, he had never ventured much beyond the wharf district. Their explorations ultimately landed them at a luxury hotel called The Empress. They had tea served in flowery cups in the hotel's gilded tea room surrounded by an array of fancy chandeliers, brightly colored carpeted floors and properly attired patrons. Mary was in her element—more appropriately dressed than her escort.

By noon, they had returned to *Channel Runner* to load their cargo. Bud suspected that he was no longer Jake's sole non-maritime customer. He even theorized to Mary that the makeshift pulley elevator carried more alcohol these days than marine supplies. Lifting the last case of whiskey aboard, the rope-tethered platform began its ascent. Jake bid them safe passage from above before shutting them out.

Halfway to Rosario, Bud took note of a boat some distance ahead running on a course other than their own. Keeping it under surveillance, he was aware of who it might be when the other boat slowed and change direction. It was becoming obvious that if *Channel Runner* maintained her heading the boats would meet. The gap between the boats continued to close. Finally, Bud confirmed the oncoming craft as the revenuers.

Looking into Mary's green eyes, Bud asked, "Are you up for some excitement?"

Unmasked concern crossed her face, "Do I have a choice?"

Unable to hide a perplexing look in his own eyes, Bud said, "'fraid not."

Bud maintained their speed and course as he sized up their options.

The feds had chosen a good place to intercept boats coming from Canada—leading oncoming craft into a narrow pass separating two islands. A reef running along one of the islands further restricted safe passage. The boats were now close enough that Bud could detect a smirk across the face of one of the enforcers. It looked as if the feds had finally corralled the Shaw Islander with the fast boat.

Bud had fished the area for rock cod many times as a youth and knew it well. Being low tide, much of the reef areas were either glistening in the midday sun or hidden just below the water surface. Ribbons of flowing kelp identified the remnants of an outgoing ebb tide.

Mary looked scared.

Bud looked contemplative.

"Don't panic Mary," Bud said, trying to calm her.

The two boats were nearly upon each other when Bud veered into a kelp laden area. Peering over the side into the water, Mary could see jagged rocks. Birds fiddled about nearby feeding on the exposed mussels and other delicacies. While some of the feathered bystanders gave the intruders little notice, a few of their kind fidgeted at *Channel Runner's* approach.

Taking the boat out of gear, they drifted while Bud reached for a fishing pole stored in the cuddy cabin. Checking the lure, he cast it out over the top of the canvas-covered crates that filled the stern. Handing the pole to Mary, he challenged, "Count to 50. I bet you don't make it before you have a fish on."

Mary obliged in wide eyed disbelief.

The revenuers began to cautiously follow *Channel Runner*. Craning their necks, mimicking the many of the long-legged waterfowl, the revenuers hesitated. Magnified by the water, submerged rocks appeared everywhere.

When Mary reached a count of 39, the pole bent slightly signaling a hooked fish.

Bud said, "Hold on. I know another way out of here."

Vroom!

The roar of the engine and frothing water quickly transformed the placid banqueters into flocks of screeching objectors.

Channel Runner leapt atop the water making her getaway—skimming across the shallows. Taking aim at a point where the kelp met the craggy tree lined shore, their course appeared it would end in sure destruction. Dancing atop the water's surface faster and faster, *Channel Runner* tore through the kelp beds.

Mary's eyes were like saucers. Mouth draped open in disbelief, her white-knuckled hands held on for dear life. Dropping the pole, it caught on *Channel Runner's* gunwale. A surfing rock cod trailed behind in their wake.

Pulling Mary down as an overhanging tree approached, Bud yelled, "Duck," as branches scraped the cabin top like fingernails on a blackboard.

Free from the confines of the shallow inlet, a shit eating grin crossing Bud's face. Hollering over the engine noise, Bud shouted, "I told you that you might get more than you bargained for by taking a boat ride with me."

Mary forced the corners of her mouth up slightly as she slid next to Bud trembling.

"Relax, I figured we had a good two feet of water under our rudder when we cleared the reef," Bud said knowingly.

After a time, Bud slowed and turned the controls over to Mary. Reeling in the fishing line he found their rock cod, not unlike the feds, was nowhere to be seen. Unlike the fish, the revenuers knew where to look for the *Channel Runner*. Bud considered their options. They could head directly to Rosario but questioned if there would be time to unload before their pursuers might come looking. They could run to Roche

Harbor, but Bud was uncomfortable with that option as well. What if their chasers decided to go directly there for some reason?

Bud had taken a risk running during the broad daylight and that decision had come home to roost. Instinctively, he headed for his boyhood haunt, Blind Island.

Channel Runner snaked into the isolated cove. Looking at Mary, Bud said, "Sorry to bring you here, but we have few options."

Mary snuggled closer, "I'm okay. It holds bad memories, but it is where I found you."

As the anchor hooked the sandy bottom, Bud rigged a set of lines to play the boat in and out permitting an easy re-boarding as the tide changed.

Removing his shoes and socks, Bud rolled up his pant legs above his knees and jumped into the water as close to the beach as he could manage. Not unlike the last time he had been in the cove with Mary, he misjudged the depth as the water reached almost to his waist. Yelping out in agony as the cold water infiltrated his pants, Bud considered abandoning Mary.

Picking his giggling passenger off the boat, Bud turned and headed for the beach. Only managing a few sure-footed steps, he stumbled on the uneven bottom dropping Mary head over heels. She surfaced spitting water. Without missing a beat, around his neck, she dragged him under. Grabbing her wrists as they came to the surface, Bud tried to kiss her.

Playfully resisting his advances, she teased, "You may have seen your last kiss after that stunt. Besides, I would have thought the water might have cooled you off."

Wadding to the beach, Bud said with a knowing look, "We may want to shed some of our clothes to dry in the sun."

Mary looked at him sternly, nose crinkled, wondering if he had intentionally dropped her in the first place. "Seems every time we get together my clothes end up wet as a prelude to you getting them off me."

Bud stripped to his shorts and bounded over the logs to his old fort. He found the driftwood structure relatively still intact. As he hoped when he had headed for the island, the fort would make a good spot to stash their cargo. Returning to the beach, he found Mary lying on the pebbled beach—her outer clothing neatly arranged over a log to dry.

Beginning the unloading process, he stacked the boxes on the beach before lugging them up to the fort. Watching fondly, Mary's eyes watered thinking of the boy who had saved her life.

The last case of whiskey squirreled away, Bud joined Mary. They sat and talked while he stroked her wet darken auburn hair into long kelp like ribbons. Noticing her hair comber's shorts unable to conceal what lie beneath, Mary began to remove the remainder of her clothes.

Uninhibited, they made love in broad daylight. Afterwards they drifted to sleep.

Pulling the *Channel Runner* closer to the beach so as not to replay the antics of their arrival, Bud gathered their semi-dry clothing and carried them and Mary to the boat. Once on board, they donned their clothes, lifted the anchor and steered a heading toward the Shaw Island Store.

Announcing their arrival with the ever-present squeak of the rear screen door, Mary and Bud found Mabel stocking shelves from an array of boxes strewn in the aisleways. Mabel left her chore once she recognized Mary and the two exchanged warm greetings.

"What about me," Bud asked in a pitiful voice tinged with sarcasm.

Mable rolled her eyes before responding, "I see you often enough to already know you're someone special."

Mary beamed at the declaration.

"Besides," Mabel said, "I wonder what my son is up to these days? The revenuers came by today inquiring about the young man with the fast boat."

"Where's Cleo?" Bud asked by way of a response.

"Oh, he's gone to the mainland to visit his ailing sister. Quit trying to change the subject," she pressed.

"Mom, I'm just having some fun with those guys. There's no need for concern."

Mabel touched her cheek. She didn't buy his story but said nothing further.

"I ran into Mary the other day and took her for a boat ride."

Noticing his mother glancing at Mary's somewhat unkempt hair and wrinkled attire, Bud stammered, "We also went fishing and took a swim before deciding to stop by to say hello."

Mabel let the explanation suffice without further comment.

Bud proposed, "Mom, I thought it would be a good time to pick up the weekly order for Rosario. It'll save a trip since we're heading that way."

"I've only just gotten the list and haven't taken time to fill the order yet," Mabel responded. "Can't it wait until tomorrow?"

"Come on mom. I'm here. We'll help."

They took the next hour to box up the ordered items pausing from time to time to catch up on a bit of trivial chit chat. No one seemed in a hurry to rush the visit.

Bud pulled a tarp over the boxes once he had loaded them aboard *Channel Runner*. Bidding their farewells, *Channel Runner* and her substitute load headed for home.

As Bud and Mary neared Rosario, Bud could see the Feds tied up at the dock talking to Yansen. To Earl's dismay, Bud did not hesitate to head directly to the runabout's accustom moorage spot, the same float opposite the revenuers' boat.

Earl looked nervous as he nonchalantly tried to get Bud's attention and wave him off.

Bud jumped on the float with line in hand as one of the men boarded *Channel Runner*. Grabbing the tarp, the lawman yanked it back revealing the store supplies.

Earl's face went from panic to a broad smile.

"Thanks," Bud said as he held out his arms for the man in the boat to hand him a box.

The overweight man gruffly declined and uneasily climbed back onto the float.

Mary remained quietly seated trying to suppress a grin.

The other man with the brimmed hat, the leader of the two, looked perturbed. "How come you sped away from us earlier this morning?"

Bud looked at them quizzically and said, "Were you the boat in the pass earlier?"

Bud looked at Yansen as if speaking for his amusement, "Oh, we stopped in the reef near the pass because I bet Mary that we could catch a fish by the time she could count to 100…. or was it 50?" looking to Mary.

"It was 50 and I lost the bet," she piped in happily.

"We did leave the area rather quickly after catching the fish, but I was only trying to scare my girlfriend."

Mary looked at Bud affectionately, being referred to as his girlfriend made her smile. "And it turned out he was right."

Bud asked, "Do we know each other?"

"Not at the moment, but…," the man paused for effect, looking *Channel Runner* over, "I speculate that we'll soon get to know each other far better than you may want."

The two revenuers got into their boat leaving with nary another word.

Yansen turned to Bud and asked, "Are you trying to give me a heart attack?"

Bud's response was a grin.

"Mary and her family are visiting Roche Harbor. You may remember the Pickards? I believe her folks still visit the Morans from time to time."

Yansen affirmed he knew the family.

It was nearly 6:30 in the evening when Mary and Bud finally headed back to Roche Harbor. Long gentle swells lifted *Channel Runner* as she sped along effortlessly. Little was communicated except their closeness. Mary wrapped her arms around Bud when they passed Blind Island in the distance.

Mary's mother happened to be in viewing distance aboard the family yacht as the *Channel Runner* motored into the harbor.

"I suspect she is not going to be all that happy with me. I didn't talk to her last night when I returned to change my clothes," Mary explained

"Will I see you again?" Bud asked.

"You don't have a choice," Mary responded. "I will write you when we get back to Seattle and we can figure something out."

Tying up at the same moorage as the night before, Bud offered, "Do you want me to walk you to the yacht?"

"It would probably be best if you didn't," Mary replied.

They parted as they had in the past, each returning to their own world.

A few nights later Bud retrieved the liquid cargo from Blind Island.

Channel Runner was Bud's. He had completed the twenty-fifth successful run on a white capped stormy night in October. Unsurprisingly, there had been no sign of the feds that evening. With prohibition dragging on, revenuer sightings became infrequent during periods of blustery weather. Clearly a fair-weather bunch, it also seemed they gave Bud an ever-widening berth as he became Roche Harbor's sole distributor.

Earl and Bud's illicit alliance thrived. Taking all the risks, Bud had assumed the role of senior partner, negotiating lucrative agreements with Roche Harbor as well as other area destinations. Yansen's piece of the pie was commensurate, and then some, with his numerous contacts in the shipping and lumber industries. As the managing partner, Bud's share was significant. They weren't getting rich by Moran's standards, but were doing very well.

Bud had set up an office on the second floor of the boat maintenance shop. As his base of operation, he managed to keep his fingers in enough of the activity around the boat basin that no one questioned his comings and goings. Robert Moran didn't seem to notice or care.

As time passed, the enterprise sought expansion opportunities throughout the Puget Sound area. While the uniqueness of Jake's marine store continued to provide a source, the establishment of additional Canadian suppliers significantly cut acquisition costs. Additional means of moving the alcohol across the border and onto distributors were sought. Contributors included individual fast runabouts, fishing boats whose cargo holds carried more than salmon, as well as tugboat crews who plied the water between Canada and the States. Aboard *Channel Runner*, Bud occasionally made deliveries, but generally the transport was left to others.

Bud's and Mary's relationship continued to flourish. She would often come to Rosario or they would arrange to meet in other coastline locations north of Seattle. Bud also traveled to Seattle from time to time for business. They spent Christmas together in Victoria and New Year's Eve back at Roche Harbor. Yet, there seemed to be an underlying vagueness to their relationship. Bud didn't like routine and couldn't, or wouldn't, fit into the Seattle crowd. Mary was drawn to the luxury surroundings and social activities that had pampered her since birth. They attended a New Year's Eve bash at a posh Seattle hotel where Mary seemed to be driven to seek out and socialize with all of Seattle's elite. Bud withdrew to the bar leaving Mary to renew acquaintances with those of her kind. Bud and Mary argued later that evening about Bud's aloof mannerisms at the party—not unlike what he once endured at the hands of Rosario's blue bloods when he was younger.

Mary's parents remained standoffish. Whenever Bud did travel to Seattle, her folks were never part of the equation. Never invited to their home, it was clear they did not condone the relationship. Often visiting Bud at the estate, she officially stayed at the mansion, but roomed with Bud in his cabin.

"Do your parents know that I love you Mary?" Bud asked one day as they sat on a log at Blind Island.

"Yes, I think they assume so."

"And what have you told them about your feelings?" Bud pressed.

"I think they believe I want to be with you," she replied, not totally answering his question.

"But they think I'm a backwards island boy who's not good enough for their daughter," Bud offered hoping for a rebuttal.

Her eyes glistening, she said in a whisper, "It's hard to explain. You know I love you."

Bud gazed at the kelp bulbs bobbing in the afternoon sun. A lone seal surfaced as if searching, possibly for a companion, before disappearing alone. Bud wondered if it might be a telltale sign of his future.

That evening, as Bud held her tight for fear that she might escape, Mary told him that she needed to return home. No explanation was offered, nor did he ask for one. Never shaking his upbringing, maybe it was just not meant to be.

Standing on the dock the following morning, waiting for Mary's passenger boat to tie up, Bud reached into his pocket and withdrew the arrowhead he had found the day fate had brought Mary to him. Placing it in her hand, he told her that it would help her find her way back.

Bud tasted the salty tears that crept down her cheeks and across her lips. She started to say something, then stopped. Then she was gone.

The scene was surreal, reminiscent of the day Helen had left, never to be seen again.

❊

1926

Seasons came and went while Bud continued to reap the rewards of prohibition. As spring blossomed, like nature itself, Bud felt a yearning to branch out from under the winter shadow of the estate. Restless, his current living arrangement providing little to enhance his independence or providing the creature comforts he could well afford. It was time to find a place of his own.

Bud had not heard from Mary since the day she left on the passenger boat bound for home. Initially, he tried to contact her, but without success. Mary's mother, visiting Rosario, ultimately sealed his fate when Bud and she ran into each other.

"Hello Mrs. Pickard. Nice to see you," Bud managed to say with a friendly smile.

Her less than enthusiastic response was short and to the point, "Hello."

"A beautiful day for sure. I trust all is well with everyone. How is Mary?" Bud said trying to start a conversation.

"We're all fine, as is Mary. I wasn't sure if you are aware that she has started a family of her own," Mrs. Pickard replied sourly. "Please don't try and contact her again."

Bud was devastated but accepted the news without response. Parting, he said, "Please wish her only the best from me."

That evening Bud drank himself into a stupor with Earl.

Spending a portion of the next week aboard *Channel Runner*, Bud motored around the islands looking for a piece of property. He wasn't sure exactly what he was looking for but knew he would know when he saw it. Returning late one afternoon without success, he went to Earl's office to see how his day was going. Over a scotch, Bud lamented about being unable to find what he was looking for.

"Have you been around the entirety of this island?" Earl asked

"Most of it," Bud responded. "Had intended to circumnavigate it the other day, but got side tracked to Waldron Island."

"I know of a piece of property that might be had," Earl said, as he pulled a map of Orcas from the shelf. Unfurling it on a nearby oak table he pointed his finger on a jutted-out portion of the shoreline and said, "Take a look at that area."

The next afternoon Bud was on his way in *Channel Runner* to search out the vicinity Earl suggested. Nearing the area, he maneuvered past a large jagged rock point that jutted from the shoreline. Rounding the other side, a driftwood covered crescent beach came into view. Thin strands of eel grass swayed in the shallows while ribbons of kelp marked the cove's boundaries. Except for being on a significantly larger scale, the setting made him think of his boyhood refuge on Blind Island. The property was located on the less traveled side of Orcas. It would give him access to Rosario but afford him privacy and what he desired most of all, the space to build his own life.

Anchoring, Bud dove off the bow and swam towards shore. The water was cold as hell, but he hardly noticed as the exhilaration of the discovery filled his senses. Scrambling ashore, he discovered a weathered rowboat with shore grass peeking through the planked bottom. Stranded above the high tide drift, it was a sign that someone once had interest in the area.

Exploring the nearby shoreline area, he discovered a creek that emptied into the bay. He traced its source to a small nearby lake. Returning to the beach, finding himself cut off from the point by a narrow tidal flow, he waded up to his knees and scaled the other side. With seasonal area tide swings of up to twelve feet, he figured the crossing would be roughly seven feet deep at high tide and dry when the tide was out. From the point's crest, Bud had a 180-degree view from east to west. Sitting down on the dried-out grass, he stared out across the expansive blue straits to Canada beyond. A pod of killer whales frolicked off shore on their quest for salmon. Lying back, eyes closed, he felt peace...he felt at home.

Bud inched his way down the steep rocks just above *Channel Runner*. Finding his route petering out about six feet above the water, he peered into the clear depths. The visibility was good. There was no kelp or eelgrass. It looked deep. Jettisoning off the point, the water grew colder as he let himself drift downward. Reaching the bottom some fifteen feet below, he could hear the distant soundings of the whale pod. Pushing off from the bottom, Bud kicked calmly toward the shadowed outline of *Channel Runner*.

CHAPTER 10

Bud found Earl in his office finishing up the daily accounting. Excitedly, he told Earl the place he had sent him was perfect to build a home. "Do you know who owns it?"

"I do know who owns it. Why do you think I suggested you look at it? The ownership of Broken Point includes 34 acres of surrounding property."

"Do you know how to get a hold of them?"

"I do. Fetch the two of us some of that ill-gotten scotch," Earl commanded as he moved to the comfort of one of the overstuffed chairs.

"Bud, I acquired that property long ago when the mill was still operating. During those early years, I was captivated with the setting and had hoped to build a home on the property. But, it never came to pass. I've turned down a few offers for the land including one from Moran himself who wanted to build a cottage retreat away from the estate. I believe Moran was jealous of anyone owning a picturesque setting rivaling Rosario."

Earl and Bud talked and drank late into the evening. Earl was in a reflective mood and, hoping a possible sale might be in the making, Bud let him ramble on. Finally, Earl said, "Bud, you and I have a special relationship. You are more than just a partner or friend. I consider you more like the son I never had."

"I feel the same fondness toward you Earl," Bud replied as he attacked the sentimental feeling overcoming him with a swig of scotch.

Appearing to be considering the fate of mankind, Earl lit a cigar watching his first exhale drift. Earl spoke again with a tone of uncommon tenderness, "I'd like to see a house built on my point, but I'm no longer the one to do it. The Point is yours with the stipulation that it has to remain in your ownership while I am still alive. I would hope you would keep it beyond then, but I won't be in any position to have a say."

A lump in his throat, Bud was speechless.

Bud rose from his chair, bent over and drew Earl near.

"Thank you, Earl."

Over the remainder of the year and into the next, Bud threw himself into the construction of his homestead on Broken Point. His priority was to build a large workshop to support the home's construction. The shop was built near the craggy shore edge of the point where it fell away to the tidal crossing. Included within the structure was a small bunkroom so he could maximize every available hour towards the undertaking. Paned hinged windows were installed to capture summer breezes and the setting sun. A potbellied wood stove, not unlike the one at Shaw's Store, sat in one corner.

Working on the home's design, Bud found himself drawn to a naturally concave area in the bedrock. The irregularly shaped depression was roughly 12 by 15 feet in size with a variable depth of five feet or so. It was connected to a long narrow trough of similar depth towards the shoreline beneath the new workshop. The final design would incorporate the bedrock depression into a secret room under his new home. Once the raised subfloor was constructed, the dished-out area would have nearly eight feet of height. That portion of the trough extending beyond the boundaries of the house foundation to the workshop would be topped with rough cedar cut boards between the two structures. The adjoining passageway beneath would provide an unassuming planked walkway from one building to the other. The plan would require Bud to relocate the shop's entry door to align with the new connection.

Over the next weeks, the house and fireplace foundations were placed, and the secret room readied for the subfloor above. Bud excavated centuries of dirt deposits from the bedrock irregularities before placing beach gravel to level the uneven areas. Next, large floor timbers were set over the entire area topped with planked subflooring. Moving beyond the boundaries of the house, Bud built the bedrock passageway cover to the shop and realigned the shop's entry. Finally, he installed a trap door in the shop's floor to gain access to the connecting tunnel.

Inside the house, the secret room would gain its access from under the stairway to the second floor. A section of the lower stairs would hinge upward exposing a steep stairway to access both the secret room and passageway to the shop.

Bud did much of the home's construction himself. His skills had been honed by helping Frank tend to carpentry tasks around the store and the years that followed at Rosario. But, there was one job for which Bud lacked the confidence or experience. It was the construction of the home's three fireplaces—one each in the living room, library study and second floor bedroom. While it didn't seem all that complicated, he was unsure. The fireplaces had to draw properly, or one could expect smoke backdrafts from the Point's swirly winds.

Over their usual scotch, Earl and Bud talked about the home's progress. When the issue of the fireplace construction came up, Earl suggested a jack-of-all-trades craftsman that Bud already knew. In his early seventies, Clyde still puttered around Rosario tending to some of the repair and maintenance of the mansion. Among other things, Clyde had been originally responsible for the construction of the estate's numerous fireplaces. Like Earl, Clyde had stayed on to work for Moran after the mill was shut down.

Clyde eagerly accepted the job. Their first order of business was to find a local source of stone. The vision Bud had in mind meant fireplaces constructed of large round rock like Rosario's. Through Clyde's inquiries, they were recommended to look at a rock deposit accessible just above the beach on nearby Decatur Island. The inspection was made aboard *Channel Runner* at the narrows of Lopez Pass. Inching close to shore, Clyde and Bud were able to get a good look at the tide washed stone. It looked perfect. The large round multi-colored deposit had been left behind by the glaciers when they carved the San Juan Islands.

On the way back to Orcas, Clyde suggested, "Now you know where there is a good supply of rock with decent access. Have you thought of building more of your house out of rock than just the fireplaces?"

"Well I hadn't, but it's worth considering. I want the overall house appearance to have a Craftsman look. Probably no reason not to include more rock other than it's going to be a bitch getting it to the site."

"There's a guy on Henry Island that has the equipment to get it there. I'll get a hold of him," Clyde said.

As it turned out, the guy Clyde ran down could do the job. He had a small barge built to be run up on a beach. A fisherman by trade, he supplemented his income by hauling pretty much everything and anything. The barge was pushed and towed about by his overbuilt gillnet boat with a more powerful engine than the norm.

Bud reviewed options for adding more rock to the design—favoring a plan that rocked a portion of the home's first story. The remainder of the first and second elevations would be sided with beveled boards available from an island sawmill. The roof would be split cedar shakes.

A crew was assembled to transport the rock. Offloaded onto Broken Point's beach, it was hauled up to the building site by cart via a make-shift ramp. No simple task, it took a crew of five, including Bud, a week of back breaking work.

The fireplace construction began before the last of the rock was piled around the decked over foundation. Retaining the hardest worker of the hauling crew to help, Bud began laying rock. While Clyde was too hunkered over to actually set any stones, he was on-site to lend expertise. Bud learned quickly that placement of a specific rock was as much an art as it was structural. Clyde's guidance was especially apparent during the construction of the fireplace flues. A design to draw smoke out the chimney while radiating heat into the house was skillfully overseen by the elderly craftsman. Still, there were times that Clyde's continuous flow of mundane directions bordered on grounds for mutiny. He felt the need to be constantly verbalizing since he no longer could perform the actual labor. There always seemed to be a rock that might have a better shape or color than the one Bud had already lugged over from the pile. Or maybe the mortar was too stiff or too wet. Bud did his best to balance Clyde's incessant deliberations while still maintaining a sense of harmony between the two of them. He learned if he challenged Clyde with good nature ribbing and acquiesced to his thoughts from time to time, the work continued at a steady pace and the old man seemed pleased with the results.

Once the fireplaces were finished, Clyde still stopped by from time to time with Earl in tow to check on things. Earl seemed especially pleased that his Point would finally grace a home worthy of its stately location. Bud additionally hired two brothers on the island to help frame and roof the house to make it weather tight by winter. As with most projects, the construction took longer than expected. It didn't help when Bud decided to add a spiral stair tower extending above the second story patterned after a Coast Guard lighthouse. The view from the narrow circular outside catwalk was exceptional. During its construction, they were rewarded with a bird's eye view of the annual gray whale migrations.

After more than a year, the house was finally complete. Little expense had been spared. Dark walnut paneling adorned the walls of the library as well as part of the living room. Granite floors graced the entry. Polished wood plank fir floors were laid throughout the house except the upstairs and downstairs tiled baths. Multi-colored Persian rugs were scattered throughout. Copying Rosario's details, brass nautical looking light fixtures were hung. Many of windows included a leaded-glass design. Furnishings included dark oak mission furniture. Walls throughout the house were a bit bare, as were the library's shelves, but time would resolve that.

Bud escorted his mother on the first official tour. While proud of her son's accomplishment, she had mixed feelings about the source of funds that built it. A few weeks later a gathering of folks were invited for an old-fashioned house warming. Guests included Mabel, Cleo, Earl, Clyde, the Morans, all the workers who contributed to the effort, as well as a few other acquaintances. Fresh salmon as well as other seafood delicacies were enjoyed by many.

While the house was not overly large or pretentious, Moran cornered Bud to tell him he loved the place and would like to buy it. Bud responded, winking at Earl, who overheard the conversation, "I intend to own this place until the day I die."

Eventually, everyone drifted away. Alone, leaving only the sounds of waves against the shore, Bud's thoughts turned to Mary and what might have been.

CHAPTER 11

THE NEXT 10 YEARS OR SO PASSED QUICKLY FOR BUD FOWLER. DURING the period, he maintained a close relationship with his mother and Cleo, as well as Earl, but few others. His ties to Rosario had been left behind when the estate was sold to new owners. Earl still maintained his residence there but had relinquished his authority to others. Mabel and Cleo continued to operate the Shaw Island Store with seasonal help paid for by Bud. Uncle Frank had lost his life when he had been washed overboard from *Lorne's* stern during a storm. A headstone marked his life in the Shaw Cemetery even though he was never found.

Bud pursued a few relationships over the years, but nothing seriously developed. For a time, he had courted an island school teacher, but ended it when she began pressuring him to get married. Besides, she was too damn prim and proper for his tastes.

Mary had become only a pleasant memory. Her photo which once occupied a prominent corner on one of the library book shelves, was now buried amongst the shelved books.

Prohibition had ended in 1933. Finances no longer an issue, Bud began to explore the world beyond the confines of Shaw Island—a declaration he once had made to the lady of the *America*. Having first booked passage on a fancy ocean liner crossing the Atlantic, he concluded that he didn't fit in well with the pretentious fellow travelers. Finding travel aboard tramp steamers more to his liking, he continued to experience cultures throughout the world.

After a couple of years exploring, Bud returned home. Having no one to ground him, he became anxious and bored. He signed on as a deck hand aboard an ocean-going tug bound for Guam. By 1937, he had attained his Merchant Marine Officer License. Continuing to find life onboard merchant ships his preferred mode of travel, he became First Officer on a vessel bound for Australia. On his travels he sought out treasures from ports of call that ultimately adorned his home on Broken Point. One of the more noteworthy items he brought home was a kangaroo. The young marsupial had originally been destined for some two-bit zoo in the States. During the voyage, Bud took pity on the small eared creature's cramped caged existence, freeing her to roam the ship's decks. Within days, her savior and the long-tailed oddity had taken a mutual liking to each other. She took comfort in Bud's attention and began following him wherever she could. Before long, to the dismay of the crew, she had a pile of blankets heaped in the corner of the galley for her to nestle in. Bud even wrestled her up to the pilothouse once, but only once—the goodwill gesture having been rewarded with a pile of shit under the chart table. In time, the ship's manifest was doctored to reflect the kangaroo's destination as Orcas Island. Old Yansen had in jest referred to the kangaroo's new home set atop Broken Point as the "Kangaroo House." Somehow the name stuck. Likewise, the gangly misplaced animal became known as Karoo.

During Bud's periods of absence, Earl typically took up residency at the Point. It gave him an opportunity to enjoy the setting for what could have been if he had built his own home. With Bud's approval, he remodeled and expanded a portion of the shop into a very nice studio he could call his own. As time went by, Earl lived full time at the Point. He resided either in the shop or house, depending on if Bud was home, as well as becoming Karoo's surrogate caretaker.

Bud was still plying the oceans of the world in 1939 when Germany declared their supremacy over the rest of mankind with the invasion of Poland—the beginning of WWII. Having been defeated and humiliated at the end of WWI, Germany now sought to reclaim their place in the world order. It had taken nearly two decades for the country to rebuild after their 1918 loss. During this period, confidence in the governing republic had eroded, fueling political extremism, turmoil and runaway inflation. Splinter groups formed within; all vying for power. A transplanted Austrian began to rise within one such political faction. His zeal and radical behavior invoked a following. His oratory performances captured the imagination of his listeners and spurred the formation of the Nazi Party propelling him into power.

By the early 1940s Nazi submarines were roaming the waters around Europe and the mid-Atlantic in their efforts to destroy shipments of goods destined for the Allied war effort. Upon the United States entry into the war in 1941, the U-boat stealth prowls expanded to include the Atlantic coast of the United States and Canada. Their targets were indiscriminate—left up to the will of an individual U-boat commander.

On a dark 1942 night, one such U-boat patrolled the waters in search of prey. Eager to prove himself, the youthful officer felt any vessel was fair game to reduce support for the war effort against the Motherland. Consequently, on that very night, Captain Bud Fowler commanded a freighter transporting coffee and other agricultural products from Columbia, South America. His ship was bound for New Orleans. Onboard passengers consisted of merchant seamen as well as civilians returning from working in South America and those seeking a better life as immigrants. Evasive maneuvers had been become common since the Nazi's stepped up their efforts in the region, so Bud had posted lookouts to watch for U-boats. Additionally, the vessel was running without lights and traveling in a zigzag pattern. Aware there had been U-boat sighting near the Mississippi River, Bud was fidgety as they closed in on their destination. His only comfort, if one could categorize it as such, was that mounting seas swells were a deterrent to a successful submarine attack.

A partial moon broke through the drifting cloud cover providing the U-boat command sporadic visibility of the surrounding seas. The shadowy outline of Bud's freighter materialized in the distance. Positioned on the surface, the submarine's low profile enhanced their ability to remain undetected by their prey. The U-boat changed course to advance ahead of the freighter's path. Having maneuvered into firing range, one of Bud's lookouts spied the threat and sounded the alarm, but it was too late—torpedoes were already bearing down on them.

The freighter shuddered as a torpedo found its mark. A second torpedo seemed to lift the vessel slightly upward as it exploded under the ship's keel creating a detonation shock wave. The hull ruptured opening a violent pathway for the ocean's intrusion into the engine room. The engine crew died immediately as the ocean snuffed out the freighter's life-blood.

The ship was doomed—the fate of those remaining up for grabs. Ordering the lifeboats deployed, the freighter began to list to port. Disoriented crew and passengers struggled topside as the sea surged upward from below. As his perch sank away, Bud grappled to hold on to the small deck railing outside the wheelhouse as he shouted orders to abandon ship. A black wall of water entombing him, he lifted off from the foundering freighter. Gripped by the descending vessel's turbulent plunge towards the ocean floor, his lifejacket fought to provide enough buoyancy to save him from a watery grave. Near surrender, lungs bursting, seawater beginning to creep into his nose, he finally broke to the surface. Gasping for air, he grabbed a nearby panicked woman without a lifejacket and guided her towards a nearly empty life raft. Leaving her to others, he sought out a lifeless body floating nearby. While the individual wore a lifejacket, the gash across his face had taken its toll. Bud recognized the corpse as one of his crew.

A searchlight penetrated the darkness from a nearby U-boat now less than 50 yards away. Satisfied, the stealth vessel motored away, distancing itself from the carnage. As daylight approached, only seventeen of the original twenty-nine crew and passengers had survived before being rescued by a Navy patrol boat.

Bud returned to Broken Point despondent. Haunted by the memory of the sinking and those lost under his command, he obsessively relived his every decision leading up to the tragedy. He began to drink heavily. Alone, pushing those he knew away, he hardly ever left the house except for provisions and alcohol from the Orcas store. He hadn't been over to see his mother in ages and as time went by, it became the norm. Late one afternoon, a rap on the door jolted him from an all too common stupor. Making his way from the library, he heard the door open before reaching the hallway. Rounding the corner, he was startled to see his mother's petite silhouette framed against the light streaming through the open doorway. Straight away, she headed to the kitchen to make a pot of coffee without speaking. Bud stepped back into the library in hopes of straightening it up somewhat before his mother's return.

Continuing her silence, Mabel entered the usually spotlessly organized room and gave it a cursory once-over. Bud could tell by her eyes that she was unsettled. Handing her son a cup of coffee, she took a seat across from him and sipped her own.

Finally, she spoke, "Bud, we've got do something about your situation. I refuse to accept this is what you want for yourself."

The room was quiet again except for the crackle of the fire. Bud was embarrassed and didn't know what to say. Intent on waiting him out, his mother said nothing further. An uneasy silence continued as they sipped their coffee.

Finally, Bud got up the courage to say something. "I'm sorry. I promise I will put this behind me, but it won't be easy."

"I'm staying a few days. My bag is on the porch. Please get it while I start dinner."

Over the next few days, the two talked about years gone by and life's twists of fate. They walked the beach together and ventured here and there on the island. She even seemed to take a liking to Karoo—her presence a reminder that her son had a good heart.

It was time for Mabel to return to home and to Cleo. She had done what she could to show her son that she loved him, and it was up to him to mend his ways. About to board the ferry back to Shaw, Bud promised he would strive to look to the future. They hugged and wiped away tears in their eyes.

Over the next year, Bud struggled to put his life back in order, puttering around the Point or venturing out in *Channel Runner* for days on end to points in the South Sound or north into the Canadian Gulf Islands. With a tarp extension to *Channel Runner's* cuddy cabin, he found he could endure most weather conditions. From time to time he would find moorage to his liking and remain in a remote seaside community for a few days. But generally, he was on the move seeking internal peace. In time, he returned to the open sea.

CHAPTER 12

1945

A WALL OF WATER BROACHED THE SHIP'S BOW IN A THUNDEROUS ROAR. Decks awash, wind howling through her rigging, the freighter shuddered to right herself. Shedding the relentless onslaught, she slid into the next murky trough. Battling to keep the *Adventurer* headed into the mountainous waves of the Atlantic Ocean, Captain Bud Fowler and his crew braced for yet another assault.

Suddenly, amid the clash, the pilothouse door flew open as a stubby man bolted in from the night darkness. Bud eyed the soaked German with a sense of disdain as the intruder fought to close the door behind him. Wire rimmed glasses fogged-over, the outsider stumbled over a stool leg toppling to the deck. Struggling to his feet, the man looked like a drowned rat trying to find the high point of a sinking ship. Having told their only passenger to remain in his cabin for his own safety, Bud, his first mate Griff and the helmsman looked at the man in disbelief.

Having taken an immediate dislike to the arrogant Nazi when he boarded in Spain, Bud hadn't said two words to the guy since their initial meeting. Swayed to give the sawed-off Kraut passage by his willingness to pay generously for himself and crated cargo, Bud now regretted it.

The German's eyes darted around nervously. Finally, he spoke in broken English, "I fear for my shipment below deck."

Having all they could handle trying to survive the storm's fury, Bud nor anyone else in the wheelhouse gave him any mind. While *Adventur-*

er was seaworthy enough, having been built originally to ply the Great Lakes, at 268 feet she was on the on the smallish side for her current skirmish.

Agitated no one was giving him the consideration he thought he deserved, the German demanded, "Do you hear me?! Go below and make sure my crates are secure!"

"Kitchen utensils and supplies my ass," Bud thought recalling the passenger's shipping manifest. His tolerance at the breaking point, he bellowed, "We're trying to stay afloat! Keep your goddamn mouth shut or get your Nazi ass back to your cabin!"

Unhinged, the man's mental state began to mimic the storm's rage. Ranting and raving, words spewed from his mouth in a dialect foreign to all. If looks could kill, the German's menacing stare would have taken Bud down. A prelude to battle, the wheelhouse visitor threatened, "You have no idea who you are dealing with and someone better do as I say!"

Having had enough, Bud crossed the deck, opened the door and shoved the German back into the slate-colored storm.

"You need to go back to your cabin where it is safe! And I don't want to see you until we come and get you," Bud shouted slamming and locking the door.

Standing his ground on the small pilothouse platform, the Nazi relentlessly tried to pound the door into submission.

"Goddamn it. What a stupid son-of-a-bitch. Someone's going to have to take him back to his cabin," Bud said with disgust.

Crossing the swaying deck, nearing the door, Bud was able see that the ostracized Kraut had upped the stakes—a gun appeared in the door's porthole along with the outsider's frenzied face.

Bud stopped in his tracks, "What the fuck?!"

"Okay Griff, I'm going to let him back in, but we need to disarm him. If we don't, I'm afraid he may go find someone else to harm. Be ready."

Roaring thunder in concert with lightning shards illuminated the unfolding events as Bud reached for the polished brass knob. His timing couldn't have been worse, or better as might be the case, as the bow of the ship plunged forward, knocking him to his knees.

Adventurer wavered at the bottom of the walled torrent. Unsure she would be able to drag herself up out of the hellhole, the crew held their breath. Fighting the abyss, she slowly began to inch her way toward the unseen sky. Clutching the door knob for support, Bud stood. Warily, he peered through the porthole. The outside landing was empty.

Maintaining his footing, Bud turned, grabbed the chart table and muttered, "You stupid Nazi. Go join Hitler in hell."

The disbelieving helmsman's mouth agape, Griff stepped towards the door, "Now what? Should I take a look?"

"That last one seemed like a rogue wave, wait to see if it settles down at all," Bud commanded.

After a time, the waves did seem less treacherous, but it would be short lived. Timing his exit with ship's rising bow, Griff said, "I'll go take a quick look, but I'm not going very far."

"Be careful. There is no telling what he might do if you find him," Bud cautioned as his first mate pushed the door closed behind him.

Returning within minutes, Griff, mimicking a wet dog, tried to shed the rain from his oilskin slicker. "I only checked the near deck area and cabin. I couldn't see any sign of him Cap," Griff reported. "His possessions are still in the cabin, but he isn't. Frankly, I don't see any chance he could have survived when he was washed off the platform outside. The wall of water would have taken him across the deck and over the side."

The storm kept up its merciless attack throughout the night. Everything it could muster tested both the ship and her crew to their limits. Not until subdued light peeked beyond the horizon, did the sea's intensity show signs of waning.

Damage to the ship was limited to flooded passageways, shifted cargo and a void where a missing lifeboat was ripped from its davits. It was sobering to think the small craft could have provided any aid during the storm's height.

Bud had acquired the tramp steamer *Adventurer* for a song towards the end of the war. Her crew totaled eight. His friend and first mate, Griffin, or Griff as he went by, was a big Scottish fellow who bore all the skills to command the ship. Three quartermasters, two brothers, Ron and Ken, and Hawk, an American Indian with a bird of prey nose, stood watch at the wheel, loaded cargo as well as other deck responsibilities. The ship's engineer, Skinner, and his oiler Bernie kept things operational in the engine room. And, finally Mick, a kid just out of high school who despite his youth, grew up around a shipyard and had good seaman instincts. Mick's duties included cooking, decking and man of work, where needed. Mick reminded Bud of himself at an early age.

Taking him under his wing, Bud saw that he received every opportunity to excel at his assigned tasks.

Still manning the wheelhouse, Bud's mind drifted back to Broken Point. Visualizing her peacefulness, he longed to be home for a time—it had been too long. Knocking, Griff stepped into the wheelhouse breaking Bud's train of thought. Griffin could be relied upon for absolute and unwavering allegiance. He had been with Bud the night the Nazis sank their merchant ship. Towering over the rest of the crew at six and a half feet and some 250 pounds, he was a gentle soul unless he felt the need to defend himself, his principles or his friends. Bud tended to only address Griffin by his formal name when things were of a serious nature.

"Go get something to eat Skipper," Griff said. "There's some hot grub in the galley. By the way, I looked everywhere for our passenger and can't find a trace. Be careful, it's still howling out there."

"I will, but first I want to take a good look at everything," Bud replied.

Donning a set of stiff canvas rain gear that hung on the bulkhead, Bud stepped to the quartermaster's side to check their compass heading. Satisfied, the legs of the oil cloth noisily announced he was on the move. Stepping onto the platform, closing the door behind, the straps of his rain cap tugged against his neck. Pondering the German's death defying last stand, he descended the wheelhouse steps onto the slippery deck. Rain and wind buffeting his back, he advanced carefully towards the stern. Something caught his eye jammed up against the outer deck lip near where the lifeboat once hung. Tying off the set of swinging empty lifeboat davits, holding on for fear of being blown overboard, Bud crouched down and grasped a swastika adorned Luger. A chill ran up his spine as he pocketed the gun. Hat turned up like an inside-out umbrella, coat and pants slapping, he trudged forward towards the galley.

After finding something to eat, Bud made his way to the cargo bay hatchway. The ship's hull and cargo creaked under the strain of the rolling sea as he started down the steel ladder into the ship's bowels. Crowbar in hand, caged light bulbs casting menacing shadows, he stepped onto the wood crated cargo part way down. The shipment he sought came aboard near the end of the cargo loading. Knowing it should be isolated along the upper outside port wedged against the ship's hull, he unsteadily crawled atop the cargo. He spotted it.

Wielding the pry bar, the crate's top broke free exposing an inner-crate wrapped in canvas. Bud pulled a knife from its sheath and sliced the top. Peeling back the canvas, Bud could see something written across the inner-crate. Squinting, he stepped to one side hoping to improve the visibility in the poor lighting. Grimacing, the metal bar raised for protection, Bud jolted back stumbling before regaining his footing. Burnt into the top, a swastika threatened impending doom. There were also some other words that, based on their arrangement, likely said "Property of the Third Reich." Inching forward, as if Hitler himself might rise from within, Bud cautiously dislodged the wood top exposing rows of vertically slots.

Removing the top padding of one of the compartments, Bud slid out a rectangular-shaped item roughly three feet square by four inches thick. He unfurled the object's wrapping. It was a painting with a gilded frame. Twisting it to gain better light, the art's composition came into view—a man at a table with an outstretched hand touching a globe of the earth. Inspecting the portrayal, Bud was able to identify the artist, Jan Vermeer 1668.

Carefully repacking the painting, Bud nailed both the inner and outer crates lids back on. On all-fours back to the ladder, he grasped the cold steel rungs pulling himself upright. There were a total of three crates of varying size. Confident his missing passenger hadn't come about them by honest means, he mulled his options. "Should I take it all or just part?" he pondered. At the same time, he needed to be careful or he might be in store for more than he bargained. The rewards could be worth the risk.

Recalling a recent newspaper article following Adolf Hitler's suicide, Bud headed topside. The article had explored Hitler's rise to power when he seized control of the Nazi Party. Coupled with his zest for racial purity was his obsession to own the world's great works of art. Thousands of paintings, sculptures, silver and other religious treasures were systematically looted, crated and shipped to Germany as his Nazi forces pillaged Europe. Hitler's ultimate plan was to create a world class museum. At the same time, he intended to expand the private collections for himself and a few chosen elite.

Cautiously, as if someone might be waiting for him on the other side, Bud opened the missing passenger's cabin door. The confined space reeked of vomit—clearly the previous occupant did not cope well with the sea. Scanning the area, Bud turned his attention to the two bags the man had brought aboard. Rummaging through them, the only thing he found of interest was a box of bullets that likely fit the Luger. Ripping the padded bottom of each travel bag, finding nothing, he moved on to a stack of books in the corner of the bunk. They were written in German. He thumbed through the pages to no avail.

"The guy must be traveling with some money. Maybe he carried it with him," Bud wondered, spurring him to poke into every nook and cranny of the cabin. He came up empty handed. Conflicted over what to do, he finally decided the prudent thing was to erase the passenger's existence. Gathering all the German's possessions, Bud headed along the leeward side of the ship toward the stern. Dropping one of the books, its wind driven pages thrashed about wildly in a race to nowhere. The wayward book corralled, Bud stepped to the rail. Hesitating, he dropped the whole mess onto the wet deck and knelt. He fingered the book's rear cover. It seemed unusually thick. Fishing out the books one by one, he set them aside. Jettisoning the clothing and other sundry items overboard, he watched a shirt catch an updraft as if possessed. Against the natural order, it rose towards the heavens. Damned, it fluttered for an instant before descending into the depths of the ship's trailing wake.

Bud picked up the six books and headed to his cabin. Wanting to inspect them more thoroughly later, he placed them on his desk. But, some unexplainable feeling caused him to gather them and shove them under a pile of dirty clothes heaped in the corner. The luger and bullets were stashed beneath his bunk.

Captain Fowler paced around the wheelhouse running through various scenarios of absconding with the German's shipment. The man who met his untimely death was a long way from Germany. Since the sea tended to wash away one's past, if ever questioned, Bud and his crew could simply deny that the German was ever aboard.

Later in the day, Bud returned to the cargo hold to see what the other two wooden crates held. Knowing the origin of the crates gave him the creeps. Opening the largest of the three, he discovered it held several boxes filled with various antiquities, silver and other adornments. The third crate had been constructed around a single piece of furniture. It appeared to be a simple stand or pedestal of some sort. Yet, as it rose from its base to the top it appeared incomplete—it beckoned for some sort of pinnacle. Considering the company it was keeping, there was little doubt that it was both significant and valuable. The piece was compelling—he wanted it. Lowering and scooting the crate into another area of the cargo hold, he eliminated the German's name from view by turning over some of the boards. Next, he dipped a rag into the oily bilge water rubbing it over the crate making it appear it had been around the ship for a while. He then threw a dirty, ripped tarp over it.

Bud turned his attention to the crated paintings, carefully removing the painting of the man and the globe. Leaving nine others in place, he replaced the crate lids before heading topside with the wrapped prize.

Locking his cabin door, Bud stepped to his bunk and flipped its mattress on end against the bulkhead. Withdrawing the upper bunk drawer released a lock mechanism for the mattress support panel. Sliding his knife between the panel's edge and its frame, Bud lifted the hinged panel revealing a five-inch deep compartment above the drawers with an overall width and length of the mattress above. He had reworked the cabinetry below the mattress on a previous trip to hide some items he had obtained in Hong Kong. Placing the painting in the space, adding the luger and bullets, Bud closed the lid, entombing the man with the globe.

Captain Fowler sought out Griff. Finding him in the wheelhouse, he told the quartermaster to maintain their heading and led his first mate to his cabin.

"Griff. I've cleaned out the German's cabin and dumped his possessions overboard. I believe the best course of action is to just deny he ever sailed on their ship."

"What about the crates he brought aboard? Shouldn't we check them out?" Griff questioned.

"It's tempting, but what if there is someone waiting for him?" Bud said. "Until we know one way or the other, we should probably just leave them untouched. That way, we can maintain the flexibility to claim the crates were delivered unaccompanied for shipment. Besides, what could that pip-squeak have of value?"

"Yeah, I suppose," Griff responded with a hint of disappointment in his voice.

"I'll talk to the crewmembers," Bud said as they headed back to the wheelhouse.

Bud felt a bit guilty lying to his crew but felt the fewer individuals who knew about the crate contents, the better he could control the situation if someone showed up for them. Later he changed the manifest paperwork to two crates instead of three. If no one showed up to claim them, he could easily hold back the paperwork.

The dethroned Nazi gazed blankly at the windowless bulkhead as he contemplated the turn of events. Tiring of the cramped jail-like quarters he had been confined to, he was a man without a country—a state attributable to the failures of others. His quest to right the order of mankind had failed.

Compelled to save himself, he had sacrificed his companion of seventeen years leaving her and an impostor behind in a burnt-out bunker. Twenty-three years his junior, her devotion had been unwavering to the very end. Willingly, she had bit into a cyanide capsule in the misguided belief their lives would end together—their vows "till death do us part" becoming a reality only 40 hours after they wed.

CHAPTER 13

Captain Fowler was having difficulty maneuvering his rust-streaked freighter alongside the Brazilian wharf. Having gotten a stern line secured, his deckhands had failed to get the bow line ashore to the waiting dockhand before *Adventurer* began to wander.

"That's as close as I can get her in this goddamn tide!" Bud yelled down to Griff.

Toiling in the South American heat and humidity, Ken quickly flung a small line in the direction of the dock worker. It fell short and plopped into the water. Griff retrieved it, recoiled and threw it again. This time it reached its mark. The small diameter line, with the braided ball-like weighted end, was called a monkey-fist. Attached at *Adventurer's* end was a large tie-up bow line. The line was dragged across to the wharf and its braided eye dropped over a piling. The line went taut as the freighter's capstan began winching her towards the wharf.

Griff raised and shook his fist to signal all was secure. Telegraph bells ringing out, *Adventurer* shuttered to a stop. After weeks of constant vibration and noise, the silence was disquieting, almost dreamlike.

Standing on the platform where the German defied the sea and lost, Bud scanned the dockside. Seeing nothing out of the ordinary, he headed down to the deck and crossed over the gangplank to the wharf. After conversing with the dock foreman, he proceeded to a nearby office to complete the paperwork to offload the cargo.

A man dressed in khakis sitting at a cluttered desk looked up as Bud entered the office. "Good afternoon. I'm the captain of the *Adventurer*. We have cargo to be offloaded."

The man acknowledged and welcomed Bud in broken English.

Bud handed him a stack of papers minus the sheet listing two of the three crates that had belonged to the German. As the papers slipped from Bud's fingers, a blond man with cropped hair seemed to materialize from nowhere. Blocking the doorway, his large frame cast a shadow into the room. The impeccably white suited arrival announced, "I'm looking for a passenger who sailed aboard the ship that just docked."

Bud turned and replied, "I'm the ship's captain and we carried no passengers."

The man's expressionless blue eyes narrowed as he moved in on Bud. It wasn't the response he was expecting after having been confined to the two-bit town for the past three days waiting for *Adventurer's* arrival. Displaying a heavy German accent, the man said, "You must be mistaken. I have it on good authority that he boarded your ship."

"I sure as hell ought to know who was aboard my ship, for Chrissake," Bud responded indignantly.

The man making the inquiry didn't look like he would be easily spurned. Standing his ground, he stroked his neatly trimmed beard. He said nothing, as if contemplating the next move in a game of chess.

Masking his emotion, the German said, "The man's name is Hans Ribbentrop."

Instantly recognizing the name as that marked on the three crates, Bud knew he better thread lightly. He didn't know what the German's next move would be.

Stepping to the office desk, Bud retrieved the shipping paperwork and subtly placed the previously relinquished sheets atop others on his clipboard. Ribbentrop's manifests now amongst the lot, he slowly thumbed through the papers.

"We do carry two crates labeled with the name Ribbentrop," Bud announced.

"Show me the crates," the man demanded.

Leaving the manifests with the dock supervisor, Bud and the German headed across the rutted wood wharf towards the *Adventurer*.

Bud said, "You'll need to wait until the crates are off-loaded."

"Do you know where they are at?" the white-suited man challenged.

"I may be able to locate them, but I don't..." unable to finish his thought, the Nazi cut him off and stated, "Lead the way."

"What good is it going to be for you to see the crates? You can't haul them off the ship on your back."

"I don't have all day. I want to see what it will take to get them offloaded."

"Fine," Bud replied in with an air of scorn.

The crew was at work cabling the huge steel deck covers in preparation of their removal for crane access to the cargo hold. Bud lifted a nearby small hinged deck hatch. Positioning himself on the vertical steel ladder within, only his upper torso in view, Bud signaled Griff to continue their work before disappearing into the shadowed depths. Apprehensively, the German followed.

Bud knew it was a waste of time heading below. Even if he should decide to show the crates to the intruder, what was he going to do with them until they were offloaded?

The ship creaked and shook as the winch rigging tugged a steel hatch trying to separate it from where it had been tightly nested during the voyage. As the huge deck cover broke free, the sound of thunder reverberated throughout the ship. Cowardly, the German embraced the ladder. Bud snickered—the visitor above him appearing ghostlike in his white attire as traces of paint and rust danced in the sunrays.

Visibly annoyed, the German resumed his descent into the ship's guts. Reaching the point Bud was waiting, the visitor unsuccessfully tried to brush the tiny specks from his finely tailored clothes. Bud smiled—who in the hell would wear white to the docks?

Bud moved atop the crates pretending to search for the two containers marked Ribbentrop.

"Like I said, you may have to wait until we begin unloading before they can be found."

The German's face turned sour at the prospect.

Finally, Bud unceremoniously announced, "Here they are."

The man barked, "Remove them first!"

Not wishing to start an all-out war with the asshole, especially under the circumstances, Bud said, "Alright."

Bud rode the sling suspended crates as they were hoisted up out of the hold. Standing next to them on the dock, Bud spotted the white-suited high stepper marching down the gangplank. As exhibited by his furled brow and angry gaze, the newcomer's controlled nature was all but gone.

Bud yelled to the dock foreman, "I've delivered the goods to their destination. It's up to you to determine who takes possession."

Leaving the foreman and the German to resolve the matter, there was little doubt in Bud's mind as to the outcome. Glancing back, Bud could see the German's outstretched finger jutting in the air near the foreman's chest.

Hoping he had put an end to the matter, Bud watched from *Adventurer's* deck as the deceased Nazi's two crates were loaded onto a flatbed truck and it left the wharf. As the truck disappeared, he felt a tinge of remorse knowing the third crate remained onboard.

By late afternoon, *Adventurer* had been off-loaded and was sitting high in the water. Sentenced to the confines of the freighter for weeks on end, Bud gave the word to his crew they were free to disperse. Far from always condoning an individual's conduct while on shore leave, he did little to sway them one way or the other.

Showered and shaved, Bud dug a lightweight pair of tan pants and a white short-sleeved shirt from the rear of his closet. Donning the transforming attire, he glanced in the small wall mirror above his sink to run a comb through his gray-kissed hair. Partially the consequence of his constant squinting into the sun's reflective rays off the water, deepening crow's foot wrinkles were beginning to appear. "Oh well, maybe it adds worldly charm?" he considered with a grin—a look that hadn't deterred women in the past.

Assured by one of the dock workers who gave him directions, Bud strolled along cobble-stoned streets towards the best restaurant in town.

"Not bad," he thought as he was being seated.

Scrutinizing the patrons, he observed many were not of local descent.

A nearby table sounded as though they might be speaking German. "So, South America is where the Krauts have run to hide," Bud surmised. "That explains the shipment we carried."

A waitress dutifully came forward and after a bit of back and forth deliberation, Bud ordered some sort of white fish. Gulping a swig of scotch, he scolded himself for not hiding the books under his bunk with the painting. It probably didn't matter. Who would find them? Ordering another shot, a Greta Garbo look-alike sleeked by, breaking his train of thought—a long-legged looker out of his league. Glancing to and fro, she seemed unaccompanied. Wistfully, she sized Bud up as she strutted conspicuously past. In contrast to most of the Hollywood starlets back home, Bud guessed her long hair was indeed naturally blond. He smiled as he considered the one true way to test the theory.

Curious, after finishing dinner, Bud headed for the bar in search of the blond he had seen earlier. Surveying the area, he spied the flawless beauty seated alone stirring a martini. Planting himself next to her on an empty bar stool, he ordered a scotch for himself and another martini for his stool-mate. Declining his offer, she seemed standoffish and left soon after.

"Oh well," Bud thought to himself as he finished his drink. "Nothing ventured—nothing gained."

Bud was about to pay up when the elusive blond reappeared and took her previous seat. "Is the drink offer still open?" she asked.

"Sure," Bud said ordering them both another round wondering why the lady had a sudden change of heart.

Flirtation charging the air, she led the conversation as if they were old acquaintances. Speaking impeccable English, Bud was unable to detect any hint of an accent that might disclose her nationality. Her name was Katarine. Bud guessed she was in her mid-thirties. While her simple white dress fell nearly to the floor, a side slit exposed crossed legs that appeared to run forever. At every opportunity, she touched Bud's arm or squirmed about on her stool soliciting Bud's eyes to follow. She claimed to be from Switzerland visiting friends in the area. Her manner of speech seemed almost too perfect.

They made small talk and had another drink. Learning the reason for Bud's visit, Katarine proclaimed, "I would love to show you around tomorrow if your ship will still be here."

Unwavering, Bud replied, "A day or two of rest for the crew is a good idea. Sure, I'd appreciate a guided tour."

Agreeing to meet for brunch the next day at the same restaurant, Bud accompanied her to the street and hailed a cab. Parting, Katarine gave him an unexpected hug before slipping into the taxi. Sliding across the seat, her dress pulled tight highlighting her curvaceous features. Bud's eyes followed. Uninhibited, she glanced down to confirm what had caught her admirer's attention. Her smiling eyes caught Bud's as she closed the door.

Watching the vehicle disappear, Bud wishfully wondered, hoped, what might be in store for him the next day. On the other hand, he wondered why she had initially rejected his advancement. Dismissing his internal debate, another taxi pulled up. Waving it off, he set out in the general direction of *Adventurer* on foot.

A few blocks later, Bud decided to retrace his steps to see about obtaining a bottle of scotch to take back to his cabin. Rounding a corner, a large black sedan was pulling away from the restaurant. If he had been there only minutes before, he would have observed his new acquaintance stepping from her taxi into the departing luxury car. He would have noted that her language of choice was German. It would have registered to him that one of the two men in the vehicle was the fancy dresser who had picked up the two crates that morning. Seeing none of this, none the wiser, Bud purchased a bottle of his preferred whisky and started out once again towards his freighter.

Climbing the first few steps to *Adventurer's* upper deck, bottle in hand, Bud caught a glimmer of a light in his cabin. He froze. Stepping back to the lower deck, he moved cautiously under the ladder-like stairs to wait. Not having to bide his time long, footsteps sounded across the upper deck.

Hovering in the darkness, Bud hardly dared to breathe as someone began their stealthy descent. Dressed in black clothing, the perpetrator was clutching something in his arms—something stolen from Bud's cabin. Bud was sure that the intruder's build was not that of any of the ship's crew. Whoever it was, the larcenist was clearly up to no good.

Bud yanked the intruder's legs through the stair openings catapulting him into space. A dull thud sounded onto the steel deck. Books scattered about the motionless body—neck skewed to one side. He was dead.

"Jesus Christ. I didn't mean to kill the son-of-a-bitch," Bud said aloud.

Admitting an audible sigh, Bud ran his fingers through his hair. Taking hold of the man's feet, he dragged the lifeless body to the ship's outer rail positioning it at the deck's edge. Knowing he had little choice, he shoved the corpse into the void between the ship and wharf.

Ricocheting, it slammed off a heavy cross timber with a deadening blow followed by a splashing sound.

"What the hell have I gotten myself into?" Bud wondered remorsefully as he gathered up the books.

His cabin was in utter disarray. The mattress had been flipped up, but the bottom support panel was still intact. Unable to shake off the mental vision of the dead man, he needed a drink to calm his nerves. He unscrewed the cap of the bottle still dangling from his fingers and took a healthy swig. Nearly stepping on a glass, he retrieved it and poured a generous portion of the amber contents. Righting his overturned desk chair, he plopped onto the spindled sided hardwood seat. Tipping the glass to his mouth, he noticed it was cracked, but gave it no mind.

After a bit, Bud went about straightening the cabin back to what might be considered normal. It wasn't particularly organized, but everything was more or less in its place. Grasping one of the books he had thrown on the small bulkhead hung table, he inspected its rear cover. The binding material along the inside length had been carefully cut creating a pocket like envelope. Bending the book beyond flat, Bud slid the blade of a knife into the space. Gently withdrawing the blade, a five-hundred-dollar bill followed. Slicing the lower edge of the cover, peeling the back apart, he found a mix of crisp one hundred and five hundred-dollar bills.

"And to think, I almost sent the whole lot overboard," Bud said to himself.

All six books' rear covers contained cash. The final tally was twenty-nine thousand dollars. There was also a piece of paper in one of the books written in German. It contained a list. Bud surmised it may be an inventory of the three crates.

Bud hid the money and the list with the painting. Gathering the books, he headed for the boiler room. Apart from the crate located below deck, any evidence that the German had ever been aboard his ship would be suppressed in the cavity below his mattress.

The books ignited in the boiler's fire box instantaneously.

Returning to his cabin, Bud tried to sleep. Tossing and turning, questioning if he should have kept the crate with the unusual-shaped piece of furniture, he knew the die had been cast for second thoughts. But more importantly, should *Adventurer* and her crew be on their way?

CHAPTER 14

THE CREW ASSEMBLED IN THE GALLEY TO FIND OUT WHAT THE DAY ahead held. Bud advised them they were going to stay in port for a day or two to see if he could line up a shipment bound for the States. Previously wondering if the decision was prudent under the previous evening's circumstance, he had decided it was best not to bring undo attention to his ship since he had already set the ground work to find a consignment. Assigning a few routine maintenance tasks, Bud announced the rest of the day was theirs do as they wished but expected them all back the next morning at the same time.

While in port, Bud always required his crew to be up by 6:30 a.m. ready to carry out the endless chore of keeping the ship operational. Although not always successful, the morning roll call was a way of keeping the crew somewhat in check. Bud's mouth curved up slightly at the thought of the intoxicated quartermasters, Ron and Ken, boarding the ship just minutes before. It was going to be a tough morning for them.

Pulling Griff aside, Bud said with a shit-eating grin, "By the way, I've been offered a tour of the area by a rather attractive lady. Don't exactly know when I'll be back, but I'm hoping it's not too soon."

Strolling across the wharf, Bud detoured to the local stevedore company to check on his previous consignment inquiry and to listen for any scuttlebutt about a missing man. Bud was told to check back in the morning regarding the possibility of any near term outgoing shipments in the region.

Bud had just been seated when Katarine entered the restaurant. Seeing him, she moved confidently in his direction while turning heads followed her progress.

"God," Bud thought to himself, "She certainly is gorgeous."

She was dressed head to toe in white again. The pantsuit was of a conservative nature with the first couple buttons of her loose-fitting blouse strategically unbuttoned. She gave Bud an unexpected light peck on the cheek before sitting. They talked briefly about how nice a day it was before a waiter arrived with menus. She waved the menus off, ordering for them in what sounded to be perfect Portuguese, although Bud knew nothing of the language except for a few words. Even the way she drank from her cup had a sophisticated flair. A take-charge woman, her brashness made Bud a bit uncomfortable considering the recent events.

Guiding them from the restaurant, Katarine's arm entwined Bud's as she steered them across the street to a late model Mercedes two-seat convertible matching her attire. Leading Bud to the driver's side, she waited for him to open the door. Sliding into the red leather seat, she started the engine.

The engine revved as Bud walked around to the car's other side. Quickening his step, he had the feeling he might be left standing in the road if he dallied. Tires spinning in the gravel, his door barely closed, Katarine gave her passenger a knowing glance that conveyed he was in for more than a two-bit tour of the town's civic buildings.

Barreling along a narrow road that clung to the rugged shoreline, Bud watched Katarine's long legs maneuvered through constant braking and gear changes. Sun dancing off her windblown hair and flimsy cotton blouse, the expansive blues of the ocean and sky beyond melted into the horizon as one.

They sped along through the late morning into the early afternoon stopping only briefly at a vista point and to get a drink in a small fishing village cantina. Clearly, the driver had a destination in mind. Finally, turning off the main road, Bud's chauffeur wound down a two-wheeled beat-down path.

Parking the car on a grassy knoll, Katarine announced, "We're here. There's a basket in the trunk with food and a bag of towels."

Leaving Bud, she set out on a narrow trail leading to a small deserted beach nestled in the rocky coastline.

"This beach is only a short distance from my aunt's and uncle's home. It has become one of my favorite places to visit."

Katarine pointed Bud toward a small dory pulled up on the sand and stated, almost commanding, "We will use it to row to a nearby reef for a swim."

"I failed to bring a swimsuit," Bud questioned.

"Swim attire is optional on my beach. But, if you think you need one, there might be one in the bag."

Ruffling through the bag, Bud did find a suit, but it was far too big when he positioned it against his waist. Turning, Bud found Katarine had removed her clothes and was walking away towards the water's edge. Her perfectly proportioned ass distancing itself, he shook his head in disbelief, stripped down and pulled on the ill-fitting suit.

Katarine grinned as Bud joined her holding the suit up with one hand. Pushing the dory into the surf, taking a dunking, they were able to get beyond the breaking waves and scramble aboard. By the time Bud had pulled himself over the stern, his suit was down round his knees.

Unabashedly, Katarine took the rowing seat. Bud sat in the stern facing her. Beaded glistening droplets of water dripped from her hair across her breasts, onto her lower belly where they disappeared into a blondish tuft—his earlier internal query about her being a natural blond no longer in question.

Once the row boat was anchored, Katarine slipped into the water to explore the reef. Finally, weary of trying to hold his suit in place, Bud let it drop to the dory's floor and followed.

The warm water around the reef was brimming with rainbow colored fish. They swam for a good hour before returning to the dory where they clung to its side in the afternoon sun. Dropping below the water's surface, Katarine resurfaced between Bud and the boat's side. Her legs moved to encircle him at the waist. While Bud held onto the boat's side, they floated gently up and down with the rhythm of the swells.

Returning to the beach, reclaiming his ill-fitted swimwear, they sat down to a meal of fried chicken, cheese, bread and wine spread atop a red and white checkered cloth. Katarine on the other hand, took the opportunity for the sun to dry her naked body. Finally, they dressed, gathered their belongings and headed back up the path.

Speeding back onto the roadway, continuing to distance themselves from their original departure point, Bud looked at his driver quizzically.

She smiled, "I hope you weren't planning on returning to your ship this evening."

"Ah, I guess not, but my crew will wonder," Bud replied as if he had a say in the matter.

"I will have word sent to them," Katarine responded.

A few miles down the road, the sports car turned into an elaborate stone walled driveway. Coming around a bend in the drive, Katarine slowed as they approached a gated guardhouse. The expressionless guard acknowledged the driver, opened the gate and waived them through. A bit further a sprawling white stucco house poised on a bluff came into view.

Katarine advised, "This is my aunt's and uncle's home. I hope you will be sufficiently impressed."

Barely rolling to a stop, they were quickly met and ushered to the house by a rather stocky fellow with a deep scar across his cheek. Off to the rear of the house was a parking area full of vehicles. Making their way through the lavish formal entryway, Katarine led Bud to an outdoor veranda where she waved to a couple surrounded by a gathering of early dinner guests. Quickly assessing that their attire did not match the assembled crowd, Katarine spurred Bud away to change. Leaving him in a guest bedroom where he was shown a closet jammed full of men's clothing, she left to seek out her own metamorphosis. The closet contained everything from tuxes to patterned shirts and chinos in a wide variety of sizes. There was also a variety of shoes. Showered and shaved, Bud donned a formal styled shirt and pair of creased khaki lightweight pants. He was just buttoning the top button of his pants when Katarine entered his room from the hallway. She looked striking in a flowery red dress that matched her highlighted full lips. Bud wrapped her into his arms under a whirling ceiling fan that struggled to offset the South American heat. Squirming, she freed herself, commanding, "It's hot. Let's go find a breeze."

Katarine moved ceremoniously through the crowd while Bud retreated to the edge of the gathering. Making small talk along her way, exuding confidence, it was clear she was comfortable with the setting and knew most of the guests. During Bud's perusal, he made note that while a few of the guests were local, the majority weren't. To his dismay, like their comrade lost at sea, he had the feeling they were mostly former brown and black shirted Nazis who had adapted to their new surroundings like chameleons. Wincing at the possibility, Bud heard Katarine speak German. "Shit," he said under his breath.

Before long, Bud recognized one of the men as the one who picked up the shipment at the dock. When they later brushed against one another in the crowd, they both nodded their heads in recognition and moved on. Unknown to Bud, the man was Otto Günsche, former Nazi Major and Hitler's adjutant to the SS, an elite force restricted to those who were pure Aryan Germans. Günsche had been one of those present at Hitler's headquarters in Poland, the Wolf's Lair, when an assassinator's ill-placed bomb failed to rid the world of their crazed leader—an unfortunate outcome for all mankind.

The SS, formally known as the *SchutzStaffel,* wore black shirts to distinguish them from the brown shirts. Functioning as Hitler's body-guards, they were responsible for seeking out and dealing with those who opposed or were a perceived threat to the leaders of the Nazi Party. Hitler later formed the Gestapo, a secret police force given the task of establishing concentration camps for the incarceration of Jews, gypsies, homosexuals, disabled and other perceived undesirables. At the out-break of the war in 1939, members of the Gestapo made up the major-ity of the mobile death squads that followed their armies into Poland and Russia to rid the countries of Jews and other inferiors. By the end of Hitler's war in 1945, forty million deaths could be attributed to the aggression of both the Nazi war machine and the Allied resistance. Of those that perished, half were civilians.

Bud left the area to find a bathroom. Standing in the marble adorned room and staring into the mirror, he mouthed, "My God, I've gotta get out of here."

Passing through the living room on his way back outside, Bud cast his eyes around the expansive room. The place was adorned with Euro-pean antiques and art. Like the three crates of cargo that had shipped aboard *Adventurer,* there was little doubt the origin of the furnishings came from the systematic pillaging of museums and private collections. There was no doubt that the pretentious bunch of warmongers were carrying on their lavish lifestyles without a second thought as to the suffering they inflicted upon the world—Katarine presumably one of their own.

Bud returned to the outer edge of the crowd where the manicured grounds faded into the rocky shoreline. His eyes swept across the open ocean to the other side of the compound where an impenetrable stone fence, like that of the compound's entry, contrasted sharply with white lawn furniture, green grass and flowered landscaping. Stationed near an iron gate interrupting the linear fence stood what appeared to be a sentry. Beyond the fence, the treed shoreline notched inward.

As the evening waned, the self-appointed elitists slowly bid their farewells. Katarine stood amongst the well-wishers extending her personal adieus to each departing guest. Off in a corner, Alfred and Otto, the German who picked up the shipment, were conversing by themselves.

Alfred said, "I can't shake the feeling that Bud Fowler doesn't know more about what happened to Hans than he lets on. Hans wouldn't have gone to all the effort to smuggle the shipment out of Germany and onto the ship only to be left behind. There has to be foul play involved for him not to catch up to us."

"I have my methods to get to the truth. But, can't guarantee he will survive the ordeal," Otto surmised.

Alfred nodded without words.

Katarine later found Bud at the edge of the compound's vista gazing into the moonlit ocean. Taking his arm as if nothing was out of the ordinary, she said, "I hope you weren't too bored. I'll come to your room once the house has quieted down."

Bud was about to respond when Katarine's Uncle Alfred and the man they called Otto approached. They talked briefly until Alfred suggested they move to the study for a nightcap. Abandoning Bud, Katarine proclaimed, "I'm tired and think I will just retire for the night. I'll see you all in the morning."

The study was nicely appointed with a subtler opulence than found in most of the compound. Possibly, the room was off limits to the design whims of Katarine's aunt. The trio's conversation remained mundane until drinks were poured.

"Are you aware we were expecting a gentleman to book passage aboard your ship?" Alfred inquired bluntly.

Günsche watched Bud intently.

"We do carry the odd passenger from time to time, but no one booked passage on this trip," Bud responded.

Aware the passenger had paid cash wanting no record of his boarding, Bud asked, "Have you tried getting in touch with the shipping company at our last port of departure? I can get you a contact after I return to my ship."

Alfred took another sip of his drink holding it in his mouth for an unusually long time before swallowing it. He did not respond to Bud's offer.

Günsche looked as if he wanted to add something but remained quiet.

Feeling he might be the target of an inquisition, Bud maneuvered to leave. Draining the last of his drink, he said, "Thank you for your generous hospitality, but I must excuse myself and head off to bed. I need to get back to my crew first thing in the morning."

Alfred and Günsche acknowledged their guest with non-verbal stares as Bud stepped towards the door and left.

Uneasily, Bud entered the darkened room he had been assigned for the night without turning on the light. Tossing his shirt onto the bed, he sat on a small side chair to remove his shoes. As his eyes became accustomed to the darkness, he saw Katarine quietly sitting in his bed. Traces of moonlight through the open door licked her naked body.

"Why'd you bring me here?" Bud demanded.

"I'm sorry. I thought you would find the experience to your liking. A welcome change from the cramped quarters and routine of your ship. I'll take you back in the morning."

He knew he shouldn't trust her, but what could he do other than play along with the charade and hope for an opportunity to get back to his ship alive. Removing the rest of his clothes, Bud got into bed with the anticipation it wouldn't be the only thing he would be getting into.

Finding his eyes open a bit after 3:00 in the morning, Bud laid listening to the cadence of waves against the shoreline. Katarine slept deeply alongside. Unable to get back to sleep, he got out of bed, pulled on his borrowed attire, and snuck out onto the grounds of the compound.

The night was warm, but a breeze had kicked up. His curiosity getting the better of him, he thought he might see what lay beyond the stone fence line.

Walking toward the outer edge of the yard, Bud was startled when a man appeared out of nowhere.

"What are you doing?" the sentry asked bluntly.

"Oh, I was having difficulty sleeping and thought I would take in some night air. I was about to return to the house."

Even more intrigued now that someone appeared to be on guard at this hour, Bud tried to generate a conversation, "Nice night, huh?"

"Go back in the house. You will not like the consequences if I find you out here again."

"My apologies. I didn't realize I wasn't allowed here," Bud replied turning to make his leave.

Reaching the far end of the house out of sight of the hostile sentry, Bud jockeyed his way down rocky shoreline. On all-fours, he cautiously made his way beyond the spot where the German had intervened.

Hunkered down near the water's edge, Bud peered into a basin with a narrow entrance. It contained a few moored boats against two floating docks. One of the vessels was partially blocked by what looked surprisingly like a military gunboat.

Bud moved deeper into the rock-bound cove.

"What the hell?" he said under his breath as the unmistakable outline of a Nazi U-boat came into view. Moored substantially under an overhanging cliff with draping vegetation, it would be virtually unrecognizable from above.

Bud froze. A figure lurked just ahead, then turned to move in his direction. He was trapped. If he retreated on the same route he had come, he would surely be seen. Slithering into the water, he hoped to retreat. Instead, he was instantaneously bucketed into the throat of the cove nearer his foe. Submerging, he let the current carry him inland. Lungs bursting, he came to the surface behind a large rock. Fighting to maintain his hidden position, he embraced the rock as swells pitched him about. Losing his grip, he was plummeted against the rock like a rag doll. Pain shot through his ribs.

Adrift again, Bud moved further into the inlet where the water fanned out and calmed. Warily dog-paddling near the shore's edge, he scanned the area for any sign of the unknown assailant. Lapping waves doused the sounds of his advancement. Rib cage throbbing, he began to gingerly scale the rocky bank. Reaching a small ledge, he saw the sentry.

The Nazi flinched as if he had heard something. Looking around, he scanned the area for whatever might have drawn his attention. Seeing nothing, he retreated toward the cove's flotilla.

Bud moved awkwardly amongst the rocks up and out of the cove. By the time he reached the patio outside of his room, it was past 4:00. Removing his wet shoes, he crept into the bedroom. Fumbling in the darkened bathroom, he hung his clothes in the shower wishing them dry by morning. He felt along his rib cage—it felt soppy and warm to the touch. Quietly, he closed the bathroom door and turned on the light. The extent of the pulsating wound jolted him. The dripping from his shirt had begun to streak the shower floor a light reddish color. Folding a wad of toilet paper, he fashioned a bitch-rigged dressing of sorts. Placing it gingerly over the ragged cut, he topped it with a white wash cloth.

Settling onto the bed, his hand over the wound, Bud closed his eyes wishing relief from his throbbing ribs. Katarine stirred slightly placing her arm across his chest. The added weight hurt like hell, but with minor shifting, he was able to find a bearable position.

Bud lay awake trying desperately to concoct a story that might account for his injury. Still lacking a clear plan, welcoming sleep finally came.

Katarine awoke. In a rambunctious mood, she pulled off their cover and swung across Bud on all fours positioning his face between her breasts.

Bud winced as pain shot through his body.

She giggled and sat back causing Bud to let out an audible cry of pain. It was then the blood-soaked cloth, peaking from under her inner thigh, caught her attention. Recoiling, her face expression one of distrust, she exclaimed, "What the hell?"

Fumbling for a response, Bud tried a bit of humor, "If I had known you thrashed around so much in your sleep, I would've thought twice about you as a bunk mate."

She did not smile.

"Look, I woke up last night and decided to go for a short walk and get some air. Along the way, I clumsily stumbled and fell down on some rocks along the shoreline."

"My uncle is a doctor. He can look and see how serious it is. Get dressed," she ordered.

Lightly kissing Bud on the mouth, Katarine left through the patio door. Stumbling over his damp shoes, she asked herself, "Stumbled along the shoreline? What the hell were you up to last night? And what did you discover? "

Bud showered, put on his own clothes and headed for the kitchen where he found Katarine. She poured them each a cup of coffee. They just sat down when Alfred came into the room, "Good morning. I trust you both slept well?"

"Okay," Katarine responded casting her eyes towards Bud. "Uncle, our guest tripped last evening while we were walking along the shoreline. I think his rib area may need your attention."

While appreciative, Bud wondered why his Nazi sympathizer placed herself with him at the time of the fall.

Alfred rose from his seat and directed Bud to follow.

Walking down the hall toward the same study they had a drink the previous evening, Alfred said, "I find it rewarding from time to time to be able to utilize my past medical training.

Don't worry, I'm quite good."

And in fact, Alfred was a competent doctor and surgeon. In real life, he was the notorious Dr. Josef Rudolf Mengele. Known as the Angel of Death at the Auschwitz concentration camp, he had honed his physician skills on human experimentations. In addition to unimaginable medical procedures he inflicted on both young and old, he was responsible for selecting which inmates would be put to death or forced to work until death became their salvation.

Passing through an adjoining door of the study, Alfred and Bud entered a small room that contained the modest accommodations of a medical examination room. Bud removed his shirt and gingerly peeled away the toilet paper from his wound while Alfred hunted down a pair of glasses. Turning to his patient after retrieving his eye ware, Alfred's eyes narrowed suspiciously at the extent of the injury.

After a painful examination, Alfred said, "I suspect that you have cracked two or three ribs. You're also going need stitches to close the wound."

Alfred gathered the necessary medical supplies from a cabinet.

The procedure brought tears to Bud's eyes as the doctor knotted the last of thirteen stitches. Alfred then tape bound Bud's rib cage while inquiring, "How did you say you did this again?"

"Just clumsy I guess," Bud responded trying to be non-specific. "I injured it after our nightcap yesterday evening but said nothing because I felt I could tough it out. Besides, I didn't think there was anything that could be done."

After Bud made his disclosing statements, he chastised himself for not thinking his answer through. Maybe it was the pain. Maybe it was the lack of sleep. Clearly, his story was dubious.

Katarine had told her uncle that she had been with Bud when he fell, yet she had supposedly left to go to bed prior to their nightcap. And, now that Alfred has seen the extent of the injury, there is no way that his patient wouldn't have suffered significantly at the time of the fall. Why wouldn't his niece have sought her uncle out the previous evening?

"I suspect it's painful. Is that the reason you were up in the middle of the night?" the doctor asked skeptically.

"Yes, had a hard time sleeping," Bud said anticipating the sentry had made the doctor aware of their contentious nocturnal face-off.

Alfred suggested, "You should return to your room to lay down for a while. I will send word to your crew that you will be delayed a day or two."

After Bud left, Alfred sought out Günsche.

"What are we going to do with our guest?" Alfred asked the former Nazi Major in rapid German. "I don't like the fact that he was wandering around in the middle of the night. Who knows what he found. And I doubt very seriously that our comrade never left Spain with the shipment or we would have been contacted though the normal channels. Not to mention that one of our own turned up dead after I had him go aboard the captain's freighter."

Günsche stated with contempt, "I'll see to it that he never returns to his ship alive. But first, I have a place I'll have him taken to for a little discussion."

"Is Katarine's relationship with him going beyond her assignment?" Alfred asked.

"I have her under control," the Major responded. "She has done what I have told her."

Katarine was straightening the room when Bud returned. The clothes he had left hanging in the bathroom the night before were gone. She said, "I don't know what you were up to in the middle of the night, but it is clear your explanation is bullshit. You're on the verge of getting yourself in serious trouble."

"Wasn't that your plan when you brought me here?" Bud responded stoned faced.

Katarine didn't acknowledge Bud's query as she closed the curtains, turned out the lights and left.

Bud's thought processes began to fail him as the pain medicine administered by Alfred began to dull his ability to think clearly. All his instincts told him he needed to be wary of her and yet, she appeared to be protecting him. Maybe it was all part of a plan hoping he would take

Katarine into his confidence. There was something more to this place than a retreat for a few Nazi war criminals and their ill-gotten loot.

"Stay awake," he told himself. "Why would they have a Nazi submarine? Why…," his mind shutting down as he drifted off.

The bedroom door cracked open ever so slightly. Groggy and unsteady, Bud tried to sit up. His mind foggy, thinking the worst, he reached for a brass bedside lamp for defense, but in the attempt, knocked it to the floor with a crash.

The perpetrator pushed the door all the way open. It was Katarine balancing a lunch tray. She had been gone nearly three hours. Exhibiting a puzzled look on her face, she moved to the edge of the bed and placed the tray between them. She said nothing.

"I'm really tired," Bud said with a slur.

Sipping her coffee, she studied Bud before finally breaking the silence, "One of Alfred's acquaintances has been found dead floating along the shore at the port. There's speculation that foul play may have been involved. It seems coincidental they found the man near your ship."

"I need my crew," Bud managed to say as he drifted away into a groggy vagueness.

Katarine departed for the boat basin.

The guard, familiar with her routine, greeted Katarine matter-of-factly as she approached the pathway to the basin. Once aboard the submarine, she passed through the hatch and descended the steel-rung ladder into the steel gray vessel. Exchanging a few words in Portuguese with a lady, she proceeded down the narrow passageway. Grasping the knob to one of the cabins, she swung the door inwards following its path. Startled, she stepped back into the passage. Otto Günsche blocked her entry. His cold chiseled gaze focused on her face. Turning and casting a look to a man sitting in a chair, he stepped by her into the passageway without saying anything.

Katarine entered the cabin and locked the door.

The man in the cramped quarters acknowledged Katarine in German and beckoned her to him. His face and head were wrapped with white medical gauze. His words and mannerisms failed to hide that he seemed peeved by her tardiness.

Taking a few steps to the man, she leaned down and kissed him on the mouth.

"Now don't be upset with me. I haven't had a chance to break away until now."

"Have I heard correctly that one of our comrades did not arrive with his consignment and another has been found dead?" he asked in a demanding tone. "I expect you to keep me informed of such matters as soon as you are aware of them."

"Yes, I too have just learned of our loss. As you know, the Major doesn't see why he needs to inform me of everything," she replied obediently.

Katarine soldiered forward. Unbuttoning her blouse, she exposed her breasts for him to fondle. Dropping to her knees, she unbuckled his pants, withdrew his hardening penis and began stroking him. The sequence seemed routine…mechanical. Rising to climax, she covered his erupting appendage with her other hand.

The patient satisfied, Katarine washed her hands in a small corner sink and turned to leave. As she headed for the cabin door, the man called out, "I want him dead."

If not for the *fraulein's* calming visits, the patient would conceivably languish into a precarious mindset that bordered on insanity. Expecting others to bow down to his every whim, demanding their allegiance—Katarine should be honored in her daily devotion.

Bud had been asleep for hours when he was awakened by Katarine announcing that dinner was about to be served. More or less clear minded, Bud felt fortunate he was still alive.

The strained dinner conversation with Katarine's aunt and uncle made it clear to Bud he had over-stayed his welcome. Assuming he had a say in the matter, it was time to leave.

While after-dinner drinks were served, Bud announced, "I really need to think about returning to my ship before I have a mutiny on my hands."

"Leaving the troops to their own devices has been the downfall of many a leader," Alfred agreed.

Unexpectedly, because of its quickness, Alfred said, "Summon a car for our guest."

"I think I will go along," Katarine announced.

"No," Alfred commanded. Katarine started to respond when Alfred raised his hand, not unlike a Nazi salute, indicating there would be no discussion. She slouched back in silence.

Bud excused himself to use the restroom while Katarine stayed.

Nearing the room from the hall, Bud hesitated when he saw the stone-faced German who had picked up the crates from his ship. He had Katarine cornered in a one-sided conversation. She looked unnerved—submissive. The discussion ended abruptly when he saw Bud.

Katarine walked Bud to the car, quietly, in a whisper she said, "I will try to get to town tomorrow. Do you think you might still be there?"

Bud responded, "Yes, we still should be there for at least one more day." It was a lie. He intended to leave port as soon as he got back to his ship.

Katarine gave Bud a brief parting hug. As she stepped away, Bud could feel something left behind in his trouser pocket. Casting a reluctant wave, her worried eyes met his as his chauffeured car accelerated down the stone walled drive.

Bud fingered the object Katarine had placed in his pocket. It was a small derringer. He felt gratified that he had some sort of defense if needed but alarmed that he might.

Bud scrutinized the driver as they raced along the narrow shoreline road. An overly large muscular man with blond hair, he exemplified Hitler's super race. Careening around one bend to the next, the Nazi was clearly in a hurry.

"The road is treacherous. Don't you think you could slow down?" Bud suggested. Receiving silence in return, maybe the driver didn't speak English.

Without warning, the car screeched to a halt along a sharp bend near a steep cliff. Motioning Bud to get out, the driver said, "We need to check one of the tires."

So, he can speak English.

In reality, it was the driver's intent to subdue Bud by tying him up before he figured out their destination was not the Captain's ship.

Clutching the small derringer, Bud opened the door just enough to view his adversary in the side mirror coming around the back of the car with gun in hand.

As the Kraut reached for the passenger door, Bud emptied the derringer's two bullets into the man's chest before he had time to comprehend his fate. The driver went to the ground squeezing off a shot as he fell. The bullet winged past Bud's temple.

Springing into action, Bud kicked the gun from the Nazi's hand as he began to raise it. Quickly retrieving the Luger from the dirt, Bud pointed it at his stone-faced assailant.

Supporting himself against the car, the German defiantly struggled back to his feet. Locking eyes with Bud, taking his final step, he spewed something that included the word Hitler. Bud squeezed off three rounds dropping the man back to the gravel shoulder of the road.

Bud felt the Luger's embossed swastika handle before tossing it on the car seat.

Straining audibly, his ribs hurting like hell, Bud dragged his would-be killer to the cliff's edge. As if a tourist taking in the view, Bud gazed out to sea thinking about what he had been through over the last few days. The fact that two men were now dead because of him was unsettling, but what choice had he had? The fuckin' Kraut started it all by getting himself washed overboard. He had been caught up in some larger plot and these were the consequences he would have to live with. Moving his foot, he nudged the lifeless body into the emptiness beyond.

Bud then drove a couple hundred feet back toward the compound before turning around. Pulse surging, he sped toward the sharp bend in the road. "Closer, closer," he said in quick succession, slamming the breaks and skidding to a stop.

"Jesus, that was cutting it close," he mumbled, the front car's wheels poised near the face of the drop off. Taking the gun off the seat, Bud awkwardly slid part way out of the car keeping his foot on the brake. Pulling away and stepping back, the car rolled forward for a reunion with its driver. A loud explosion and a blaze of flames engulfed the near shore as the car hit the rocks below.

Without guilt, Bud briskly headed away from the Nazi compound. Having only covered a few miles, he could hear an unseen vehicle narrowing the distance between them. Hoping that it wouldn't be any of his new acquaintances, Bud ran ahead and crouched behind a boulder at the edge of the road.

An old beat up truck sluggishly rounded the preceding bend. Bud shoved the Luger in the back of his waistband and stepped onto the road's edge. The farm truck cautiously inched forward. Bud waved. Wondering if the truck would stop, he stepped into its path.

Brakes screeching, metal to metal, the truck halted some twenty feet away.

The corners of his mouth turned up in a wide grin, Bud closed the gap. When Bud approached the diver-side window, the driver let out a tirade of angry Portuguese which slowed when Bud held up a few reais and made a vague gesture that he needed a ride. With the exchange of some reais, a ride was negotiated back to the *Adventurer* and the safety of his crew.

CHAPTER 15

Tʜᴇ ʟᴇᴀᴅᴇʀʟᴇss ɢᴀᴛʜᴇʀɪɴɢ ᴡᴀs ᴀssᴇᴍʙʟᴇᴅ ɪɴ *Aᴅᴠᴇɴᴛᴜʀᴇʀ's* ɢᴀʟʟᴇʏ as Bud stepped in from the passageway. Heads turning in staggered unison, mouths agape, wide-eyed astonishment swept over the collective faces of his crew.

Griff's mind flashed back to the previous morning when Otto Günsche had appeared. Otto had stated without emotion, "I am sorry to advise you that your Captain Bud Fowler and his lady friend have been in a horrific accident. Their car left the road and plummeted down an embankment to the water's edge. A resulting fire left only traces of the vehicle's occupants, but there is no doubt that it was them. At this point, the rising tide has swept away all traces of the remains."

Coincidentally, the scenario was not unlike that staged by Bud on his escape back to the ship.

Griffin broke the dumbfounded mood, "You look pretty goddamn healthy for a dead guy."

Griff said, "I had a lot of questions for that Nazi when he told us of your death, but he seemed to have all the right answers. We were still trying to decide what to do to be sure that you were in fact dead. For starters, we were going to hang around here for a week or so in case you showed up."

"Those Nazi sons-of-bitches played me from the beginning. I was a dead man from the start." Noting a variety of whiskey bottles in the middle of the galley table, Bud said, "I sure as hell hope that you were giving me a proper wake instead of just using the occasion to get drunk."

Sitting down at the table, Bud poured himself a stiff drink and re-capped a few highlights of the preceding couple of days. Of particular interest was the recounting of the German U-boat discovery.

The crew reacted in disbelief at Bud's tale of the Nazi war-mongers' enclave.

Pouring everyone one last shot, Bud raised his glass and announced, "It's time we get *Adventurer* and us the hell out of town."

Telegraph bells called out as the crew released the freighter from her moorage and her props pulled her slowly astern. Glancing at the pilot-house clock, its hands recorded their departure at straight up midnight. Bud said to an empty wheelhouse, "I hope that's a good omen. We sure as hell need it."

By daybreak, *Adventurer* had plowed her way a fair distance up the coast. Their destination was a port two days away where Bud hoped to find a consignment of coffee.

Reaching for the engine room telegraph, Bud pulled the brass handle from FULL to STAND BY to SLOW AHEAD and then to STOP. The return arrow, triggered from below, followed suit as the ship slowed to a drift. Hawk, the on-duty helmsman, looked at Bud questioningly while the reincarnated captain hunkered over a navigation chart rolled out on the bulkhead table. Pulling another from the collection of those pigeon-holed beneath, he hoped to find a larger scale chart of the immediate area.

Griff, tailed by another crewman, entered the wheelhouse.

"Griffin, call down to the engine room and tell Skinner to get up here," Bud barked.

Pointing out a small island off the coast harboring a narrow inlet on its seaward side, Bud explained, "We passed this island about an hour back. I'm thinking we should go back and see if we can anchor *Adventurer*."

Griff, looming over Bud, asked quizzically, "What's up skipper?"

Stepping to the telegraph, Bud signaled FULL AHEAD triggering Skinner to high-tail it back to the engine room. As *Adventurer* began a large sweeping circle back towards south, Bud finally answered Griff, "I'm not sure I'm done with my would-be assassins. We'll talk about it later, but I have yet to revenge them sinking the merchant ship we commanded, and the innocent lives lost. And now, they have threatened my life again."

The jungle canopy walling the narrow island inlet looked impenetrable beyond the shoreline. Unsure, *Adventurer* held back while a workboat swung over her side and dropped towards the gentle ocean swells. Griff and another crewman scrambled down a rope ladder to board the paint spattered craft as she bobbed against the freighter. They carried a sounding line to check the depth of the entrance and narrow inlet beyond.

Adventurer, treading water to maintain her stationary position, waited patiently as the workboat crew surveyed the depths beyond. It took almost an hour for them to complete their task. After taking the tidal swing into account, Griff yelled up from the small boat, "Cap, there sure as hell isn't an excess of width nor depth, but I think we should be able to squeak by. It's a damn good thing we're running empty. The soundings indicate a soft bottom for the most part, so we shouldn't get into too much trouble."

Overhanging vegetation scraped along the freighter's starboard side as she crept into the constricted waterway. Griff led the procession in the workboat shouting out directional information to Ron stationed on the bow. Course corrections were then relayed to Bud. Griff, virtually within spitting distance of *Adventurer's* bow, went unseen from the wheelhouse. A rapid series of telegraph signals to Skinner in the engine room emulated the difficulty Bud was experiencing maneuvering the gangly vessel in the tight quarters.

Once *Adventurer* was positioned to his liking, Griff gave the order for the crew to drop the bow anchor. The sound of rumbling chain exiting the hawse-hole engulfed the inlet, causing a flock of treed birds to lift from their perch. Forcibly dragging astern, Bud gave the order to tighten the bow chain before the stern anchor was dropped. The anchor chains were then winched to limit the ship's swing.

Serenity returning to their haven, engines gone quiet, two brightly colored parrots glided overhead scrutinizing the intruders.

Gathering his troops for a late breakfast, Bud began, "I want to find out why that band of misplaced Nazis have a submarine."

Griff countered, "I gotta ask why in the hell we would want to go poking about in a nest of hornets? It sure seems the odds of getting stung are high."

"You may be right." On his soapbox, Bud continued, "If nothing else, I would like to sink their fuck'n turd shaped vessel. I want revenge for the sinking of the merchant ship you and I were aboard. Not only did they slaughter innocent women and children, but they left us all to die as they no doubt toasted the event. It also doesn't help their cause that the bastards tried to kill me. It pisses me off to no end that they are just lounging about without a care after nearly destroying the world as we know it."

"I don't think we have to assume too large a risk. If we approached from the water at night, I believe we can take the sub. If nothing of significance is found, we shouldn't have any trouble escaping before their U-boat takes her last dive. At the same time, I don't want to see any more lives lost, so we need to be prepared to subdue and hogtie anyone we might encounter. And who knows, we could discover something that would make the trip well worthwhile."

Ron, the old man at sixty-seven, piped up, "How in the hell would we be able to haul anything of significance away from the site? The only thing we have is that measly runabout of yours stored below deck."

Bud answered, "They have a number of boats moored in the basin." Hesitating, a smirk crossing his face, "Or we always have the option of taking their U-boat."

Scoffs and wrinkled brows communicated that most thought their skipper's statement was a hair-brained idea. But, Griff seemed to ponder the thought. Actually, Bud had made the U-boat comment in jest.

"Hell, we can run that sub if it's seaworthy," quipped Griff. "I spent a couple of years aboard a submarine in the Navy. I hated it so finally got myself reassigned back to the surface. But not before I learned enough about their overall operation."

"But can you make a Nazi sub dive and, more importantly, can you make it resurface?" Skinner rebutted sarcastically.

"There can't be much difference from one to other unless she'll only respond to German commands. Shit, we'll figure it out. That is if you can operate her engines."

Skinner shot back defensively, "There ain't an engine or electric motor built that I can't run."

Most of the crew watched the debate with blank stares.

Griff went on to explain that operating a sub was not much different than running a surface ship. While on the surface, a sub's diesel engine makes operation pretty much like any other vessel. And running underwater wasn't a whole lot different than operating blind in the fog with a compass and chart. Submerging was a simple matter of opening a few valves and filling the buoyancy tanks—kind of like taking on ballast if a ship's running empty.

"What's the damned difference other than you can't go outside for a smoke?" Griff smirked.

It was probably best that only Griff knew nearly 800 U-boats were lost during the war. Bud wrapped it up, "I know it may seem foolhardy and a risk we frankly don't need to take. For that reason, I want you all to consider the unknown consequences should we fail. Discuss it amongst yourselves. If anyone doesn't want to get involved, it is perfectly okay with me. No questions asked. No judgments."

Katarine tried to act indifferently when Günsche told her that both the driver and Bud Fowler had been killed when their car plunged off a cliff. Considering the events of the last few days, she doubted the deaths were purely accidental. She had enjoyed her time with the American skipper regardless of the fact that the man delivering the news had orchestrated the entire sequence of events from their "chance" meeting to her bringing him to the estate.

"I'll go tell him," she said setting out for the submarine.

"Is he dead yet?" the gauze-faced patient asked as she stepped into his cabin.

"Not yet. You have to give me more time," Katarine replied meekly.

"I want him dead before my bandages come off," he demanded. "He's one of the few individuals alive who knows my true identity. And it's been reported he escaped from Germany and is in hiding somewhere in South America. There are many who want to hunt him down to stand trial for his transgressions. And, if he is found, I have no doubt that he will bargain away my life to save his own. We will also need to dispose of the nurse."

The patient continued, "I will not leave anything to chance. I went to great efforts to erase my existence. I won't let anything, or anyone jeopardize that belief."

Katarine reported what she knew about the previous evening's car accident that killed both the driver and the American visitor. The Nazi seemed indifferent to the fact that one of his own had been killed but pleased that the captain of the freighter was no longer in the picture.

Channel Runner glistened in the bright sunlight as the winch cables raised her out of the ship's depths. A shiver ran down Bud's spine thinking about what she had meant to him over all the years—for better or worse, she'd had a profound influence in shaping his life. Having not seen the light of day for months, Griff and Bud jumped aboard to make a run around the island. The starter hardly turned over before she roared to life.

The circumnavigation complete, *Channel Runner* approached *Adventurer*. From their view point, it was clear the steel freighter was woefully out of place in the tight quartered setting. Tied off, Bud and Griff ascended topside via a rope ladder to prepare for the assault.

Assembled around the galley for an evening meal, Bud began, "As I told you before, I hold no ill will for those that wish to stay behind while I return to the Nazi compound. In fact, some of you need to remain aboard. If the raiding party doesn't return in a reasonable amount of time, the others need to be able to get *Adventurer* underway.

I propose Ron stay behind as the leader. Ken and Mick will remain to crew. Bernie will man the engine room. It won't be easy, but I think you can manage in calm seas. There's a port city about twelve hours northward. You could anchor in its bay and take the workboat to shore. Give us a week, if we don't meet up do as you wish. If you run into trouble getting *Adventurer* out of here, there's some small fishing village a couple hours up the coast that could be reached with the workboat."

CHAPTER 16

Clouds obscuring the night sky, Bud, Griff, Skinner, and Hawk prepared to embark aboard *Channel Runner*. They would have roughly a three-hour run back down the coast. Calm seas and warm temperatures were expected to make the trip uneventful. Still, there was an air of uncertainty amongst the runabout's passengers—an unspoken feeling that the odds might be stacked against them.

Their assembled arsenal consisted of a small handgun, two rifles and Bud's recently acquired Lugers. At the last minute, Ken shouted from the deck above as he began his descent, "Wait a minute. I have something that might come in handy!"

Climbing down, it didn't take those aboard *Channel Runner* long to identify Ken had a Thompson submachine gun strapped across his back.

"Jesus Christ, Griff! What else does this band of ours have squirreled away that we should know about?" Bud said with a wide smile. "I'm certain I don't want to know how he came to have that particular toy."

Stepping aboard, Ken exhibited a shit-eating grin as he handed the weapon to Bud. Bud returned the offering with a closed smile and dubious look across his face before stating slowly, "Ken, Ken, Ken… somehow I'm not surprised."

Ken went on to show the raiding party how to use the Tommy-gun as well as producing several magazine rounds from a pouch dangling from his neck. Bidding farewell, he scrambled back up the ladder as *Channel Runner* motored out of the inlet.

The old excursion boat approached south of the sub's moorage well beyond any chance of detection. It was nearly 2:00 in the morning. Positioning *Channel Runner* for a fast getaway, they anchored within wading distance of the shore.

The overcast weather endured, lending aid to the stealth mission. Advancing steadily along the upper shoreline, the inlet containing the sub finally showed itself. With its overhanging cliff and weeping vegetation, the moorage took on an eerie appearance.

The crew lay motionless, scanning the area for nearly ten minutes. Finally, Bud detected what he had been looking for—a cigarette's glow pin-pointing a sentry's presence. Having reviewed their assault plan earlier, the raiding team proceeded without words. Staying together in a rag tag bunch, they neared their quarry until only Bud continued on.

Bud synchronized his boarding with the up and down rhythm of the waves as he crept onto the stern of a boat near his prey. Slinking forward on the narrow deck along the vessel's cabin, he paused within mere feet of his victim. The guard slumped unconscious from the brunt of the Luger before the ripples created by Bud's thrown rock diversion had flattened across the water's surface. The quickly repeated flicking of Bud's lighter signaled the invasion party forward.

Emitting a glow from within, the open hatch of the submarine's turret beckoned them. Hawk fell away to gag and bind the sentry. He would remain topside to stand guard. The others scurried down the steel ladder into the sub.

Further up the passageway, a dark-haired woman sat in the galley dressed in baggy night-clothes. Her back to them, Bud and Skinner ventured toward her, leaving Griff at the ready. They looked at one another and silently recognized that she didn't look German. In fact, she looked Brazilian, but that didn't determine her allegiance. She was gently subdued and gagged. First attempting to reassure the wide-eyed woman that she would not be harmed, Bud whispered a few questions that only required minimal response.

"Are others onboard?"

A nod.

"How many?"

She initially showed four fingers, but subsequently added a single digit pointing up which Bud interpreted as the sentry they had already captured.

"Will you alert the others?"

A turn of the head indicated she would not.

At the ready to take whatever action was required to keep her quiet, Bud motioned Griff forward with a head gesture as he removed the woman's gag.

"There are two crewmen in the forward quarters and one patient in one of cabins," she explained. "There is also a guard outside. I am a nurse held against my will." Her voice was soft and her accent strong.

"Show us the cabins where the men are. I am sorry, but I need to gag you again. I need to be sure," Bud said.

Positioned between Bud and Skinner, the nurse shepherded them to the patient's cabin. Hovering outside in the corridor, Bud gestured Skinner and Griff forward to the sub's crew quarters with the woman in tow.

Bud slowly turned the brass handle. Opening the door ever so slightly, loud snoring could be heard. Squinting into the room as the door arched open, a widening beam of light overtook the darkness within. The person lying in the bunk appeared to have a white bed sheet pulled up around his head. No, his head and face were totally bandaged with exception of eye, nose and mouth cutouts.

Bud stepped silently next to the bunk's occupant and turned on a bulkhead brass lamp. The body stirred saying something in German before his disbelieving eyes announced his intentions. Reaching under his pillow, the patient stopped when he felt the hard jab of Bud's Luger against his bandaged temple.

It wasn't necessary for Bud to say more than, "I'll blow your fuckin' head off!"

The man understood, withdrawing his empty hand. Bud retraced the patient's path and withdrew a gun from under the pillow. It was identical to the others he had confiscated.

Skinner entered the patient's cabin. Stepping to attention in jest, he flashed a stiff-armed salute, "We now have two sailors that appear ready and fit to help operate the vessel—sir!"

After hog tying the patient's hands and feet, they quickly tore the cabin apart to be sure there were no other weapons. Satisfied, Bud and

Skinner returned to the vessel's command station where Griff guarded the two captive sailors. With a bit of prodding, one of the captives spoke a few words in broken English.

Bud directed, "Give Hawk a status report, then familiarize yourselves with the vessel. Find out how to open the seacocks in case we want to sink her. I'll be back in a minute."

Bud found the woman in the galley where she had been taken. Sitting across from her, he removed her restraints. Her oversized frumpy housecoat and unkempt appearance disguised a hint of beauty. Her name was Ana. She had responded a few months prior to an advertisement in Buenos Aires for an experienced nurse to care for Alfred's aging mother. "I was hired by a tall blond-haired man they call Otto. I've also heard him referred to as Major Günsche."

A fleeting sense of fear gripped Bud as his mind raced believing he recognized the Major's name from a recent newspaper account of Hitler's top military brass. Günsche was a ruthless Nazi who had been unaccountable at the end of the war—an at large war criminal of the highest degree.

A jumble of thoughts clouding his mind, Bud tried to refocus on what the nurse had said, "My god, what has he gotten his crew and himself into?"

"I came to what I was told would be an estate. Instead, I found myself a prisoner required to assist Alfred during surgery and care for his patients. I have not been permitted to contact my family since arriving six months ago."

"What kind of surgery?" Bud asked.

"We perform facial surgeries to change the appearance of the patients," she said. "I can show you the operating room here on the boat if you want." Bud nodded.

The nurse led Bud to a nearby locked door. Withdrawing a key from her pocket, they entered what once might have been a Situation Room where the officers plotted their combat tactics. It had been transformed into a modern medical operating facility.

"So, Alfred's performing surgeries to change the identity of his Nazi comrades," Bud stated not expecting a response.

"Is there anything else about the sub that I should know?" Bud asked.

"I think there are a lot of valuable items on the boat. Old paintings and things. They take stuff to a room towards the back of the boat that has a locked door. I don't have a key for it. They added some items just the other day. He has also gone down a few times to an area that I think they call the torpedo bay."

Bud thanked her and replied, "I promise that you won't be hurt, and I will do everything within my power to see that you get home."

Bud hurriedly returned to the helm and told his crew, "It looks like the sub has a locked cabin where they store their loot."

"I can get the door open. Where's the cabin?" Skinner said.

Bud cautioned, "I am beginning to believe this band of dethroned Nazis may be high ranking war criminals. Be on your toes."

Bud led his engineer down the passageway to the door. Skinner pulled a folding knife out of his pocket that had a variety of other odd shaped implements connected to it. Selecting a slender hooked tool, he inserted it into the key opening. The lock clicked open with little effort. Pushing the door open, he groped and snapped on the light.

The cabin appeared to have been turned into a storage room. Canvas covers concealed a collection of randomly shaped items. Bud pulled off one of the covers exposing a long row of neatly compartmentalized paintings. Skinner yanked the canvas off a rectangular shaped object in one cabin corners uttering, "Jesus Christ. It's a stack of gold bars."

Returning to the helm, Bud commanded, "We've been aboard nearly fifteen minutes. We're pushing our luck. This sub is loaded. Paintings, gold bars and who knows what else. There also may be more down in the torpedo bay, but we don't have time to hunt it out. I say we take it, but it will be dangerous. Griffin?"

"The vessel looks virtually new. She had to be one of the last to come out of the shipyard. And better yet, I believe she's a scaled down version of some of her sister ships. I'm with you Cap, let's take her."

"If anyone isn't up to this, speak now," Bud offered, not expecting any takers.

No one said anything.

"Griff, the nurse wants to go with us and for now the guy in the cabin and the two crewmen have no choice. Bring the two Nazi seamen to the helm to help. Skinner, when you get a chance, fix the lock on the bandaged guy's cabin so it can't be unlocked from the inside."

"I am going to lag behind," Bud advised. "I think it would be downright unfriendly of me not to pay a visit to my old friend Alfred since I'm in the neighborhood. I would like to personally let him know that my death, no doubt at his direction, was ill conceived. Give me ten minutes before you start the engines and cast off. I'll be along in *Channel Runner.*"

Rechecking the sentry's bindings and dismissing Hawk to go below, Bud headed towards the rock-walled fence separating the basin from the rest of the fortress. Just as he entered the house through the room where he had slept a few nights prior, the compound erupted into turmoil. High beam lights illuminated the night as if the sun had risen from the sea. Gunshots sounded near the boat basin.

Otto Günsche streaked down the hallway past Bud's temporary refuge. No doubt reporting the unfolding events to Alfred, Bud could hear a frantic German conversation.

Like a cat would a mouse, Bud laid in wait for Alfred to emerge from his burrow. In an instant, Alfred scurried down the hall.

Günsche exited the house in the direction of the boat basin.

Undetected, Bud stood behind the kneeling Alfred as he transferred the contents of a safe into a black doctor's bag. Taking two swift steps, Bud placed the barrel of his gun against the back of Alfred's head, "Where do you think you are going?"

Turning, Alfred briefly locked eyes with Bud before glancing into the safe where a gun laid.

"Don't even think about it," Bud commanded.

A look of loathing etched across his face as Alfred contemplated his next move.

Slowly, Alfred inched his hand toward a concealed gun on the floor between his knees. Then he hesitated. Looking past Bud toward the door, an undetectable sense of relief flooded his well-being.

Deafening shots rang out—the standoff was over.

Bud whirled around expecting the inevitable, but felt no pain while Alfred crumpled against the safe, blood oozing from his chest.

Katarine stood poised in the doorway dangling a gun at her side. She had carried out the bandaged man's order—Josef Mengele was dead.

Neither knew quite what to say or do.

Finally, Katarine launched into an attempt at a plausible explanation, "He's not my uncle. He's Josef Mengele. I am only a pawn in their efforts to hide from the world."

Again, recognizing Mengele's name as another notorious war criminal, Bud considered the irony at being present at his execution—a closure of sorts for all those innocent lives persecuted by Auschwitz's Angel of Death.

Bud asked, "Whose idea was it to contact me?"

"Otto directed me to become acquainted with you," she responded. "He hoped that I might find out something about the missing man who was supposed to be onboard your ship. Later, I came to hope that you would be able to help me escape."

Bud said nothing. Although skeptical about the authenticity of her Oscar winning portrayal, he felt relieved she hadn't instead placed the bullets in him.

Near what had been a concealed safe behind a book case, the bag lay open partially filled with cash. Alfred was obviously readying himself to make an escape. The safe still contained a substantial amount of currency.

Kneeling, Bud scooped up a set of keys lying next to Alfred, grabbed the bag and stood up. The bag seemed heavy for its size. "It would be less risky if you stayed and didn't bring undo attention to yourself. Give me your gun. They will assume I killed Alfred. Take what you want from the safe and go back to your room. I suspect Alfred's wife is around here somewhere so beware."

Jockeying around Katarine frozen in the doorway, Bud took the gun from her hand and left. She touched his arm momentarily as he passed by, no longer the strong confident woman.

Exiting the house, Bud dashed by Alfred's terrified wife. Neither spoke. He jogged inland a hundred yards or so before making his way undetected back to *Channel Runner*.

The boat basin took on the sights and sounds of an all-out war zone—muzzle discharges lit the night as the Nazi sub maneuvered its way from the confined space. The German's artillery, both small and larger firearms, had little effect against the steel hull vessel. The tommy gun helped keep the frantic guards at bay even though the shooter, Hawk, kept his head below the sub's conning tower randomly returning a volley of fire. Upon clearing the bounds of the boat basin, *Adventurer's* crew immediately began to submerge.

A searchlight lit the area searching in vain for the submarine, but only able to briefly identify the upper tower as she slid beneath the surface.

Major Otto Günsche took command of a patrol boat. Shouting orders, the boat leaped into action and was at full speed before clearing the basin's entrance.

Her throttle commanding it, *Channel Runner* likewise roared out of the water a few hundred yards down the shoreline. Intent on making a large arc to avoid the lights from the Nazi's search vessel, Bud headed out to sea.

Günsche was lucky. Amid all the confusion, the swiping light beam somehow found the black hulled runabout. A hail of rapidly fired bullets danced in the nearby waters accompanied by splintering wood. Bud's partner in crime had been hit. The barrage intensified, blowing out one of Channel Runner's side windows.

Giving all she could, nearly leaving the water's surface at times, *Channel Runner* leaped atop ocean swells in a zigzag pattern.

A large caliber gun sounded.

Bud closed his eyes, their fate hanging on the spin of a roulette wheel, he cranked *Channel Runner's* spoked helm hard to starboard.

Their luck held. The nearby ocean surface violently spewed showering the escapee.

The Nazi's continued to volley their weaponry in vain as the old Rosario excursion boat bolted away, distancing their would-be slayers. In time, a course change had the old excursion runabout on a heading back to the *Adventurer*.

Scatterings of morning sun fought through the low clouds as *Channel Runner* progressed northward. Continually looking over his shoulder for any advancing watercraft, Bud could see sunlit bullet holes along the port side. As if consoling *Channel Runner* for her injuries, Bud said, "Oh girl, I know where there are some very pissed-off Nazis."

Satisfied he had succeeded in ditching his pursuers, throttling to an idle, *Channel Runner* bobbed aimlessly in the open sea. Taking hold of Alfred's satchel near his feet, Bud set it on the seat. Reaching into the bag, past layers of cash, he felt a heavy square-edged object with a roundish relief. Removing and pushing aside some of the currency, he pulled the object from the bag. As if choreographed, a gold crucifix broke the binds of the Nazi satchel as the sun exploded through the clouds shrouding the boat.

Mesmerized, Bud reflected on the realization that the crucifix had likely been stolen from a place of worship of great importance. The intricately crafted figure was so heavy Bud could only assume it was solid gold. The cross was secured to a dense wood base that seemed inadequate to balance the top-heavy piece.

Contemplating, Bud decided to hide the satchel and crucifix in the overhead of the cuddy cabin. Gingerly, pain radiating from his rib area, he bent and inched forward carefully sweeping broken glass aside with the satchel. Feeling his ribs, he came to the realization that his shirt was damp with blood. "Damn!" His stitches had torn. Shaking off the jabbing sensation, he hunched uncomfortably as he inspected the overhead section of the cabin. Unscrewing four screws, Bud removed a segment of board.

Flattening the satchel of money, he crammed it in a void between the overhead and deck above. Removing his bloodied outer shirt, he wrapped the statue of Christ and placed him into the same cavern-like hollow.

CHAPTER 17

In excited anticipation Bernie, Ken, Ron and Mick shouted out greetings from above as *Channel Runner* slid alongside *Adventurer*. There was no sign of the sub. Clambering gingerly up the freighter's rope-wood stepped ladder, Bud failed to reach the top before the barrage of questions started. Climbing over the rail, slightly winded, he faced the inquisition. Holding his hands up in a defensive position, the crew retreated slightly. After recounting the events since the raiding party's departure, he finally dismissed himself to tend to his rib area as best he could and don clean clothes.

Captain Fowler was beginning to get anxious. Where was the rest of his crew? Buttoning his shirt while he stood outside his cabin, he gazed beyond the cove. About to find a scotch to calm his jitters, the Nazi U-boat broke the surface offshore. "Well, so far, so good."

Triumphant shouts could be heard as the sinister craft maneuvered astern of *Channel Runner*.

His rib area still under the grip of a dull persistent pain, Bud carefully trailed his crew down the suspended ladder to the returning victors. Griff, ascended from the turret displaying a tooth-filled grin as he greeted Bud with a bear hug. Bud grimaced, shutting his eyes as if it might lessen the pain.

"The three Krauts are presently confined to their cabins," Griff said as if it was just another day. "They were fairly cooperative when given the proper incentive. And our guys are now a bit more confident in their ability to operate the sub. I also told the troops to stay the hell out of the cabin with the paintings and other things."

"Oh, by the way Cap," a smug look on Griff's face, "There's a shit-load of gold bars down in the torpedo bay."

"How much?" Bud asked.

"Hell, I don't know. A shit-load."

Two bottles of cognac materialized from within the swastika tainted vessel to help celebrate their mastery at outfoxing the Nazis. While they had stolen the sub and its cargo, taking it from the warmongers didn't seem like they had done anything wrong.

Bud directed Mick to take their female passenger to the cabin that once housed the German lost at sea. Mick led her topside with her bag of clothes.

"Now what the hell do we do?" Bud contemplated. "Griffin, don't let these guys get too carried away. We need to meet later to discuss our next move. Right now, I'm going to go talk to the nurse and see what else I can learn."

Bud found Ana in her cramped cabin. Her shapeless garb and unkempt hair was no longer a disguise. While she wasn't drop dead gorgeous, she was striking—pulled back raven colored hair highlighted deep dark eyes and a pretty enough face. Her dress was tight at the waist and loosely buttoned, showing a hint of what lie underneath. The transformation left Bud a bit tongue-tied. He stammered, "Can you tell me more about the extent of the medical procedures Alfred performed?"

"Yes, of course," Ana replied. "From time to time, the doctor bandaged cuts, set a few broken bones and even delivered a baby. And, we performed an appendectomy on one gentleman. But, our primary focus, and the reason for the operating room was the performance of facial plastic surgery. We performed the procedure on seven men over the last five months. I believe they all were Germans. The man recuperating in the submarine was operated on nine days ago. He is scheduled to have his bandages removed in the next few days. But at this point, they could come off anytime."

"Who visited him while he has been on the sub?" Bud inquired.

"The doctor, Otto and the blond woman they called Katarine were frequent visitors," Ana answered.

Bud reassured her everything was going to be okay before he left to return to the submarine.

Stepping into the "vault," as named by the crew, Bud scanned the visible and yet to be opened bounty. Numerous oddly shaped wood containers lined one side. A metal bookcase attached to the steel bulkhead contained shelves full of smaller boxes. The row of stacked paintings numbered twenty-nine. Bud guessed the crated painting that had been aboard the *Adventurer* were now among the lot. Recovering the paintings with the cloth that was cast aside earlier, he noted that someone had already replaced the canvas tarp over the gold bars.

A stout metal desk with drawers running down one side and a chair filled one corner of the sparsely dimensioned room. Bud took one of the heavier shelved boxes and placed it on the desk. Opening it, he found it contained jeweled necklaces, bracelets and the like. Still another held a matching set of engraved silver flintlock dueling pistols. Shuddering at the thought of the innocent lives annihilated by the Nazi war machine, he closed and returned the boxes to the shelf. Bud removed the loose wood top off one of the crated containers. It contained a two-foot-high vase of unknown origin, maybe Egyptian based on the symbols adorning it.

Bud tried opening the desk drawers, but they were locked. Remembering the keys he had taken from Alfred, he removed the clutch from his pocket. The center desk drawer opened on the third attempt. The narrow drawer contained another Nazi Luger, ammunition, a pair of glasses, magnifying glass, jeweler's loupe, blank paper and an assortment of pens and pencils. Each of the two side drawers required its own key to work the lock. Bud unlocked the drawers without initially opening them. Sliding open the upper side drawer revealed it to be totally engorged with high denominations of American currency. Bud slid the drawer closed and moved on to the bottom double drawer finding it partially filled with files in addition to more money hailing from various countries. There had to be thousands upon thousands of dollars, likely hundreds of thousands, stashed in the desk.

One file contained what appeared to be an inventory of paintings as guessed by recognizable names of artists. Other files appeared to contain other listings he could not make heads or tails of. Possibly, they were associated with the boxed items.

There were seven files identified only by a series of numbers. Each contained a few pieces of handwritten notes Bud could not decipher. It appeared all the files contained pages of notations in a similar format. The seven files coincided with the number of facial surgeries recounted by Ana spurring Bud to wonder if they were Alfred's surgical notes.

Relocking the drawers, Bud left the cabin. After trying a couple of the larger keys in his ring, he found one that locked the passageway door.

Bud turned the key in the cabin containing the German and entered. Having been released from his bindings after Skinner reworked the door lock, Bud found the man sitting at the desk staring at the blank bulkhead.

By all appearances, except for a slight eye twitch, the man seemed composed.

"Do you speak English?"

"Some," the man communicated.

"You need to answer a few questions. Your comrades tried to kill me."

The man nodded slightly leading Bud to wonder if the man had understood him.

"Why are you in a German submarine with your face wrapped in surgical gauze?"

While the two struggled somewhat trying to communicate, the man's response was that he was Austrian and a spy for the British during war. His name was Frans Bernheim. He was changing his appearance in hopes of beginning a new life.

"Who are you hiding from?" Bud asked.

"I'm not sure who to trust."

If the story was true, Bud thought it ironic that the remnants of the society that was helping Frans slip back into society may have been those that he helped bring down.

"Who is Otto Günsche?" Bud questioned.

"He seems in charge." Wanting to appear cooperative, Frans added, "Günsche was a major in the German forces."

Bud brought the conversation to an end, "You will remain in your cabin until your bandages come off."

While Frans' story might be conceivable, Bud re-locked the door as he left the cabin.

Bud gathered his crew around the galley table. "Our easiest route would be to simply unload the gold and other valuables from the sub onto *Adventurer* and leave the area. On the other hand, we should anticipate the Nazis are already organizing themselves to track us down. Major Günsche, the guy in charge, doesn't appear to be a man who is easily daunted from his duty.

"My guess is they will be looking for the *Adventurer*," Griff chimed in.

"If that is the case, we should consider taking the sub," Bud responded. "Can we run the vessel without the Germans' help?"

Quartermaster Ken said, "Maybe we should take the two Krauts along and dump them later."

Griff responded, "Should, could, like I told you bunch of doubting bastards before, we can run that sub ourselves. Let's get rid of them now and be done with it."

Bud spoke, "We can probably operate the sub on our own, but where do we go and how do we go about laundering a few tons of Nazi branded gold? But, first things first, we need to provide safe passage for the nurse to a point she can return home. We also need to decide when and where to dump the bandaged guy and the two crewmen. I won't kill them in cold blood even though their kind tried to do me in. We need to find a place remote enough so they can't bring the wraths of hell down upon us. For now, get the sub ready for departure in the morning. Top her fuel tanks off from *Adventurer's*. Transfer the food, water and any other supplies we will need. And Griffin, I want this crew to practice submerging in the bay to become more familiar with her operation. It will only be a few feet down to the bottom, but they better goddamn learn the routine because our lives may depend on it. Use the two Germans for training. Tell them we will set them loose unharmed in a day or so if they help without trouble."

Late that afternoon, Bud was present as Ana removed Frans' bandages. Other than some swelling and redness, he could be the next guy you pass on the street. Wondering what inner turmoil might be masked behind his expressionless eyes, Bud asked him, "What do I do with you?"

Frans responded, "I only want a new life."

Frans would continue to be confined to his cabin.

Ana dined with Bud and the crew that evening. While talkative with Bud, she was restrained in the company of all the exuberant men.

After dinner, Bud asked Ana to join him for a walk around the deck. "I have some things we need to talk about," Bud said. "I intend to run you up the coast in my powerboat before morning's light. There's a small village less than an hour away. From there, you should be able to make arrangements to return home. I'll give you some money for the trip."

"How can I ever thank you? You have saved me from what I feared would be my ultimate death. I had come to believe I would never see my family again. Each day I prayed that my nightmare would end."

"Are you married?" Bud asked.

"No," stopping short of providing any further explanation. Tears forming at the corner of her eyes, Ana leaned forward to kiss Bud on the cheek. Placing her hand squarely against his wounded rib area, Bud winced noticeably.

Ana recoiled. "What have I done?" she blurted, surprised at his response.

"I cracked some ribs a few days ago and the stitches of a wound have begun to separate."

"Let's go to the submarine operating room so I can take a look," she insisted.

"First, I have a couple of items that need my attention," Bud replied.

"Then I will gather some bandages and other supplies from the operating room and come to your cabin in an hour," Ana said forcefully.

Bud watched her retreat across the deck confirming what he had already surmised—a nicely shaped lady. Ana turned and smiled at him before disappearing into a corridor.

Bud found most of the crew still hanging out in the galley area. Bud told Skinner that he wanted *Channel Runner* fueled before nightfall so that he and Ana could get an early start for the nearby fishing village.

Skinner said, "Have you decided what we're doing with the patient? Are we releasing him in the morning?"

"I don't think so," Bud said. "I am beginning to think that he might actually have value until we're sure we have eluded our German friends. He was obviously important to them. And, it won't hurt to keep the two sailors for a few days in case any operational questions come up."

Bud dispatched the crew to finalize the submarine for an early morning departure. While they headed for the door, Bud told them, "Remember, we may never see *Adventurer* again after tonight."

By 9:30, the ship fell silent. Having got caught up in a discussion with Griff, Bud had missed his appointment with Ana.

Because of the lateness, Bud decided it was a good time to retrieve the satchel and cross. Gingerly descending down the rope ladder, he settled behind *Channel Runner's* steering wheel to weigh his options. The satchel, cross, painting and the crated pedestal in *Adventurer's* cargo area could end up being a fall back pending an unsuccessful escape. After due consideration, Bud left the cross in *Channel Runner* and took the satchel of money.

Having placed Josef Mengele's satchel into the bunk cavity with Jan Vermeer's centuries old painting, Bud settled in for the night. Sleep did not come easy as he considered his crew's plight. Just as he was beginning to drift off, he heard the cabin doorknob click and the door began to inch open. Jumping out of his bunk, moving swiftly across the deck, he grabbed the doorknob and flung the door wide open. Taking the intruder to the floor, Bud immediately felt a softness.

Her frightened face flooded with moonlight, Ana sputtered, "I had been by earlier and found no one. I was going to wait, but ah…," her voice trailing off not knowing quite what to say.

Her robe having fallen open, Bud saw she wore only undergarments. She was clearly not the frumpy nurse he had initially mistaken her for.

"Sorry about that. Not a very good way to welcome someone to my cabin," Bud apologized.

"I guess I should get off you," Bud said, inching away.

Ana made a concerted effort to close her robe before kneeling to retrieve the scattered bandages and other medical supplies.

Bud shut the door and turned on the light.

"Please lay down," she requested.

"Really?" Bud answered with kind of a cocky grin.

In a businesslike manner, Ana replied, "Do as I say. You want me to have a clear mind and steady hand."

Greeted by the subdued light of dawn, the bunk's white sheet slipped away as Ana sat up in bed in response to Bud's rap on her cabin door. Having already checked to ensure *Channel Runner* was ready for their departure, Bud announced, "We leave in fifteen minutes. See you on deck."

Ana acknowledged, "I'll be ready," and began packing her small bag of belongings.

Channel Runner's engine interrupted the stillness as Bud and Ana left the sun starved inlet into the light of a new day. Wishing he had more time to know the lady next to him, he placed his arm around her shoulder to ward off the chill. Ana moved slightly closer unsure of his intention—was he her savior or just being friendly?

Their destination in view, Bud throttled back to a crawl as they wove their way among brightly painted dories heading out for a day's fishing. Steering the throaty runabout towards a pile supported structure, Bud squeezed *Channel Runner* in at the end of a dilapidated floating dock. Gathering Ana's tattered travel pouch, Bud led her across the tipsy float.

Finding a small inn less than a block away, Bud slapped at a bell hanging in its open doorway as they entered the confines of the tiny lobby. Ana called out in Portuguese, "Is anyone here?"

A thin, unkempt man stepped from behind a curtain. How may I help you?" he said, trying to straighten his wrinkled shirt or night clothes as might be the case.

Having been previously instructed by Bud, Ana stepped forward, "We will need a room for the next two days while my husband conducts some business."

Bud paid for the room in advance.

The uneven floor, drab painted walls and faded bedspread of their room were certainly less than ideal. Fortunately, neither of them would be spending the night as long as Ana could find a way out of town yet that day.

Bud sat Ana down on the sagging bed, took her hand in his and said, "I wish I could see you safely home, but I need to return to my crew. Life is unpredictable and who knows, maybe our lives will cross again someday."

"I owe you so much," she whispered leaning her head against his shoulder. "Take this," handing him a slip of paper. "It has directions to where I live," she said wishfully.

Bud directed, "You should keep yourself clothed as a peasant during your travels so not to bring undo attention to yourself."

"Yes, I know," Ana responded.

Taking Ana's travel bag, Bud set it on the bed and removed its contents. He then showed her that he had fashioned a false bottom in it.

"There is a significant amount of money between the outside and inside layers. You'll have to pull the bottom apart to access the money so leave it be until you get home. You really need to leave today if all possible, even if you go to another village. The Germans will likely be looking along the coast for us. An inland destination would be best. Here are enough reais to provide for your needs until you get home."

Kissing her softly on the forehead, Bud left the room without looking back.

Tears trickled down Ana's cheeks as the door closed, leaving her alone.

By the time Bud got back to *Channel Runner*, he had to weave himself through a throng of locals gathered on the float. The presence of such an unusual boat made for much attention—a worrisome circumstance should the Nazis come looking.

Bud stepped aboard, started the engine and motored out of the bay mindful of his wake. Once beyond the limits of the bay, *Channel Runner* sped off in the direction from which she had come.

Slings poised below the water's surface, *Adventurer's* hoist engaged as Bud positioned *Channel Runner*. She was to be condemned back to the dark chamber of the freighter's bowels. Bud rode up with her. Rising, rivulets of sun-sparkled like tears dripped off her hull dimpling the surface below.

CHAPTER 18

THE EXILED U-BOAT LEFT THE PROTECTIVE SOUTHERN HEMISPHERE INLET for points unknown. Taking one last look, Bud glanced from the conning tower to see *Adventurer* swallowed by the surrounding jungle vegetation. It had been a difficult decision to leave her and *Channel Runner* behind, but there was no way to take her with them and the submarine offered the best hope for a successful escape. Turning with a sigh, hoping someday it might be safe to retrieve his freighter and beloved runabout, he scanned the open sea before them.

Barely underway, in the distance, a lone plane was flying along the shoreline. Weighing if the plane might be searching for them, it veered away from the coast. "Nazi bastards," he yelled to his crew.

"There's a damn good chance that plane is hunting for us. We'll proceed north on the surface until they are no longer in view. Then we will drop out of sight and head south."

Keeping its distance, the plane eventually swept southward out of sight.

"All right," Bud commanded, "They know we are on the move. Our goal is to round the tip of Cape Horn into the Pacific and ultimately onto the west coast of the United States."

Having considered taking an easier route northward via the Panama Canal, he and Griff figured the less frequently used route might help throw the Germans off their tail.

Turning to Griffin, Bud placed a Nazi officer's cap atop his friend's head. Saluting sharply, he proclaimed, "Other than the two Germans, you're the only one who really understands what the hell you're doing. Thought this hat might help fool the sub into thinking you know up from down."

"Griffin's in command! We damn well better heed his word if we want to get through this ordeal alive."

Stepping up to the task, Griff immediately began barking orders in preparation for submerging. Sounding a piercing alarm that penetrated every nook and cranny of the vessel, he ordered, "Everybody below deck! Telegraph Skinner to kill the diesels and engage the electrics! Secure the hatch! Flood the mid-ship tanks!"

Her buoyancy tanks filling and horizontal stabilizers rotated downward, they began a slow decent into the obscure depths of the Atlantic Ocean. While the two Nazi seamen lent a hand, it was clear *Adventurer's* transformed crew had risen to the challenge.

The claustrophobic sea entombing them, Griff reassured the crew that there was nothing to be concerned about. Leveling out at a depth of seventy-five meters, Griff rattled out over the ship's intercom, "This vessel is hereby christened the *Fort Knox*." Cheers erupted signaling the crews approval of depth sounder reading.

Undetected, *Fort Knox* continued south throughout the day and into the next. They motored mainly on the surface unless they detected another vessel. The fact was that they had little choice since the electric propulsion batteries had a fairly short life without being recharged by the diesel engines. On the other hand, they made better headway with the diesel engines. Depending on weather and sea surface conditions, the two diesel engines could thrust the U-boat along at nearly eighteen knots while the batteries propulsion system provided less than half that speed.

Surfacing on the second night, they scanned the nearby shore with binoculars. Bud was looking for a drop point for their captives. Within an hour, he had identified a site that was to his liking.

"Griff, it's time to lighten our load of extra passengers."

"All three?" Griff asked.

"I kind of hate to bundle them together. Just the two sailors for now. The shore area looks uninhabited and according to the charts, we should be able to move in fairly close. I'm betting they won't contact their comrades. I suspect they would be in a shit-load of trouble for aiding and abetting us."

The Nazi seamen were brought on deck looking extremely apprehensive. They seemed relieved when they were handed life jackets and a small lifeboat was inflated.

Bud scrambled down the steel ladder from the sub's turret. Even though he harbored a general hatred for Germans as a whole, the two sailors he was preparing to set adrift had been cooperative—sailors, not unlike others throughout time, who had followed their command into battle. Bud gave each man a small amount of currency.

Eleven long days passed uneventfully as they pushed southward and rounded South America's Cape Horn. The noteworthy event allowed the crew to relax a bit as *Fort Knox* distanced their pursuers. Having found the vessel to be exceptionally well maintained and her operational systems trouble free, the crew became confident in the sub's operation.

Navigating northward along South America's west coast, Bud set course for Costa Rica. Once there, their plan was to abandon *Fort Knox* for a less conspicuous vessel before continuing onward toward home. Running on the surface under diesel power at 15 knots, their next leg was expected to take some two weeks

Frans was showing signs of heightened aggravation. There were instances when he could be overheard in his cabin raising his voice as if preaching to some unknown following. No one could understand what he said, but there was a blazoned righteousness about his demeanor. At meal time the ostracized German seemed fidgety, eyes always in motion, in a constant state of turmoil. He began pressing Bud regarding what the future held for him. Each day that passed convinced Bud that Frans' involvement in the Third Reich was not what he claimed. The fact he was associated with the likes of Otto Günsche and Josef Mengele, additionally did help his case. If he had successfully pulled-off a spy's double life, he wasn't exhibiting the wherewithal to blend into whatever surroundings he might find himself.

Fort Knox was approaching the northerly reaches of the continent when Griff yelled to Bud from the turret, "There's a large ship ahead at 11 o'clock."

Joining his mate, Bud scanned the horizon in search of a vessel. "My God, it looks like an American destroyer," Bud blurted lowering his binoculars. "And I think she is heading our way. Shit! Take her down."

Dropping through the hatchway, spinning the wheeled locking mechanism behind them, *Fort Knox* pitched forward. "Level out at sixty meters and cut the propulsion," Griff snapped. "Everyone shut the fuck up. No sounds."

The band of pirates hovered in the depths of the Pacific hiding from their own countrymen. Trusting it would take some time for the destroyer's command to sort out the protocol, Bud hoped they would escape further detection.

Fort Knox's radio cracked to life dashing their wish.

"Submarine located 5 degrees north latitude by 80 degrees west longitude, identify yourselves. You are in an area patrolled by the United States Navy to assure the security of the Panama Canal. I repeat. You must identify yourselves."

Griff looked to Bud, saying with a nervous chuckle, "Do you think they will let us keep our new toy and its ballast if we radio back?"

Bud, brow furled and lips drawn tight, was about to respond when the impact of a distant depth charge shook *Fort Knox* slightly.

"What the hell is the deal with that?" Griff sputtered.

Everyone's eyes focused on Bud for direction.

"Oh, they're just fucking with us to get our attention," Bud surmised with no assurance whatsoever.

The radio again sounded, "Do you understand the situation? Take that as a shot across your bow. The next one will rattle your teeth. I repeat, identify your vessel."

"All right," Bud spoke to his crew, "If we identify ourselves, we'll end up broke with nothing to show for our efforts. If we say nothing, they may decide to get serious, but it's doubtful their commander wants to sink an unknown vessel in peace time."

Bud reached for the radio transmitter and raised it to his mouth, "This is the unidentified sub returning your communication. You do that again Commander and I'll think about shoving a torpedo up your ass. We are on a mission for the United States government. You damn well better chose your next move carefully or you will be spending the rest of your days swabbing out the Admiral's latrine."

Griff shook his head and said, "Oh that'll work."

Bud shrugged his shoulders.

A few moments of silence went by before the destroyer came back, "How do we confirm your mission?"

"You don't," Bud barked.

"Your appearance and soundings lead us to believe you may be a German U-boat," the destroyer replied.

"So," hesitating for affect, "What's your point?" Bud said curtly. "If the United States Navy wanted you to know my mission, they damn well would have told you. Now get off my back."

Bud commanded, "Start the engines. I'll bet they will attempt to get clarification from higher command. And after all, the war with Germany is over."

The destroyer followed their progress without trying to make further radio contact. After forty minutes or so of cat and mouse, indications were that the seas were gaining strength.

Rising to periscope depth, *Fort Knox* hovering just below the surface, Bud confirmed that the weather had taken a turn for the worse. "Let's go back to cruising depth. I doubt the destroyer can continue to monitor our whereabouts," Bud said.

Within a half-hour, the destroyer could no longer be detected. Bud refigured their course giving a compass bearing for Costa Rica.

Griff tipped his Nazi cap before taking it from his own head and placing it on Bud's.

Hours later, less blustery weather prompted *Fort Knox* to surface. Hunkered over charts they had brought along from *Adventurer*, Bud figured they were near the Peninsula De Osa at the southern end of Costa Rica. Bud asked Griffin to remain topside before relieving the helmsman to go get something to eat.

"We're sitting on millions of dollars of gold and rare art," Bud began. "Yet if we aren't careful, we could have the entire lot taken from us. Then there's Frans. What the hell do we do with this guy?" not expecting an answer.

After substantial discussion, it was decided they would put Frans ashore at the next opportunity with a few bucks and bid him farewell. Little did they know their reluctant comrade would not necessarily consider such a benevolent gesture to his liking.

With the decision concerning Frans made, the conversation turned briefly to the distribution of the wealth amongst the crew.

Griff indicated, "I am not interested in any of the paintings or other stuff. Just the gold, assuming it can be converted to cash. And I suspect most of the crew will have similar thoughts."

"I don't have any interest in the jewelry. Well figure it out later," Bud replied.

The helmsman returned from below. Bud dismissed him telling him to come back in an hour.

Griff and Bud next hatched a plan that would put Griff and Ken ashore with enough cash to purchase a vessel that could handle some estimated 9 tons of gold. Once the bounty was loaded onto the new vessel, they would scuttle *Fort Knox*.

Bud and Griffin disclosed their plan to the crew later that evening. There was little feedback from the crewmen other than Bernie, who spoke up, "I would like to settle in Costa Rica. Back home there's the potential of a six by eight-foot room with a rather shitty view. Could I be paid off now?"

Not wishing the others to start thinking about options and be left without an adequate crew, Bud replied, "We'll discuss it later, but I'm not in favor of it."

Aided by the light of a half moon, the shoreline in sight, the sub maintained a northeasterly heading that brought them near the coast of Costa Rica. Finding the shoreline favorable, Griff and Ken scrambled into a rubber raft and shoved off for the beach. *Fort Knox's* crew lingered long enough to see the figures make land and disappear. Moving roughly a thousand yards offshore, they would wait.

Griff and Ken wandered into the small coastal village of Quepos in the late morning. Only some sixty kilometers from the inland capital of San Jose, the area was a significant supplier of fish for the region. Spanish was generally the language of choice, so the two seafarers hoped they could get by with their scant mastery of the language. Seeing a fairly large boat rigged for fishing moored in the local basin, they sought out its owner. Two men working on the boat directed them to a ramshackle building nearby. Within the structure was a man past his prime, yet he still seemed to have the twinkle of youth in his eyes.

As best he could, Griff asked, "Your boat?" pointing to the craft in question.

The local nodded.

Unaware of the local currency, Griff withdrew a substantial amount of paper pesos from his pocket as well as some US dollars. "Buy?"

The man said something in return that neither Griff nor Ken understood.

Griff next motioned for them to go to the boat and started to walk in that direction. The man followed.

Once aboard, the man clearly understood the two gringos wanted to purchase his boat as they moved about inspecting the craft. The elderly man said something to one of his deckhands and the boat roared to life as its diesel engine exhausted a black cloud of smoke. The old man, no doubt hoping to fund his retirement, smiled a semi-toothless grin and nodded.

Griff and Ken looked at each other bewildered. Speaking in English, Griff said, "Fuck, we should have brought Skinner with us. She looks seaworthy enough," as he pounded his fist against her inner hull.

"Fuel?" Griff asked.

The owner took a stick and inserted it into the diesel fuel fill port. It registered about half.

"How much?" Griff asked producing the wad of cash he flashed earlier.

"More," came the response.

Having no stinking idea what the boat was worth in these parts, Griff mistakenly produced all his money.

The man, probably a better judge of what the currency's value was, bent down and stacked the denominations by origin on the weathered deck. On his knees, figuring numbers in his head, the owner swayed back and forth in deep concentration. Looking up he nodded agreement.

"Shit," Griff exclaimed, "I shouldn't have shown my hand." Bending down next to the man, Griff slid away a portion of the US dollars. The man moved most of it back. Griff moved some back to his pile. The man reached over and took a lone fifty-dollar bill from Griff's pile and smiled in contentment. Griff shrugged and reached for the man's hand.

As the sun began to fade the following evening. Bud and his crew were beginning to worry—there was no backup plan for finding or retrieving Griff and Ken. Finally, they identified a sizable boat in the distance, but who was it? Binoculars unable to determine the vessel's identity, Bud told the crew to stand by to submerge. About to pull the plug, a figure could scarcely be seen waving a white cloth on the approaching craft. Bud gave the order to standby.

Griff emerged from the wheelhouse of his new acquisition grinning ear to ear as the crews scrambled to tether the two dissimilar hull configurations together. The new arrival looked to be about 85 feet and rigged for deep-line fishing. Her name scrawled unevenly on her bow—*Cara Mia* had seen better days. But, if Griff thought she was up for the task ahead, it was good enough for Bud.

The crew conducted a quick inspection of their new home. Skinner spent the time checking out *Cara Mia's* running gear. Finally, a consensus was cast. The vessel appeared more or less seaworthy and likely up for the task ahead. Even the naturally doubtful Skinner seemed okay with the old tub.

Next, the crew began the backbreaking labor of moving the swastika-branded gold to the hold of the fishing boat. They worked well into the night before all the bars were stored away. Bud even managed to draft the reluctant Frans, who seemed strangely wistful as he handled the gold. The paintings and other boxed items eventually clogged the crew quarters and galley leaving barely enough room for their intended purpose. Lastly, the sub was stripped of her charts, food and other useful supplies while Skinner topped off Cara Mia's diesel and water tanks.

Bud, acting alone, located a space behind the stern's rudder shaft to stash the cash and files from the sub's desk drawers. The area was damp, but hopefully out of the crew's reach. Not wanting to alert the crew about the hoard for fear they might want to debate their share, Bud made the transfer undetected while the crew was busily carrying out the final organization of their quarters in hopes of actually finding a place to bunk.

Griff emerged from *Fort Knox* announcing, "Skipper, we've made a last sweep of the vessel and she's ready to make her final dive."

Bud gave the go ahead. Griff, joined by Skinner, disappeared below where they would open *Fort Knox's* sea-cocks allowing the Pacific Ocean to flood her. Reappearing within minutes, the two hurriedly scrambled across to join the ceremonial gathering aboard the *Cara Mia*.

Cara Mia backed off.

A hushed somberness fell over the sub's adopted crew as the sea began to entomb the stealth craft. She would join the rest of her scuttled fleet as had her sister boats at the war's end.

Her devotion to her adopted crew notwithstanding, she had failed to overcome her tarnished lineage. Betrayed, fighting her destiny, she was dragged into the murky abyss.

CHAPTER 19

A SMALL FISHING VILLAGE APPEARED IN THE BINOCULARS AS EVIDENCED by the chart Bud had laid out before him. The sighting initiated the helmsman to say, "Hey, Cap. Any chance we can see if our shore legs still work?"

Deep in thought, Bud didn't answer. Having concluded that Frans was to be released, he was thinking about Bernie's departure as well. Yet to talk to his oiler about parting financial arrangements, Bud was torn. His gut told him dropping off Bernie and Frans in the same town was unwise, but Bernie was pressing to leave, and Bud wanted Frans gone.

Moored, evening descending over the basin, Bud gathered the crew, "Okay, a few rules. Loose lips do in fact sink ships. I will not stand for any behavior that could jeopardize our mission." Looking squarely at Griff, Bud directed, "Griffin, I expect you to herd the flock back here after you've had a chance to stretch your legs and get something to eat. It's 8:15. Everyone goddamn better be back for an eleven o'clock departure. And, you all better be in good enough shape to crew this boat. I have no qualms about leaving anyone behind. It's also my intention to release Frans before we depart. It's time to get this guy off our backs."

Bringing his attention to the oiler, Bud said, "Bernie, we have a couple of things to sort out. I don't know about the two of you being left in the same town. I want to give you time to get a jump on this guy."

Bernie and Bud remained at the galley table as the rest of the crew headed up the dock. Handing Bernie a canvas bag, Bud advised, "There's $85,000 in the bag."

"This isn't enough! The gold's worth millions." the seaman protested.

"Goddamn it, then stay and look to a bigger payoff when and if we reach the United States! You're the one who decided to jump ship. As it is, you're taking virtually all our cash reserves," Bud said trying to suppress his rising anger.

"I'm at least entitled to take a few gold bars with me," Bernie pressed knowing his fellow crewmembers would likely receive substantially more once the gold was disposed of.

"You're entitled to what I say you're entitled to," Bud shot back indignantly. "Do you think I want to have you parading around advertising the fact the Nazi gold even exists?"

"Alright," Bernie responded somewhat disheartened.

As Bernie stepped off the *Cara Mia* to make his new life, Bud said, "If I were you, I wouldn't hang around this two-bit town. Frans will be following in your footsteps shortly."

Bud waited until Bernie disappeared into obscurity at the wharf's end before heading below where Frans was being held.

"We need to talk," Bud said expressionless as he removed the captive's bindings. Moving to the galley, Bud poured them a whiskey. Facing Frans, yet to decide his fate, Bud studied the man's soulless eyes.

Sensing the magnitude of the situation, Frans seemed jittery. Finally breaking the silence, the subdued Nazi spoke, "I'm glad you hold no ill-will."

Bud said nothing as he poured himself another shot.

After another lengthy silence, Bud said, "I don't believe you are as innocent as you say. Frans, or whoever you are, I don't trust you. My instincts tell me that I should have probably left you in the sub. What would you do with me if the circumstances were reversed?"

Shifty eyes evading confrontation, Frans wiped the perspiration from his brow, carelessly spilling some of his drink with his other hand. Not catching every word Bud had communicated, he said, "Thank you for helping me escape the Nazis and start a new life."

Another prolonged period of silence followed.

"All right," Bud ruled. "Here's $5,000. My conscience is clear. There's enough to get you by for a while wherever you choose to go."

Frans looked both relieved and distraught over the news. Relieved his life was being spared, but near crazed to find himself having to kowtow to the likes of Bud Fowler. His departure would take place once the crew was reassembled and ready to shove-off.

While the crew returned at the appointed time, it was apparent that all but one had drunk too much. It seems the bunch had pooled a share of their money, and with the single draw of a card, a winner had enough to ante up the favors of a lady. The winner of the draw had been none other than the youngster among them. Mick not only returned to the boat sober but sporting a shit-eating grin. It would be up to Mick and Bud to shoulder the load getting *Cara Mia* underway.

An uneasy feeling ran up Bud's spine as they motored away from the float. Looking back to the wharf, he could make out the shadowy profile of Frans in the darkness. Glaring back, the Nazi vowed, "This is not the last you have seen of me Captain Fowler."

Cara Mia made good headway over the following days on her quest northward past Nicaragua, Honduras, Guatemala and on to Mexico. Other than needing to keep on top of a leak around the shaft stuffing box, the old fishing boat plugged along with only routine maintenance. For the most part, the crew spent the time relaxing in the warm weather or taking their turn at the helm. While they had commercial fishing gear aboard, sport fishing became a daily ritual providing for their meals as well as breaking the drudgery of their push home. Conversation naturally drifted to discussions about what each would do with their share of the wealth nested below. Paramount in those discussions was how they might convert the gold into dollars, so its use would be something other than ship ballast.

Sightings of other vessels were few. Bud thought he saw the reflection of a plane near the coast at one point but paid it little mind one way or the other. All in all, they were confident their foes had been left well behind. The pressing issues bearing down on them in the near term were dwindling fuel, water and food reserves.

On a lazy afternoon, Bud directed the crew to spend the remainder of the day fishing with the commercial gear. Their goal would be to take on a catch that would help disguise their illicit cargo when they made port. Their heavy payload causing them to sit low in the water, a few fish could help decrease the possibility of any suspicion and provide a means to stock up on necessary provisions.

For seamen who did not routinely make a living at the trade, *Cara Mia's* crew did especially well when they stumbled onto a school of tuna. In fact, the event turned into sheer chaos. The entire crew took part hooking, pulling fish in, unhooking the lines and sending them back for more. Constantly in the way of each other, lines were tangled, fish flopped about underfoot, decks became slippery and foul language reigned supreme. The crew was banged and bruised by the time the tuna headed elsewhere, but no one suffered unduly. Griff even broke out a couple of bottles of whiskey to celebrate their success.

Bud fretted about making landfall in Mexico—worried an over-zealous official might demand to see ship documents, or even worse, search *Cara Mia.* While the entire crew had their seaman credentials, they were still subject to the whims of local regulations. There was also the obvious question as to why a bunch of gringos would be crewing a run-down Costa Rican fishing boat? It was decided their best course of action would be to land after dusk when anyone of authority would likely be long gone for the day.

Cara Mia took aim for the dim lights of what was expected to be a sizable fishing village. Nearing, they were able to spot a wharf where other fishing boats were berthed. A nearby building with a swaybacked roof appeared to have the makings of a cannery of sorts. Surrounded by discarded fishnet, float lines and two wheeled carts strewed about, it was a reasonable assumption that *Cara Mia* might be able to offload her scaly cargo.

Bud headed up the gangway toward the building in question. In addition to its disheveled appearance, the structure seemed to lean to the point one might wonder how long it could remain structurally standing. If it ever had paint, there was no longer any sign of it. Only a single bare light bulb shining through a cracked window hinted the place was occupied. Of more importance was the existence of what appeared to be a couple of large saddled fuel tanks nearby.

Approaching the cannery through the obstacle course, Bud could smell the familiar odor of fish. He knocked on the planked door. Almost immediately, a hunched-over elderly man opened the doorway. Not seeming particularly surprised to be looking at an unshaven gringo, he asked in Spanish, "What the hell you want?"

"We have tuna and need fuel," Bud managed to communicate.

Not responding one way or the other, the fishmonger shut the door leaving Bud perplexed.

Bud, having been joined by Griff, was about to knock at the door again when a nearby large barn style door fought to open.

"I don't have all night." The proprietor waved his hands vaguely in the direction of a jumble of weathered carts. It was enough of a communication effort that Bud understood.

The crew had their catch loaded, hauled and weighed in under an hour.

A pile of pesos was counted out on the worn counter and pushed toward Bud. Bud considered arguing about the amount but decided otherwise.

"We need diesel fuel," Bud said.

The man pointed to the slightly elevated tanks at the end of the cannery and asked, "How much?"

His hand extended rocking side to side, Bud said "2,500 liters,"

"There's not enough to pay for fuel," the man responded referring to the pile still bunched on the counter.

Bud nodded and showed a wad of pesos.

The cannery man dipped a stick into the top of the larger tank. Backing it out unceremoniously, he thrust it toward Bud. Bud squinted in the poor light in an attempt to verify the wetted notch indicating the tank's fuel level. Not really caring if his customer was satisfied or not, the stick was set aside.

Bud signaled Skinner to place the nozzle into *Cara Mia's* fueling port as the old man turned the valve sending the fuel on its piped journey.

After about 25 minutes, Skinner called out that the tanks were full. The man closed the valve halting the flow, but not before a pint or so of the olive-brown liquid dumped out of *Cara Mia's* tank vents, ran down the deck, through the scuppers and disappeared. In the moonlight, a rainbow of diffusing colors spread out across the dark surrounding water surface.

Reaching for the still wet dip stick from its earlier plunge into the fuel tank, the fish merchant stepped to the tank. Bud spotted a dry stick and grabbed it. The old man snickered quietly as he held out his hand for Bud's chosen measuring devise. Bud declined, inserting the stick to the tank's bottom. Since Bud could only guess at the tank's capacity, the difference between the two sticks told him little other than wishful thinking that the drill wasn't a complete ruse. It mattered little under the circumstances. At least, the fuel total was in the ballpark of Skinner's guesstimate as to what they needed.

Squaring up the payment, Bud joined his crew at the top of the gangway and led the way to a nearby cantina. What the establishment's food lacked in variety was offset by quantity. Never questioning the issue of currency, the crew was either a poor judge about the price of fish, fuel or simply didn't care as long as they were getting a night off the boat. Having eaten enough, Bud announced he was returning to the boat and expected the rest of them within the hour. Griff began to stand up, but Bud placed his hand on his shoulder and told him to wait for the others. Snatching up one of the half empty wine bottles, Bud left.

Taking up sentry duty on the bow of the *Cara Mia*, Bud took a swig of wine. Stars peeked through the light cloud cover as his thoughts drifted to the Kangaroo House. Finding himself thinking about home often, he wondered when he would see the islands again.

Bud sensed a slight movement near the cannery. Cocking his head toward another area of the wharf, he strained his eyes sideways. In the subdued lighting, he could make out a figure leaning against the building—a tall figure. A bit paranoid, Bud thought he had a build not unlike Otto Günsche.

Welcoming the broken silence, familiar voices could be heard making their way back to the boat. Whoever Bud thought he saw lurking had disappeared.

Early the next morning, the crew was sent out with pesos to stock up on food supplies. Bud and Skinner stayed behind to ready the boat for departure. Gone longer than Bud would have thought necessary, they finally reappeared brimming with provisions for the continued push north.

Cara Mia sputtered and billowed smoke as Skinner fired her up. Having hoped to get under way earlier, Bud spurred his crew into action. It was too late. Their lackluster effort left them still dockside by the time a rather stout, well-dressed local arrived with an entourage.

Bud stepped from *Cara Mia*.

The man extended his chubby hand and introduced himself as the town mayor. "I heard that there were some Americans in town and came to extend our welcome," the official proclaimed.

Bud replied, "We are honored that you would take time from your busy schedule, but we are just preparing to depart."

"I offer an invitation to you and your crew to stay and sample the delights of our town. I rarely have an opportunity to practice my English. Surely you can stay the morning," the portly bureaucrat said.

"I must decline your gracious invitation," Bud stated as he turned and placed one foot upon *Cara Mia's* rub rail.

"I must insist," the man responded pulling a swastika adorned Luger from his coat.

In a blink of an eye, Bud swung his foot from the boat's rail up through the man's crotch cascading him off the narrow float. Falling spread-eagled into the water with a mighty splash, the official's gun discharged, breaking one of the wheelhouse windows.

The overweight man bobbed to the surface spitting and sputtering. But, that was the least of his concern. He was going to have to face the wrath of the German who had paid him off and provided the gun which was now at the bottom of the basin.

Bud stepped on the gunwale with one hand on the rigging as the *Cara Mia* moved away in a cloud of black smoke. Scanning the dock area for some sign of further aggression, he saw none. While general pandemonium erupted near the wailing official, no one seemed to direct their efforts toward them. Bud hustled up to the wheelhouse asking himself how a man in a two-bit Mexican town would come to possess a German Luger.

Haunted by the drastic measures taken in an attempt to detain them, the crew obsessively scanned the horizon for the rest of the day. As a precaution, *Cara Mia* maintained her northward-bound quest miles away from the Mexican shoreline. Progress was uneventful until a nasty squall hit. To make matters worse, the engine sputtered to a stop. The fishing boat rolled precariously as Skinner worked feverishly to correct their plight. Diagnosing the problem as a blocked fuel line, he back-flowed the fuel delivery system with diesel fuel. The reek of spilled diesel permeated the air as *Cara Mia* rolled and fought to remain upright.

A large wave, larger than the others, smashed against the side of the low-slung wheelhouse leaning *Cara Mia* over precariously. If not for the added weight of their golden ballast, the old workhorse may have breached on her side.

"So, this is how it ends," Bud thought, as a wall of water busted a window and sent a sheet of steel-gray water into the wheelhouse. The swirling sea around his shoes, Bud braced for the next surge as the diesel engine cranked over spreading renewed life throughout the ship.

Fighting to bring *Cara Mia* about into the waves, Griff burst through the door. "Jesus Christ, if we'd taken on much more water that gold would have taken us down."

"Shit, and now we're missing a window," Bud said sweeping jagged shards of glass away from the steering station with his foot.

"Well at least it was the window with the bullet hole," Griff replied with smirk.

As evening approached a few days later, the foggy outline of San Francisco could be seen on the horizon. Their arrival into the States could have been further south, but Bud felt they might gather less notice up the coast a bit. Besides, he had another reason to make port in San Francisco. Waiting until nearly midnight in hopes of again evading any custom officials, they cautiously entered the large wharf community. Burying themselves amongst a covey of other fishing boats, *Cara Mia* shouldered up against a dock.

They had made it.

CHAPTER 20

Looking the proper businessman, Bud left the men's clothier in his new gray suit, white shirt, dark blue tie, and black oxfords. His mission was to find Jonathan Pickard. If unable to do that, then he would begin the search for other opportunities to dispose of the gold bars. Mary had told Bud years prior that her cousin had fled to San Francisco after his evil deed on Blind Island. There, he had supposedly graduated from college before being hired by a local bank. It was unknown if he still resided in the area, but it seemed probable the large and diverse community would have continued to provide the anonymity he sought when he initially left Seattle.

Griffin and the others remained aboard *Cara Mia*.

Having failed to find anyone who knew of Pickard in the first two banks visited, Bud was beginning to wonder if he was wasting his time. Entering the next financial establishment, taking note of a wall plaque identifying the bank president among others, Bud stepped to a teller window.

"I have an appointment with a Mr. Owen Taylor," Bud said with authority.

Without further inquiry, Bud was escorted to an adjoining room by a quiet woman he could only assume was the secretary. Mr. Taylor arrived promptly and asked how he could help.

Bud began, "I'm sorry to bother you with your busy schedule but wonder if you might help me locate an old acquaintance who you may know. His name is Jonathan Pickard. I believe he is involved in the local banking business?"

The president's helpful demeanor now soured, he said, "Yes, I am aware of who he is, but don't personally know or conduct any business with him."

Not surprising to Bud, he had the feeling that the man didn't hold Jonathan Pickard in high esteem. Learning Pickard's whereabouts, the meeting came to an abrupt end as the bank president left, leaving Bud to find his own way back to the lobby.

Within a short walk, Bud stepped up to a barred oak-framed teller window and announced, "I have business with the bank's president, a Mr. Pickard I believe?"

The female teller looked Bud over and smiled. His new duds yielding the desired outcome, she asked, "Do you have an appointment?"

"I believe my assistant scheduled it," Bud responded.

The lady replied, "Mr. Pickard is our vice president. The president is out of town. I am sure Mr. Pickard will be able to assist you."

"I believe he can," Bud said.

Bud was ushered to the president's office and told, "Please make yourself comfortable. Mr. Pickard will join you momentarily."

While waiting, Bud perused the impressive office surroundings. The book-matched walnut paneling, inlaid desk and other adornments provided the tasteful ambiance of a trusted and successful establishment to carry out your business. The wall paintings looked impressive. They were likely originals, but not the caliber of those currently residing in the old fishing boat down at the harbor.

A side door opened, and a distinguished gentleman entered the office. Older, heavier and graying at the temples, Bud instantly remembered the expressionless dark eyes that showed no mercy on that fateful day on Blind Island. Crossing the richly colored Persian carpet, he extended his hand and introduced himself as Jonathan Pickard, acting president. Even though some thirty years had passed, Bud immediately renewed his disdain for the guy. He was the degenerate who attacked his Mary. Briefly taking Pickard's hand before wiping his own on his new suit pants in thinly veiled disgust, Bud introduced himself as David Jones. Taking a seat in front of the expansive walnut desk as directed,

Pickard settled opposite him into an oversized leather arm chair as if it were his throne.

Bud spent the next few minutes tantalizing the vice president's greed. Spinning a tale, he rambled on about controlling a fortune in gold bullion that had been hoarded away since the days of the California gold rush. "I'm seeking help to liquidate the gold. I am concerned if the bullion became common knowledge, there would be others who would unjustly claim they had an interest in its ownership."

Reaching into his shiny new briefcase, Bud withdrew a bar of the Nazi gold. Placing it on the desk between them, the telltale swastika turned down, it resounded with a thud.

Pickard stretched across the desk and drew the bar near for a closer look. Looking like a rat inspecting an ear of corn, never lifting it from the desk's surface, he anxiously smacked his lips and shifted in his seat.

Pickard said, "You say you have a large quantity of these?"

"I do," Bud simply responded.

"Do you mind if the bar is taken to another room to confirm its authenticity?"

"That's fine as long as I go along," Bud said picking up the golden relic.

Pickard led the way down the hall to a scrawny gentleman with bug-eyes hunkered over a pile of bank receipts. Donned in an elastic banded sleeve white shirt and gold half-rimmed glasses set low on his nose, he struck the perfect image of a bank accountant. A shaded green visor over wisps of hair completed the portrayal.

Instinctively knowing his assignment, the man took the bar from Bud without saying a word. Crossing the room, he placed the bar on the workbench like surface of an oak watchmaker's desk. Positioning a tall stool just so, he climbed atop it. As if preparing to begin a piano concerto, he extended both arms out adjusting his sleeves before sliding out one of the side drawers. Withdrawing a wet stone, he drew it across the edge of the bar leaving a trace amount of color on the stone. He next retrieved a small bottle of liquid from another drawer. Squeezing an eye dropper deposit of the clear liquid onto the gold rubbing, he studied the results. Showing no acknowledgment one way or the other, he placed the bar on a rather elaborate scale atop the workbench. The accountant carefully adjusted the various counter weights until satisfied with the results. Next, the mathematician calculatingly rotated the bar to measure its dimensions. Bud was relieved that the little man gave the bar's origin no mind. Scribbling figures on a sheet of paper, a single nod of his head conveyed his findings.

Bud intercepted the bar's intended handoff to the shifty eyed Pickard, who tried with little success to conceal his enthusiasm. Returning to the President's office, Bud placed the bar back on the desk where it continued to cast its spell over the greedy banker. Bud thought to himself, "I hope I have the opportunity to work this bastard over."

Pickard began the conversation. "How much gold do you have?"

Bud nonchalantly responded, "Well, I haven't calculated it precisely, but I would estimate it to be more than nine tons."

"Surely you jest!" scoffed Pickard.

Face drawn tight with no hint of emotion, Bud responded, "No."

Pickard swiveled in his chair and began feverishly pounding on a Burroughs mechanical action adding machine. "Let's see, nine times 2000 would be 18,000 pounds. Times 16 equals 288,000 ounces at the current rate of $34.71 an ounce." The noisy calculator droned on before finally going silent. Pickard stared briefly at the results before exclaiming, "The market value of the gold would be nearly ten million dollars!"

Taking his cue from the accountant, Bud simply nodded without expression.

Pickard fidgeted behind the desk clearly plotting his next move.

"You realize I, I mean the bank, doesn't have such reserves just sitting in the vault. In addition, such a transaction would carry a substantial discount."

"How much of a discount," Bud questioned.

Obviously scheming to leave the bank out of the transaction, Pickard nervously taped his pencil on the desk as he struggled for an answer. "I'm unsure of a bank's federal reporting requirement."

"If that is an issue, I don't want a bank involved," Bud answered.

Pickard's head and shoulders began to bob up and down repeatedly as he considered the hefty commission for such a transaction.

Extending his hand, Bud's foe said, "I can make it happen."

Aware that Pickard never did answer his question regarding the gold's discounted value, Bud reached past the outstretched hand to pick up the bar.

"I'll be back first thing in the morning. If you are unable to handle the transaction, I'll go elsewhere."

Bud turned and left the office leaving Pickard trying to extract himself from behind the desk.

"Is there a way I can contact you?" Pickard called from the hallway.

"No," was the final fading communication as Bud crossed through the marble floored lobby.

The next day, Jonathan Pickard was pacing the inner-teller area as Bud entered the bank's expansive lobby. Upon seeing Bud, the waiting vice president darted around in an attempt at looking authoritative. An obvious sham, the collective faces of the tellers exhibited wonderment as they eyed their substitute leader. Hurriedly passing through the area's swinging gate, ushering Bud away from inquisitive ears, Pickard spewed, "I have access to the funds."

"Fair enough," Bud responded indifferently as Pickard motioned toward the entrance door.

Out to the sidewalk and down the block, Pickard strutted ahead like a rooster leading his flock. Getting into a newer dark blue Cadillac, they drove about a dozen blocks arriving at a five-story luxury hotel. Surrendering the car to a valet, they proceeded through double brass doors across a marble lobby and into a sparsely occupied bar. Halting, Pickard scanned the room before getting his bearings then heading off to a dimly lit table at the back of the establishment.

Seeing no need to look anxious, Bud trailed at a discrete distance as if he wasn't with his guide. Lingering, Bud waited until he was asked to join Pickard and two well-dressed thugs at a smallish round table. One wore a blue striped suit, the other a black ensemble.

A few pleasantries followed, without exchanging names. One of the men asked if Bud wanted a Bloody Mary. Before waiting for a response, the bartender was signaled by a revolution of an outstretched finger.

"So," one of the mob guys began, "We understand you have a rather significant amount of gold to dispose of."

"That is correct," Bud answered.

"How did you come to possess such an accumulation?"

Bud reacted defiantly as he sat upright in his chair, "With no disrespect, how I came to have the gold is really no concern of yours. The question is do you want it, and do you have the means to pay for it?"

The man who had been doing the talking thus far began to respond when the other heavier set man moved his hand onto his associate's arm, silencing him. Leaning across the table, fixated on Bud's face, the new spokesman said, "Don't mess with me."

"Is the meeting over?" Bud questioned placing both hands on the table within inches of the man's.

Pickard shifted in his chair nervously, wanting to arbitrate, but wisely kept his mouth shut.

The man moved back from his hovering posture and ran his hand through his slick black hair. Hesitating, he appeared to be considering his next move. "All right, I guess we've flexed a bit and can call it a draw for now," the man responded with a grin, breaking the tension.

The waiter appeared as if on cue with his gleaming silver tray to distribute the morning beverages. Obviously relieved, Pickard proposed a toast, "To a profitable transaction for all."

No one acknowledged the banker's interruption.

Having previously done his homework, Bud started the negotiation, "Mr. Pickard's accountant's calculations of an individual bar would set the total weight at 18,750 pounds. At nearly 35 bucks an ounce, that's a bit less than ten and half million dollars."

The striped suit man took a drink of the blood colored liquid from his glass. Traces of the beverage remained on his graying mustache as he set the glass on the table. Drawing his hand down across his upper lip as if the remnants of his drink were a grooming aid, he asked, "I trust you brought one of the bars along for me to look at?"

Bud produced the same bar of gold he had shown Pickard the previous day and laid it on the table. "All the rest of them are exactly alike."

The man took the bar, felt its weight and turned it over. Pickard gasped audibly. The slicked-haired man looked up at Bud with wonderment, but initially remained silent. Finally speaking, "Based on the bullion's origin, it will have to be re-melted at a substantial cost."

"That's understandable," Bud replied. "I think ninety cents on the dollar would be a good number. That's a bit less than $9,400,000. You'll make a million plus.

Jotting some numbers on a piece of paper the ringleader took from his inside suit pocket, he countered, "$8,500,000 and I want to see the gold if I am going to go to the trouble to accumulate the funds."

"Alright, I can live with that," Bud responded knowing the amount was somewhere in the ballpark of eighty to eighty-five percent of the gold's market value.

"I'm not willing to disclose the gold's whereabouts until the funds are placed in a bank of my choice. The actual transfer of the money into my account will be conditioned on assurance that a representative of your choice has possession of the gold."

"Seems you have this all figured out," the would-be buyer said guardedly.

Pondering, the man responded reflectively, "The funds will be available within a day."

Still hoping to get a piece of the pie, Pickard piped-up and said, "My bank can handle the transaction."

"I don't think so," Bud responded. It was apparent that Pickard wasn't in charge of the transaction and whether he got anything out of the deal was of no concern.

Upon hearing this, Pickard's downtrodden expression resembled a hound dog on the wrong side of a kitchen screen door while bacon fried in a cast iron skillet.

Boarding *Cara Mia* with a bottle of whiskey in hand, Bud was met eagerly by his shipmates. Gathering the crew around the galley table, he poured everyone a double shot of Scotch before announcing they had a buyer. Distributing the rest of the bottle's contents, Bud explained, "I will meet with you individually to discuss your fair share. All shares will not be equal. I've lost both *Adventurer* and *Channel Runner* to get us to this point. Once the funds are transferred, we will abandon *Cara Mia* with her cargo to the buyers. Each of our shares will be placed into an individual account at the bank. Each will then be free to go their own way."

"Griff, come to the wheelhouse," Bud directed.

Bud began once they were alone, "Griffin, we need to determine a fair split of the $8.5 million dollars and other valuables. I propose you take $2 million. We'll give Skinner a million. Each of the crew will get $300,000 for a total of another $1,200,000. That will leave me $4.3 million. I hatched this, and you know what I left behind."

It was also Bud's intent to take ownership of the paintings and other antiquities. Their lineage possibly clouded even before the Nazi's absconded with them, Bud would just happen to become their keeper at this point in history.

Summarizing, Bud said, "I have no interest in the jewelry. I do in the paintings and crated items. Who knows, I may even try to find a way to return much of it to the rightful owners."

Griff said, "That all sounds fine to me. I may grab a gold pocket watch or two, but it's okay with me if we let the others take the jewelry. But, if I spend all my money on loose women and drink, I may come knocking at your door someday for a handout."

"Fair enough," Bud said with a smile, extending his hand to seal the deal.

Bud met separately with Skinner and then the remaining four as a group. Skinner was elated with his share. Ron and Ken voiced they weren't getting enough. Hawk said nothing. Wide-eyed, Mick looked more than satisfied.

"I am telling you your $300,000 share is not up for negotiation. You are getting upwards of four times what Bernie got and for good reason. Remember, you guys signed on with me a while back for a few measly bucks with room and board. I'm sending you off with enough money to last a lifetime if you don't squander it. There is also a box containing a fair amount of jewelry. Griff wanted a watch or two, but other than that, the four of you and Skinner can divide it as you see fit."

Bud took the pause in the conversation as a signal to leave.

With the help of the crew, Bud spent the afternoon crating up the paintings and other historical items for shipment. Once the task was complete, they located a reputable shipping company operating out of the dock area. The crates were forwarded on to Seattle, Washington where they would be put into storage under the name Earl Yansen. The contents of the crates were listed as household goods of minimal value.

That evening the entire crew went out for their last night together. Their restaurant of choice had a clear view of *Cara Mia's* moorage. During after-dinner drinks, Bud theorized, "Someday, I may try to return to South America and try to retrieve *Channel Runner*."

"That seems pretty damn foolhardy," Skinner challenged. "She's probably worth less than it would cost to ship her back to the States."

"It sounds like a good way to get killed by those fuck'n Krauts," another stated.

Griff said, "Let me know if you go. Who knows?"

Bud alone knew *Channel Runner* and *Adventurer* still held valuables. But that wasn't the reason—he wanted *Channel Runner* home where she belonged. The retrieval made for interesting discussion as the evening wore on. Finally calling it quits, they filed out of the restaurant.

On the way back to the *Cara Mia*, Bud talked with his young deckhand, "Mick, most of your life's ahead of you. When you get your share of the money, leave the area and head for home immediately. Don't hang around here for a minute. I know little about the men we are doing business with and don't know if they can be trusted. You have the means and intellect to improve your future. Find a trustworthy banker to invest your money and go to college. Here's my address on Orcas Island, write and let me know how you are doing."

"Thank you, Bud. I can only imagine what a difference this will make for me to move beyond just being another poor kid from New York."

The next morning the crew was up early readying themselves for their final departure. If all went as planned, they would be financially set in a few short hours. Bud would ultimately carry a leather satchel and seaman's bag containing a few of his clothes, his Coast Guard License, passport, a Luger pistol, the files and some of the remaining cash from the sub.

Shortly before ten o'clock, Bud and Skinner headed up the wharf for their clandestine meeting at the Wells Fargo Bank. Griff and the others would remain aboard *Cara Mia*. Bud wore his new duds while Skinner managed to look presentable in a pair of his own pants and one of Bud's shirts. Once the availability of the funds was confirmed, Skinner would lead the buyer representatives back to *Cara Mia*. Upon satisfactory inspection of the cargo, word would be sent, and the transfer of funds would be finalized.

Upon arriving at the bank, a large black automobile pulled up to the curb containing the two men from the previous day as well as Pickard and his accountant. The gangster who had controlled the negotiations for the gold set the stage. Decked out in an impeccable pinstriped summer suit with matching white shoes and brimmed hat, his ensemble heightened the mood for a successful transaction.

All the players accounted for, Bud directed Skinner to stay alert and remain in the lobby with the bug-eyed number pusher who had instinctively taken a seat in the area. The accountant held a case containing the necessities to test the gold's purity and a small scale. Greetings were exchanged by the others before being escorted to a private conference room by a homely woman who introduced herself as secretary to the bank president. In all probability chosen by her boss's wife, her efficiency likely made up for what she lacked in first impressions.

With little fanfare, a high-ranking bank official introduced himself before ceremoniously asking Bud under what name the $8,500,000 was to be deposited. Bud drew the deposit slip near and printed his real name on the form. The bank official signed the slip and the transfer of the funds was nearly complete.

Skinner was called from the foyer. He would accompany Pickard's accountant and the lesser ranking thug to the gold's location. The striped suited man and Pickard remained with Bud to await a call confirming the gold's existence.

Twenty-five minutes passed with little conversation until the conference table phone rang. The bank official picked up the receiver before the initial ring finished sounding. Only holding the instrument for a moment, he handed it to the man in the striped suit. Listening intently to his associate at the end of the line, a quizzical look crossed his face while his free hand stroked his clean-shaven chin. "It's in an old fishing boat down at the wharf?"

"The gold's container is free of charge," Bud responded with a slight smirk.

The man said, "Okay," into the phone and hung up.

Bud extended his hand to his short-lived business associate who warily took it, completing the exchange. Painfully, Bud thanked Pickard, but did not shake his hand.

Within a few minutes, Griffin, Skinner, Mick, Ron, Ken and Hawk arrived at the bank by way of two taxis. Bud redistributed the funds into separate accounts before transferring his own share to a Seattle bank. Hardy handshakes and goodwill gestures were exchanged, but not before Bud cautioned, "I don't know a lot about the guys we just did business with, so my recommendation is keep your mouths shut and get the hell out of town as fast as you can. Good luck."

Bud was just finishing dinner in an upscale hotel on the outskirts of San Francisco's business district when he noticed a young couple across the room. They were celebrating the evening with a toast. Bud's thoughts went to Mary. Maybe he would stop by the bank tomorrow and find a way to prod Pickard into a conversation about his roots and extended family. Even if the Pacific Northwest transplant had been cut-off from his uncle's side of the family, he might offer something. He could even offer to take the son-of-a-bitch to lunch.

Then again, Bud reflected, "Do I really want to know that Mary was married with a dozen kids? That her life was much better than if she had stayed with me? Besides, her mother had once said she had a family. Christ! I'm grasping at straws. Maybe I'll just tell the degenerate what a piece of lowlife scum he is."

Bud was jolted back to reality as the waiter placed the evening's bill on the table. Once paid, he headed up to his room. The door closed behind him as he cast his jacket on the bed. Standing in the middle of the room, he sensed something seemed out of place. He couldn't put his finger on it. Whoever had been there went to careful lengths not to disturb anything.

Hurrying to the bathroom, he pulled the neatly stacked towels off the shelf and sorted through them. The files were gone. God only knows why he had even kept them in the first place—no real explanation what impelled him to at this point. Obviously, his hunch to hide them had been correct even if he had chosen a poor hiding place.

Moving quickly across the room to the closet, he lifted his satchel onto the bed. It appeared at first glance that the bag's contents including the money were still intact. Whoever had been in his room could not have overlooked the bag. The intruder was obviously not a typical thief.

"Wait a minute," Bud said aloud as he was looking around the rest of room. Returning to his bed, he dumped the contents of the satchel across the bedspread.

"Christ almighty, they took my Coast Guard License!" Had they wanted Bud to know that the current order of things was not yet concluded?

Having spent a restless night, the next morning Bud walked on a route generally in the direction of Jonathan Pickard's bank. Grabbing breakfast along the way, he debated with himself about completing the trek knowing the likelihood of learning anything meaningful concerning Mary was remote. The loss of his license was weighing on him. Putting aside the jumble of thoughts clouding his mind, he lost his way for time. The sun-drenched walk amongst the hustle and bustle of the crowded streetscape seemed to have a calming effect on his wellbeing. Deciding to make his way back to his hotel, he stopped to get his bearings at a busy intersection. About to head off in the correct direction, he glanced up one of the streets and saw Pickard's bank but a block away. Stepping off the curb, he walked in that direction.

Bud stalled at the bank's entrance to consider abandoning his attempt to see Mary's cousin, but didn't. Inquiring within, he was told Mr. Pickard was in his office with a business client. Bud took a seat to wait. After waiting about fifteen minutes, about to give up, a shot rang out from the walled area behind the tellers.

Springing to his feet, Bud bolted for Pickard's office while wide-eyed tellers and customers followed his leap to action. The customer passage gate splintered and flew open as Bud charged the familiar hallway in the direction of the gunshot's origin.

Glimpsing a figure carrying a large tan envelope exiting through a rear door, Bud sprinted down the corridor shoving aside the bug-eyed accountant along the way. Charging through the back exit, Bud found himself on a raised stair landing next to an alley. Taking the stairs down in two steps, he stood in the middle of the narrow alley.

Tires screeching, Bud spun around as a car careened towards him. Leaping aside, there was no mistaking the vehicle driver's identity. Fleetingly, the penetrating blue eyes of Otto Günsche glared back.

Bud raced back up the stairs and grasped the doorknob to the bank. It was locked. Pounding relentlessly for someone to let him in, he was about to give up and run around to the bank's entrance when the door finally swung open.

Sailing past the accountant, Bud headed into Pickard's office to find a screaming secretary hovering over the vice president's lifeless body. Pushing her aside, he dropped to his knees next to Pickard. The banker struggled for a breath as blood seeped from his mouth fading indistinguishably into the ruby-colored Persian carpet. The shroud of death cast, Jonathan Pickard gasped his last words, "The files."

Feeling no emotions one way or the other, Bud was aware that Pickard's death was the result of seeking him out a few days prior. His thoughts went to the girl in the boat on Blind Island—her cousin's ruthless behavior was finally avenged.

Bud rose to his feet as a uniformed policeman entered the room with gun drawn. Trying to respond to the cop's interrogation, Bud's own questions jumbled his mind. How had Günsche tracked him to San Francisco? Had Pickard taken the files from his room?

A senior officer arrived to interrogate those gathered while Bud continued his internal deliberation. Did the files disclose the identity of the Nazis who had face altering surgery? Had Pickard disclosed the sale of the gold to Günsche?

The officer spoke to Bud, "Sir, I need your full attention. You need to answer my questions."

"I came to the bank to discuss a business transaction with Mr. Pickard and got caught up in this unfortunate event."

"No, I have no idea why he was shot but I did see a man racing out the back door."

"The only thing I saw in the alley was a car speeding away."

"It was blue."

"No, I was only able to get part of the license plate number. It was FID6 something."

Walking back to the hotel, Bud came to the realization he should have heeded the advice he had given his crew. Even if for a different reason, he needed to leave the area immediately.

Bud warily turned the key in his hotel room door and swung it wide open. Standing in the doorway, he scanned the room. Housekeeping had been in to make up the bed. Entering a few steps, he stopped when he could look directly into the bathroom. Once satisfied that the room was empty, he stepped back and shut the door.

Hurriedly gathering his belongings, Bud considered that both Griffin and Skinner were lodged in a nearby hotel. He needed to advise them of the recent events. The rest of the crew had disappeared the previous day and there was no way to find them. Mick had said he was leaving for home that afternoon and hopefully, the three helmsmen had followed suit.

Bud walked briskly to the hotel. Asking the staff to call both Griffin's and Skinner's rooms, he was told both checked out that morning.

Bud thought it odd that Griffin had not at least tried to contact him before departing. His whereabouts unknown, Bud had a bad feeling. He hoped his senses weren't correct. He hoped his longtime friend had heeded his words to leave town.

Standing back at the front desk of his own hotel, Bud scrawled off a note to Griff in case he should check back. Exiting the hotel with his sea bag and leather satchel, he barely acknowledged the doorman's greeting. Stepping to the curb, a cab pulled up. Opening the back door of the cab forcefully, Bud tossed his bags across the surface of the back seat, "Let's go. Take me to a Chevrolet dealership."

Stacking the hundred-dollar bills onto the salesman's desk, the man took the money and recounted it. Satisfied, he handed Bud the keys and title to a used dark gray 1944 Chevy convertible.

San Francisco falling behind in the rearview mirror, Bud breathed a sigh of relief. Stretching back into the cushioned leather seat, an unexplainable shiver ran up his spine.

CHAPTER 21

Summer 1945

HER BRONZE HORN SOUNDING A LONG DEPARTURE BLAST, THE FERRY *Vashon* pulled away from the mainland on route to the San Juan Islands. Bud went topside. Taking an isolated seat near the bow, he reflected on his life as familiar land masses came and went from view. Shaw Island passing on the port, he could make out the familiar profile of the store that had shaped his youth. Tears formed in his eyes as he thought of his mother's passing the year before. Word of her death had caught up to him aboard *Adventurer* long after she unexpectedly died while digging clams. It was assumed she'd died from a heart condition. Vowing to visit her the next day, he questioned the life choices that led him to miss her burial. Earl had been there in his stead, but it should have been him.

Two short blasts of the vessel's horn startled him back from his thoughts and signaling their arrival at Orcas Island. Swiping at his nose, Bud headed down to his car.

Dust trailing behind along the road, the Kangaroo House came into view. It had been almost two years since he had laid eyes on his home. Removing his shoes and socks, he forded the narrow reach and climbed the rocky trail. Wincing as rocks dug into his bare feet, it mattered little—he was home.

Down the beach, Karoo was poking along the drift line the retreating tide had left earlier. Like her master, she seemed drawn to the tailings left by the ebb and flow. Over the years, Bud had amassed a significant collection of net floats, fishing plugs, the random oar and the like from his high tide explorations. While his discoveries had little monetary value, there was always the anticipation of finding something to make the trek seem worthwhile. Never able to figure out what drew the kangaroo to execute the same routine, she did seem to nibble on something amongst the clumps of seaweed from time to time.

Cigar smoke drifted from the porch. His eyes closed, face turned up to gather the sun's warmth, Earl seemed at peace. Quietly, he studied his old friend not wanting to interrupt the serenity of the moment. Furrowed wrinkles and gray wisps of hair bearing witness to his advancing years, a slight smile formed on the weathered face as if dreaming a pleasant thought. As if sensing someone's presence, he slowly opened his eyes. Squinting into the sun, startled, he enthusiastically rose to greet Bud.

During their noisy exchange, Bud caught a glimpse of Karoo bounding up the beach. Stepping off the porch, Bud braced himself for her greeting as she closed the distance. Only slowing slightly before her arrival, she knocked Bud to the ground. Picking himself up, Bud ruffled the small-headed creature's ears before dusting himself off and rejoining Earl.

"You know, she thinks she's a dog," Bud said.

Bud and Earl spent the remainder of the afternoon and well into the evening filling up on salmon, crab, Scotch whiskey and conversation. Bud caught Earl up on his most recent exploits. Not going into detail concerning the description or value of his assemblage, he did indicate that it substantially exceeded the value of his freighter left behind. At intervals during the storytelling, Earl's wrinkled brow, clenched teeth and chastising eyes did little to disguise his disfavor with the risky undertakings.

The next morning Earl sheepishly announced he would be traveling to Seattle for a day or two to visit a friend. After Bud's prodding, he confessed he had been seeing a lady friend from time to time. She and her husband had frequented the Moran estate as guests over the years where they had become friends. The husband had died about a year ago and Earl had recently begun making the journey to visit her.

Earl's departure was fine with Bud since he had some things to attend to. On the other hand, he didn't want to let his old friend too easily off the hook. "Don't worry about me. Why should I be a priority over some lonely, love-starved, damsel?"

Earl shrugged his shoulders. An overnight bag in one hand and shoes and socks in the other, he set out down the trail.

Watching Earl gingerly wade across the gravel spit towards his beat up old pickup, Bud called out, "Wait a minute."

Grabbing the keys to the convertible, Bud headed to the spit grinning at the thought of the old coot heading off for a romantic interlude. Bud trailed Earl as far as he could without getting wet.

"Here, use these," Bud said tossing the keys to Earl.

Cushioned by the soft sand, Earl landed on his butt trying to make the catch. Rising triumphantly with keys in hand, Earl yelled, "The keys to the Ford are in the ignition."

"Now I know what it must feel like to see your son off on a date with your new car," Bud thought as he headed back to the house.

Bud puttered around Broken Point the rest of the morning, reacquainting himself with his surroundings. Walking the beach with Karoo, they were rewarded with a cork line float. Interrupting its journey, he chucked it up beyond the high tide limits where it caught a craggy fir's overhanging limb before dropping amongst the logs.

Early afternoon found Bud launching the small skiff. His destination was the Shaw family store. While the store became his upon his mother's death, it was a given that Cleo could live above and operate the store as long as he wished. As before, Bud helped financially with the enterprise's well-being as needed.

The small outboard putted along slowly giving Bud the opportunity to take in the grandeur of his upbringing. Turning off the engine, the skiff drifted aimlessly. Without thought, Bud found himself taking up the oars and quietly rowing toward Blind Island.

The familiar sounds and feel of gravel rolling against the bottom of the skiff took him back to his youth. Stepping ashore, he stripped to his undershorts before plopping onto the warm beach. Closing his eyes, the sound of the lapping waves reeled off images of his past. He replayed the frightful day Mary nearly drowned before shedding the thoughts for more pleasant ones. Sleep ultimately came easily.

Bud awoke with a bit of a start as the incoming tide licked his feet. Feeling truly rested for the first time in recent memory, he sat up and squinted in the bright sunlight. Two ducks which had meandered ashore scurried back into the water.

Turning his attention to his fort, Bud headed across the logs. Somewhat surprised to find the structure had weathered the years relatively intact, he poked through the accumulation of tide treasures before heading back to the beach.

Donning his pants, Bud threw his shoes, socks and shirt into the skiff and shoved off. Rowing placidly through the eel grass, he could see a sizable salmon moving about. Hesitating, he wondered if he could somehow bag it for dinner. Dismissing the notion, he pulled the outboard to life propelling the skiff noisily out of the cove.

The green weathered rowboat slid alongside the dock just as the mail boat was pulling away. A young man, about twenty, who had made the mailbag exchange, dropped the bag and reached out for the line to secure the skiff. He introduced himself as Michael. A brief conversation followed wherein Bud learned the newcomer was helping Cleo at the store for the summer before returning to college in the fall.

As the two walked up the dock, Bud spied Cleo sitting in the shade in an Adirondack chair braiding eyes in ropes to sell as tie-up lines. Upon seeing Bud, Cleo rose to meet him with a warm hand shake. While spending little time together, Bud had learned to genuinely like the guy. He had made life simpler and less lonely for his mother.

After a bit of reminiscing and a beer, Bud said, "I'm going to walk up the road to see mother."

"Do you want company?" Cleo offered.

"Thanks, but I'd rather go alone."

It was late afternoon when Bud finally set out for the island graveyard. Years had passed since he had last been to the resting place of his family. He thought back to times he had walked the same route with his mother while she reminisced about her early years on the island. Both grandparents had died by the time Bud was seven years old, so his memories were few. He did remember going out in the woods with his grandfather a few times to watch him target practice with an old revolver. He'd even gotten to fire the clunky thing a couple of times, his grandfather's hands covering his own in guidance. His grandfather would dig the lead out of the tree after he was done shooting. Bud was unsure if the lead was reused or a kind gesture to the wounded tree.

There was little in Bud's life these days to rekindle the memories of his grandparents other than a bible that sat on the shelf above the roll-top desk back at the Kangaroo House. F. E. Fowler, initials for his grandfather, Frank Eugene, highlighted the cover in gold lettering.

There were a few written inscriptions in the back pages of the bible replicating the names and dates chiseled on cemetery headstones. The bible itself had little overall wear attesting that his grandfather probably didn't refer to it all that often.

A faded red Chevy pick-up approached as Bud unlatched the gate and entered the graveyard. Halfheartedly, he raised his hand in a wave without looking to see who it might be. He was familiar with most of the folks who lived on the sparsely populated island so chances were they knew each other.

Finding his mother's place of rest, Bud meticulously tidied up the area around it. Casting aside a few wayward fir cones, he wetted his handkerchief from a nearby mason jar containing wilting flowers to erase away a weathering of debris from the flat granite marker. He then pulled a bunch of dried spindly grass that had entrenched itself over one corner of the stone record. Studying the headstone's simple inscription, he was disappointed that it stated only her name and the dates of birth and death. If he had been home, she would have had a nicer stone with a declaration about being a wonderful mother. Maybe he would add a larger upright monument someday. Satisfied with his tidying efforts, Bud took a moment to wander the small graveyard rediscovering his roots.

The name Fowler was more visible than any other name in the graveyard. At this point, Bud was the only Fowler left on his branch of the tree. He was forty-four and the only thing he had to show for it was a house filled with stuff. And the closest thing he had to a family was Yansen, Cleo and a kangaroo. He knew his mother had been disappointed with aspects of his life. While she kept her feelings to herself, there was little question she wished he had chosen a more commonplace existence. As of late, often wondering the same, the boy from Shaw no longer had anything to prove to anyone.

Wandering back to his mother's resting place, Bud knelt to bid his mother farewell. Wiping his eyes, Bud rose and headed across the dried grass toward the road.

Part way back to the store, the red pickup that passed previously could be seen making its way around the bay in his direction. The vehicle slowed as it neared to lighten the cloud of dust trailing it. Bud glimpsed Michael sitting in the passenger side of the truck as waves were exchanged. Because of the reflecting sun across the windshield, Bud only got a vague look at the woman driving. She seemed intent on focusing on the road ahead disappearing around the bend. Yet, there seemed something familiar about her. Bud turned his thoughts to earlier years when he delivered groceries along that same route on the back of their dirty-white horse, Queen.

Cleo twisted the slender legged key in the front door of the store and hung it on the inner frame of a nearby window. Locking the door was merely a formality to keep non-islanders out. The locals knew where the key was and could be trusted to square up for anything taken during times no one was manning the place.

"Michael's mother just gave me some fresh caught bass for dinner and there's plenty for the both of us," Cleo stated seeing Bud approach.

"That sounds great if you'll throw in a beer," Bud replied.

Cleo unlocked the store and grabbed two chilled beers.

They ate their dinner and drank their beer on the small deck facing the setting sun. Conversation naturally included anecdotes that expressed feelings about the extraordinary mother and partner they both had been fortunate to have shared. Tears creeping from their eyes from time to time, they reminisced while the setting sun exploded the sky and channel into a brilliant canvas of oranges and yellows.

Cleo untied the skiff as Bud yanked the old engine into action with a single pull of the cord. Shaking hands as the boat began to move ahead, they silently parted.

Cold water slapping at the skiff's bow, as if conveying a message, Bud looked to the sky. A narrow-sliced moon paled to the incandescence multitude of stars. Maybe it was time to settle down. Who knows, maybe he could even find someone to share it all.

The skiff tied off at Broken Point, Bud was startled by Karoo coming to greet him, "Dumb marsupial," he blurted regaining his wits and touching her head fondly. Bounding alongside, Bud chuckled thinking about some poor soul who might stumble on to her in the dark.

Without turning on any lights, Bud poured himself a double scotch and settled into one of the library's overstuffed chairs.

It had been a good day.

CHAPTER 22

Bud watched a large ship in the distance making its way to Canada as he sipped his morning coffee. He needed to keep track of the time, having promised to meet his shipment of household goods arriving on the 9:35 ferry. There would be a total of five crates—two containing paintings, while the others held boxed antiquities that could have adorned civilizations as far back as the Egyptian pharaohs. In time, Bud expected he would try to donate many of the items to a museum and let them determine their fate.

Draining the last of his coffee, Bud set out on foot to borrow a flatbed truck from a nearby farmer he had known since his youth and working days at Rosario. He had considered using Earl's pickup but would have had to make more than one trip. Cutting through neighboring fields and woods, the morning dew wetted his shoes and pant legs. He felt at peace and knew it was time to stop gallivanting around the world.

Flagging the delivery driver, Bud jumped on the truck's side running board as it lumbered up the ferry dock. Pointing the way, Bud directed them up the hill to the waiting flatbed. The heavy crates required them to use levers to skid them from one truck to the other. The transfer complete, the driver hastily maneuvered his vehicle around and accelerated down the hill to the waiting ferry.

On the jaunt back to Kangaroo House along narrow tree canopied roadways, Bud pondered the likelihood of the truck's cargo finding its way to a rocky island in the middle of nowhere. Arriving, he positioned the truck as close to the crossing as possible without getting stuck. Scrambling atop the truck bed, he was eager to begin the task ahead. The top of the first crate broke free with encouragement from a crowbar. Karoo watched intently nearby. Pulling a wrapped painting out of the crate, his excitement grew as if a youngster on Christmas morn. As luck would have it for the time being, the tide was low, but on its way in. "Let's get to it," he said to Karoo.

To minimize any chance of a mishap, Bud ferried a few pieces at a time in the skiff pushing it across the moat like waterway. Once transported to the house, he began to stack the paintings in a row along the wall in the living room. The boxed items would come last. Bud gasped for breath on the last few crossings as the frigid water seeped into the crotch of his pants.

Climbing back into the borrowed flatbed, wet pants and all, he headed inland. Knowing the farmer would put the boards to use, the empty crates remained in the bed of the truck. There was a good supply of lumber in his own workshop or he might have tried to salvage the wood himself. Declining the farmer's offer of a return ride, Bud headed on foot across a newly hayed field in the direction of Broken Point. On the way, he mentally constructed the storage framework he would need for the paintings as his growling stomach reminded him he hadn't taken time to eat lunch.

As the light of day began its transformation to night, Bud confidently began to boil water on the stove before going down to the rocky point. Grasping the line that led into the water where he had dropped the pot that morning, he looked forward to the trapped bounty at the other end. He hadn't had fresh crab in ages.

With the remnants of dinner out of sight, he opened the lower second floor stairway section to the aptly named kangaroo pouch. Brushing away cobwebs, he descended the stairs and flicked the light switch, illuminating the space. The cavern was cool and dry. Even though darkness had overtaken the point, he went about gathering lumber and materials to construct the necessary storage areas. A simple framework made expressly to vertically store paintings was easily assembled. Next, a raised planked over area of the cavern floor was constructed for the other antiquities. Working late into the night, the Nazi plunder was systematically relocated below Kangaroo House. All but three of the paintings and a few other antiquities were safely stored away as midnight came and went. The task complete and the section of stairway back into place, Bud headed up the same steps to bed.

Rising to another blue-skied day, Bud made a pot of coffee before shifting some items on the library walls to make room for the three elaborately framed paintings. Standing back admiring the works, he wished he had not left behind his favorite—the man with the globe. An Egyptian looking vase found a prominent place in the foyer. Other pieces found their place here and there.

Puttering about the house, Bud revisited memories from his past. Each chair, book, rug or the like told a story of its origin and the adventure of its acquisition. Pushed back in one corner of the library's bookcases, amongst the volumes, was a silver framed photo of Mary. She had given it to him the Christmas prior to that fateful day she had left the islands never to be seen or heard from again. Taking the photograph in hand, Bud leaned against the windowsill overlooking the channel. He studied the image of his lost love as the reflecting sun danced on the photo. Shaking it off, he went about straightening the shelves.

By mid-morning, Bud found himself pulling on the oars of his rowboat. The tranquility of water lapping against the bow and rhythmic creak of oar blades heightened the sense there was no need to have a destination. A bald eagle soared overhead scanning the placid water's surface. Bobbing amongst kelp ribbons, a seal's oversized eyes followed the sounds of the skiff. The inquisitive mammal disappeared only to reappear just astern in the surface tailings left by the boat.

Bud rowed for an hour before finding himself across the channel from his boyhood home. Turning the boat, he began heading back in the same general direction he had come. Hesitating after a few strokes, he pulled an oar to align the bow setting a course for the store.

Michael was stacking feed sacks in the warehouse when Bud found him. Handing him one of the two bottles of soda that he had retrieved from the store cooler, Bud suggested the boy take a break. Michael obliged, climbing atop a pile of sacks.

The two talked of nothing in particular. Bud shared youthful memories of stacking feed bags on the very spot. Eventually, the conversation included the Fowler family lineage. Prodding a bit, Bud asked Michael about his family.

"I am an only child as well," Michael offered.

"My mother never really talked about my father," Bud replied.

"Mother mentions my father from time to time when I ask," Michael said. "When she does, she talks fondly of him. I guess their lives just didn't match up," he surmised, looking out one of the building's pane-less openings to the channel beyond.

"She said her family used to visit the Rosario estate years ago when it was still owned by the original family. Who knows, maybe you even met some of them back then."

Bud asked, "Michael, I don't recall you mentioning your last name."

"Pickard."

Bud took a swig of soda, "My god," he thought. "Is it possible?"

"Is your mother's name Mary?"

"Yes," Michael responded thinking Cleo must have disclosed it.

Bud choked down another gulp. Clearing his throat, he started to say something, but didn't.

"Thanks again. But I better get back to it. That Cleo is a slave driver," Michael said with a chuckle.

Leaving Michael, Bud headed for the planked walkway to the store. When asked, Cleo told him where Michael and his mother were staying. It was a house just across the bay he knew well from his childhood.

Bud bid Cleo farewell. Walking down to the float, Bud glanced back in the direction of the store to see if Michael might be watching. He was not. Pushing off, he began rowing on a course different than the one to Kangaroo House.

Stroking slowly across the bay, turning to view his destination, the oars went silent. The sun reflections off the water made it difficult to clearly distinguish the house. He was unsure—he hadn't heard from her for years. The oars began to move again without changing direction. Some hundred yards from the beach, squinting into the sun, Bud could make out a figure sitting atop a log.

He wondered what he would say.

He wondered what she would say. "She came to Shaw. She had to have considered the odds of seeing him. Is Michael my son? What if he's not? What happens if I'm not welcome?"

Carried by a wave from a passing fishing boat, the skiff surfed onto the beach. Bud removed the oars from their locks, placing them at his side. Still in the rowing position facing the stern of the boat, he heard her footsteps in the gravel closing the distance. Taking a deep breath, Bud lifted his feet and slowly turned around on the seat.

Standing at the rowboat's bow, her misty eyes telling him what he had hoped, Bud clumsily made his way out of the unstable boat. A gold chain with the black arrowhead hung around her neck. Burying her face in his chest, her muffled sobbing was barely distinguishable over the sounds of waves against the shore.

Mary and Bud spent the rest of the day on the front porch retracing the years. They talked about Michael. They talked about Bud being spurned by Mary's mother. They talked about the mistakes they made not trying to bridge the wedges between their lives.

Barely audible, unable to control her rising emotions, Mary said, "You know I never stopped loving you,"

"And I you. We should have tried harder," Bud replied.

"Why didn't you ever tell me about Michael?"

"I tried to the day we last saw each other many years ago. I was already pregnant but, the words just didn't come. At that point in your life, you were a bootlegger living in a one room cabin. It didn't seem like you were ready for a wife and child. I did hear about you from time to time from my parents or other friends who visited the estate. As time went by it became harder and harder to just show up on your doorstep. I never found anyone to replace you. Then there were my parents," she stopped short of further explanation.

As dinnertime neared, a familiar red pickup motored its way round the half-moon shaped bay. When it turned down the driveway, leaving Bud on the porch, Mary crossed the yard to greet her son. Timing her arrival as the truck rattled to a halt, she stepped onto the driver's running board and stuck her head through the open window.

The two conversed for what seemed an eternity to Bud. His pulse quickening, Mary stepped back to the ground as the truck's door opened. Michael's eyes locked onto him as he stepped from the vehicle.

Arm in arm, mother and son strolled up the beaten down grassy pathway to the house. Bud stood as they ascended. Her eyes glistening, Mary lead her son towards him. With only a step or two separating them, Mary said, "Michael, I would like to introduce you to your father, Bud Fowler."

Bud resisted the urge to pull Mary near as he extended his other hand to his son. Michael took his hand firmly and guardedly uttered, "I'm glad to finally meet you."

Acknowledging the day had been a significant event for all, Bud said, "I hope it's not too late for us all to be a part of one another's lives."

Concealing his thoughts, Michael's conversation was wary and uneasy.

"It's probably time for me to head back home," Bud said. "Tomorrow's Sunday. Why don't you both come over to the Broken Point for the day?"

Mary looked at him curiously. "We would be happy to, but I have to admit that I have no idea where that is."

"The answer to that question can wait," Bud responded. "I'll be by to pick you up about 10:00."

Mary walked Bud down to the beach while their son retreated into the house. Before stepping into the boat, Bud faced Mary and said, "I want to kiss you."

Knowing Michael was probably watching, their lips touched briefly like school kids sneaking a first kiss. Rowing away, they remained focused on one another until the rowboat disappeared from view.

Restful sleep did not come easy for Bud that night. In all likelihood, the same held true for Mary and their son. Up early the next morning, having straightened the house, Bud shoved off in the motorized skiff to retrieve his newly-discovered family.

His destination reached, the bay went quiet as the engine sputtered to a stop and the paint chipped skiff met the beach. Bud stepped out awkwardly getting one of his shoes wet as the boat started to retreat. Giving the boat a slight pull inland to keep her from floating off, he headed up the trail towards the house and noticed the old pick-up was gone.

Mary emerged through the screen door, letting it slam loudly behind. The morning sun framed her youthful jubilance as she strolled toward him prolonging the moment. She wore a low-cut print dress that caught the breeze coming off the bay. With a few steps to go, she impetuously flew into Bud's arms giving him a forceful kiss before finally releasing her hold.

"I've missed you," she stated emphatically taking his hand leading the way to the beach.

"What about Michael?" Bud asked.

"This is my day," she answered.

"Is he okay?" Bud queried.

"It's difficult to tell. He seemed quiet last evening. I think we just need to give him some time. I also don't think he is particularly happy that I didn't tell him about you long ago. He's nearly a grown man and I believe he understands that life choices aren't always easy. It's confusing for him now, but I believe, and hope, he won't harbor any ill-will."

Mary sat in the triangle shaped bow with one hand draped over the side cutting and curving through the water. Her fingers had no course in mind other than the freedom of the moment. Her eyes closed, face tilted towards the sun, a slight smile crossed her mouth.

"What are you thinking about Mary?"

"Well, I was remembering the time we outran the revenuers and you took me to your special island. The beach felt so good against..." She stopped herself from ending the sentence and slowly opened her eyes.

Abruptly, Bud changed their heading and revved the engine.

"And what do you have planned?" she asked.

As if time had stood still, the small pebbled beach caressed their naked bodies under the sun's warming rays.

After dressing, Mary headed to the edge of the drift line while Bud watched. Eager to discover unknown treasurers, she skipped like a youthful schoolgirl. Squealing out, she reached down amongst the drift to retrieve a greenish tinted glass net float. Inspecting it closely to ensure that it had made its long journey across the ocean without mishap, she held the globe high and announced, "We're rich."

Bud responded with a large grin, thinking at this very moment he did truly feel like the richest man on earth.

"Time to head to Kangaroo House," Bud stated without really thinking about his reference to their destination.

Mary tilted he head quizzically, "Kangaroo House?"

Bud, realizing what he had said, replied, "Oh, you'll see."

As they motored along, Mary asked, "Not that I am complaining about this boat, but whatever happened to the *Channel Runner*?"

"I still have her, but she's halfway around the world."

Mary was just about to ask a follow-up question when they rounded a bend and Broken Point came into full view. "Wow. Whoever owns that place must have one of the most beautiful properties anywhere," she exclaimed.

Continuing her gaze at the surrounding beach area, an unfamiliar upright animal bounded along the beach not forty feet away. Mary turned questioning green eyes to Bud's knowing ones. Bud said nothing as Karoo continued to parallel the boat's progress toward the point where the house reigned.

Veering away as if they were going to pass the point, Bud instead made a full circle heading directly toward the float. "Mary, I built this place as I tried to move on after you left. Yet, I always hoped someday you would come back to me."

Mary's eyes were brimming over as Karoo appeared on the dock startling her. Letting out a nervous yelp, she jumped to Bud, nearly tipping them over the side. Bud laughed as Karoo moved cautiously toward the boat eyeing the intruder. The long-tailed marsupial closed the distance causing Mary to move ever tighter against Bud.

"Don't worry, she won't hurt you. I rescued her from an unhappy zoo life." Taking Mary's hand, he extended it for the strange looking animal to inspect and introduced the two by name, "Mary, this is Karoo. Karoo, meet Mary."

Apprehensively Mary stepped from the boat constantly looking for reassurance as the trio headed towards the house. Along the way Bud explained how Karoo came to live on Broken Point. To Mary's relief, Karoo seemed to know her limits and fell back when they reached the porch.

Taking in the panoramic setting, Mary stood on the porch and said nothing.

"Look around. I'll find us something for lunch."

"What a glorious place," she exclaimed when Bud later found her in the library. Holding a picture retrieved from the fireplace mantel where Bud had placed it the evening before, she asked, "And how long did it take you to dig this out of an old box?"

"I'll admit it hasn't always been located exactly in that very spot, but it has never been far away," Bud responded. "It's always been tucked away safely just as you have been in my heart."

She looked up at Bud lovingly, said nothing and placed the picture back on the mantel.

"It's time to eat," Bud announced.

Walking arm in arm to the living room, they sat on a leather couch next to where Bud had laid sandwiches and drinks on a finely carved coffee table.

After lunch, Bud showed Mary the remainder of the property and beach area. Returning to the house, Mary methodically revisited each room inquiring about every detail and object that adorned the structure. She took special interest in a figurehead prominently stationed in the large entryway. Bud explained that he had rescued her from a dying clipper ship in a small Mediterranean seaport.

"I feel certain she was carved by the same artist who had created the lady from the bow of the *America* over at Rosario. I've even considered on more than one occasion trying to negotiate an exchange of the two with the estate's new owner but have yet to do so. Afraid he might turn me down. Yansen and I have even discussed the possibility of a kidnapping and replacement when the owners are gone for a few days. We think we can trust the hired help not to expose us and question if the family would even notice the difference."

Intrigued, Mary enthusiastically proclaimed, "I stand willing and able to be part of the raiding party."

Mary took Bud's hand and led him toward the second-floor stairway. Since they had previously toured the upstairs, he wondered about her intentions. Climbing the stairs, he wanted to share his secret of all secrets with her but thought better of it.

The expansive bedroom contained a massive four-pillared bed that had come from New Orleans. Mary plopped herself onto the middle of it with outstretched arms taking in the grandeur of it all. Bud leaned against one of the large pillars watching her. She motioned for him to join her where they entwined themselves and drifted off to sleep.

That evening they dined on fresh salmon cooked over an open beach fire and wine chilled in the Sound. Later, Mary phoned Michael. She told him she was considering staying on Orcas until the following day. Michael took the news with minimal comment.

"I think he is okay." Mary reported to Bud. "He seemed better. He even said he loved me before we hung up."

Later, as the fire diminished to glowing embers, they stretched out on the beach and watched the brilliance of a starlit sky.

"Make a wish," Mary said as a shooting star crossed overhead.

"I wish for nothing more—I found you," Bud responded.

The night chill finally chasing them off the beach, they made their way up the path. Following close behind for a time, Karoo knew the routine as he veered off to the workshop with Bud. Mary continued to the house.

By the time Bud ascended to the second floor, he found Mary in the oversized cast iron bathtub. Joining her, Mary floated off to sleep in his arms. Nearly an hour passed until Bud finally woke his bathing partner. Retreating to the poster bed, they made love as peaceful sleep overtook them.

Bud stirred before morning's first light to find Mary gone. Donning a pair of pants, he made a futile search of the house. Ascending the spiral stairs of the tower, peering out from its vantage point, he was able to make out a figure sitting along the lower reaches of the point where it transitioned to the sea beyond. Next to her lay Karoo.

The setting was almost surreal as moonlit rays poked through the clouds casting a shimmering trail across the water. Wrapped in a blanket to ward off the cold, she seemed to be staring out into the depths beyond. Unsure whether he should interrupt her tranquility or rescue a damsel in distress, he took up residence in the tower to watch over her.

Ultimately, as the sun began to peak over a distant island, Mary rose and headed back towards the house. Bud hurriedly descended the tower stairs back to bed as a board squeaked on the stair landing. Carefully, Mary slipped next to him. Bud could feel her chilled body even though they were not touching. He rolled to his side facing her back. Reaching around her waist, he drew her against his warmth. She began to cry softly as he tightened his hold and stroked her hair.

"Is there something I can do?" Bud asked

"Another time," Mary said bringing the discussion to a close.

The morning brought no hint of why Mary had been upset a few hours previously. They had breakfast before deciding to drive around the island in Earl's old Ford. It had been some twenty years since Mary had been on the island and a sightseeing tour seemed fitting. For the most part, the island had remained relatively unchanged except for a few more cleared fields and constructed homes. They stopped along the way several times, including a vista on Mt. Constitution that looked over the islands and beyond. Ultimately ending up at the ferry dock, they stopped at the only café on the island for a late lunch.

Acknowledging few locals in small eatery, Mary led the way to a window table to her liking. Their overlook included the nearby ferry landing and the distant Shaw store across the channel. A hairy-armed waitress appeared thrusting two glasses of water on the table. Impatiently, pad and pencil in hand, she stood poised waiting. Mary asked what was good. Forcing a smile, hoping to mask her weary eyes, the table visitor jerked her head toward the chalkboard next to the kitchen entrance. Bud ordered a ham sandwich. Mary chose an egg salad.

They were just finishing lunch when the *Vashon* came around the bend marking its arrival with two blasts of her horn. As it neared, Bud recognized one of the cars parked on the forward bow as his own. The top was down, and he could see a figure, no doubt Earl, seated behind the wheel. Hoping to improve the waitress's outlook on the day, Bud left a generous tip. Taking Mary's hand, he leisurely led her down to the landing to watch the arriving passengers.

Mary commented, "Look at the convertible on the front of the ferry. I bet it's destined for Rosario."

"Likely so," Bud agreed, indicating, "Probably needs that fancy car to compensate for some sort of character flaw."

Mary was surprised that once the driver cleared the dock area, he waved to them pulling onto the shoulder.

"Do you know the guy?" Mary asked.

A look of indifference, Bud shrugged his shoulders. Extracting himself from the car, the first thing out of Earl's mouth was, "Boy was I ever a hit with the old ladies in Seattle. I think I need to buy this car from you before someone figures out it's not mine."

Mary glanced up at Bud with a knowing look of disapproval—a look Mabel might have given her son if she had been there.

Bud reintroduced the two by reminding them of the time the revenuers had searched *Channel Runner* at Rosario only to find a load of groceries. They all had a good laugh recalling the event. Bud explained Earl sometimes house sat while he was gallivanting around the world. He then told Earl that he would see him later back at the house.

Earl offered to exchange vehicles. Bud declined, "But, don't get too attached to it."

Bud and Mary boarded the ferry for the short crossing to Shaw. "You know I am perfectly capable of walking on and off the ferry by myself. It's not necessary for you to see me home."

"I know," Bud replied. "I'm not willing to give you up quite yet. I'll catch a later boat back."

Remaining on the car deck, Mary and Bud talked to one of the deckhands during the short crossing. They learned that there was some excitement up in the Purser's office. A lady on the way to the mainland to have a baby looked as if she might not make it. Luckily, she has a nurse with her as well as her husband. The expectant mother's husband worked for the ferry system on one of the other boats. "He's driving us all nuts telling us how to load and unload in record time. I suggest you don't dally getting off the boat," the deckhand reported.

Before the boarding slip came to rest on the ferry's bow, Bud stepped up onto it with Mary in tow. Hearing a departing hay truck's engine rev when they were only part way up the dock, Bud glanced back to confirm the truck was in motion. In the spirit of the situation, Bud began to trot pulling Mary along. Urging her to get the lead out, the noisy truck continued to close on them. Reaching the end of the slip, they stepped aside as the truck's horn honked a salute.

Laughing, Bud turned to receive the shock of his life. Mary's face was bright red, and she began to wheeze uncontrollably. Swooping her up into his arms, briefly considering the nurse on the ferry, he saw the *Vashon* was already backing away from the piling wing-walls. Running as best he could carrying Mary, he yelled out as he went. Michael emerged from the feed storage building sprinting to catch up. Converging outside of the store's entrance, Cleo opened the door to see what the commotion was.

The gathering quickly moved inside where Cleo swept a table clear of loaves of bread, so Mary could be placed onto its surface. Placing a cushion taken from a nearby chair under his mother's head, Michael decreed on his way to the wash sink, "Just give her time. She should be okay." Snagging a newly shelved towel on the way, he wetted it under the cold water before returning to place it on his mother's forehead. Obvious to the bystanders, it was clear the two had been through the routine before.

Mary looked up at Bud and mouthed, "I'm sorry."

Taking a blanket from Cleo, Michael placed it over his mother, "Now close your eyes, mom."

Bud, showing fear in his eyes, looked to his son for guidance. Motioning his father to follow, Bud tailed Michael out the back door. Once on the porch, Michael said, "My mother is dying. Her lungs have all but given out. Before you ask, I can assure you that she has seen the best doctors available. We came to the islands so she could enjoy the last of her life in a setting that held fond memories for her. The doctors say she has just a few months, hopefully more. I can say that finding you has been very difficult for me but a godsend for her. I guess it's not your fault since you didn't know I existed until a couple of days ago. But, I blame both of you somehow. I guess I'll need to get over it."

Despair overwhelmed Bud. Michael stepped forward and placed his hand on his father's shoulder before stepping away. Bud shook off his feelings of gloom and trailed his son back into the store. Bud now knew why Mary was so emotional in the middle of the night at Kangaroo House. Was her illness the reason she tried to bring her family together after all this time?

Mary's color returned within a few minutes. Sitting up, she took a sip of water.

Within an hour, Michael and Bud moved Mary to the summer residence and settled her in the living room. Objecting unsuccessfully to the special attention heaped upon her, by early evening she seemed her old self moving about the house appearing no worse for the wear.

Before Michael drove his father back to the ferry, Bud suggested, "Why don't the two of you consider relocating to Broken Point? There's plenty of room. Michael could ride the ferry over to work each day, or Earl has a boat he would be pleased to offer up. We could entertain and keep an eye on each other."

Michael looked to his mother who smiled and said, "I'll discuss it with our son."

Instinctively, Michael headed out to the truck, leaving his parents to say good-bye. Mary and Bud embraced for a long time before Bud left to catch the approaching ferry.

Hesitating, Bud turned and said, "I love you. I always have."

That evening, mother and son talked about Bud's offer. "Michael, I know you are upset with me for not telling you about your father. While we loved each other back then, our lives just didn't seem to be in tune. Your father was a poor kid from Shaw and I had your grandparents to deal with. They certainly didn't make it easy. I should have done more, but at the time I was used to living a privileged life and I was concerned about moving to Orcas. Besides, I didn't think your father was ready for a family. As time went by, it was just easier not to tell him, or you, of his existence, and make our way in Seattle with your grandparent's support. I love you and your father and hope you both will forgive me."

Michael took his mother in his arms and said, "You're forgiven."

CHAPTER 23

Michael stood gazing at the Kangaroo House and its surroundings. Smiling at his parents, he said, "Who would've thought?"

Bud returned the look with a satisfying grin. "Let's get your belongings across the spit before the tide comes up. Mary, drop that stuff and get yourself up to the house so you can tell us where to put everything when we get there."

Mary responded by sticking out her tongue, crinkling up her nose, advising, "You're not my boss," as she waded across in the shallows on up to the house.

While they had not discussed the sleeping accommodations previously, Mary directed that her clothes be taken up to the second-floor bedroom. Bud was pleased that she took the initiative without embarrassment or explanation. Michael headed upstairs with an arm full of her clothes without hesitation. Bud leaned over and kissed her cheek before following.

Michael moved into a vacant room on the ground floor. By now, the elderly house guest had shifted back to his own living quarters in the expanded shop.

That evening, having all retired to the library, Mary brought up the whereabouts of *Channel Runner*. The conversation drifted to how Bud had come to own the runabout followed by Mary's favorite story about eluding the Feds. Reciting the details of the encounter, she had everyone laughing in no time. She embellished the surfing fish incident, described stashing the whiskey on Blind Island and culminated with trying to get the revenuers to help unload their groceries back at Rosario. Reaching over taking Bud's hand, she concluded the story by stating, "It was that day on Blind Island that I came to love your father."

"All right, enough," she said, "Where's *Channel Runner?*"

"Hopefully, she's still sitting in the hull of a rusty freighter anchored in an island cove off South America."

Bud spent the next hours recounting the exploits of the last few months. He did not tell them everything but provided enough detail one would have difficulty misinterpreting the danger of such an undertaking. Mentioning they had confiscated some paintings and antiquities, both Mary and her son cast their eyes toward the seemingly out of place wall art. Glossing over the deaths of men by his own hand, Bud's depiction of the ordeal left little doubt there were Nazis who likely perished. At the same time, he clearly established that the renegades had eluded justice for their atrocities on innocent families. He did not mention his reunion with Mary's cousin in San Francisco.

It was nearing 10:30 when all agreed it was time to call it a night. Mary and Michael headed for their new accommodations. Bud indicated he wanted to check on Karoo to make sure she was bedded down in the shop as well as seeing how Earl was doing. After having a quick nightcap at his old friend's urging, Bud headed back to the house.

The bedroom was dark when Bud entered. He could see the outline of Mary already in bed. Quickly washing up, he got into bed trying to take care not to disturb her. Once situated ready to doze off, he felt a bare leg swing across him and a whisper, "If you think you're going to get away that easy, you're sadly mistaken."

Life began to fall into a comfortable routine. Michael caught the ferry if the weather was blustery, but otherwise took Earl's outboard boat to make the crossing to the store. Mary and Bud continued to grow closer, looking forward to each day. They usually did nothing out of the ordinary, just being together was all that either wanted. Their day might include a short beach walk or a boat ride.

Mary's energy began to slowly wane. She had good days as well as those that were not.

One day, Mary said, "Let's go over to Rosario today and see the figurehead off *America*."

"Great idea. We can take the skiff and pack a lunch," Bud replied.

"I'll size up your ship's figurehead for comparison," Mary said in a take-charge manner.

"Aye Captain," Bud responded with a sharp salute.

When she first mentioned the adventure that morning, Bud pretty much dismissed it as a good way to while away the day. It had now become clear she was serious. The conspiracy seemed to give Mary renewed energy, so they began to plot the heist. Bud knew he better get onboard with a plan or she might just figure out how to pull it off without him.

The last time Bud had seen the lady of *America*, as he now referred to her, he noticed that she had begun to show signs of wood deterioration. Her time for weathering out the winters in the elements was over if she had any chance of survival.

Motoring into the bay, the statuette came into view—a scene Bud had looked upon many times. "Now don't look too obvious," Mary commanded. "You need to figure how to make the switch."

Bud replied, "I'm sure I can figure it out. Without getting caught may be another matter."

The estate's new owner, an industrialist from California, stood watching from the dock as Bud and Mary approached. Once he recognized Bud, he shouted a greeting and stood ready to help rein in their boat. Their welcoming party owed a debt of gratitude to Bud and it showed. Bud and Earl had voluntarily spent a significant amount of time helping to guide Rosario's transition after the new owner took possession. Having spent a good part of their lives managing the complex, neither wanted it to languish under new ownership. Earl had stayed on call more or less permanently to provide history and continuity as requested. For his efforts, it was not unusual to see him there during a mealtime or as a whim guided him.

Donald Rheems and his wife kept the estate more private than the previous owners. She frequently stayed on the island while he returned to California for business. They seemed nice enough, although Mrs. Rheems did seem a bit eccentric. Being a fair distance from their California home led Earl and Bud to speculate why her husband might have acquired Rosario.

Joining her husband, Mrs. Rheems invited the new arrivals up to the house for afternoon tea. Mary seemed delighted with the prospect of lounging away some of the afternoon on the large open porch. Bud could have cared less. He did hope, however, that the occasion might afford an opportunity to learn about their comings and goings. Earl, who happened to be visiting, obliged when he too was asked to join the gathering.

Mary and Mrs. Rheems carried on an exhaustive conversation concerning the lack of social activities available on the island. Mary agreed with every insignificant point the wayward socialite put forth. Bud was beginning to wonder if his accomplice was forgetting their mission when she winked at him and said, "I couldn't agree more with your belief that one needs a break away from the backward ways of the islands. I miss the theater the most. Not to mention that there are hardly any events that give one an excuse to buy a new gown for an evening out."

"Oh, you are so right," Mrs. Rheems replied. "In fact, we are leaving the day after tomorrow for a visit to our home in Los Angeles. I have a thousand things I want to do that I can't do here. We have scads of dinner parties scheduled and we plan to attend a movie premiere. You know, Donald is a significant shareholder of Paramount Studios in Hollywood. When I get back, you will have to come over and I will tell you all about it."

After a bit more carrying-on between the two, Mary said, "This has been most enjoyable, but we must go. Please don't get up, we can see ourselves off."

Leaving their hosts and Earl, Mary and Bud departed down the same pathway they had taken to the beach so many years ago. Squeezing Bud's arm, Mary said, "So how did I do?"

"I'm glad I'm on your side," came the response.

They stopped for a minute next to the lady of *America* before continuing to the dock. Bud bent to retie a shoe that didn't need attention while Mary sized up their quarry.

It had been a good day for Mary.

A few days later, Bud arranged to borrow the same flatbed truck he had used to retrieve his shipment at the ferry dock. He had known the truck owner's family almost as long as he could remember. In those early years, Bud often helped harvest the family's field hay in exchange for a portion that would later be sold at the Shaw Store. Back then, Bud had worked for the current owner's father, Don. Now, his son Roderick had sons of his own to help work the 160-acre farm located in the island's central valley. As was common in the close-knit island community, once

Bud disclosed his need for the truck, Rod readily offered his and his eldest son's help to carry out the exploit.

Mary was up early the next morning preparing breakfast as the accomplices gathered. Being Sunday, Michael was home and looking forward to the day's adventure. The crew fed, Mary herded them to the foyer.

By mid-morning the intricately carved statue that had graced the foyer on Broken Point was crossing the tidal flow headed for her new home. The adults rode up front while the boys steadied their cargo in the rear.

"Now remember," Bud said as they all piled off the truck at their destination, "Just act like we know what we're doing and let me do the talking if challenged."

Carefully freeing lady of *America* from her concrete base pedestal, Bud's brow furled. The extent of rot along her back became painfully evident as black saw bugs scurried about in the soft damp wood. Shaking his head, he said, "We've rescued her none too soon. I can rebuild her, but she was nearing her life's end if she'd stayed."

The estate's caretaker sauntered down the pathway. A friend of Earl's, he had assumed Earl's oversight when he had moved to Broken Point.

"I'll take care of this," Mary said stepping in front of Bud to greet him.

"Good morning! What a great day!" she proclaimed.

"Hi everyone," the man replied. "What do you think you are doing?"

There was an authoritarian edge to his question disguising the fact that Earl had already done the legwork to foretell the caper.

Mary, unaware the new arrival already knew their mission soldiered forward undaunted, "Oh, as you can see the figurehead is rotted badly and nearing the end of her days. The one in the back of the truck is very similar and has a relatively full life ahead. But it's a secret, so don't breathe a word of it to anyone. The Rheems wouldn't want others to be aware it isn't the same statue looking over the estate as always."

Winking at Bud, the caretaker said, "She does look like she's in need of repair. And being Sunday, I'm pretty much the only guy around other than a housekeeper. I'll talk to her and direct her to keep her nose out of it. Mr. Rheems may have previously noticed the rot and bring it to my attention when he notices it miraculously repaired. I'll deal with it if he does."

As the caretaker headed back up the walk towards the house, Mary turned, looked at her crew and said, "Get back to work you bunch of loafers."

"I thought I was going to do the talking," Bud exclaimed.

"You're here because you have a strong back and nothing more," Mary announced happily.

They spent the next couple of hours positioning, trimming and fastening the substitute figurehead into place. They were especially careful to ensure the joint between her underside and the concrete stand was weather tight. Mary finished the effort with a generous coat of white paint while the men loaded *America's* lady for her trip home to Broken Point.

It was mid-afternoon by the time they forded lady of *America* across the ebbing channel to the workshop. Bud started to reach for his wallet, but Rod stopped him by raising his hand, "Don't you even think about it Bud. Just make sure you invite us over to help put her in the house. We signed on for the entire mission."

Rod and his boy were preparing to leave when Mary came around the end of the house and handed them a fresh salmon she and Bud had caught off the point the evening before. "Take this home and tell your wife you'll cook dinner."

"I'll gladly take it home," Rod replied. "I'll negotiate the cooking when I get there, but my guess is we would all be better served if I only do the eating."

Dust hanging above the two narrow-wheeled ruts leading away, Bud and his family watched the truck disappear inland.

It had been a good day for all.

Over the next few weeks after the exchange, Bud rose early each morning to restore lady of *America* back to her glory. Lovingly renewing her from her deteriorated state, he wished his Mary's health could be as easily mended with similar results. Afternoon outings became less frequent as her well-being steadily declined. Weight began to slip from her body as she ate less each day. Some days, Bud simply carried her petite frame down to the beach where the warm sun and soothing sounds of waves against the shore provided a sense of peace. They talked of earlier years and plans to bring *Channel Runner* home. It was on one of those outings that Bud knelt in the sand to ask Mary for her hand in marriage.

The wedding would be a simple affair taking place on the point beyond Kangaroo House. On the afternoon of the nuptials, guests, including Mary's parents who had come from Seattle, were greeted with a foot of rising water to traverse. Shedding shoes and socks, rolling up pants or hiking up carefully ironed summer dresses set the lighthearted mood of the day. A few guests resorted to the use of a rowboat for the crossing but suffered good-hearted jeering for their actions by those who had not. By the time Rod's oldest son and girlfriend arrived late, the crossing depth had risen above their knees. Carrying his lady above harm's way, the assembled guests rang out chants of support urging them forward. Stumbling, they settled not-so-gracefully into the glimmering blue water. Cheers rang out as the latecomers emerged triumphantly dripping head to toe whereupon they were ushered to their host's closets. Knowingly, Mary and Bud looked into each other's eyes—the reenactment reminding them of the day on Blind Island when they made love on the beach the first time.

The lady of *America*, having taken her place of honor in the entry hall, cast her spell through the open double doors as Michael steadied the bride to Bud's side. Taking Mary's arm from their son's, Bud whisper, "I have never seen you more beautiful."

By the end of the vows, when Bud bowed to kiss his Mary, there was nary a dry eye amidst those gathered. Mary's mother was especially emotional asking the happy newlyweds, in so many words, to forgive them for not believing love could have conquered all. It seemed the boy from Shaw had finally won them over.

The joyous event continued throughout the afternoon as adults mingled and children dressed in their Sunday best underwent a happy transformation playing tag with the waves and exploring the tide pools.

Coinciding with the setting sun melting into the horizon, transforming the sky to a yellow-orange glow, the accumulation of well-wishers slowly began to wane. A flood tide's rising waters having isolated them from the realities of life, Mary knew in her heart she would never see many of them ever again. Tears trickling down her cheeks, she sat in a chair watching everyone take their leave. With Michael positioned on the opposite side of the channel from Bud, the departing guests made their way in a rope tethered rowboat.

❈

The time had come for Michael to return to college in Seattle. But as expected, he was finding it difficult to leave his mother. At her insistence, he reluctantly agreed to start the fall quarter. He would take the convertible his father had given him. On the morning of his departure, mother and son held each other while she lay in the upstairs four poster bed. Unable to say the words in his heart, he rose from his knees choking back his sorrow. Struggling, he said, "I love you mom," and bolted for the stairs. Muffling his sobs of grief, Michael hurried past his father, waiting at the bottom of the stairs, and out onto the porch.

Pausing at lady of *America's* side, Bud waited for his son to gather his composure before joining him. Walking the trail together to the crossing, they said their somber goodbyes.

Mary's health continued to decline over the next few weeks. One morning sensing her time was near, Bud cocooned her frail body in the comforter atop the bed and carried her to the beach. A light rain began to fall. Her deep-set eyes looking longingly into his, she sensed their time together was coming to an end.

Cradling Mary's doll-like body, Bud dropped to his knees in the wet sand. Uncharacteristically, Karoo slowly approached, nuzzled Mary and dropped back.

A faint smile crossed Mary's lips as her labored breaths were no more—flowing red hair gently blowing about, *Channel Runner* carrying her across waves of blue towards the light.

Mary was laid to rest in the Shaw Island Cemetery near Mabel. The two women who held Bud dear would wait together for him to join them someday.

Over the next few months, Michael returned home to the Kangaroo House nearly every weekend. Initially bound together by their mutual loss, the friendship and fondness the two shared grew into a close father and son relationship. Bud was especially heartened one evening upon Michael's return when his son handed him a piece of paper documenting he had legally changed his last name to Fowler. Mary never leaving their thoughts, over several months her family's focus began to shift to the present and future instead of dwelling in the past.

Swirling snow whitewashed Broken Point sculpturing accumulations atop dock pilings and edges of the covered porch. Seemingly oblivious to the grand display, a legion of ducks fidgeted aimlessly in the raven colored waters. Waddling onto the near shore, triangular-shaped impressions trailed behind. An eagle swooped from the whiteness scattering the close-knit congregation in an unsuccessful attempt at snagging a meal. Not a bird of prey's first choice to curb an appetite, but winter required adaptation to one's surroundings.

In the last year of his engineering studies, Michael had arrived home for the holidays just as the shoreline's white transformation had begun. It had been just over a year since his mother had passed. As the snowfall continued to spin its tranquil spell, Bud and his son retreated to the library to the warmth of a blazing fire.

"Michael, I'm thinking about going back to South America to reclaim *Channel Runner*."

"You should go. I know that boat meant a lot to mom and you. She would have wanted you to bring her back home. But if you go, I'm going with you."

Bud said nothing nor took his eyes off the hypnotic flames. While pleased his son would want to be with him, he wondered what dangers could lay ahead.

Michael, sensing his father's concern, blurted, "Dad, I know mom wouldn't want us separated."

"We'll cross that bridge when and if the time comes," Bud replied.

Talking well after nightfall had obscured the view beyond the eaves, they finally headed off to bed after Michael caught one of his father's yawns.

Bud lay awake until after midnight. It was time to fill Michael in on the details surrounding his abandonment of the *Adventurer*. His son needed to understand all the potential pitfalls in their quest to retrieve *Channel Runner*.

The next day after breakfast, Bud asked Michael to come to the library. Once they were seated and had fresh cups of coffee in hand, Bud began, "When I previously told you and your mother the story of leaving the *Adventurer*, there were many details I didn't disclose. We need to talk about the danger should we decide to go."

Bud spent the next hour filling in the blanks concerning everything leading up to his seizure of the submarine and his ultimate return to Kangaroo House. He told of the men killed along the way, leaving out only the death of Mary's cousin in San Francisco. As he recounted his belief that there were those who would possibly kill to get back what they thought rightfully theirs, Michael listened intently to Bud's account of the events without uttering a word.

Finally, Bud stood and motioned his son to follow, "I have something to show you."

Hesitating at the beginning of the stairway to the second floor, Bud said, "No one knows of this, not even your mother."

Bud leaned down, lifted the lower stair section revealing a dark emptiness. Wide-eyed, as if having discovered the entrance to Tut's tomb, Michael followed his father into the mysterious unknown.

Part way down the steep stairs, Bud found the switch that lit the rock passageway. Reaching the heavy door that guarded the cavern, Michael pushed up against his father with anticipation. Thrusting the door open, the dimly lit void ahead beckoned them on. Lights illuminated, Michael was spellbound.

"Michael, I don't exactly know what the value of all this stuff is, but I can tell you that over the ages many have sought to possess it. I thought once about showing this room to your mother but decided she would only worry. And God knows she already carried enough of a burden."

After a cursory look at the room's contents, another door indicated there was more. Opening it, Bud showed his son the connecting access to the outside workshop.

Back in the library, Bud revealed there were still a few valuables left behind in both *Adventurer* and *Channel Runner*.

"Dad, when do we go?"

"We have some time to think about it. If we go, it will be after your graduation."

That June, Bud watched from the audience as his son graduated from college with honors in Civil Engineering. Tears trickled down his face as Michael raised his diploma over his head and looked to where his father sat. His chest heaved in jubilation for his son then turned to grief for Mary as an audible sob rose uncontrollably from within.

CHAPTER 24

1947

The Pan Am Clipper's four massive engines revved ever faster propelling the huge silver plane across San Francisco Bay. Plowing water as if she might never take flight, Michael turned to his father and said, "I guess it's too late to change our minds, huh?"

Bud tried to disguise a nervous grin. With the plane's overall length exceeding 100 feet and a wingspan of just over 150 feet, it was a wonder the gangly machine could fly. Picking up speed, the clipper began to break her binds unsteadily across the wave tops in the sundrenched mist. Finally, the slapping echoes against the aluminum hull eerily stopped as the craft lumbered into the sky. Gaining elevation, clearing the Golden Gate Bridge, a postcard view lay beyond her wingtips.

The plane's destination was Rio de Janeiro. Flying at a cruising speed of one-hundred and fifty-five miles per hour, the flight time would take some forty hours. They would stop twice to refuel and sleep.

Once aloft, the passengers settled in for the first leg of their long flight while stewardesses shuttled about serving breakfast. It was the first flight for either Bud or Michael. Bud was a bit nervous while his son seemed eager for the adventure. Michael sat next to the window taking in the views while his father was content just being on an adventure with him.

Later in the morning, wanting to stretch his legs, Bud stood and headed down the narrow passageway toward the restrooms. Snickering to himself, he wished there was a way to nail a seagull out of the air with the crap he was about to take—retribution for being at the end of their deadly aim over the years. Meandering back to his seat, Bud took note of some of their fellow passengers. Most were nicely dressed to match the elegance of flying. Noteworthy were a family with three daughters, an elderly couple returning home as hinted by their intermittent speaking of both English and Portuguese, and a pair of newlyweds made obvious by their love-struck cuddling.

Nearing his son, Bud stopped. His empty seat was occupied by a stewardess. Reversing his path, he wandered back to the galley area. Draining the last of his coffee cup, Bud was beginning to wonder if he was destined to make the rest of the trip standing at the rear of the plane. As if hearing his thoughts, the young woman vacated his seat. She a bit red faced, the two smiled at each other as they jostled past one another in the narrow confines. Sitting back down, noting the telltale lingering warmth of the previous occupant, Bud looked knowingly at Michael. Leaning his seat back, closing his eyes, he said, "Well at least she has a warm butt."

Having previously cautioned Michael about discussing any aspect of their journey to anyone or anywhere they could be overheard, their long flight passed uneventfully. They ate and drank well, read newspapers and magazines, napped and conversed about nothing in general.

Finally, the Captain broadcast over the cabin speaker that they were beginning their final approach to Rio and that everyone needed to be sure their seat belt was buckled. The announcement spurred the stewardesses to gather wayward glassware and such, taking special note to be sure everyone was indeed strapped in. When Michael saw the same attractive stewardess that paid him a visit heading down the passageway, he glanced sidelong at his father, smiled and unbuckled his seat belt.

Upon reaching Michael's row, the blue uniformed flirtatious maiden stopped and directed, "Please buckle your seat belt sir."

To his father's disbelief, Michael fumbled with the two ends of the belt and announced, "I can't seem to get it to work. I believe I could use some assistance."

Even more surprising, the stewardess leaned across, took both ends of the belt and buckled them together giving the top of the clasp a little pat. She then announced with a southern drawl, "There, that should do y'all for now."

Michael beamed as she continued down the passage. Bud thought the stewardess' playful antics were reminiscent of something Mary might do.

Low over the water, the gleaming flying boat passed directly overhead of a small flotilla of fishing boats plying the harbor. Michael pointed out a man and a boy in one boat as the great ship descended. The boy waved as the plane touched and skimmed atop the bay's brilliant surface. If it weren't for the radiating echo of the water on the craft's hull, one might not have detected that they were no longer soaring above the clouds.

Engines slowing, the plane settled heavily into the sea. Then, all was quiet as the propellers stopped their rotation and the craft drifted alongside a float to a waiting shore crew.

Humid air cascaded inward as the plane's door swung open. Michael and Bud gathered their few belongings and jockeyed for the exit. Stepping onto the floating pier, Bud made his way over the walkway connection to shore.

It took Bud a moment to realize that his traveling companion was no longer behind him. He had been detained by the playful stewardess.

Waiting, his son finally zeroed in on his whereabouts and caught up.

"Guess what," Michael exclaimed, "The crew is staying at the same hotel as us and I…ah, *we*, have a dinner date."

"*We* have a dinner date?" Bud questioned.

"Well, ah…, if you want to join us," came his son's less than enthusiastic response.

"I can't believe I'm being dumped for a set of gorgeous legs," Bud muttered within earshot of his son. Taken off guard by his father's knowing response, Michael followed with a Cheshire Cat grin.

Sitting alone at the hotel bar that night, Bud ate before whiling away the rest of the evening walking a few blocks either way of the hotel. Returning about 10:00, he decided to get a nightcap before heading up to his room.

Entering the bar, he noticed Michael and his dinner companion cuddled in a far corner.

Taking a seat at the polished wood bar at the opposite end of the room, Bud ordered his customary scotch. No sooner having taken possession of his drink, an attractive lady of local descent took the next stool. Her revealing attire hinting at her probable profession, Bud consumed his drink in one swallow. Leaving a five-dollar bill, he told the bartender to keep the change after buying the next stool's occupant a drink. The lady looked dismayed at Bud's hasty exit, thanking him in broken English.

Bud took note that Michael and his lady friend were nowhere to be seen.

The next morning, his face partly covered in shaving cream over the bathroom sink, Bud was interrupted by a single rap on his door. Thinking that Michael was up and about from his room across the hall, Bud nonchalantly left the bathroom.

A piece of paper had been slid under the door. Stooping to retrieve it from the floor, Bud gingerly unfolded it with wet hands.

The note, written in clear English, simply said, *"If you expect to see your son alive again, be in the lobby in 30 minutes."*

Throwing open the door, Bud bolted into the hallway. The stairway door at the end of the corridor was just closing. Dressed only in boxer shorts, Bud ran down the hallway and shoved open the door. Hesitating on the stairway landing, straining for a sign to go up or down, he heard a door close below. Vaulting down the stairs three at a time, he flung the door open on the next landing only to find himself standing in a vacant hallway.

A couple exited their room and headed his way. While they both displayed quizzical looks on their faces, she alone gave Bud the once over and raised her eyebrows as they passed.

Bud hurried back to his floor via the same route he came.

Racing to Michael's room, Bud pounded on the door. There was no answer.

Reentering his own room, the door still wide open, Bud washed the remaining lather from his partially shaven face, dressed quickly and headed down the hallway to the elevator. Changing his mind, he took the stairs. Upon entering the lobby, he spied the crew from the previous day's flight assembled for breakfast in the coffee shop. Michael's dinner companion was among them.

Briskly crossing the room, Bud approached the stewardess. Taking her arm with little conversation, he led her away from the group. Startled by the forcefulness of his actions, she nevertheless went along without causing undue alarm.

"When did you last see Michael?" Bud demanded.

Looking around to be sure they were out of range of the others, she stammered, "Well ah," hesitating, "Why do you need to know?"

"Listen," he said. "Michael is missing, and I need to know when you last saw him!"

The stewardess flinched and said quietly, "Michael escorted me back to my room about two-thirty this morning."

"Thanks," Bud said leaving her standing alone while she and the other crew members watched him disappear into the lobby.

Bud scanned the area for some acknowledgment from the room's few occupants. Receiving none, he paced nervously back and forth across the varnished mahogany floor. "How could I have been so fucking stupid to have brought Michael along on such a foolhardy adventure? How'd they know I was back?"

More than a half hour had come and gone since Bud had received the note. Fearful, another agonizing ten minutes passed as incoherent thoughts muddled his mind.

Then, on cue, an evil looking man with piercing blue eyes rose from a chair in the far corner and walked towards Bud. The recognizable figure had been disguised the whole time by a hat and newspaper. It was Major Otto Günsche.

The German accent was prominent as the man simply said, "Your son awaits."

Günsche headed towards the lobby exit, not even bothering to see if Bud was trailing. Like an obedient dog, Bud followed his foe out into the bright sunlight. The doorman signaled a taxi, stepped to the curb and opened the rear door of the vehicle. Placing some coins in the door-man's hand, the Nazi stepped into the cab.

Bud faltered at the curb.

Günsche looked at his quarry with an expression that conveyed what they both knew. Smirking, the former high-stepper was back in command.

Bud got in the waiting vehicle.

The taxi ride lasted only minutes before pulling up in front of what appeared to be an older building undergoing extensive renovation. With exception of the upper floor, a caged framework held locals scurrying about their trade.

Günsche stepped from the car with an unwilling Bud in tow. Weaving their way through the jumble of construction debris, Otto led Bud to a waiting elevator. An operator inserted a key into a brass panel triggering the elevator to life. Jerking to a start, the occupants began an upward journey measured by an arrow arching across a brass numbered face.

Heartless eyes riveted on the elevator's prisoner as the door slid opened onto the fifth-floor penthouse. "So, our paths cross once more Mr. Fowler. Welcome back," Frans said. "Did you really think you could return without my knowledge? Are you so naïve to think I don't have associates in customs watching for your name after what you took from me?"

Without hesitation, stepping from the brass adorned caged platform, Bud scanned the room for his son, "Where's Michael?"

"Patience comrade," gesturing the new arrival towards an adjoining room. The chamber's opulence was over the top. Richly decorated furnishings, Persian carpets and antiquities suffocated the space. Heavy gold framed paintings hung everywhere.

With the help of a henchman acting as translator, Frans began, "You have something I want, and I have something you want. Are we not intelligent men who should be able to arrive at a mutually acceptable solution to our quandary?"

"What do you want?" Bud said.

"You know what I want. I want what was mine before you absconded with it."

"You're going to have to be more specific," Bud replied.

Nazi eyes narrowing, Fran's blurted impatiently to Günsche in German, "I am not in the mood for a give and take conversation! I want the paintings, antiquities and whatever money he has left from the sale of the gold. I intend to see that he suffers for his foolhardy ways."

Fran's undecipherable statement to Otto heightened Bud's nervousness as his eyes fell upon a small narrow pedestal near the dining area. It was the piece he had confiscated from the ill-fated German passenger and left onboard the *Adventurer*. Carved with simple upward sculpturing, it brought one's eyes to a point that seemed to lack a final pinnacle.

With Günsche aiding as an interpreter as necessary, the dialogue between Frans and Bud continued.

"I guess there is no reason to deny I have some of the paintings you seek. What assurance do I have that you will let my son and I go unharmed if I identify their whereabouts?" Bud asked.

Frans studied Bud for an uncomfortably long period before responding, "You spared my life a number of months back when you didn't need to. And, I suppose there is some honor among us that would deem that I do the same for you. That is, if I get what I want."

At that instance, a side door opened, and Michael entered the room accompanied by none other than Katarine. Bud stood from his seated position. She looked gorgeous as usual, cloaking her manipulating and conniving ways. Nevertheless, Bud was shocked to see her still associated with the Nazi clan.

Signaling her allegiance, Katarine cast an expressionless glance toward Bud, walked to Frans' side and took his arm.

Bud wondered if Frans had any idea about the intimacy he and Katarine had experienced while he had been holed up recovering from his surgery. Bud looked directly into Katarine's eyes until she uncomfortably turned her head away.

Michael's face showed his fear.

"My son knows nothing of the items you want. Let him return to the United States. When I have confirmation that he is safe, I will make arrangements for the paintings and other valuables to be returned. I have some of the money from the sale of the gold, but not all."

"Secondly, if you are going to strip me of all my possessions, I need agreement that you will let me retrieve my freighter without obstruction."

Frans responded, "You obviously know that we are aware of your vessel's location. You disclosed that when you recognized the pedestal in the corner of the room. While a reckless act, I understand why you attempted to possess it. It is of significant religious and historical value. Unfortunately, the gold crucifix that once adorned the top is nowhere to be found. Dr. Joseph Mengele was last to know but can no longer convey its whereabouts. I must ask you, Captain Fowler, if you ever saw or know where it could be?"

Bud simply shook his head as he glanced at Katarine's expressionless face.

Without responding to Bud's last offer of exchange for Michael's freedom, Frans said something in German without aid of translation and the captives were escorted to a room down an adjoining hallway.

Bud gave his son a fatherly hug as the door locked behind them, "I should have known better than to come back. It was stupid."

The windowless room was generally void of amenities other than a narrow bed without covers, a table with two straight-back chairs and an empty chest of drawers. A small adjoining bathroom contained a toilet and sink. Bud and Michael sat down at the table and talked through their predicament and, more importantly, how they might escape if Frans didn't accept their offer of exchange.

Frans' concocted story of wanting to escape the clutches of the Nazis was clearly a ruse. And, there was little doubt in Bud's mind that the Nazis would most certainly kill them once they got what they wanted. He knew what Frans looked like after he had gone to great length to change his identity. Katarine had presumably killed Josef Mengele because he could identify Frans before and after surgery. And, unbeknownst to Bud, Frans thought Bud may have discovered his identity before his face altering procedure.

Of additional worry was the possibility that Frans would devise a plan to force his captives to disclose the antiquities' whereabouts. Torture was not a concept that had eluded the Nazi regime. Having Michael in the mix made Bud fearful at the possibilities. He had to do something and had to do it soon.

Accompanied by one of the Nazi goons, Katarine brought the prisoners a few morsels of food later in the day.

"So, you're just going to stand by and watch him kill us?" Bud asked in a traitorous voice. She looked at him without emotion as she set the tray down and left the room followed by her gun wielding accomplice.

With a look of disbelief, Michael said, "She isn't the lady you mentioned in your story before stealing the sub?"

Bud dropped his head slightly forward signaling affirmation. If only I had disposed of him when I had the chance," Bud said. "Not only do we need to escape, but I now know Frans is their leader and we will never be free of him if he's still alive."

Pacing the floor of their cell-like room, Bud tried to devise a plan.

Finally, Bud said to Michael, "What do you think about this?"

An air of nervous anticipation permeated the hot, humid room. It was late, and the captives had been expecting someone to either bring them something for their evening meal or conduct a final check for the night. Waiting, the scene was set. Michael sat in a wooden chair next to the table. Prone, Bud hugged the floor between the bed and the wall. Palmed in Bud's hand was a small-diameter metal rod taken from the workings of the bathroom toilet tank. The flapper of the toilet tank had been propped open gurgling as though someone had just flushed it. Slightly ajar, the bathroom door emitted a narrow beam of light into the dimly lit room.

A key sounded in the lock followed by one of Frans' lackeys entering the room carrying a tray of food. Glancing at the bathroom, the Nazi fixated on Michael as his intended target. A window of opportunity presenting itself without having to deal with the senior Fowler, the guard stepped up his game. Quickly setting the tray on the table, he motioned with a wave of his gun towards the hallway beyond. Michael did not respond to his silent command.

The German's back towards the bed, Bud sprung from his hiding place. Taking two noiseless steps, he grabbed the guard from behind and jabbed the toilet rod forcefully against his neck. Instantly at his father's side, Michael slammed their assailant's gun wielding hand with a chunk of busted wood from the chest of drawers sending the Luger rattling to the floor. Together in quick motion Bud and Michael lifted the Nazi onto the bed and pushed his face into the mattress to muffle any outcry.

Probing the thin steel rod nearly to the point of penetration, the enemy went limp. Taking a wad of cloth from his shirt pocket, Bud crammed it into the man's mouth. Michael retrieved the gun from the floor. The Nazi's hands and feet were bound with strips of cloth torn and made ready from the underside of the mattress.

Sneaking cautiously into the darkened hallway, Bud and Michael hesitated to plot their best means of escape. Beyond the elevator down the hallway they could hear muffled voices. At the opposite end of the corridor, lights beyond beckoned them to a large partially open window.

Bud pushed the window fully open and poked his head out. The street below was teeming with crowds of locals making their way to and from the area restaurants and drinking establishments. About a half floor down and slightly to one side laid a run of scaffolding. They could no doubt make the jump to the platform, but at what cost? Bud placed his finger to his lips and held his open palm up signaling Michael to stay.

Returning quickly to the room they had just left, Bud found their captive thrashing about on the bed trying to break his bindings. Placing the confiscated gun against the wide-eyed man's temple, the Nazi stopped moving—the message conveyed without a sound. Grasping the mattress, Bud lifted and dumped the Nazi onto the floor.

The mattress trailed Bud out of the room and down the hallway. Dangling it out the window, Bud swung it side to side gaining momentum before launching it towards the scaffolding. Landing on its edge, the mattress teetered before finally toppling flat atop the platform.

Poised on the window ledge, Michael was ready to make the jump when an adjoining hallway door opened. Katarine stepped into view. Her choice of hot weather sleepwear did little to disguise her ample tits. She held a gun to her side.

"And where do the two of you think you are going?" she whispered softly.

"So," Bud thought, "At least she hasn't raised the troops yet."

Knowing that someone would be looking for the guard at any minute, Bud said nothing prodding Katarine to make the next move.

"Help me," she mouthed without explanation.

Bud did not reply for fear of being heard by others. He motioned his son to jump.

The scaffolding shook violently as Michael collapsed onto the mattress-covered platform. Quickly signaling he was okay, he beckoned his father.

Bud stepped upon to the ledge. Katarine raised her gun in his direction tightening her finger on the trigger. Firing, the gun shattered the window frame near his head. Giving her a look of gratitude, Bud propelled himself off the ledge as another wayward round sounded.

Landing, quickly assuring Michael he was not hit, they began a panicked descent. A volley of bullets splintered the wood framework around them part way down. Horrified, Bud could tell Michael was the intended target.

As the crowd dispersed in terror, Frans shouted, "Thieves, we've been robbed."

Two of the next barrage of bullets hit Michael from below dropping him instantaneously to the deck of the second-floor scaffolding.

"Surrender!" a man aiming a gun from the sidewalk shouted out. It was Günsche.

"Save your son. We will send for a doctor," Frans added from above.

Bud yelled, "Hold your fire," as he moved down to comfort his son. Michael had been hit in his upper leg and side above the hip. Pain etched across his face, pleading eyes searched his father's face for help.

An open second story window was only a step away. Bud whispered, "We're going through the window."

Michael nodded as Bud squeezed off a rapid-succession of bullets into Günsche, lifted and dragged Michael through the opening.

Crumpling, the SS Major dropped to the ground.

An exploding gun from above rained a hail of bullets in vain.

Bud half carried, half dragged, Michael to the rear of the unoccupied building and down a set of stairs where they disappeared into a garbage-clogged alley.

Frans knelt next to the religious pedestal moving his hand across the area where the missing crucifix once reigned. Listening in anger, one of his henchmen relayed they couldn't find the two Americans. Becoming more agitated as the events unfolded, the Nazi leader began ranting and raving incoherently—furious that his band of incompetents had allowed Captain Fowler to pull off such a stunt.

Exhibiting little remorse for Otto Günsche's grave state, Frans shouted, "How dare they continue the deception. Find them. Search his ship again."

Katarine entered the room as the informants were escaping into the elevator. Recognizing Frans' impaired state, having been the brunt of his recurring wrath in the past, she turned to leave. But before she could break away, Frans grabbed her by the arm, whirled her around and shouted, spittle hitting her face, "Have you heard the news?! Your American has vanished without a trace!"

"Well, you both seem to have something in common," she said mockingly as she tried in vain to twist herself free.

Yelling, Frans tightened his grip, "Where is your loyalty *fraulein*? How is it your Bud Fowler always seems to be one step ahead of us?"

Knowing she had already said too much, Katarine did not respond.

His unbalanced state escalating, Frans demanded, "I know you to be an expert marksman. How did you miss them at such a close range?"

"How can you question my allegiance? I have done everything you have asked of me, including killing Joseph Mengele."

Trying to mask her fright, she stepped to him obediently.

"Enough," he shouted wildly throwing her to the floor. Hovering, fists clenched, he dropped to the floor and grabbed her hair. Wrenching her head to face him, he bellowed, "I have given you everything and you repay me with treachery!"

Terror etched across her face, Katarine knew she was about to suffer the brunt of her Fuhrer's instability. Thrashing and kicking to free his clutches, her foot struck the holy pedestal knocking it crashing to the floor.

Reacting as if it were he who had been injured, Frans moved to cradle and comfort the splintered wood stand as if a fallen child.

Sensing the opportunity, his back to her, Katarine dragged herself beyond his reach. Struggling to her feet, she bolted down the hallway. Consumed by panic, hearing his footsteps in pursuit on the marble floor, she charged into her bedroom slamming the door. Her trembling hands fumbled with the lock as time ran out. At the last instance, as the knob was grasped from the hallway, the lock clicked into place.

Echoes reverberated throughout the apartment as Frans attempted to beat the door into submission. Katarine frantically groped for her Luger on the night stand.

"Open it," he demanded wildly. "Open it or I will kill you bitch!"

Knowing it was only a matter of time before the door gave way, in a state of peril, she fired round after round into the door until there was only the sound of an empty clip.

Was he dead?

Eyes and nose streaming, needing to escape before his henchmen returned, she listened at the door. There was no sound. Holding her breath, she turned the key and cautiously twisted the knob. The mechanism felt tight as if there was a weight against it.

Fearing the worst, she fumbled to relock it, but it was too late. The door burst open catapulting her to the floor. His face contorted in pain, blood oozing from a gaping neck wound, Frans wavered defiantly before hurling himself atop her.

Crying out in agony as if somehow it might ease the pain, Katarine knew her life was over.

Salvation—his body was nothing more than dead weight.

Straining, she pushed him off and rose to her feet.

Wailing out like an injured creature, grasping at freedom beyond her reach, a death-like grip seized her ankle.

CHAPTER 25

AN OLD BEAT-UP PICKUP HEADED SOUTH THROUGH THE NIGHT distancing the Fowlers from their captors. The vehicle came from a somewhat inebriated couple who claimed ownership. More than the jalopy's worth, Bud's gold watch and a fistful of dollars drove the exchange.

In obvious pain, his gut area bloody, the bullet that hit Michael in the side appeared to have entered and exited. The other bullet remained lodged in his leg.

By daybreak, they came upon a town with a clinic. Having Michael under a doctor's care was paramount, but Bud knew they were still in dire straits. Asking little, as if routine, a young doctor inspected Michael's wounds. Attending to the entrance and exit path of the gut shot, the doctor stitched and dressed the torn flesh. He felt no vital organs had been imperiled. Moving on to his patient's leg, the doctor inspected the bullet's entry in the upper thigh muscle. No exit of the bullet was found.

"I am going to have to find and remove the bullet," the doctor said. "It will be painful as we currently have no drugs to dull it."

Bud grimaced at the news. "Michael, you heard the doctor. Are you up to it or do you want to continue on and try to find another clinic?"

"Let's get it over with dad."

The doctor gave the patient a cupped piece of rubber and asked Michael to place it in his mouth between his teeth. He next strapped

Michael down to the table over his hips and at the knee. "This is going to hurt. Please help restrain your son."

Bud leaned over Michael in a bear hug position announcing they were ready.

The doctor cut deep into the entry wound with his scalpel. The sudden sharp pain caused Michael to twinge, bite down on his mouthpiece and wail. His eyes watered. Next the doctor pushed his finger into the wound as far as he could. Michael stiffened in pain while Bud held him tight.

"There you are," the doctor announced as he removed his finger and grasped a long pair of forceps. Inserting them into the pathway of the bullet he explored the area momentarily until closing the handles together and removing a lead slug.

Michael nearly blacked out from the pain.

"The worst is over," the physician announced as he drenched the area in antiseptic and began stitching the wound. Given time, the doctor indicated the only lasting effects of the ordeal should be a few scars.

The physician warned the Fowlers, "These wounds need to be attended often. They will need ongoing antiseptic treatment and clean bandages for the next couple of weeks to ward-off infection. He also needs a pint of blood but, we have little reserves."

"I'm his father. I should be a match."

Michael received a transfusion after a confirming compatibility test. While his son rested, Bud was able to negotiate a pillow and blanket from a nurse for their continued southward escape. After a few hours, against the doctor's advice, Bud made the difficult decision to get back on the road in an effort to distance themselves from those who might be in pursuit.

Helping transfer Michael into the truck's crammed cab, the doctor again cautioned the patient's need for rest and care. Placing fifty dollars into the doctor's shirt pocket, Bud said, "I ask that you say nothing should anyone inquire about us."

The clinic receded in the rear-view mirror as the old truck continued unimpeded. A few hours later, Michael, needing a reprieve from the constant joggling of washboard roads, they came upon a sizeable coastal village. Searching the dirt side roads, they found a dilapidated hotel. Making Michael as comfortable as possible in their tattered room, Bud went in search of something for them to eat. In less than twenty minutes, he was back juggling a smorgasbord from a nearby cantina. Having eaten little over the last twenty-four hours, the parolees devoured the local fare before settling in for night.

While Bud considered trying to get Michael on the first flight home, he was also cognizant their would-be captors might have the area airports and ports under surveillance. And clearly, Michael's condition wasn't conducive to traveling incognito.

Over the next few days, Bud and Michael continued their trek in the direction of Buenos Aires. Never missing a beat, their pickup plodded onward as long as she was fueled and received generous amounts of engine oil to replenish her smoky trail.

Some three hundred miles north of Buenos Aires, the escape vehicle rolled to a stop at another objectionable looking inn. Once Michael was settled in their room, Bud returned to the hotel desk. A tarnished desk bell prodded the attendant out of his stupor—his appearance a match for the seedy work surroundings.

"What wrong?" he muttered to Bud in broken English.

"We're fine," Bud replied unconvincingly as he unfolded a small piece of paper on the counter. "I need directions to La Paloma."

Shuffling through the clutter surrounding him, the clerk produced a dog-eared map. A variety of sundry stains and scribblings was a testament to it having endured more than its intended use. Repeatedly rubbing the back of his hand across his unshaven stubble, the local tried to jog his clouded mind. Leaning over the map, the reek of alcohol and body odor emanating from the proprietor caused Bud to retreat a step. The man studied the seemingly unfamiliar territory as if an uninformed tourist.

"Paloma. Paloma. There," the man spewed, placing an unkempt finger on the spot.

The town was located about 75 kilometers further south down the coast.

"Thanks," Bud said on the move seeking refuge from the tainted air.

Upon returning to their room, Michael stirred and asked, "Well, what'd you find out?"

"A friend I hope may be able to help us is not that far from here. I'm going to run down the coast and see if I can find her. I shouldn't be back too late. You need to rest anyway. I'll go across the street to the cantina to find something for you to eat later."

Arms filled with provisions, Bud jockeyed the room's door closed. The variety of foodstuffs included fruits, a bottle of red wine, can of spaghetti and some bread. Placing the items within Michael's reach, Bud said with a smile, the first Michael had seen in days, "And last, but not least, here's a can opener with a cork screw handle. Sorry the spaghetti will be cold. If I get back early enough, I'll find something else."

"Michael, if for the unlikely reason I don't return by morning, I want you to contact the U. S. Consulate and have them make arrangements for you to return home. The drunk manning the desk should be able to summon the local official. It goes without saying you need to be careful who you trust. There's nothing to worry about, but who knows, I could get run down by a horde of donkeys."

"I don't like the idea of separating," Michael replied with a concerned look.

"Everything will be alright. It's just that I want to make sure that my contact is still in the area and hasn't been found by the Nazis."

Rattling to a stop, the old pickup arrived at the sleepy village of La Paloma as the mid-afternoon coaxed children home from their daily lessons. Having brought the piece of paper Ana had scrawled some two years prior, he had little difficulty deciphering her directions. He strolled up a cobble-stone path. The area was far from affluent, but the folks milling about seemed content as they went about their daily lives. A few of the locals eyed Bud curiously, but most acknowledged him with a smile or wave. Rambunctious children dressed in white shirts and blue trousers or skirts happily accompanied him on his way.

Wavering when the neatly kept white washed cottage came into view, Bud wondered if he should have come. Paying little mind to his short-lived deliberations, he proceeded toward the house.

Knocking on the frame of the open door, a young girl bounded up the stairs as an aged, motherly type appeared. Calling out, the girl rushed across the porch to her waiting arms.

After dismissing the blue-skirted girl, the plump lady said to Bud in her native language, "Can I help you?"

Bud nervously cleared his throat and replied, "Ana?"

Hesitating, the lady looked at him suspiciously and said, "No, don't know her."

While Bud only understood a word or two, he handed her the piece of paper with Ana's directions to the house. Placing his hand on his chest, he said, "Bud Fowler."

Identifying her daughter's writing, and possibly Bud's name, the women stepped forward and shook Bud's hand, "Of course. I am Ana's mother. She's at the clinic and will not be home for another hour. Please sit," pointing to a chair on the porch.

Bud accepted the invitation and sat down as she disappeared. Momentarily she returned with a glass of lemonade. While Bud downed his drink, Ana's mother said, "This is my granddaughter Yvette. Her father drowned three years ago."

Bud understood little and struggled to make small talk. Finally, he rose from his seat and said, "Thank you. I will come back later."

Walking to the town square to while away some time, Bud took a table in an open-air cantina and ordered a beer. Observing the comings and goings of the locals, he found himself suspiciously considering if anyone seemed out of place. Tipping his bottle up for the last swallow, she came into view. Her conservative white uniform, complete with a little cap, did little to disguise her beauty. He watched her saunter confidently through the marketplace. Should he wait until she reached home, and her mother had a chance to warn her or should he approach her now?

Setting aside the tomatoes she had gathered, Ana scanned the crowd as if she somehow knew.

Bud stood. Could she see past his unshaven face and pulled down hat? Her eyes locking onto him, she moved through the crowd towards him savoring the moment. Only a step or two separating them, she flung herself around his neck burying her face in his chest. "Well, I guess this answers the question of if you'd be glad to see me," Bud said.

She laughed through her tears and briefly put her lips to his. Bud wasn't sure how he felt about the kiss but made no gestures one way or the other.

Three nearby women who no doubt knew Ana whispered something to each other.

"I hoped I would see you again," she said quietly.

Returning to Bud's table, they ordered an early dinner of bread and fish. He advised her he had already been to her home. Partially through their meal, Bud began to highlight some of the events of the last few days. He talked briefly of his encounter with Frans and his henchmen disclosing that his son had accompanied him back and was laid up in a hotel. Ana's quizzical eyes disclosing her inner thoughts, Bud indicated that his son's mother had passed away.

Ana was awestruck that Frans and Otto would go to such lengths to capture Bud and his son.

Bud asked, "Do you think Frans or Otto could ever trace you to La Paloma?"

"I do sometimes worry about being found. But I had used my mother's maiden name when Otto falsely hired me to care for Alfred's mother. I also told them that I was from Buenos Aires. My father taught me to be leery of strangers until I am sure."

"Good girl," Bud responded.

"Why not bring your son to our house? I can help nurse him back to health. There's room. My daughter Yvette can double up with me."

Words Bud had hoped to hear when he set out to find her, he responded, "I could wish for nothing more. What about your parents?"

"There will be no concerns. My parents are aware that you saved my life. I also used some of the money you gave me to help pay for our home. In a way, it's your home. Besides, my mother and father are leaving in a few days to visit my grandparents."

Grandmother and granddaughter were sitting on the steps waiting as Ana and Bud made their way towards them. Yvette ran to her mother as they neared. Ana's mother rose and disappeared into the house. Climbing the few steps to the home's small veranda, Ana introduced Bud to her daughter as a very dear friend. Leaving Bud to fend for himself, she disappeared.

If Bud had difficulty conversing with Ana's mother earlier in the day, he was equally unprepared for the man who walked through the door onto the porch. Introducing himself as Ana's father, he asked Bud point blank, "Why have you come to La Paloma? And why have you come to see my daughter?"

Bud was gathering a response when Ana reappeared to rescue him. She looked beautiful. Her raven hair no longer bunched atop her head, she had discarded her uniform for a clingy low-cut dress as if needing to remind her guest what lie beneath.

Her father's furled brow didn't hide he wasn't particularly enamored with the transformation.

"I hate to go so quickly, but I need to get back," Bud said. Exchanging good-byes with everyone, he headed down the porch stairs with Ana. Strolling back to the truck, he reassured her that he and his son would return the next day. Rising on her tiptoes, Bud accommodated a brief parting kiss. The truck fired up and left her standing in a haze of exhaust.

Torn with thoughts of Mary, Bud was unsure what to think about Ana's not so subtle romantic sentiments. It appeared she wanted them to be more than just friends.

Michael was still awake when his father entered their hotel room.

"I don't mind telling you that I've been worried," Michael exclaimed gruffly.

"Hey," Bud responded, unscrewing the cap off a bottle of scotch whiskey. "I told you I would be back before it was too late. And 9:20 sure in hell isn't all that late."

Handing Michael a shot of whiskey, he went over the day's events, including locating his friend who offered to put them up for a while. They would leave in the morning. From there, Bud would begin the quest for *Channel Runner*.

Ana arranged to take the following day off from work. By the time Bud and Michael arrived in the late morning, Yvette's room had been reorganized into makeshift lodging for their guests. Ana's father was fishing, her mother had gone to the market and Yvette was in school.

Ana greeted Bud with a hug. Sensing Bud's restraint with his son present, she shifted her attention to Michael, ushering him into the house. Once Michael was settled into bed, Ana's nurse training kicked into play. Wasting little time, she demanded that she be allowed to inspect Michael's injuries. The leg injury appeared fine under the circumstances. She grimaced at the sight of the torso wound.

"I am going to go to the clinic to obtain some iodine and dressings to clean and bandage the area. I will be back shortly."

Michael looked to his father once she had left and asked, "Is this your friend? She sure seems nice. You didn't mention how pretty she is."

"Yeah," Bud replied without emotion, "She's the nurse from the Nazi sub I was telling you about. Now try to get some rest."

By the time Ana had returned from the clinic, Michael was asleep. Concerned about her patient's well-being, she pushed past Bud standing in the doorway without a word other than telling him to leave and close the door on the way out.

Ana spent the next hour with Michael cleansing and dressing his wounds. By the end of her nursing, borderline mothering, there was little doubt in Michael's mind that Ana considered his father more than just a friend. She didn't say anything, but he could tell by her comments and attention to his own care that she harbored feelings for his father. Michael wasn't quite sure what to think of the situation, but also understood his father had had a life before he and his mother unexpectedly reentered it.

Ana's family returned home in time for dinner. Bud ate at the table with the group while Michael took his dinner in bed. No doubt the outcome of Ana having talked with him, there were no more interrogating questions from her father.

The next day with Michael in better hands, Bud traveled further south where he had been told he could find an air service. Having little to choose from, he was able to locate a plane for hire. The pilot seemed competent enough when Bud inquired about his experience. The two-seat single engine plane on the other hand had clearly seen better days. Hoping the aviator didn't have some sort of death wish, Bud just had to trust the unseen mechanics of the craft. He told the pilot he was tourist and wanted to view the surrounding area. While having no destination in mind, he anticipated flying for an hour or so—first down the coast and then returning cross country. Hoping to seal the pilot's opinion that his passenger was just another sightseer, Bud asked a few dumb questions and agreed to a gringo rate that seemed high.

As Bud adjusted his backside to a poking wire in the tattered seat, the engine revved and responded to the pilot's command. Bud grabbed the plane's exposed interior frame and took a deep breath. Bounding down the grassy runway gaining speed, Bud stared transfixed at an approaching tree line. Finally, the plane lifted off, sputtered, touched back to earth, regained full power and soared up, barely clearing a grove of mango trees. Sober faced, Bud looked at his pilot who responded to the nonverbal communication by indifferently shrugging his shoulders.

Once aloft, they followed the coastline at about fifteen-hundred feet. The aerial views were truly spectacular as small fishing villages bordering brilliant blue waters came and went. Time had passed uneventfully when Bud spied the island on the horizon where he had abandoned *Adventurer.*

Nonchalantly Bud suggested, "Let's fly over that island."

"It's your trip," the pilot acknowledged banking the plane.

Bud perspired in nervous anticipation.

Nearing the anchorage site, the pilot dropped to just a hundred feet or so and began a tight circle around its jungle like perimeter.

"Look," the pilot exclaimed as they rounded the seaward side of the island, "There's an old freighter."

Bud simply nodded in agreement as the plane regained altitude on a westerly heading. Upon reaching the shoreline, the pilot suggested it was time to think about heading back. Hearing agreement, the aviator maneuvered the plane on an overland course towards their take off point. Along the way, Bud had the pilot sidetrack from time to time further instilling the idea their flight was nothing more than random.

Lost in thought, Bud contemplated the options ahead.

The plane's engine throttled back as they quickly lost altitude. Touching down, bouncing, the plane rolled to a stop off the side of runway in the taller grass. Thankful to be back on solid ground and having already paid for the flight prior to their departure, Bud headed for his truck.

The pickup jerked forward only to die. Revving and on the move again Bud steered across the end of the field towards the road back to La Paloma. Chugging along the coast roadway, Bud's mind was filled with questions surrounding *Adventurer.* From the brief sighting, it was apparent she was sitting low in the water. Her engine room could well be flooded. She might even be resting on the bottom of the cove. As for *Channel Runner,* her condition was entirely up for grabs. Contemplating the Nazis may well retrace their steps back to *Adventurer,* his trip's purpose was becoming increasingly clouded—should he just abandon *Channel Runner's* recovery? The painting and crucifix weren't worth losing a life. On the other hand, chances were Frans' troops hadn't discovered the area below his bunk or they would have mentioned it during the interrogation.

Ana bounded down the path towards Bud quelling his thoughts of *Channel Runner's* pursuit for the time being. Embracing, he felt fortunate to have someone back in his life. Her parents, taking Yvette, had left to visit relatives up the coast where they would be spending the night.

"How are you doing?" Bud asked his son.

"He's doing better," Ana chirped before Michael could open his mouth, "But he still has a way to go before he will be up and around."

Knowing he was in no condition to do much of anything else, Michael complained, "I'm already tired of doing nothing, but on the other hand, the food has been outstanding. I did hobble about a bit this afternoon."

Bud recounted the day's explorations disclosing his intentions to somehow still get aboard *Adventurer*. He would be leaving in a few days but didn't want to be in too much of a hurry for fear of running into Frans' henchmen.

Michael told his father that under the circumstances, the plan was foolhardy. Ana's face expressed the same. She began to voice her objection when Bud brought an end to it, "My mind is made up. It's something I'm going to do."

Looking squarely at his son, Bud said, "I think you need to get back to the States where you can stay with your grandparents."

Before Michael could offer opposition, Bud talked him through the facts, "We need to think of Ana and her family's safety as well as our own. The longer a couple of gringos are in the area, the higher the risk that Frans and his troops might stumble onto us. Besides Michael, if it becomes necessary to relocate or run, you will only slow me down and jeopardize any chance of escape."

Michael reluctantly agreed. He would return to Seattle as soon as practical.

After dinner, as the evening drew to an end, Michael was left to sleep while Ana and Bud retired to the cramped living room. Entwining, they talked well into the night before retreating to their respective sleeping accommodations.

CHAPTER 26

THE COASTAL FISHING VILLAGES BLURRED AS BUD DROVE THROUGHOUT the entire day toward his hopeful rendezvous with *Adventurer*. A day had passed since he had placed Michael on a homeward bound flight. It was gratifying to know that Michael was by now safe and sound in Seattle. At least regardless of the outcome of his own daring, if not foolhardy, mission, his son should no longer be in jeopardy.

Blending into the local surroundings, Bud wore baggy worn clothes, a straw hat atop unkempt hair and sported unshaven graying stubble. As darkness overtook the day, Bud reached the very town where he had left Ana those many months before. He found lodging for the night in an out of the way hotel—accommodations beneath the Nazi elitist's self-ordained stature. Once settled, he walked to the boat basin where he found a nondescript eatery. His disheveled appearance providing little draw to the locals inhabiting the establishment, he sat alone.

Up early the next morning, Bud donned the same disguise from the previous day and set out for the local flotilla of fishing dories. With him, he carried a gunny-sack containing a few provisions. Upon reaching the dilapidated wharf area, he found it alive with fishermen preparing for their daily ritual with the sea. The boats scattered throughout looked as if they had been crafted from the same set of design principles handed down over generations. Nearly all the multi-colored wood dories were powered by a single sail wrapped around an irregularly cut pole. All had rowing oars. Very few had outboards.

Bud walked amongst the orderly activity trying to identify a fisherman to his liking. Passing a well-weathered boat with a man of like characteristics, Bud was moving on when the old man gestured to him. The man's tanned face, wrinkled by years of enduring and surviving whatever life placed before him, was framed by snow-white hair. His calloused hands curved unnaturally, no doubt a result of pulling lines from the sea well beyond the length of time nature had intended.

Bud knelt alongside the dory and handed the boatman a dented rusty bucket of bait sitting on the dock. The old man placed it on the salt bleached deck under his rowing platform. Silence followed. No further acknowledgment of Bud's presence. Finally, raising his aged face, squinting into the morning sun, the old man said in surprising good English, "You're not from around here." He then returned to the task at hand.

Bud was about to respond when the man looked back to Bud and asked, "Did you find the food to your liking at the cantina last night?"

"A good eye, I like that." Surprised his cover had been blown so easily, Bud continued, "I have an offer for you that will earn you a week's worth of fishing. Do you know the offshore island about fifteen kilometers due south of here?

"The one with the freighter in its seaward cove?" the old man acknowledged glancing up to read his visitor's face.

"Yes, that's the one. How do you know of it?" Bud said guardedly.

"Some time ago there were some men who came to the village asking if any of us had seen anyone who might have come from the ship. None of us had. Few have gone to see it. Most find fishing better to the north," the man stated.

"How did you learn English?" Bud asked

"I was orphaned at an early age and raised by American missionaries."

Taking care not to disclose his actions to others still puttering about the area, Bud placed a few coins amongst the coiled fishing lines laid out on the paint worn seat.

The old man took Bud's sack setting on the float. Placing it in the stern, he motioned for Bud to follow. Retrieving the coins, he dropped them in the bucket amongst its herring-sized bait. It was only after this, that Bud learned the boatman's name was Juan.

The patchwork sail pulled them away towards the warmth of the rising sun as Juan worked the meager winds. Their destination finally sighted on the horizon by early afternoon, the white-haired man read-ied hooks and baited a few lines. Hand spooling out the lines, Juan said, "Just looking like fishermen isn't enough. You never know who might appear."

Nearing the inward side of the island, the fisherman landed three siz-able fish in rapid succession. Ignoring Bud's attempt to pick out a land-ing point, the old man headed directly into a small reef area containing a patch of sand at its end. It was apparent the boatman had visited the spot before. The sail dropped as the dory caught the sandy bottom.

Stepping into the warm tidelands, Bud surveyed the dense foliage beyond. A brief conversation ensued wherein it was agreed that Juan would return the next day. For his efforts, he would claim twice the *reais* received for bringing Bud to the castaway island. Either, he would be picking up his passenger and the *reais* or just the coins. Bud handed the money to his new friend who stashed them under a rock to his liking.

Pondering, as he watched Juan row away, Bud ate some dried fish and fruit and watched until the dory's discolored sail rose against the bright blue backdrop of the waters and sky beyond. Painfully aware his only means of escape from the island was now gone, he was putting his trust, and maybe his life, in the hands of someone he met but a few hours before. Taking one final look at the distancing fisherman, Bud stepped into the lush vegetation.

The humidity and suffocating tree canopy choked the sunlight as Bud pushed aside the undergrowth and groped forward. Adding to the trek's formidable toil was the abundance of winged insects drawn to the sweating explorer invading their sanctuary. Sporadic rays of light beck-oning him onward, Bud moved cautiously as he neared the inlet. The wait nearly over, *Adventurer* and *Channel Runner* were within his grasp.

Stopping before reaching the lagoon, Bud sat watching and listening for nearly half an hour for any signs of intruders. Unable to detect any drifting motion, Bud's spirits took a turn for the worse at the disheart-ening discovery that *Adventurer* was grounded.

Trying to push aside the possibility that *Channel Runner* may still be lashed in her cribbing entombed underwater, Bud warily stepped from the jungle into the shallows. An array of bird life eyed his every move as he waded up to his armpits and began to paddle. His feet had barely left the bottom when the roar of a powerful sounding boat shattered the calm. Frantically, he swam under an overhanging tree as a large gray vessel swung into view.

The intruder was some sort of military cruiser. A canvas tarp covered what was likely a large caliber gun on the boat's bow. The craft could well be the same one that had fired upon *Channel Runner* the night Bud and his crew absconded with the Nazi submarine. As the engines were cut and the boat rubbed alongside *Adventurer*, Bud made out the guttural sounds of German as two Nazi crewmen scaled the rope ladder that hung from the side of the freighter.

Heart pounding, Bud spotted one of the crew poised on the bow of the gunboat with binoculars scanning the shore in an arc toward his hiding place. His gunny sack at the water's edge almost in plain view, Bud tried to melt into his surroundings—nose barely breaking the water's surface hardly daring to breathe.

The seaman's binoculars seemed to stop directly in line with the bag. The inquisitive crewman lowered his field glasses and called out to the assembled crew in the stern. A figure, likely the band of misfits' leader, strutted forward. Failing to move the strap over the head of his underling, he grabbed the binoculars jerking the sailor's head sideways. Following the sightline of the pointing finger, the take charge Nazi dismissed the exercise with an arrogance of disgust.

The crew of the dull colored boat milled about abiding their time waiting for their comrades' return. Finally, the boarding party reemerged on *Adventurer's* deck and shouted a few words. Back and forth communications were exchanged until finally the two descended to their waiting crew. The vessel rumbled awake. As she came about in the inlet, the crewman with the binoculars remained focused on the area where Bud's sack lay.

Secure the loud engines would drown him out as the boat distanced itself, Bud sounded out in a loud voice, "Fuckin' Nazis."

A wasted effort at this juncture, the gunboat unlikely to return soon, Bud still waded ashore and positioned his bag behind a tree. Reentering the water, he swam toward his ship as the drone of the German boat faded.

Bud grasped the rope ladder dangling in the water, scaled the side of *Adventurer* and dropped over her bulwarks. Making his way to the cargo hole, he peered into the dark crevasse, but was unable to detect anything. Eyes straining to adjust from the surrounding brightness to the dimness below, he tried to make *Channel Runner* materialize. He feared the worst. Unable to conjure her up, he descended into the ship's bowels. Eyes slowly adapting to the vague conditions, he shouted for joy, "She's afloat!"

Reaching the bottom of the ladder, Bud plunged into the dark oily water without hesitation and swam to the drifting runabout. Pulling himself aboard, he moved about in the dimness to determine her state. Finding seat cushions and life jackets had been cast aside to inspect her storage compartments, he inched forward into the cave-like cuddy cabin and felt the overhead for some sign of breach. It was intact. She seemed no worse for the wear other than an area of her starboard rub-rail chafed down to the screw heads where she had been against *Adventurer's* steel bulkhead.

Sitting behind the wheel, Bud removed a key from his pocket and inserted it in the ignition. He turned the notched brass piece to the on-position. Taking a deep breath, he pushed the start button quickly as the engine began to engage.

"Good girl."

Sliding back into the murky water, Bud swam to the rusty ladder and climbed to daylight.

Ascending the steps to the upper deck area, he felt confident that the fate of his cabin and its hidden contents would have a like outcome. He was wrong. The face of his bunk had been pried off and the hidden compartment was empty. Frans had reclaimed the painting of the man with the globe as well as the money left behind.

"Shit, I was rather fond of that painting," he sighed, wondering why his Nazi captor had only disclosed finding the religious pedestal.

Heading back below to tackle *Channel Runner's* freedom, creeping storm clouds began to darken the skies. A deluge of rain followed. Ducking into a passageway, Bud hoped the old fisherman would find safe harbor. Considering his next move, should he just retrieve the cross from its hiding place and disappear into the jungle to await tomorrow's rendezvous? No one would be the wiser that he had been there. But no, he had promised Mary. He had to try to take *Channel Runner* home.

Bud spent the next several hours locating, dragging and floating the tools he needed to extract *Channel Runner* from her tomb. Positioned on her stern, a subterranean eeriness spread throughout the cargo hold as an acetylene torch attacked the freighter's hull. A piece roughly eight-foot square would need to be cut away. The incoming tide lapping the lower sections of the box shaped cut, Bud cautiously moved the blue flame along the final upper leg of the bulkhead. Positioning *Chan-*

nel Runner, stretching from her stern, the torch assaulted the last few inches. Shearing into the water, a short lived steamy sizzle marking the event, their escape route to freedom was open.

By now, the heavy downpour had subsided to a cleansing shower dimpling the surface of the inlet. Bud dove beyond *Adventurer's* cave-like portal to wash away the sweat and filth of his labors. Swimming back, he wondered, "Who freed *Channel Runner* from her cradle?"

By ten o'clock, the tide had risen sufficiently for their escape. Pulling *Channel Runner* through the gaping hole, Bud readied her for the journey ahead. Raising the engine cover back, he primed the carburetor and switched on the key.

"Okay, here we go," he said aloud.

Bud pushed the starter button. Agony followed as the engine barely cranked without firing.

"Goddamn it all!" he screamed out taking his finger off the button. The batteries were low after all the time that had passed, but it never took much to get the old excursion boat to fire.

From *Channel Runner's* port storage locker, Bud removed a hand crank and attached it to the engine's flywheel, "Alright, let's get your juices flowing old girl."

Straining, Bud struggled to turn the flywheel over and over in an attempt to get all her systems fully lubricated. Knowing he probably only had one last opportunity for the exhausted batteries to crank her over, Bud began to softly speak to her, "Come on old girl, you can do it. You've gotten us out of binds tougher than this."

Removing the hand crank, he lovingly patted her flywheel as one might a woman's ass and pushed the starter button. The engine groaned and hesitated.

"You bitch. You better start, or I will punch a hole in your ass-end and sink you here and now," Bud wailed in desperation coaxing the starter to manage one last revolution.

Channel Runner's engine sparked and roared to life.

Chuckling, Bud said in triumph, "So, you like a little dirty talk before you're in the mood, huh?"

The storm heightened once again as darkness fell and *Channel Runner* cleared the inlet on a northward heading. While the rain was not all that heavy, the winds had turned the sea into a roller coaster of swells. Repeatedly, Bud skillfully maneuvered his craft to the crest of one white tipped wave only to disappear down the backside trough toward the next. His thoughts drifted to the old seafarer, hoping Juan had sought refuge. If not, he would surely be battling for his life against the mounting onslaught. Bud did something he seldom did. Looking to the heavens, he said a prayer for the old man.

Channel Runner had been fighting the storm for nearly an hour and a half when Bud got a glimpse of a triangle-shaped outline in a wave trough ahead. Rising to the peak of the next swell, Bud could see a small sailboat laboring up the next. It had to be Juan.

The weary helmsman, initially startled at *Channel Runner's* presence, broke into a semi-toothless grin. Motoring with difficulty to within a few feet, Bud threw Juan a line. The sail dropping, the seamen struggled to bring their crafts together. Scuttling the dory, too dangerous to take her in tow, Bud dragged the half-submerged fisherman aboard as raging waves separated the boats. Rain plummeting him, tears ran down the old man's weathered face as his dory rolled and was swallowed by the sea.

For the next few hours, they fought the relentless barrage. Never wavering, the old excursion boat made steady progress. Finally, sparse lights ahead signaled their salvation—the wayfarers had beat the odds.

Channel Runner secure in the village boat basin, Bud accepted his new friend's invitation to accompany him home to dry out and get something to eat. Plodding up the hill, soaked to the bone, it was nearly 3:00 in the morning. Nearing Juan's house, the rain clouds began to dissipate exposing hints of starry skies.

Upon entering the humble tin and wood structure, Juan disappeared behind a curtain where voices could be heard. Reappearing, a short round woman closely in tow, Juan introduced his wife who shyly dipped her head. Excusing herself, she stepped to their meager food preparation area to fix something to eat.

The bungalow exhibited traits like that of the old man's devotion to his fishing dory. While sparse, it was clean and neatly organized with everything in its place. The single room structure was made up of a combination living space, kitchen and curtained off sleeping area.

The boatmen sat at a table on homemade stick chairs as hot coffee flowed into their cups and a cooked mixture of fish and vegetables was scooped onto their plates. Having their fill, Juan directed Bud across the room where they took up residence in two well-worn chairs.

Bud closely surveyed the room assuring the old man that his promised money was still under the rock back at the island. In addition, Juan would be compensated for the loss of his dory. Unexpectedly, Bud spied a familiar straight-backed chair in the corner of the room with a blanket draped partially over it. It was his cabin desk chair from *Adventurer*.

Bud looked into the old man's eyes, "Juan, you know that I am in your debt. Are you the one who found the painting and money under my cabin bunk?" Bud asked.

Juan rose from his chair, more hunched over than before, and motioned for his guest to follow. Bud trailed him behind the sleeping curtain where a single hanging bare bulb cast a soft glow. Overwhelming the small space, a gold gilded-framed painting hung on the wall—a man sitting at a table with his hand on a globe.

Bud grinned ear to ear. The old man reached into a nearby chest and withdrew Alfred's satchel handing it to Bud, "I have only spent a few *reais*."

Bud handed it back. "The money is yours. But be careful how you spend it so not to bring undo attention to yourself. And never disclose how you got it. The painting is very valuable. Never tell anyone of its existence. Someday, I hope to return to buy it from you."

Passing back through the curtain, they sat in the same chairs as before. Juan recounted how he had stumbled onto *Adventurer* while she was still afloat. A week or so later, he was fishing in the vicinity when he saw a large gray boat in the distance. After the craft rounded the island to the ocean side, he heard a loud gun fire several rounds. Having spent the night on the inward side of the island as he had done on other occasions, he summoned enough courage to visit the inlet where he found the freighter sitting low in the water, but still afloat.

"Yes, I saw your boat in the freighter's great hold. She was straining to be freed from her cradle. I cut her binds. It didn't take me long to discover the hidden compartment under your bunk. The space between the bottom of the mattress and the drawers didn't seem right."

"I would expect nothing less from a man of such wisdom," Bud proclaimed.

The white-haired man chuckled as he got up and went to the kitchen where he produced a partially filled bottle of sugarcane liquor and two chipped glasses.

Over their drink, Bud asked, "Can you watch over *Channel Runner* until I have an opportunity to return for her? It should only be a few days."

"I know a spot where she can be moored out of the sight of others," Juan replied. "I will take care of her. Don't worry."

"I would be indebted," Bud said. "If anyone asks about her, tell them that some stranger gave you a few *reais* to watch her until he returned. Be careful. There are those who would wish to see me dead," Bud concluded.

After shaking hands, Bud headed out into the morning sunrise as sporadic rain cast a rainbow arch over the bay. Walking down the path toward the basin, the dazzling display of colors looked to be coming from the position of *Channel Runner's* moorage.

Stopping briefly to retrieve the crucifix from its tomb, giving *Channel Runner* one last endearing look, Bud climbed into his truck setting the bloodied shirt wrapped statue of Christ next to him on the seat. Unfurling the cloth as he drove along, he was struck by the awe-inspiring beauty of the piece. Wetting his thumb from his own saliva, Bud wiped away smatterings of his dried blood from the religious icon—and it seemed to Bud that he had to rub a disproportionate smudge from Christ's outstretched wrists and feet.

The welcome Bud received from Ana as he passed through the front door was disproportionate to the time he had been gone. Aware of the caliber of scoundrels Bud was defying, she had been duly worried. The tears and kiss were especially unexpected when Bud realized that her parents and Yvette were all watching.

When questioned, Bud responded that *Channel Runner* was safe and out of harm's way for the time being. Appearing outwardly frustrated, Ana would not leave his side. While Bud had similar feeling, he did a better job of disguising it.

Finally, without consulting Bud, Ana announced, "We are going to go to the square and I am not sure when we will return."

Bud looked at her with a startled expression as did her family. Making no further explanation, she headed for the door with Bud closely behind. Having made her intentions known, she allowed Bud to stop long enough at his truck to retrieve a bag containing a clean set of clothes and shaving gear. While he wasn't sure if he would need them right away, he wanted to be prepared for whatever Ana had in store for him.

Ana and Bud did in fact go to the town square, but directly to a hotel. Later they wandered the square and had dinner.

The next morning Bud lay in bed watching her sleep. Without doubt, he felt fortunate to have found her, but struggled with his feelings. He had come to care for Ana, more than just a friend, but wondered if he might be taking advantage of her feelings. Was it the beginnings of love or just an infatuation of sorts? Either way, it was clearly not what he had with Mary. A tear crept into the corner of one eye as his thoughts went back to the day on the beach that Mary died in his arms. Shaking off the memory, Ana opened her eyes and reached out to him.

The next few days were a flurry of activity. Bud arranged for *Channel Runner* to be loaded onto a freighter and shipped to San Francisco under an alias.

Bud confided to Ana, "You know that you are very important to me. But, I need to return to the States to ensure Michael is safe and well. Until Frans and Otto are dead, it's dangerous for you and your family to be associated with me."

"Take Yvette and me with you," Ana asked.

"No, it's not safe," Bud replied, avoiding the heart of the matter.

As expected, the morning of Bud's departure set the scene for an avalanche of Ana's emotions. Hiding his identity, Bud again looked the part of a local peasant rather than a gringo. He would take a bus to Buenos Aires and from there find a flight home.

Walking the short distance to the bus depot together, he told Ana that under her bedroom pillow she would find a crucifix to protect her until his return. Advising her of its history, he cautioned her against anyone becoming aware of its existence. Lastly, Bud handed her an envelope containing a bank account registered in the States with enough funds to provide for her and Yvette's security for many years to come.

The bus trip to Buenos Aires was crowded, unpleasantly hot and dusty. Unshaven, and having donned an old hat and worn clothing, no one seemed to give him any mind. The first flight Bud could find to the States was bound for New York the next day. He would be detained four additional days if he wanted a flight to the west coast. Not wanting to hang around thereby increasing the Nazis' chance of finding him, he bought the ticket for New York.

Spending the night in a rundown hotel, Bud was up early the next morning and set off on foot. Grabbing a bite to eat at a hole-in-the-wall café along the way, he arrived at the waterfront departure point with plenty of time to spare. He walked hunched over, pulling his worn hat down just above his eyes.

Engines revving, the clipper moved away from her boarding float. Entombed in a mist created by the propellers' air draft atop the surface of the water, Bud's mind was awash in the events of the last few days. He was leaving Ana but driven to see Michael. A smile crossed Bud's face picturing an old fisherman sitting in a new chair—the man with the globe looking down on his weathered face.

Telltale rivulets trailed as the plane broke her watery ties to drift upward. Settling back in his seat, Bud closed his eyes and prayed silently for Michael, for Ana and her family, as well as for Mary's understanding.

The Statue of Liberty's head peaked through the top layer of fog as the relenting drone of the engines lost their edge dropping them into the whiteness. Peering out, unable to distinguish the end of the wing tip, streaks of moisture wandered aimlessly across the Boeing 314's oblong shaped windows. The sensation unnerved Bud. Tightening his grip on his armrests, the aircraft continued to lose elevation. Finally, after what seemed an inordinate amount of time, the gray waters of New York harbor unveiled themselves.

Cool air greeted Bud as he exited the plane. It felt like home. Still wearing his panhandler disguise as a precaution, he hailed a cab asking the cabby to take him to the best hotel in the heart of the city. Because of his appearance, it took some doing to convince the doorman to allow his entry. Having just been through a similar routine with the cabby,

Bud simply handed the uniformed sentry a five-dollar bill. The man nodded and held the door open. Bud received similar disapproving gawks as he crossed the lobby to the registry desk. Figuring he was about to receive the same welcome he had encountered at the entrance door, Bud blurted, "Don't worry. I just arrived from out of the country and I can assure you that I have the means to pay for a room." Once checked in, Bud made his way towards the brass adorned elevator calling out his floor to the operator as he did so. The room was nicer than he needed, but he figured why not mark his safe return by splurging a bit?

Bud was elated when he heard Michael's voice over the phone, "Yes, everything is okay dad. The grandparents are spoiling me."

"Great. I will be home in a couple of days. Just stay put." Before hanging up, he said, "I love you Michael." Being as how it was the first time he had made that declaration; his voice choked a bit.

It took Bud a few tries before connecting with Earl, "Earl, I'm back and expect to be home in a few days depending on connecting flights."

Earl responded with a grunt. He seemed distant. Then the phone went dead.

"What the hell was that all about?" Bud thought, concerned about Earl's health. Earl had confided in him just before Michael and he left the States that he had been diagnosed with liver disease. A lifetime of heavy drinking had finally caught up to his Norwegian friend, rewarding him with a grave prognosis.

Bud scheduled a flight to San Francisco for the next morning before venturing out to buy new clothes.

Descending the wheeled stairway on the San Francisco tarmac, Bud fell in with the rest of the passengers accessing the airport structure like milk cows bunched at the barn door. Originally intending to take a connecting flight on to Seattle, he had decided he would make the drive instead. If he drove straight through, he should be able to reach Seattle in something less than 20 hours. The timeline wouldn't be much different than if he waited to board a flight the next day. Besides, driving up the coastline would give him time to clear his head and focus on the future. Hailing a taxi, he returned to the same dealership he went to many months prior when he purchased the convertible. Setting out immediately upon taking possession of the used blue flatbed truck, Bud was on the road by four in the afternoon looking forward to home and reconnecting with his son.

Fighting to keep his eyes open, he hadn't slept well in days. Stopping after dark at a roadside motel, he was up and on his way by sunrise. By early afternoon he crossed over the Columbia River on the final leg to Seattle, glad that most of the travel was behind him. Checking into a Seattle hotel, he went directly to the bar for a scotch and something to eat. In his room later, he called Michael's grandparents only to find that his son had left that morning for the Kangaroo House.

"Have you heard from Michael since he left?" Bud asked.

"We have not. And we asked him to call us when he got there."

"Well like his mother, he doesn't always listen. I told him to wait until I got there," Bud said. "I'm sure there is no need for concern. I'll leave for the island first thing in the morning. I hopefully can make ferry connections and be there by nightfall."

Michael had arrived at Orcas earlier that same day. Stopping to grab something to eat at the local diner, he learned a man with an unusual accent had been at the café the day prior inquiring about the Fowlers. Red flags raised, Michael wasn't sure how to proceed. Was he being paranoid? Should he go directly to the house? Should he try to do some reconnaissance? Maybe, he should just go over to Shaw and wait for his dad?

Bud tossed and turned throughout the night. He and his family would truly never be safe, nor at peace, until Frans and Otto were wiped from existence. Wishfully, he hoped Otto was already dead.

Darkness and rain blanketing the channel, the ferry approached the island that molded Bud's youth. Barely distinguishable, the outline of Blind Island across the bay shown as a flash of lightning lit the backdrop. He had been unable to make the connection on a boat bound for Orcas and the Kangaroo House. Churning astern, water frothing ahead, the ferry slowed towards the waiting slip. While winter storms weren't out of the ordinary, the downpour and accompanying winds were unusual. Pulling his wool coat over his head, Bud raced from the warmth of the upper cabin to the shelter of his Chevy.

Wing wall timber pilings creaked and groaned as a testament to their arrival, windshield wipers slapping, Bud let the clutch out and headed up the dock ramp to the store. It took Cleo a moment to recognize the drenched figure seeking refuge near the potbellied stove. The two shook hands as Bud juggled a cup of coffee he had already poured. Learning Bud would be unable to cross over to Orcas until the morning ferry, Cleo said, "Well there's a chicken in the oven and your old room's empty. So, you might as well settle in for the night."

Bud made a call to the Kangaroo House from the store's oak boxed wall phone but received no answer. Finishing dinner, he tried another call. Again, no answer. Maybe the weather had something to do with it? Bud told Cleo, "I am sure Michael is fine, but I can't shake the need to get over to Broken Point. The service is probably just out because of the storm, but I need to go."

Not particularly enamored with the thought of Bud heading out in such weather, Cleo questioned, "Do you think the rowboat is up to the task? The channel looks pretty rough."

"I'll be okay. Besides, once I round the eastern side of the island, the going should be more protected."

The small open boat's outboard started on the third pull, launching Bud away from the dock into the stormy darkness. Pulling up the hood on Cleo's borrowed rain gear, lightning flashed in the distance followed by running thunder. The navigation lights of a tug and its tow moving down the channel made Bud long for the warmth of their pilot house. Re-snapping the raincoat's top button that had come loose, Bud pulled the hood tighter over his head.

Fighting windblown whitecaps, the outboard's reassuring rhythm stopped. Jerking the engine back to life, it stopped again. On the next pull, the cord didn't recoil. Verbally expressing his displeasure, the rowboat bucketed about like an unruly horse. Glancing at the distancing lights of the store over his shoulder, Bud considered abandoning the crossing. Inserting the worn oars into their locks, moving to the middle seat, he began to pull into the rain on a course no different than before. While not the worst conditions he had rowed in during his lifetime, the darkness, lightning and thunder added an uneasiness. He was able to make the remainder of the crossing safely as long as he tended to the ongoing task of bailing wave slop and rain.

Rounding the leeward side of the island, having expected the storm to taper off, Bud was disappointed. Conditions just as blustery, he nevertheless felt some tension drain away knowing his destination was near. Turning from his rowing position, he pinpointed Kangaroo House's silhouette when a shard of lightning momentarily brightened the sky. For an instant, he even thought he saw a comforting flicker of light in a window.

Shifting back to face the stern, he pulled against the waves with revived purpose only to fall back as one of the oar locks snapped at its base. "Shit!" he shouted in vain, perturbed at Cleo for letting the boat fall into disrepair. But, there was no one to blame other than himself for reefing so damn hard on the old oars. Removing the remaining oar from its lock, he began awkwardly paddling canoe-like towards the wave-pounded beach.

Jumping into the surf to prevent the waves from spinning and swamping the rowboat, Bud failed to maintain control as baptizing frigid waves ripped the small craft from his grasp. Making a passing effort, he tried to retrieve the skiff from the ravages before it began to break apart against the logged shoreline.

Swirling water at his feet, Bud struggled to maintain his footing between the grounded drift and the surf's ebb and flow. Unexplainably, the closer he got to Broken Point the more apprehensive he became. Startled, a shadowy figure was heading his way. "Who's there?" No reply. "I said who's there?"

The ghostly outline closed the gap without response. Raising a piece of driftwood in defense, the intruder ever closer, Bud chucked the weapon into the surf as Karoo bounded into view. Knocking Bud to his knees, every cranny of his body that hadn't already been soaked was now. Seeming uncommonly agitated, Bud questioned what she was doing wandering the beach in such dreadful weather?

Looking to the Kangaroo House, Bud strained to find evidence of the light he thought he had seen from the boat. Seeing none, he continued with his sidekick trailing behind him.

Otto Günsche stirred the embers and carelessly threw another log into the fireplace causing sparks to spew onto the Persian carpet. The room glowed eerily with restored warmth underscoring his expressionless blue eyes. It had not been easy, but the Nazi Major had tracked his foe to the Kangaroo House on Broken Point. Having gotten Bud Fowler's Coast Guard Merchant Marine Officer License certificate from the San Francisco banker, Günsche had been able to determine it had been issued in Seattle. While he and Frans had discussed tracking Captain Fowler down months back, it had been the American's recent aggressions that had turned the tide towards bringing the larcenist to justice. Aided by inquiries within the marine industry, the high-step Nazi was able to trace Bud to Orcas Island. Once on the island, he didn't have difficulty getting directions to Bud Fowler's home from the friendly folks at the ferry dock.

Nearly catching up with Bud after he had rescued his runabout, the German was growing anxious as another day passed without the islander's return. Present during Earl Yansen's phone conversations a few days prior, he knew Fowler was on his way—an occasion that marked the old man's last words. Expecting his enemy after each scheduled ferry landing, Otto lay in wait. The unanswered phone calls gave him hope. Surely, the thief who had absconded with the paintings hanging on the wall was nearing.

Under siege, Bud tried to shield the onslaught of blowing salt spray and rain from his eyes. Squinting at the Point, detecting a faint light coming through the library windows, a violent bolt of lightning and thunder sounded. Unheeding, he plunged into the flooded neck to the Kangaroo House. Leaving Karoo behind, he feverishly struggled to reach the other side of the surging narrows. Straining near exhaustion, he crawled unsteadily onto the jagged bedrock. Crouching to catch his breath, hands bleeding, he looked back at Karoo pacing back and forth at the water's edge wanting to follow.

A sense of uneasiness gnawed at Bud. Moving warily up the trail toward the house, pelting rain and wind tried to drive him back.

On the other side of the world, Ana knelt at her bedside with a look of terror. The sacred gold crucifix Bud had left behind lay separated from its base. While she'd been holding and praying over the religious artifact, it had fallen from her hands and as it hit the floor, twisted apart. A small piece of paper hidden within covered the palm of her hand. It contained a series of seven numbers with names. Trembling, she realized the list was the key to the identity of Alfred's patients who had undergone facial surgery.

The last entry burned into her soul as tears of fear crept from within. Looking to the heavens for guidance, she whispered to herself, "Frans is Adolf Hitler."

Adolf Hitler perched on a bench along the upper cliff of his South American estate. Starring out across the ocean beyond, he now spoke in a raspy voice and shuffled along hunched over. His buzzard-like physique and twisted facial scars were a far cry from the defiant Nazi eagle he once prided himself upon. A daily reminder of those who had failed him, his impaired well-being was attributable to the gunshot wounds inflicted by the once affectionate Katarine. She, like others before her, had paid the price for her transgressions.

He chuckled. Skillfully manipulating the world on his final offensive, he was pleased that the only living being that knew his identity was Otto Günsche. The Major was necessary to find his works of art and, more importantly, wipe the Fowler clan from the face of the earth. In time, Günsche would give his life as had the others.

Spewing forth words beyond comprehension, Germany's once supreme ruler was unable to get past Bud Fowler's tactics to outwit him.

CHAPTER 27

Lightning lit up Kangaroo House as the Major stared into the hypnotic flames. His sinister features in contrast to those depicted in the paintings hanging on the wall, the Nazi puppet willfully allowed the dancing light to shroud the haunting portrayals of his past. Awake for over twenty hours, he surrendered to the fire's warmth. Succumbing to the murky depths of sleep, his face dropped from view.

The fire deceivingly illuminating the library interior, Bud cautiously peered through a window, "Earl Yansen, you old son of a bitch." Crossing the porch into the house, he passed lady of *America* and entered the library. Moving to the warmth of the fire, he extended his hands to draw the heat to his frigid body.

"Earl, where's Michael? I've been worried about him."

A brief silence, as if savoring the moment, Otto Günsche mockingly replied, "As you should comrade."

Every fiber of his being screaming, Bud froze. Slowly turning, the sinister figure faced him, gun in his hand. Filled with terror, the fire at his back, Bud took a step to the side showering Günsche with the fire's glow. No longer exhibiting the prowess of their previous clash, the ravages of Bud's bullets had taken their toll. The Major's left arm hung awkwardly, his face hardened, his eyes cold.

A roll of thunder shook the house as if God was making known his disfavor with the unfolding events.

"The führer wants his possessions back," Otto said as a sinister smirk crossed his lips. Waving his gun at the unworthy rival, he contemplated how to extract the whereabouts of the stolen antiquities. Neither said anything.

Voices from above had spurred Michael. Having been tipped off by the ferry dock agent that a man with a strange accent had been asking about his father, Michael had surmised the worse. He hadn't stuck around as he should have after giving explicit instructions that were to be relayed to his father upon his arrival. Entering the secret room below the Kangaroo House by way of the workshop, he waited indecisively, knowing someone was in the house. He thought he detected German being spoken at one point so knew it wasn't Earl.

A window rattled jarring the standoff between Bud and Günsche. Heads jerked as a dark shadow appeared outside. The Luger flashed as a shot shattered the leaded framed glass and dropped the unknown assailant. The unearthly shrills of Karoo's pain could be heard over the storm's fury.

Bud charged, hurdling himself atop Günsche. A glass faced bookcase exploded as the two violently clashed. A bullet ripped into Bud. Both fighting for their very lives, the Nazi Luger scooted across the floor up for grabs.

The stair section opened drawing Michael to the gunshot and violent commotion. Sprinting to the library, he ignored the pain radiating from his healing wounds. His father seemed to be at a disadvantage, Michael heard his father cry out, "The gun. On the floor!"

Dropping to his hands and knees, Michael cast aside a chair and frantically raked the floor. Driven face down by the weight of the Nazi Major throwing himself atop him, Günsche was nearly back in charge as he reached beyond the young Fowler.

Staggering to his feet, blood oozing from his upper chest, Bud launched into the midst of the thrashing upheaval joining the struggle for the weapon.

A muffled shot rang out.

Having won the skirmish for the swastika adorned gun, a lone figure rose to his knees. A log shifted in the burning ambers illuminating the Major's face. Mistakenly, still bent on extracting the whereabouts of the other paintings and antiquities, he knelt to see if any of the Fowlers were alive.

Surging from the mayhem, the young Fowler knocked Günsche to the floor. Landing on his bad arm, the Major yelled out in pain and gave Michael a chance to kick the pistol from his hand. Punching the Nazi in the face, briefly immobilizing him, Michael crawled away to retrieve the Luger. Outmaneuvered, outgunned, the Nazi Major rose and fled into the night.

Adrenaline pumping, the pain of a bullet in his shoulder pushed aside, Michael gave chase.

Stepping off the porch, he was unsure of Günsche's whereabouts. As if showing the way, a bolt of lightning illuminated the waters beyond outlining a figure near the Point's outermost rim.

Teetering at the cliff's edge, dazed, blood streaming from his face, Günsche knew the outcome of the standoff was cast.

Michael closed the distance, raising the Luger from his side. His hand steady, as if savoring the moment, Michael began to slowly tighten his finger on the trigger.

Defiant to the end, Major Günsche raised his arm in a Nazi salute. Another flash of lightning to mark the event, he stepped back into the void above the crashing waves.

THE END

EPILOGUE

After the storm quieted, Bud's universe still seemed to be whirling around him—everything he'd known was in upheaval. Earl was dead, he, his son and Karoo were all recuperating from Günsche's wayward gunshots, and the island folks were talking. While life at Kangaroo House was quieting down a bit, there seemed to be a constant undertow gripping the family that Frans Bernheim wasn't done with the Fowlers.

Günsche's body had washed up on the shore some distance from Broken Point one morning after a squall. The crabs had done a number on his features, but there was little doubt who it was. The islanders assumed he was some unidentified deranged intruder who had squatted in the Kangaroo House before being surprised by the Fowlers, and Bud and Michael did nothing to dissuade them. A sense of relief prevailed within the island community, but Bud and Michael who knew that Frans did not accept failure and would recruit others to take up where Günsche had left off once he figured out his right-hand man was dead.

A quiet funeral was held for all those who had known Earl. A simple wood coffin, a dram of scotch, and more friends than expected made for a good send off for Bud's dear friend. Bud buried him on upland beach near Broken Point with a commanding view of the waters beyond—he was home at last.

A month or so later, hoping to distance his son from any retaliatory action by the dethroned Nazis, found Michael preparing to move to Seattle for a new job with an engineering firm. The day before his departure, Michael wandered into the house clutching the daily post. Flipping through the letters, he handed Bud an envelope from the local doctor. Bud had been expecting a bill and smiled when he thought of the Doc's reaction when called upon not only to attend to the Fowlers, but to dig a bullet out of a kangaroo as well. Glancing at Karoo wandering aimlessly along the tide line, Bud returned his attention back to his son who seemed transfixed on an envelope. "Dad, it's from Brazil," Michael's voice was hardly above a whisper. He was clearly alarmed.

"Hand it to me son," Bud said, trying to remain calm. After all, it wasn't likely that Frans would send the duo a friendly note in the mail. Bud had to tug to get it out of Michael's grip, and he felt the paper give a little. "Let it go so I can read it." Michael sat down and breathed deeply as Bud gently tore the seal on the envelope. Inside was a one-page letter accompanied by a folded scrap of paper. He read the shaky cursive and sighed in relief. "It's from Ana."

Michael smiled and said, "Well, what does she have to say for herself? I honestly didn't think we'd ever hear from her again." But as Bud read, his knuckles whitened because the paper Ana included with her letter ruined all chance that Bud and Michael had for a normal life. Bud read aloud.

> *"Dearest Bud,*
> *Hopefully this letter finds you and Michael well. I miss you both terribly.*
> *Yvette keeps talking about the nice man who came to stay, and asking if you are coming back. I wasn't sure what to say but told her we would always be friends.*
> *Just days after you left my home, as I was praying for your safety before I fell asleep, the crucifix slipped from my hands. When I grabbed for it, the base separated from the gold statue. Thinking I broke it, I found instead that the bottom was designed to twist apart from the top. Within a small void between the pieces, I found this piece of paper and knew that you needed to see it as soon as possible.*
> *Please know that I will do anything I can to help you but hope that this information will be safe in your hands. I would beg you to please not risk your lives to follow this man but am not sure that I can ask that of you. Stay safe.*
> *All my love caro,*
> *Ana"*

Bud unrolled the slip of paper and saw a list of seven names matched with corresponding numbers. He came to the same conclusion that Ana had, that the names corresponded to those members of Nazi elite who had received facial surgeries. The last line chilled his blood. He handed the paper to Michael who read out, "Frans Bernheim is Adolf Hitler."

ACKNOWLEDGEMENTS

I am indebted to Maggie Taylor for her extraordinary support and guidance in bringing the story to print.

Meet L. G. CRAWFORD

L. G. Crawford grew up in a small Pacific Northwest island community where his ancestors settled in the 1890s. *Kangaroo House* draws on a combination of the early days of past generations of his family and his interest in historical events. He is married to his high school sweetheart of over fifty years. After traveling the world for a major engineering and construction firm, he returned his family to the roots that shaped his life. Retired, he and his wife live in a 1920s lakeside cottage with uneven floors.

CPSIA information can be obtained
at www.ICGtesting.com
Printed in the USA
LVHW020404280519
619246LV00008B/855